Commonality

Lucy's Large Lunch

Gordon Watt

"Sometimes life's like livin' a dream...and you're just lettin' it happen," Wilf sighs as he gazes with tired eyes down along the street. Ed and Sid beside him on the bench are peering, full of feeling too, toward the buildings across the way. "Then someone dies, and it's all too real..."

At that, Sid crosses his arms against his blue T-shirt, as though to hold his emotions together. His shaggy blond hair and chubby fair face are nodding slowly. And Ed, dark and rail thin, frowns deeper with painful reminder.

About then, seeing how this particular summer-evening gathering on the bench outside Lucy's Large Lunch has just suddenly collapsed from the snarls and jabs of men to mere talk, the five boys who were edging in on their bikes now back off and scramble away toward the town's nearby ball field, gloves flapping on handlebars, to honor their summer-long game.

High above, arcing right along, the late-day sun stays hot, though a breeze now and then does replenish the downtown with some fresh country air. And billowing white against the infinite blue, tyrant thunderheads silently mass eastward, well beyond the aged red brick of the buildings opposite. For a short spell, traffic gets heavy, and people fill the sidewalks as the stores close all at once... And it seems to Wilf that everyone's buzzing... well, in their heads, at least, about the murder.

Suddenly ol' Chase pushes open Lucy's squeaky screen door with a grunt. "Where's everybody?" he asks as he shuffles out and nestles down onto the last bare patch on the four-seater bench. Ablaze in a bright red plaid shirt, he is concentrating fully on the brimming paper cup of coffee he grips with both hands as he slouches back. He then tips up his old red ball cap – as though to let his white tufts of hair breathe – and repeats, "Where's everybody? – you young dinks don't know shit!" As he mutters that at the three middle-agers, his wrinkle-set eyes are straining around his low-slung bifocals up and down the street. "Where's all this town's brainpower, anyway?" he groans, then sips coffee and scowls straight ahead at the air, his lips working a toothpick and his head automatically nodding in response to every walking and driving passerby.

"Nun set yet," Ed expressionlessly observes beside him.

"Who said that?!" Chase huffs, though what must be the beginning of a grin softens his weathered face.

Wilf's wise and gentle pale blue eyes now sparkle with amusement; his lean, strong arms brace one knee crossed on the other. "More coots coming," his voice resonates as he spots three other old boys trudging around the curve where the business section ends, a quarter mile of deep-green shade trees down the sidewalk.

"That Bert there?" Chase squints along the buildings, too. "Ol' Bert, he'll have it all figured out by now, won't he? – who it ain't, anyway, and what all them police should do...ol' Bertrand-full-o'-horseshit!"

Now overly small-town anxious and upset (as everyone) when "it" is mentioned so openly again, Sid pushes slowly to his feet and stretches, tugging up the waist of his dark green work pants under his ever-expanding gut. With bright hazel eyes glancing sideways down at the others and along the walk at the three men coming, he then counts thumb against fingers while slipping inside for three chairs and six take-out coffees (Chase omitted), everyone's creams and sugars remembered (in a rare all-out admission of a turn to buy).

In delayed response, Ed scratches his thinning scalp and rules: "Chase, no one really knows the truth about anything 'round here. The best truth, we make up as we go along."

Just as sudden as the street flurried with folks, it's now nearly emptied...deep yellow sunshine on faded gray asphalt, meters standing guard for vacant parking spaces, and the occasional car heading out...somewhere; evening, suppertime: a town of people shifts to quiet back streets canopied by trees, to behind screen doors and opened drapes (for anyone who has to be so curious to go right ahead and look at what's going on inside).

Bert and Mel and Shooter soon arrive chattering. Their coffee, in paper cups, is waiting on their chairs set at the usual places on the worn sidewalk at the curb, opposite the long-familiar bench. Settled in, they and the others do not even mention "it" again tonight. Instead, they analyze the weather and farming and town stuff, and add in repeated (endless) accolades for Lucy's ever-delicious custom bean-brew. And the evening lazes on...

Then soon – quickly there in front of them from up the street – a loud rumble idles down at the only stoplight here where Sideroad 93 crosses Highway 3 at Lucy's corner... The four bikers have stopped, arms angled up to handlebars, patiently, obediently, waiting for the red light to change and for no one to cross. And Bug Doug on his bike is right up to the white crosswalk; the other three sit, sparkling, a little behind. Bug does not look around. As the light begins changing his eyes stay fixed full of thought down at the road. His left hand braces on his hip. With a twist of his right wrist he commands attention from his spotless old bike, and it echoes a growl up and down the street, making a small man seem bigger. The light turns green. With another curl of his hand Bug Doug revs hard – and the bike's front end jumps two feet high as it surges and glistens and howls through the intersection on its rear wheel...and Bug Doug's eyes and cool gaze raise sideways up to the men on the bench and with his lips set tight and that hand on his hip – with long hair fluttering and open black jacket lifting in the wind and reared back on one wheel – he blinks slowly, then peers ahead, in utter, roaring, scary indifference.

"**S**o then who did it, beanhead?!" Jackie leans down off the pitcher's mound toward the rock-and-paper-bag home plate and Kevin cocked there with his oversized bat. (Kevin's only ten, and thirteen-year-old Jack is intimidating enough out there with just that hardball he's about to fire at him, so the image of Jackie stridin' the sun-baked dust to stop eyeball to eyeball with him – which Jack likes to do – makes him regret scoffing that the killer could no way be anyone in town.)

And with his black eyes glaring and mess of black hair flying free in the breeze, Jack looks as defiant out there as he actually is. Growing up with just his mom, he is full to the rim with their poor, abandoned life – Mom was a whore, everybody knows. In a small town, who even talks to her now? – who'll take the weight of everybody inevitably and soon enough judging? And at her age, looks sagging... So he ain't about to entertain some flaky fabrication by this kid from Respectable Road, where, as far as he sees it, uppity bullshit forever misses reality.

Kevin compromises: "Some say it's Looker." He then wiggles his bat, as though to prompt Jack to please just throw the ball and forget it.

"Dipshit," Heap Henry now implores flatly from center, "throw it."

Jack droops his arms to his sides and turns sneering toward the outfield.

"Looker did it, so what?" Kenny groans impatiently from first.

So Jack gives in and returns to the stretch – to see Manny at third looking him in the eye and turning both his glove and bare hand skyward with full uncertainty against him.

"Lick my lumps," Jack mutters to the world. But again he tremors: someone is dead, someone he knew – not old, someone young, near his age, with her whole life unlived, like him and all (solidly alive) thirteen other kids here on this field. Who around town – someone everyone knows! (no way it's Looker) – would do such an unreal, way past any everyday-shitty thing..?

And Jack throws the ball, sailing it five feet over Kevin's head against the screen backstop.

The night has just blackened the midsummer, late Friday evening's sunset edge of horizon out along the dirt country road well ahead of the parked car.

"Nah, Howard..!" Gene moans from the darkened corner of the back seat, a little echo sounding from the beer bottle nearing his lips.

"Hey, seriously – just picture it!" Howard persists, his voice, from his dim silhouette, bouncing off the windshield. "You've never ever done it or even seen it done, then *choo!* – you sneeze. First you'd shit yourself with panic then seizure and die!"

There's a rustling of cardboard and a little clink of bottles as two hands reach at once into the beer case centered on the back seat and pull out cool ones. In the dark, Ba-Dee smiles unseen in the other back corner and Norm in the passenger front tries to pierce the sightlessness ahead to see Reason...while waiting for Howard's usual finalizing little laugh of true fascination.

"Hee," summates Howard.

Norm then breaks the subsequent thick silence himself. "I dreamed a mother and baby elephant were standing in these high flames. They just burned. Without moving. You know how some dreams feel more intense than reality..? It was awful, the feeling of death consuming that helpless little elephant..."

"Was the little one Janet?" Ba-Dee braves the symbolism of the murdered girl.

The air in the noise-deadened car ices. The self-consciously warped desire for something – anything! – to happen in this dead-asleep town is doused by Wednesday's hard reality of life's shocking sickness. And Norm is sorry he mentioned his dream, because now he's churning with its reminder of revelation – what he really wants to tell these friends but feels he can't: the one possibly revealing detail he knows. He is also mindful of how all past weekend nights spent out on this back road were never as heavy with such non-philosophical reality. "No," is all he answers.

"So...it's Bug Doug," Ba-Dee soon suggests his convenient suspect.

"Looker," Gene drones his.

"Fuckin' space aliens!" Howard loudly huffs – so tired already of guesses – and kills the conversation again.

"...It's Howard..." Norm poses evenly.

"Death!" Howard himself now reverberates the morbid thought. "A Great Equalizer – of peasants and princes!" he offers poetically.

"Sleep," Ba-Dee contributes another.

"Stoplights."

"Toilets..."

The Earth rolls on, through the infinite pitch. Swirling white on rich blue, chaos patterns the winds, that drive the clouds. Through a break in the cover: a patch of land, squares of green and brown – a patternless quilt of farms, and a crossroad with buildings gathered close. Nearby, around one structure, one home – amid a world of wars and births and billions of lives living: the flashing lights of four police cars, and five men and two women officers combing every square inch of its yard. Three more officers, plus Chief Cintz, self-consciously absorb the hysteria inside...

It's the morning of the murder:

"Ahhh...ahhh...ahhh..!" Margaret's subconscious screeches anguish on and on. Her husband Carl can only try to hold her, sitting with her on the sofa, as he moans his own disbelief through the searing pain. In the easy chair opposite them: the second child Jennifer – at thirteen only a year younger than her victim sister Janet – sits unheld, feeling shocked beyond tears or sobs by her mother's complete loss of control, her father's uncharacteristic utter helplessness, and her own inability to comprehend her presence in this suddenly and gravely distorted reality.

And strange to Jennifer too is how everything else is still the same: the street outside that picture window, the television's gray face there in the corner, and the bright rose pattern on her chair arm she stares at with eyes...that on their own now finally begin welling with tears – why is nothing else in this room as odd in this catastrophe as what is happening in this sequence and in her mind..? But she senses that disconnect with only a fleeting grip – an elusive grasp, that feels impossibly surreal in between each wrenching wail from this woman across the room...who she somehow knows is now forever different from her mother... Wait!, she thinks: It's only Wednesday, I should be in summer school – no!, of course not, it's a crisis... So what do we all do next – do we leave for somewhere? – we don't stay here, do we..? And then, like shocking cold, the realization seizes her mind again that Janet is dead... "dead", Chief Cintz had clearly said. And as though her very soul is trying once again to make her feel more fully just what that means, a powerful adrenalin surge causes Jennifer to twist in her chair, and the act of moving makes the thought and feeling go away. And she stares at her mother again, and then at her father – suddenly, she feels she's not even in the room!...and now again, she is... Then an officer, a lady – she's seen her around the house but doesn't know her name – drifts across the room and leans close to her with pretty, pleading eyes, and raises a hand and carefully, softly, touches her shoulder. And with that touch, that affection, that permission, Jennifer whimpers – as though that one special contact with another life releases – for her whole heart to feel – the full pain of tragedy and the swelling loneliness of loss and the first perilous glimpse of an abyss of grief..! And she collapses limply to the floor.

Outside, in the side neighbor's yard, several police officers have slowly tightened their search ring around a trampled patch of grass at the brown-stained picket fence that separates the prop-erties. The flattened grass leads them behind a nearby old tree. And one officer has found a fresh, well-chewed wad of bubble gum, within spitting distance; another is examining a faint, dew-highlighted footprint in the light dust – a small footprint on the fence's bottom rail. Someone now reminds the others what the local police said about Margaret's and Carl's complaint two weeks ago regarding young boys late-night peeping at their daughters' bedroom windows. And all of them have it in mind that it rained Monday until late evening – enough to wash away any previous footprints. And as everyone looks back over the fence at the house and then the plain impressions marking the lawn with lines leading from it – that could easily be from Janet's unconscious body being dragged away after midnight to be raped and brutalized then strangled in a shallow ditch outside of town – they each imagine now that they were the young boy who must have been cowering here last night behind this tree watching.

As Looker rounds the bend at the end of downtown, no one is on Lucy's bench to gaze back at him. But there is nothing unusual about his coming: Looker regularly walks around on Saturdays, to sit for a minute in the little park opposite Lucy's or to window shop in the bright, warm sunshine for an hour or so.

This Saturday he wears a midnight-blue T-shirt, showing his fit chest; his usual plain jeans end a little crumpled onto white, only slightly scuffed sneakers. He walks casually, and with dignity. His face is carved strong – "Ooo too cute!" girls giggle. He's about thirty. He is always clean looking, with brown, unpretentiously styled hair trimmed short (by someone expert, not the local barbers). And his eyes – those ever-watching, pale gray lenses – absorb everything that is, and glance at this and study that, and see the summer wind and comprehend the trees, the birds, the blades of grass, and scan the stars through the daylight blue...it seems.

For ten years now, Looker has lived at the edge of town, occupying the upstairs of a white, wood-siding house set on the fringe of fields at the end of a side street – where he sits on his balcony... and watches what he sees, for hours.

Looker doesn't work; some say he just has money (but doesn't bank). His landlady downstairs smiles when you ask, but she "don't know nothin' that everyone else don't know...he's very quiet"; he leaves her cash rent, held with a paper clip, inside her screen door.

And Looker never nods hello, but appears as though he's thinking it to you. He's always nearly expressionless. And never talks – ever.

Half the town figure he can't talk, the other half say...all kinds of things. But nobody seems to know the truth. (Wilf once said to a gathering outside Lucy's that there's no question Looker's a genius – must be, knowing no need to ever have to talk over anything with anyone.)

"Then there's no point asking him in here for questioning, is there?" reasons Chief Cintz as he watches from overtop his burgundy half curtains while Looker walks along across the street. (Again, he's glad he has only his assistant officer Tom Addison left to say that or anything to, now that all the other investigating officers sped the ten miles back to Elston City yesterday – for the last time – as fast as they came Wednesday when he called, three days ago.) "Anyway, Looker doesn't do much of anything. Murder is way out of his activity level."

Tom merely grins, only one side of his police (or firefighters') apparently regulation mustache curling up. (His desk in front of him, end-against-wall in the bare storefront office, is as offensively neat as the Chief's is messy against the other.) He rotates with his chair a quarter turn, and leans back. "See-see," he begins with a hint of irritation ("See-see" as in "C.C." – "Chief Charles/ Chuck Cintz", which even after three years working for him he still, like one or two others around, sometimes trips over), "are we not doing enough? – since the minute that farm supply driver found her and called, we've done all we can! We've questioned all the people. We've searched the yard and road and ditch. Her body's in the city for tests – so, com'on! No one's gonna riot!" Yet for some reason he grips his chair arms tight, his black eyebrows scrunched over his brown, intensely squinting eyes. His pressed, tailored blue shirt then heaves with a breath.

"This ain't tee-vee, Tom. Likely no one will say anything," Chuck assures him somewhat impatiently, still motionless at the window and his eyes still following Looker. His shaggy, half-grayed hair is messy from pushing his fingers through it all morning. His pale blue eyes are weary, as much from last evening spent on a Lucy's barstool talking at length with Wilf as from this unaccustomed stress. (But his full, friendly face spills out as much open and instantly likeable character as always, Tom sees.) Then as he combs his thick fingers through his hair again, Chuck finally turns his back to the street.

In his mind the Police Chief tours his town once more, thinking further along through his unspoken private list of possibilities, offering only a small, humorless smile of mutual bewilderment to Tom rigidly sitting there watching him. "Take that stupid tie off!" he snarls at his neat-dressing helper for the hundredth time, half joking. (The half that isn't knows he should wear one too.) He then strokes his chubby neck, as if to demonstrate how relaxed it is not knotted up. And sliding his hands into his dark blue pants' pockets, he puckers his thin lips as though to whistle, but just blows out air in spurts – one for each name discarded in his thoughts.

"Nohhh," Chuck finally mutters to himself. Staring at the air, he simply holds there, appearing perfectly comfortable standing straight up, like a wax statue of small-town concern.

"The boy might crack open..." Tom tries again, returning to the option of interviewing every grade school male in town – which he himself knows is a long shot. (Under the gun, he realizes, young boys will say a lot of things, much of it sure to be almost as scary as what they would be looking for, but no way they want to hear.) He plays with a pen on his desk, twirling it around on its fat center, his eyes glancing back and forth from it to his Chief.

"He's gotta come to us," Chuck again insists, though somewhat absently. "And we can't let this out – not yet, anyway. Every parent in town will be all over their kid...or quietly wondering, at least."

"The Mayor says it's young Jack – Nighttime Nancy's boy," Tom peers in earnest at the Chief, fishing only for nibbles.

"Too big," Chuck angles his eyes down at Tom. Then he adds with some anger, "And why is it the rough side of town people always start looking around first?"

"Sorry. Don't know," Tom squirms, mindful of his boss's compassion and friendship for Nancy and concern for her boy.

"But Jackie might know something," Chuck concedes. "He's like a miserable older brother to every kid in town – especially all the ones he plays ball with."

"Well, we could tell him that much, that we don't think it's him but we respect his...his position," Tom uses an argument he knows is weak. (But again he feels appreciation for his Chief, having worked for others elsewhere who were not wholly understanding or tolerant of subordinates' words. With Chuck, as he usually calls him, you can say anything, without visions of demotion making you mumble.)

"I'll see him around," Chuck suggests. "We shouldn't single him out, bringing him in here."

"True," Tom agrees. Then, after thinking a few seconds, he ventures, "Got any theories – something I can help you with?" he puts it (as though trying not to ask for something too deep, something he couldn't contribute to).

"Yup," Chuck now strolls toward his desk, eyes fixed on the floor. "It's not me, you, Looker or Wilf – Wilf promised me on our tenth beer last night," he jokes without smiling.

"I believe him," Tom laughs a little, feeling the same respect for wise and caring Wilf that the whole town seems to feel.

"It's a start, isn't it? Write 'em down."

"Ha!" Tom reacts as he imagines a final list with three thousand, two hundred and thirty-nine names on it (everyone in town – minus one) but then immediately frowns: "Chuck...you're not gonna like this one – what about Carl?" he finally says it, as though someone has to decide to routinely, officially register it: the father.

"There's an uncle, too," Chuck admits he's been thinking about it (all too aware of the sad statistics showing who causes most family tragedies).

"But he was ten miles away in Elston," Tom believes the alibi (its confirmation – being sensitively checked – not yet back).

"Right now," Chuck has to relent, stopping at his chair and daydreaming down at his desk, "I guess Carl's on that list – all alone, at the top..." But he would bet his own life it wasn't Carl. He's known him forty-some years, and there is just no way... And then, leaning on his desk and lowering himself to his chair, he recalls Wilf's thought last night: "What a delicate web of human interaction a small town is."

J ennifer leans against the back corner of their house. Young,
   pretty, she looks older, and drawn. Her reddened eyes shift
   around the fenced yard as though searching, but she can't
bring herself to walk back there. The yellow sunshine is hot.

Her mother just left for the city, to stay with a sister for a
while. Jennifer refused to go.

The thought of going back to summer school Monday makes
her shiver. It's up to her, her parents – the half strangers – had
said...

Two white butterflies frolic above the green grass, where...
Tears quickly pool again and drip down her cheeks... A warm
wind rocks the treetops. Up the street, a lawnmower buzzes; in
the yard behind, beyond the shade of maple limbs drooping with
big leaves, a barbeque fragrantly smokes, unattended.

She doesn't want to, but she imagines her yard at midnight –
Tuesday – and a dark shadow slipping noiselessly over that fence,
and her sister on her back on the picnic table sneaking a cigarette – fourteen years old, bound to do that – and searching, the
way she liked, straight up past the stars...while her parents and
younger sister sleep inside...the wind howling...

Jennifer's father, watching her from the kitchen window,
lowers his head and cries again, too.

"Tree spaying," Ed says again to Bert sitting there across the sidewalk from Lucy's bench. Bert just stares at him, raised paper coffee cup stopped halfway to his mouth. His white beard twitches. The wrinkles around his brown eyes quiver. Wilf, Sid, Shooter, Mel, Chief Chuck Cintz, Norm and Howard all sit and stand around, as eight young boys on bikes inch in closer from near the street corner to watch his face. He looks like he grasps it.

"Tree spaying..." Bert repeats, seldom speaking so few words at once.

"Sure," Ed affirms matter-of-factly.

"Your nephew..?" Bert asks again, to be sure of the source.

"Tree spayer..." Ed insists, no expression on his face, whatsoever.

Bert now says nothing, fully realizing that by doing so he is admitting to not knowing something. Yet he is wary of these boys' leanings toward fantasy.

"Spay – you know, like cats and dogs," Sid now contributes as he points his plump face up and down the street without emotion, merely tossing in a simple fact.

Bert nods slowly, appreciatively, but does not even glance at Sid. He just peers into Ed's eyes, visualizing.

"Well, it's a big business: tree leaves – getting rid of them, right?" Ed frowns back.

"Sure!" Bert humphs, his bushy eyebrows raised with indignation. As if he didn't know that!

"So they figured out a way to fix the seeds..." Ed prompts.

"And the leaves stop falling!" Bert connects and leans back in his chair by the curb. The late Saturday afternoon sun illuminates the rare (yet restrained) amazement on his years-creased face.

At the moment, the street is strangely quiet.

"Right. Spaying." Ed can't be more clear.

"But he's a registered tree surgeon – your nephew," Sid wants to remind everyone it's a professional technique... No one looks at him. Even the kids are waiting solely for Bert.

"Of course he is," Ed angles his head a bit toward Sid beside him on the bench while scowling intently down at the sidewalk. He swirls his half-emptied coffee cup held in two hands between the faded jeans of his bracing legs. A couple of the kids rock back and forth a little on their bikes. A car lazes softly by, easing through the silence. Chuck Cintz shifts his weight to his other leg and leans back on the parking meter again, blankly watching everyone as he sips his coffee.

"So...how do they...*do* it?" Bert goes for it wide-open.

Ed can't stop his lips from grinning: "A little incision..."

And they all burst with laughter at once – except Bert.

Moments later, with their last chuckles echoing away between the buildings and with Bert finally allowing himself a smirk at his own expense, Ed, somewhat awkwardly, ventures to Chief Chuck there across the sidewalk and circle of males, "You and the wife be at the dance tonight..?"

"Yup. You?" (Chuck is well aware that no one ever asks. You just show up at the Local Order of the Varmint Hall dance, or don't.)

Normally, some of the kids on bikes would be pulling on others to leave, right here, but they sense something coming. The Chief doesn't ever look as serious when he hangs around Lucy's as he suddenly seems right now.

And they're right, because Chuck can't stand the feeling of being squeezed: "Okay, I get it. No, we don't know anything more. The autopsy...well, can't say anything about it, you all know that. Least, not until an arrest is made. If there's nothing conclusive enough found anywhere, we just keep working away at it, hoping something surfaces – someone gets too drunk and opens his mouth a bit or confesses to someone close. We've searched all we can, from her yard to the ditch. But I can't say more, you know that too. And I don't want to lie to you, so please don't ask..." He pauses, meets some of their wide eyes, glances down along the street then into his cup, and adds "Still, like I said to you last night, Wilf, seems almost every case you want to read about, there's someone knows something – a wife whose husband came home late, acting just a little different, or a boss sees a little change in an employee – he's a little quieter, or something. That's what we hope for..." he hesitates again, concerned that his remarks might set the whole town on edge (though a small cost for justice – for Janet). "And so often, someone has a little piece, but doesn't think it's important enough. And so many times, there's an actual scared witness..."

All the others stare or gape at him. No one looks at anyone else. He downs the last of his coffee, then smiles timidly. "Sorry, fellas, kids. We've got to get this solved, somehow. It can get rough. But the roughest part would be having it happen again..." And raising a hand as though to hold them back, like an offensive outsider begging off, he straightens up from leaning on the meter, crushes the paper cup in his other hand, and – pushing his fingers once through his hair – turns and crosses the street.

They all stay still for a moment, watching their ambling police chief disappear into his office. Then they wade through a pensive few seconds just blinking around at each other...without a word...until Wilf spots Bert: "So you got your fall yard rakin' plans set yet..?"

And Bert throws his empty cup at him.

The summer stars shine with divine silence out the opened windows. Crossing through the car interior, a soft, warm breeze is spiced by the faint taste of farm fields full of corn and nearby bush plots seeping oxygen; it's scented with the dirt road's earthiness and carries the cricket creakings. The pleasing hot sun is long set, but the Earth still radiates its power.

In the middle of the back seat, Joseph balances last night's remaining half case of beer on top of the leg-numbing cold of a fresh one. The four shadowy forms around him reach through the blackness toward him regularly – as though curiously parched. (They don't ever do this both Friday and Saturday nights of a weekend, but Joseph had walked the new case to the dancehall parking lot, so they "broke away from the action", as though to accommodate him – like a new friend...for life.)

Sitting beside Joseph, Gene has been ridiculing him since the car stopped. Howard, a mere passenger tonight in the front, has chipped in as best he can to Gene's cause. Behind the wheel, Norm slouches down against the door. And from the other back corner, Ba-Dee has tried to change the subject six times.

"You don't know what some people have to go through," Joseph defends himself and much of mankind, there in the dark.

"Crusher," (Gene likes to call him) "we know your sad story. We've heard it enough," he adds mockingly.

"No you don't," Joseph counters flatly.

"Self-pity is not a legitimate emotion," Gene insists.

Joseph takes a long guzzle... "Fuck you. You don't get it."

"Everybody has their problems. Most people, you don't see them. Yours, Crusher, are right on the surface."

(Gene's attempt at humorous implication, inferring Joseph's strange looks, is too obvious to be funny.)

"Fuck off and die," Joseph tries again, loudly uncapping another beer in the abyss.

"Will-dew..!" Gene relents a little, for everyone's sake.

"Check your schedule," Joseph suggests, challengingly.

"It's on here. Just can't find it," Gene looks away into the night.

"See Chief Chuck at the dance?" Ba-Dee brightens, since they were talking about how to handle death anyway.

"He's always at the dance," Howard moans.

"That's not what I meant," Ba-Dee sort of scoffs. "He's a changed man."

"Hey, that's true!" Norm sits up a bit. "His eyes were on the prowl – you didn't notice?"

"He's always watching stuff. He's Looker's dad," Howard jokes.

"He knows something," Ba Dee swears.

"Like what?" Gene huffs, leaning forward to try to see Ba-Dee's eyes across the pitch of the back seat.

"He's the one who said watch for little changes in people – when they secretly know something," Ba-Dee recounts what Howard told him about this afternoon's intense moment in front of Lucy's.

"So?" Gene is still hanging out there squinting past Joseph.

"Chuck knows something," Ba-Dee insists.

(Norm cringes in the dark. He's asked himself a hundred times whether what he knows is important. And has imagined as many ways it could do the wrong thing, out in the open. He wishes again that he didn't know anything.)

"All right! What?" Gene imagines he wants to hear it, scrunching back into his corner.

"He certainly doesn't know who did it," Howard mutters, nestling down even more in the front seat as though preparing for a long stay.

"But he knows there's someone who knows something," Ba-Dee claims. "That's what Norm and Howard heard him sorta say today..."

A moment of breathing and sipping goes by; the country breeze gently slips around them, passing through the car.

"Someone over there did it!" Joseph now growls dramatically, glowering at the glow of the town that faintly lights the cloudless sky two or three miles away.

And as though each of all five of them here thinks the same thing, that it could even be someone in the car with him right now, another odd silence passes...

"Why can't it be someone from out of town?" Howard sits up and turns to face the invisible panel of three in the back.

"Who knew she'd be out there? Her sister says she always went out there late. But how would a stranger ever know that?" Ba-Dee reminds him in his characteristic uncritical tone.

"Oh," Howard says softly. "Hee," he lilts.

"Let's go ask Chuck," Joseph utters.

"What?!" two voices join.

"Why not? We'll ask him what he knows – we only want to help him," Joseph reasons. "We're citizens!" he justifies it all in a word.

That stops them for a second.

"Well..." Gene rolls it over.

"He can't arrest us for trying to help," Norm tinkers with the idea, too. "What's to lose?"

"No way!" Howard squirms. "Listen to you guys! We're beer-swilling low-lifes out here! We've got no right to – "

"We've got every right," Joseph states. "And there's lower lifes than us – in fact, most of the – "

"Crusher's right," Gene for the first time ever agrees with Joseph, interrupting him to do so.

"Whatta you mean, 'low-lifes'?!" Ba-Dee is suddenly indignant.

Three beer bottles glimmer as they raise to six lips as though on cue.

"We're supposed to be out here. It's in our teenage contract," Norm is the voice of reason.

"Then come on – let's go!" you can hear Gene grin.

"Let's drink beer," Joseph changes flags abruptly, withdrawing his crusade support at the face of reality.

Howard has a compromise: "We'll come back. Leave it on the road."

"What?!" three voices ring.

"Just put it in the trunk," Norm relents (as the driver).

"Oh, just put it on the hood!" Ba-Dee gives up, with a little laugh.

"Let's drink it all," Joseph inserts again.

Another silence then grips them, five town sons teetering between their usual selves and life's true seriousness...

"If the sun was a pea," Norm soon offers with thorough incongruence, "the nearest other pea would be ninety miles away."

The other four think for a moment.

"So how big is this car?" Joseph has to ask.

"Fly shit," Howard guesses.

"Smaller," Norm imagines.

"Amoeba shit," Gene thinks he knows.

"Teenier," Norm believes.

Howard then leans out the window a bit. Searching around the heavens, full of wonder, he humbles them to Creation: "Quark shit!"

"Yes," Norm concludes, then slurps his beer. "But, dinky grains of life that we are, we can still perceive infinity..."

...

The five pillars of youthful community concern re-enter the Varmint Hall dance in a clump. Chief Cintz sees them clearly with only peripheral vision.

Along the hall walls, stacking chairs are scattered around plain wood tables cluttered with lots of beer bottles, plastic cups, potato chip bags and purses. Half the seats have someone sitting on them; the empty ones await dancing fools tearing up the floor. (As ever, the number of chairs set out is about right: one hundred and ten, the regular summer-Saturday-night bunch.) The hall is dimly lit, the indirect light from the stage (where Brad the bouncing band-break disc jockey is grooving) being its main source. A little lamp at the right front corner of the dance floor illuminates two rolls of tickets lying flat on a small desk – red tickets for beer and blue for mixed drinks. In behind, a Dutch door's top propped open spills out a white glow of light from the small kitchen beyond: the "bar". The music (not too loud because it echoes off the bare rafters and wood floor) is oldies; the instruments abandoned on the stage by the oft-resting band are a saxophone, a pile of old drums, and a primitive electric guitar. Nobody sings.

The talking and laughing and music make for a steady roar. Almost half of the crowd are near the same age as the five returnees who have just skulked as one body in and along the back wall. (All the young women notice them; some of the young men eye them sideways. The five are obviously up to something.)

Chief Chuck finally stands, sighing and groaning in one breath. "'Scuse me," he says pointedly above the noise to his cherished wife Beth, to Wilf and his wife Sue, and to the ten other friends jammed around their front table. His gray hair neatly combed, his white, long-sleeved dress shirt left open at the collar, plus dark and baggy low-slung jeans and white-sneaker dancing shoes make him look like someone else. He frowns professionally and grins reminiscently at the five young corner-huddlers as he circles around the stomping mob toward them. He makes like he's going to walk right past them, then stops and turns. "Gene! How's your dad?" he clenches a hand on Genes shoulder, concerned about his father's heart problem.

"He's okay – fine," Gene replies appreciatively (the truth, known to at least these few, being he wishes the old monster was dead).

"Good...good. So...what's up, fellas? You look..." Chuck twirls one hand in the air a little as he slips the other into his pocket. His frown is gone, leaving only an open smile. "Go ahead, I understand everything..." he trails like a doctor.

Gene has already spoken, so it seems up to him to answer. "We were just talking about... if we could help you out, somehow. But – "

"It's pissin' us off!" Howard suddenly blurts, glaring out across the floor. "We wanna help get this over with – nail the fuckin' bastard..!" he sort of forgets himself, his own startled eyes jumping back to the Chief.

"Sure," Chuck shocks them with his easy response, all of their beer-floating eyes now popping like Howard's. "You sure can. Com'on outside."

Though a piece of all five of them right here feels they are presently part of the arrest process, they mostly feel eager with trust's potential.

Outside, Chuck leans on a car under a streetlight a few steps away from the door. He glances quickly from one to the other as they align clumsily in front of him. "There was a witness."

"Told ya!" Ba-Dee chimes.

"No you didn't," Norm pokes him hard. "You said – "

"Who?" Gene and Joseph both interrupt together.

"Don't exactly know," Chuck answers plainly.

All five are instantly confused.

"Evidence shows that someone was watching," the Chief explains.

"Yeah..?!" Joseph gasps the only reaction possible.

"And," Chuck continues, "maybe you can help me find him."

"Him?" Gene notes amid the gaping.

Chief Cintz then tells them everything, ending with a plea for secrecy, "Or I'll shoot your lips off," he adds with steely calm. He doesn't even hint at how they can go about it. He just smiles weakly, shakes each of their hands solemnly, then turns to go back inside. "It pisses me off, too," he growls at the ground as he walks away.

Gene, Joseph, Norm, Ba-Dee and Howard watch Chief Chuck pass through the open doorway, walk up the short, bright corridor, then turn left and disappear into the dark dance hall... slowly accelerating then soon running to their car, the young men are moments later speeding back out of town.

"Three hundred and ninety-five to three hundred and ninety-eight – *for us!*" Heap Henry growls as mean as a twelve-year-old can. He leans on his bat, propped on home plate, his other hand braced on his hip. He spits. He's staring menacingly at Ricky on the mound, who had just declared to all thirteen of his fellow regular players that the score "don't mean shit". Ricky's six infielders and outfielders behind him are moaning or jabbering. Six kids in the shadowed dugout are trying to drown them out. Heap chomps his gum. His round face sparkles with sweat in the sunshine, his dirty white T-shirt and sagging jeans – a trademark. His long, blond hair, halfway down to his shoulders, flutters in the dusty wind. Everyone seems to have a different score. He refuses to budge.

Outside the screened-in field, at the center of the bottom bench of the otherwise empty third-base bleachers, sitting straight, arms crossed, maybe smiling, eyes thoughtfully gazing, sits Looker.

"Start the game over again, hootheads!" Jackie mocks them all from the shade of his personal corner at the far end of the first base dugout bench. "Summer's only half over!"

"Awright, awright, lardass!" Ricky seethes at Henry as he relents to three runs down. "Jus' bat!"

The grumbling and whining dissolves. Rick gets ready to throw. All eyes turn to him. Minds are focused back on the pitch – most of them oblivious to a certain self-consciousness that Looker over there can make a young boy feel – that someone like him just seems to know that you know something, that he's someone you fear will expose you, and what you have seen...every boy here is concentrating on the ball arcing toward Henry's bat... every boy except one.

Mayor James Jimms – "Hap", as in happy, "Jolly Jay-Jay", Jimmy Jimms – is terrified. Everyone gathered on the church steps there with him and Reverend Fisk right beside him are wondering about him! – no, don't get wound up again!, he tells himself. No one really suspects anyone, specifically. At least, no outsider more than a local. (Just because you were born here doesn't mean you're pure as the country air, does it?)

The Sunday sun is brilliant. The wind is strong and hot. All the colorful dresses and plain suits clustered on the wide cement steps contrast the many younger (up to middle aged) folks wearing jeans or shorts. Reverend Fisk welcomes all – some even bring their dogs (as though just popping in from their happen-to-be-going-by obligatory family weekend doggie-dump walk).

The Mayor tries not to sweat. He wishes right then he had a wife to stand beside him. He knows everybody knows he simply showed up in town twenty years ago, and now he's acting like he knows none of them know where he came from – and they know it! And he tries not to believe that at least one of them has to have found out that he came here straight from jail. And that he had spent the first twenty years of his adulthood there. And that he was guilty. Of murder.

"Hap!" the Reverend calls his name loudly beside him, startling him again. "Hap, we've got a good town here, we all know that. My sermon wasn't meant to be a statement of hopelessness – you know how you get in a mood and then that's all you can write down?"

"Sure, Reverend," Hap smiles wide.

"It's not like nothin' ever happened here before," Sid notes from a couple of steps down.

"Sure!" Reverend Fisk fans an arm downward in sweeping agreement. "And like I said, time will let us forget..."

A chill goes through Mayor Jimmy Jimms. He doesn't believe time eases pain or guilt. In fact, he knows it.

"Well, it's Lucy time," Sid reminds them. (A traditional after-sermon coffee draws more folks than the Reverend, sometimes, somehow.) "Comin' Rev? Hap?"

With the Reverend smiling ashamedly and the Mayor grinning tightly, Sid leads the two dark-suited men along the street through the continuous shade of all the old buildings. They walk briskly, and are soon at the other end of the two blocks and right in the midst of twenty or so folks sitting on or standing around the bench positioned under the plain but honest sign painted black on white: LUCY'S LARGE LUNCH. Below "LUNCH", steady streams and big clumps of people swing open the restaurant's squeaky screen door and fade completely into its soft darkness, as though it's infinite in there. The Reverend and Jim shuffle to a stop by the bench, white Sid goes inside to fetch coffee.

Across the street, Wilf is alone with Chief Chuck in the police office. Wilf is standing, hands in pockets, at the half-curtained window. Chuck sits back in his chair watching him – communicating. (They don't always have to talk.)

"They're all guilty of something," Chuck soon suggests without emotion.

"I burned down a house once – only a falling-down shack, really. When we were kids," Wilf confesses.

"Didn't mean you," Chuck is quick to qualify his condemnation. "Anyway, I already knew that."

"What's your story?" Wilf's wise and gentle blue eyes glint as he smiles, still looking across the street. He straightens back his thin shoulders under his crisp, light denim church shirt (the best he owns).

(Right then at the ballpark, Heap Henry has notched a triple, his second hit and second RBI of the morning, vaulting his and Jack's team to four hundred total runs. Ricky's guys have yet to score today. And one of Ricky's outfielders shudders coldly when he sees, after Heap's hitting commotion, that Looker is gone but, well back between the backstop and the bleachers on the first base side, hands on hips and wind blowing his hair – having arrived somehow unnoticed and his apparently staring eyes too far away to tell their focus – sits Bug Doug on his big bike.)

Chuck opens his desk drawer and takes out the sacred bottle of vintage whisky and the two Sunday morning glasses. He pours an inch in each. "Never told ya...this is gonna sound great, now..." he squints at the drinks...

Wilf's eyes crank as far around as they can go with his face still square with Lucy's. His expression stays blank.

Chuck follows through: "I dragged a girl behind a garage, once..." he confesses.

Wilf shows a little grin. (Chuck Cintz can do no wrong, he knows.)

"She was about fifteen... I was about fifteen or so," Chuck adds, meaning he was old enough to know better.

"Yeah?" Wilf reacts matter-of-factly.

"I was going nuts. I was all over her, trying to kiss everything she owned..."

"And?"

"It suddenly hit me what I was doing – what I might do next. So I backed off, and watched her look of...her look of amazement.

I just stared at her, for a good half minute, then actually started crawling away down that dusty ol' lane..."

"What'd she do?" Wilf means long-term.

"She tackled me!" Chuck's face lights up as he squeals it. "She was climbing all over me, yanking my clothes off – right there in broad daylight..! Wildest teenage time I ever had..."

Wilf laughs a little (he has a good enough idea who she was) as he turns and crosses the office to get his drink. Taking a savoring sip, he meets Chuck's eyes then walks the few steps back to watch the street. "That was just your normal, everyday biology," he concludes in his resonant, soft way, twirling the contents of his glass in the shade of the curtain, his lean, weathered face seeming to glow in the window's bright daylight.

"I've always felt guilty over the way it started," Chuck frowns, then takes a quick drink. "It scared me."

"Wait a minute!" Wilf turns his head. "You're not talkin' the same thing at all, Chuck! God, there's two separate realities here! Doing something like what happened to an innocent girl like Janet is way over the line – not human – *the way we have to be to stay human*," Wilf strongly points out with his usual, only slightly flustered calm. Staring the Chief down, he lets that sink in. "You're talkin' about something merely red-blooded. You had the sanity to stop. But what we've got now somewhere in this town is a brain mutant, someone with some blown circuits. It's two different living things."

"But where does it begin?" Chuck doesn't really mean himself, now.

Wilf takes a thought-filled sip. He then jams his free hand into the front pocket of his jeans and grimaces at the Chief's question. "I'd bet even the best psychoanalyst couldn't be sure of that one. People are just wonky, Chuck – you know that. Sometimes, after the fact, it stops mattering what made them that way."

"Then how do we stop it happening?" the Chief anguishes.

"Shit, we tried everything – as a race. Execution, education. Kids keep getting abused, ignored, and grow up walking detonators. The world is full of violence, always was. You're talkin' about changing human nature? How do you begin to make a non-violent world? It'll be ages, yet. It's just...inherent."

"I wish it wasn't always so pessimistic," Chuck sighs.

Part of Wilf is still involved across the street: "A collection of people," he muses. "A collection, as in guns, or something. Each one, you could suppose, is potentially lethal. But most never get fired. And others are hair-triggers...

"And the way I see it, it's supposed to be this way, Chuck. Every one of those folks over there is living a life they have to live, in a world that, right now, has to be the way it is. Who's rules? – we can't know the answer." Wilf gulps his drink as though to steel himself against his own theory.

Chief Chuck raises a leg onto his desk, teetering back more in his chair. He sets his glimmering crystal-cut glass on his dune-like belly. His worried, gentle eyes raise from his whiskey to Wilf, over and over. "Good point..." he trails, trying not to feel total futility for his chosen profession. "But the reality, Wilf, is that one of those people out there has an ugly story that I think is way beyond the way it has to be, and my duty as the bouncer – and yours as someone who wants the right thing for you and yours – is to get him out of our little town party – "

"You're right. That's what it comes down to, here and now." Wilf studies the bottom of his glass as though deciding if he needs a refill. "So what do we do – what do *I* do, Chuck? You're doin' it full time, what can I do – besides rattle on about it?"

"I can't ask you to – "

"You asked those five young guys – at the dance!" (Chuck tells Wilf everything.)

"I thought they might come up with a...different angle," Chuck raises his gray eyebrows in self-defense.

"Well, we were all them, once," Wilf grins. And he takes a few steps back to Chuck's desk, clenching his empty glass in a hand hooked on a belt loop. "And I guess back then, like most, I felt I had enough common sense answers to save the world – didn't you, Chuck, good-buddy?"

"Of course."

"Growin' up in this town," Wilf then gently sets his glass at the center of Chuck's blotter, "was fulfillin'. There's always been all kinds of caring people to help you out. My family got its full share, through our rough times. I always knew the value in that – in a community, and appreciated it. And it feels just as good to me now." He waits while the Chief pours him a fresh inch, then slowly picks it up and, dangling it at his side at arm's length, returns thoughtfully to the window. "My brothers envy me, you know that, Chuck? Both tell me they wish they still lived here. City neighborhoods just aren't the same. And I've traveled around just enough to believe they're right, that a place like this can be a home you belong to... " He pauses for a moment, and sips. "Sometimes, to watch the world when you're outside of here, you feel only pessimism for the race, but comin' back here, it feels different, you know?"

"Oh, yeah, I know," Chuck smiles reflectively.

Wilf watches the people coming and going around Lucy's. "But you could worry, after your life is sort of invested here, that the memories of a secure growing up...and the heart of this town being made up of most every heart together – your own a meaningful part of it – you worry that a thing like this could make it come apart, make people just a touch mistrustful, then suspicious, then isolated..."

"Depends on who did it and if we catch him," Chuck interjects.

"But will it forever spoil it?" Wilf fears, surveying the street.

"Lots happened here over the years," Chuck reminds his lifelong friend as he stiffly rises out of his chair and waddles (just noticeably) to the window, hooking his thumbs on his belt like Wilf.

"And it changed things," Wilf shakes his head a little. "Remember the Parkin's suicide? How it got everyone down for months? That poor old woman, in the middle of a town of *caring* people... No one knew or cared just how alone she felt, her husband and son passed on. Didn't that break your heart, Chuck? Didn't you just want to move away?"

"No, well, fifteen years ago...well, I guess I felt somewhat responsible, having just become Chief. But people choose to do things, or not do things. Maybe she could have reached out..."

"Sure, but the fact is, she didn't, and she died a forlorn death, thanks to all of us. And now, how responsible are we for this murder, and especially for what this town becomes?" Wilf wants to know.

"You're asking a lot. You're asking folks to be something more than human, to carry everyone else on their backs," the Chief watches the same moving lips and outbreaks of laughter that Wilf is watching across the street.

"Ha!" Wilf bursts with realization. "You're right, you're right. Perfect paradise gets spoiled by actual reality, every time. And I know better, in my clearer moments... Hey! – you see? It's changin' me, even! I'm turnin' into the town cynic!"

"You're the town rock," Chuck insists, standing beside him.

"I hate it when I feel this way," Wilf grumbles, though unemotionally.

"You're the town donkey," Chuck insists without expression.

Both men of concern and vision watch the passing parade along the street, full of thoughts of their conversation. Both take occasional little sips of their drinks, and both rock on their feet a little, as though to soothe themselves. Finally, Wilf speaks again:

"Mayor Happy-Jim-Jimms seems a little jumpy, don't he?"

"The sky is black. Some shaded dirty clouds are pushing across. The wind is moaning. Leaves flap and cling. A tiny red glow brightens then dims right above the hard outline of the picnic table against the white siding of the house. I watch transfixed, I have no thoughts, only eyes. The cigarette reddens brighter again.

"I'm going to do it.

"I've got to do it now.

"I tighten my grip on the cool fence, ready to climb over it. Some deep part of me knows exactly what I'm doing but consequence has no meaning now.

"I stretch a foot up to the top rail then swing quietly as I can over the pickets to crouch on the ground."

(Did he make a noise? – he can't remember if he made a noise hitting the ground.)

"The grass is mushy, not wet, just stringy soft. The cigarette glows, illuminating more now a few steps closer. There's no lights in the back yards both ways.

"There's no point crouching. She can't see me, it's too dark. She can't hear me, it's too windy.

"I need to do this.

"I can feel her skin.

"I imagine her hair. Her smell. Her body."

(His heart races, remembering detail after detail.)

"This is forever. It can't be undone.

"Her face, her lips, her cheeks, glow faintly under the cigarette.

"There's a smell of farm shit mixed in the wind. If it wasn't for her, the wind would be spooky.

"I'm five steps away. I imagine grabbing her face, her mouth. I'll punch her in the back of the neck."

(He pissed himself with excitement. Remembering that, he feels even more aroused, now.)

"The cigarette smells sweet.

"I stretch out one hand. She doesn't see a thing. I tiptoe around above her head to the very end of the table, looking almost straight down at her. She's mine."

(That's all he needs to come, to get it off. He now consciously erases his mind, his memory, forcibly thinking about something else – like making it to church, or just going for a coffee at Lucy's. As soon as he wipes himself off.)

Her room is dim and shadowed, though the daylight is bright around the drawn shades. The air feels heavy with time. Her dolls and stuffed bears on the shelves are still coldly lifeless. She's crying silently, in her clothes on her back on the bed. Her short brown hair is all tangles, her small body looks lifeless, her pretty face is pale. Another tear follows the wet path down her cheek; the pink pillow has stains on both sides. The house below and around her is forlornly quiet.

Jennifer breathes shallow breaths. Her drenched brown eyes stay open for a moment, then close, as though she can't stand the sight of her gray room or the involuntary images behind her eyelids. She feels heavy, in this world. She is aching with hunger, having eaten nothing today – or yesterday. But she can't get up.

Why, her thoughts wander, is the world so cruel? Why does there have to be pain? Is it (she asks the invisible heavens) God's intent to have us suffer things to...to have us learn something? So then, is pain God's way? – a part of His heaven, too? And if so, is Janet still suffering there, the way she suffered dying? And if she was God's child, a person, a life, pure of heart and born innocent, why did He push her – and all of us – out into the onslaughts of rage, sorrow, hunger, suffering, despair, emptiness...though all only as real as creation...

Both her eyes have become wells of tears, reddened and brimming wet.

How could anyone hurt God's child – Janet was not theirs to hurt, to consume or own or change! Her life was *hers*, and His...

She sighs. And softly sniffles.

What life would Janet have lived? she wonders again. What joy and hope would have been hers? What tragedy..? What emptiness does she feel now? The same as mine..?

Outside, the birds are chirping, playing in the trees. She doesn't hear them. Outside, the warm Earth gently rolls through silent, graceful space. She feels only thoughts. She's a mere thin form atop a made bed. And in a grave nearby, a sister lies forever still – time moves all around her, but she keeps still. She cannot be heard, or summoned, or held.

Sometimes, now, Jennifer thinks about her mother and father, and feels bad for them – how sad for them to lose a daughter. (They still have one.) And she sometimes, now, thinks about the outside world – school, church (this morning), friends – and thinks she misses them...but is afraid, embarrassed, how it will feel. And she imagines there will be a time when she will not be full of Janet and death...but cannot imagine not missing her...

"What energizes atoms?" Norm asks Howard-like from the dark back corner seat.

"God," Howard in the other corner knows what Norm means.

Joseph is driving, Sunday night the only night he can get the family car. Big Gene sits in the passenger front. Ba-Dee is out by the back taillight having a leak. All five are barely sipping tonight –this isn't a beer thing. It's an emergency assembly, a challenge to young minds.

"*What?!*" Gene asks incredulously. "What the fuck are you talking about?"

"No scientist," Norm obliges, "ever questions where the endless energy of every single atom comes from. It's just 'there'."

"Oh," Gene now understands.

"So, like, God drives them?" Joseph wants clarification.

"No, God *is* the energy of them," Howard reveals.

"Why don't they even ask the question?" Norm is still brooding in the blackness as Ba-Dee opens the door again, blinding everyone with the dome light as he scrambles over legs while lifting the half-full beer case off his place in the center of the back seat.

"What question?" Ba-Dee asks innocently, settling in.

"Why people are untruthful," Gene picks a subject of his own.

"What the fuck are *you* talking about?!" Howard guffaws.

"The primary flaw of human nature," Gene elaborates a clearly favorite theory, "is its inability to be accurate – including lying: intentional inaccuracy. Imagine if people could only speak the accurate truth..."

"Utterly boring," Howard grasps it.

"We certainly wouldn't be sitting here now," Norm thinks he sees.

"You mean we couldn't lie about our age to buy beer?" Joseph is struggling with the big picture.

"No, dungwad," Howard councils him. "He means all history would be completely different. Who knows where we'd be – if even born."

"And Janet..?" Ba-Dee violently twists the mood again.

"There would still be murder, wouldn't there?" Norm apparently can't picture it too well, after all.

"It sure is part of lots of murder mysteries – picking out the liars," Gene says.

"Then that's what we have to do," Ba-Dee gathers.

"Find the liar?!" Gene somehow suddenly gets flustered again. "Well, let's just go ask everybody if they did it! We'll know the liar right off then, won't we!"

"Nohhh," Ba-Dee pushes his voice. "No one knows what we're up to, right? Just Chucky Chief and Wilf. We can talk with guys, check alibis, make kid lists – "

"Of course!" Howard agrees. "We don't have to do fingerprinting or anything. We just start with the obvious: asking around a bit."

"Better us than Chuck. They'd just seize up on him," Norm thinks.

Lightning flashes in the distance, far from the close sounds of the car interior. Outside, crickets keep cricketing; a windless silence holds the motionless car on the road.

"It's Looker," Gene once again offers up a suspect in the blackness.

"...Sid," Ba-Dee suggests a new one after a pause.

"Chase," claims Norm.

"Chuck," Howard considers.

"Joseph," says Joseph.

"Carl."

"It could be a female..." Joseph begins.

"With a little hand-held sperm shooter?" Howard ridicules him, laughing.

"Nighttime Nancy."

"Lucy!"

Run out of immediate suspects, the five of them sit through another country silence. Thirty seconds pass before anyone speaks again – a record.

"No way it's Lucy," Howard defends an institution.

"Let's go see Lucy. Lucy knows everything!" Ba-Dee proposes.

"Right!" two voices ring at once.

Then Norm shakily blurts it: "I think I know something..."

"Quantum electrodynamics?" Howard guesses blandly.

"No. Something about Janet..." He lets that sink in.

No one talks.

"She was seeing someone – "

"*What?!*" Gene screams, aware as everyone that all the testimony established there was no secret boyfriend.

"How do you know?" Howard asks with a cautious edge.

"It's my little brother," Norm lets it all out, the pain of doing so as edged as his words.

"But Jeff's only..." Gene starts.

"Fourteen. Same as her," Norm answers, staring out the window.

"Whuh," Joseph utters.

"Oh, man!" Howard slumps in his seat.

"Shit! Why'd you even say it!" Ba-Dee laments.

"I don't know... I want to do the right thing, I guess. If we're going to try to do something about this, I need to get this out – "

"You don't think...?" Joseph counters.

"No," Norm is blunt. "But I can't guarantee where he was that night..."

Howard notes, "He couldn't have been the one watching – Chuck saying the kid's only eight – "

"Or ten," Joseph tries to keep it accurate.

"Did you talk to him?" Ba-Dee asks carefully.

"No."

"Your folks know?" Howard continues with the obvious parts.

"No."

"Shit," Joseph concludes.

"Now that I've said it, I know what I gotta do," Norm almost whispers. His eyes glance around at the shadowy forms of his friends.

"What if – ?" Howard begins.

"What am *I* supposed to do?! What *if?!*It's his life, his actions. I can't be guilty for *his* actions!" Norm angrily spits the rehearsed words out the window. He's obviously spent a lot of worry arriving at them.

Another new record silence is self-consciously set. Joseph then finally ends it:

"Lucy's waiting," his lofty tone is timed dramatically with his starting the car.

On the way back into town, Norm is offered sympathy and encouragement, philosophy and advice, and promises of confidentiality. None of it takes more weight off him than his admission.

"**T**he biggest thing we got," Chuck walks in the office and announces to Tom sitting there in his usual crisp uniform, "is a disturbing lack of anything."

It's Monday noon and the results are final from Elston's lab.

"Nothing that we didn't already know," Chuck explains, sitting down and leaning back in his chair. His eyes, steady and expressionless in the mix of daylight and fluorescent, are level with Tom's. "Punched, stripped, raped. Dressed again. Dragged off to the roadside with her shoes on, likely still unconscious. Strangled, by hand. Nothing under her fingernails or on her teeth – if she came to, she probably submitted..." And, he just then chooses to hold off adding (why, he doesn't know yet): one little red thread – maybe not hers – caught under a back stud on her carved leather belt.

"Well," Tom responds after a sigh, "nothing new on the road, either." Having just got back from scouring the ditch again where Janet's body was found, he looks tired of going around in circles.

At least Janet's uncle's alibi had proved true. And, to their surprise, Carl had late last night volunteered his car to Chuck for examination. ("A father is probably always suspected," he had astutely offered in the privacy of the police office. "Better me saying it first, I guess.") Chuck thanked him, then drove him back home in it. And he has just come back from taking it to Elston

City first thing this morning. (Both he and Tom realize there's little to be expected from a car the victim rode in all the time.)

"We need to talk with Jennifer," Chuck then reluctantly says it. "We can't keep putting it off. We have to see if she can help us."

Tom's gaze lowers to his bare desk. He has said more than once how tough a call that is, imagining what the poor sister is feeling. "I'll go get her," he reacts mechanically, his eyes meeting Chuck's again as though looking for hesitation.

The Chief says nothing. Tom slowly stands and leaves.

...

Jennifer was calm, all through Chuck's sensitive questioning. Tom had tried to stay invisible at his desk in behind where she sat facing the police chief. She was friendly, though she didn't smile once. She talked at some length about Janet's friends and some of their conversations about them, but said nothing that either police officer felt was the least bit of a lead. They had her back home within two hours.

At Norm's house, Jeff is outside lying on his back on the picnic table, smoking a cigarette, staring at the blue sky.

Norm steps through the porch doorway onto the top step and sees him. He's about to growl something, the way older teenage brothers give advice, but stops with his mouth half open. Instead, he comes down and sits on the bench beside him...and just watches him a few seconds. Then, with forced calm, he asks Jeff why he even told him that he and Janet were a "thing". Jeff just shrugs. (He was just trying to reach out somewhere, it's obvious.) Norm next wants to know what else there is to tell. Jeff takes a drag, thinks a moment, then spills out that Janet and him only hung around together at school a lot and met maybe four or five times late at night in the park, smoking and talking. "Shit, we only ever kissed twice..." his voice now breaks with anguish. Still searching the sky, his face and eyes grow tense, as though to hold back a flush of tears. When Norm softly questions why they didn't meet that night – last Tuesday – Jeff doesn't answer, and clearly does not want to talk again. Though Norm doesn't suspect any wrong-doing by his brother, he knows for certain Jeff is still holding back the most important part.

And meanwhile, downtown, the bench at Lucy's is empty, waiting. The late-afternoon sun angles onto the restaurant windows; occasionally someone walks by. Folks are working in the stores, helping customers, up and down the street. In some of the houses all around, housewives, or even husbands, are preparing supper or playing with the kids.

Wilf and Sid soon walk around a corner, having parked the truck along a side street. Finished work for the day, they stride, a little stiff looking, talking about their day, through the sunshine toward Lucy's.

A few minutes later, up the street, Norm parks his parents' car in the side parking lot of Nick's Bowl (five lanes) where Ba-Dee works summers at the small burger bar (twelve red vinyl revolving stools). Inside, Howard is the only one sitting at the counter, nursing a coffee, talking with Ba-Dee. No one is bowling. Norm sits beside Howard, and immediately recounts every word of his brief conversation with his brother Jeff. The other two nod their heads as he talks, more details stirred into the mix in their minds.

On the windless, sun-baked diamond not far away, the ball-game is tied again.

And Bug Doug rides the crop-lined country roads all around, as though he can't stand being in town.

ilf coasts his new bicycle right along the top of the
curb all the way down the block to Lucy's, the new
restaurant on the corner at the stop sign. In front of
the building, under the window, he sees they've just put out a
new bench, but no one is sitting on it yet there in the summer
warmth.

There's people on the sidewalk, and he has to steer carefully.
His dad just bought him (for passing) and taught him how to ride
this red-frame balloon-tires bike, and it's a little too big for him,
too. But he stays up on the curb most of the way.

At the corner in front of the restaurant, young Wilf brakes.
Down the street, the little maples lining the road at the curve
slowly sway in the hot wind, their leaves like small green flags
flipping and flopping, he thinks. Along the street, a few cars have
parked at meters, and a couple more now slowly drive by. An elderly lady is walking away, big old handbag almost scraping the
sidewalk.

He looks down at the paint markings on the pavement. That
kid at school was right: they're finally putting in the stoplight.
(Wilf then recalls how many stoplights Elston City has, ten miles
away, and wonders how long he'll have to wait to see a second one
put in here. It's a measure of a town's size and worth, he thinks,

how many stoplights and how many neon signs liven up its night streets.)

Soon, as he tries to balance on his bike there by holding onto a signpost, two old men (maybe forty) come out of Lucy's and sit right down on that bench, holding coffee mugs and muttering. He watches as they lean back and then self-consciously survey the street. They must think everyone is eying them on that new bench right out in the open. Wilf decides to stay there a minute and maybe hear what they're saying.

"Then after the gas station," one says taking a sip, "that's when they break the window of Hargrove's Pharmacy there, but Chief Phillips figured somethin' scared 'em off, 'cause nothin' seems taken."

"That was two months ago, this is now," the other one argues, glancing at Wilf wiggling closer on his red bike.

"Well," the balding one frowns, "there's jus' too much of it for such a small town. Yuh live here 'cause it's s'pose to be safe. Now, people tryin' tuh kill people..."

The other man just slowly shakes his head, raises his steaming mug to his puckered lips, and swishes his eyes back and forth up and down the street as though wary of a car full of hit men. (Wilf imagines that's why they put the bench out here, so they don't get caught defenseless over a plate of spaghetti – like those gangsters in the movies.)

The two men change the subject. Wilf thinks it's because he's nosing in so he decides to race home and ask his mom what they were talking about...people trying to kill people.

Once again sailing the clean, gray sidewalk, every crack a new sensation, Wilf pushes down hard on the pedals. Along the store-fronts – hardware spilling out into the drenching sun, a single coat rack jammed with drab suits on sale, a man in overalls step-ping out of a doorway and two women in bright-colored sum-mer dresses going in the next – he looks for his friends (especially

Chucky Cintz) so he can show off his new bike. (But his head is full of images of the Murderous Evil suddenly undermining his town.) Turning the next corner off of Main Street, he realizes he can take a long route back, along and up all kinds of side streets, and still make it home faster than ever.

Everything Wilf passes is so familiar – each tree trunk and every porch pushing out toward the street – except he's looking more down at it all, now. He knows his town inside out, including (unlike most kids his age) lots of older folks too. He knows where many people in these houses work – in which stores – and where that car easing away from him is probably going and what dogs are fenced in or which ones might chase him.

At the next corner he chances the long puddle (that seems to always be there) and splashes through, almost losing his balance – another triumph of riding skill! He then roars down the middle of the next street at breakneck speed, leans into a turn at a death-defying centrifugal incline, and coasts forever under shade trees lining the way. (Still no kid of any significance has seen him.)

Dead ahead on the next street, a fierce, black tree rat stares him down, but scoots off the road at the last possible instant (just when Wilf loses his nerve and is about to swerve wildly). Riding on, he forgets the squirrel and calms down, and as he soars away he notices with a grin how a big pine tree looks hung with turds and behind it how the mountain range of white thunderheads in the distance seems to move with him, just like in a car... And then he remembers what the men were saying, and he wonders if it was someone in this house, or in that one... (He has no comprehension of the emotional impact of killing or murder. Violence is a word that has to do with crimes that happen out there in the cities and on television. He's seen a fistfight, but that wasn't violence, it was just men tussling out an argument. Wilf has no feeling of violence, or the rage behind it. He can't see that far into it, though he understands people can be that way. All he can picture happening here in his town is some fall-down drunk shooting at what he maybe thought was a deer, or something.) He's glad he's almost home, so he can ask his mom what happened.

His grand old house is in sight, yellow brick blazing in sunbeams patterned by surrounding tall elms. He can see there is no one in the white wooden chairs on the wide front and side porches. (It's Monday, he realizes. Dad's at work, and so are Wilf's two older brothers and all their neighbors and family friends – all the men and some of their wives.) He coasts on the uneven sidewalk, across the spill of gravel from the driveway, and up the front walkway framed by little hedges all the way to the steps. Above him, there inside the screen door, his forsaken Golden Retriever Woofer scrambles to all fours at the sight of him, eagerly wagging and panting.

With the screen door slamming behind them, Woofer bounds as tall as Wilf as they pass through the dark wood hallway to an empty big kitchen then, with a quick u-turn, run back to and up the creaky stairs. Mom's soaking in the tub, only a pile of brunette curls visible on its rounded rim just a few inches from the cracked-open bathroom door.

"Mommm?"

"Yes, honey," she answers lazily.

"Mom, who's s'pose to be dead?" His thin face is deathly serious.

"Pardon, Wilf honey?" Mom shifts a little, and water-ripples softly echo in the plain bathroom.

Wilf slumps to the hallway floor, and sits leaning against the doorframe. Woofer flops down in front of him, watching the boy's twiddling thumbs. "Two men by the new restaurant were talkin' 'bout someone *killing* someone, or somethin'..."

His mother thinks for a moment, then takes a deep breath. Perhaps she feels she's about to spoil something. "It was an attempted murder, Wilf," she answers frankly. "Elam Jacks shot his brother Elias...he'll be okay – he'll live," she explains. She has to be thinking that Wilf is now feeling the same thing she did when she heard: less secure. And maybe a disturbing doubt, a sensation against all your hopes and dreams – that you suddenly can't help but feel homeless.

"Why'd he do it?" Wilf asks, puzzled.

Mom doesn't answer.

The son senses she is holding back the most adult part, and tries to make it easier for her: "Got arguin' and tusslin', right?"

"Wilf...you're going to hear anyway," she turns her head, big brown eyes straining around to try to see his outside the narrow gap. "Elias...touched Elam's little girl..."

"Oh," Wilf reacts with a voice as mature as he can make. (Now his town feels even more spoiled.)

"Do you know what that means?" she decides to help him understand, laying her head back down on the rim.

"Sure. Uh...he, uh, touched her...uh..."

"Her private parts, Wilf. And that's a crime, for an adult to do that with a child," she tells him calmly.

Instantly flushed with self-consciousness – that she is naked in the tub right there! – he springs to his feet, greatly startling a gradually dozing-off Woofer.

"I see," he claims loudly from a few feet down the hall.

His mother smiles with realization, then adds sternly, in a slightly raised voice, "It's a real complicated thing, son, what happens between people sexually – what's right and wrong, what's perfectly okay in families, and things... We'll talk more about it later... Whenever you want," she thinks to add.

"Okay!" is all Wilf responds as he takes off down the stairs, embarrassed to even think about it in the house, anxious to get back on his bike so he can think about it over on the other side of town.

Disappointing Woofer again – left with his nose pushing out the screen of the porch door – Wilf is soon at the dead end of a side street as far away as he can get from home. He carefully lays his bike on the ground and pulls himself up onto the high tree stump at the pavement's end, then stands and peers out over the sun-soaking wheat fields.

The sky is radiant blue above the textured gold. Deep green trees fence the fields, and a brilliant white roundup of clouds chase the warm wind. Gulls circle high to float on currents, twirling toward the distant shore without flapping a wing. The air smells sweet, and Wilf takes a deep breath of it. Crickets chirp in the wheat and birds clamor in the row of bushes beside him. He finally thinks about Elam's little daughter, and cautiously imagines her rough looking Uncle Elias "touching" her – all over. He's both repulsed and curious – and immediately ashamed that he's curious at all.

And then it occurs to young Wilf that there are probably a lot of other things going on or that have happened in this town, and no one knows about them. In fact, he realizes, likely almost everyone has some hidden thing that's reluctantly – or never – talked about. (And he remembers Mom telling him about the man in a city who, distracted, suddenly stepped into traffic in front of Dad's car and died right there on the street. There was never a more innocent man, but to this day, she said, your dad can still feel the eyes of the onlookers along the sidewalk leaning near his windows and – because he had one way or another killed a man – silently chanting "murderer". Wilf remembers, when she told him that, how he felt thankful he hadn't been born yet.)

Now he's feeling really insecure. What is going on in this town? How many people does he know who could be secret murderers or rapists or molesters? Shoot! Which ones of his parents' friends – or relatives! – who he talks with all the time..?!

Wilf suddenly wants to move away, to convince Mom and Dad this town is haunted by demons and it's time to move on to... But the next town will be the same, won't it...

He searches the horizon for answers, but cannot unjumble his thoughts – until it hits him that he's looking at it all wrong! Being brought up in such a safe and normal home, he is not exposed to general human beings, and general human beings are a mess! He sees it on television all the time. And part of growing up, he bets, is accepting that humans have ugly sides, and that life is, for many, a struggle to keep themselves from doing ugly things, or trying to run from ugly things they've done. (Though he inherently understands too that there has to be rules of behavior that put a lot of strain on some humans' natures.)

So, satisfied as much as he is scared by his conclusions, Wilf sighs and squints up at the gulls in the bright blue...until another fear grips him: what about my own parents? – oh, no! he aches. What if one of them is one of *"them"* – with some ugly dark deed in their past? He can't bear the thought – until he realizes one final truth: that he himself might someday do something stupid and ugly! – God forbid! he thinks. I swear right here I never will, he promises... But, what if..?

The weight of humanity transfers to him. He takes on the pain of being human... He is no longer sure he's anxious to grow up...

Fortunately, at that somber impasse, he remembers he promised Chucky Cintz he'd play baseball on his team this afternoon. He jumps down to the ground (with brighter thoughts coming to mind – like the great new screen backstop they put up yesterday at the rough old field) and yanks up his bike, then peddles furiously toward home to get his ball glove, and Woofer, dragging his troubled mood behind him.

"Here on Earth, Crusher" Gene matter-of-factly reacts to him in the opposite back corner of the pitch-black interior, raindrop-pelted car, "we take the liquid internally." (Joseph has just discovered he has somehow tipped his beer bottle and spilled all its contents on his crotch.)

"Fuck your hat," Joseph suggests. He then yanks a fresh bottle out of the box on Ba-Dee's lap between them. "Knucklewalker," he has an afterthought.

Norm is in the driver's seat grinning, Howard's slumped low in the passenger front making about-to-burst-with-laughter noises. It's a Monday night emergency meeting.

"Crusher..." Gene lets a timed pause reverberate the name. "Go back to the start. Get a brain."

Joseph just seethes. The others fully sense...what a tirade of foul imprecations is apt to execrate...as Joseph would choose to say.

"Well," Norm breaks a brief but menacing silence, "I figure with a population of three thousand, two hundred and forty people, with the average family being four, that makes sixteen hundred and twenty kids, tops. Age six to twelve is about a third of them, making five hundred and forty. Half are girls, so we got two hundred and seventy boys to go through." (The other four are listening intently, fully caught up in Norm's logical approach.)

"And my aunt at the post office says one hundred and five families were away on vacation – lots of them at the cottage right now 'cause it's peak season, she says – and had their mail held. That means one hundred and five boys – rough estimate – from two hundred and seventy, leaving one hundred and sixty-five..."

"Whoa, Norm!" Howard roars. "Good stuff! What did you tell you aunt you were asking for?"

"I think she guessed it might have something to do with...with Janet. But I told her some of us were figuring out a summer lawn cutting business. Maybe she bought it."

"Can she get us that list?" Ba-Dee is optimistic.

"She's getting it," Norm confirms.

Howard points out, "Not all of them really fit the picture. You can't imagine six-year-olds – "

"No...well, anything's possible," Norm half agrees. "But you gotta go with the odds, meaning we do start with the most likely ages. And we need to find out the shoe size from Chuck – "

"I'm not skulking around measuring *feet* – *!*" Joseph erupts.

"No, gas-head!" Norm retorts. "We just rule out the obvious big and small ones."

Howard seems equally convinced: "Right! Just cross off the pontoon-feet freaks and teeny-weeny mutants."

"Alright!" Ba-Dee is all for it, too.

"Then what?" Gene solemnly quells their spirit.

Which causes Howard to foresee: "Wait! We can't go around gawking at kids' feet!"

Norm himself hasn't quite thought through his own plan. "Uhh...well, then we could recruit spies – a few kids – girls, maybe – to find things out about the boys."

"Might work," Ba-Dee imagines.

"Whatever," Joseph tries to stay close to doable, "it's first things first: get the postal list."

"Then start working on the actual name list," Norm agrees.

"Maybe we can invent some reason to get class lists," Howard suggests.

"Great!"

"Good."

When all agree that's what they should do next, the car interior falls silent again...for a moment.

"So..." Howard soon has a new question. "If God is the energy of every atom, why is there so much of Him in useless places – ?"

"'Tween Gene's fuckin' ears," Joseph mutters, but his timing is way off.

" – Like gigazillions times gigazillions of Him buried in the middle of the Moon for gigaeons?" Howard gets out there.

"Don't be so technical, Howie," Ba-Dee chuckles, aware that Howard hates "Howie" but mindful of how much bigger he is than him.

There's a pause...

"Norm?"

"What?"

"It's your theory," Howard still wants an answer.

"Umm..."

"It's an imperfect world," Ba-Dee helps Norm out.

"If God is capable of creating anything, why would he make it imperfect?" Howard is ready for it.

(As they talk, splattering rain glitters the town's soft light illuminating the cloud cover in the distance. The gentle drum of the drops is a soothing lullaby, and the coziness of the closed-in car is a perfect warm pool of philosophy and kinship,)

"These incessantly shitfaced questions!" Gene groans.

A cool gust fills the car. (Their conversations were always open-ended, where anything goes, with everything – sorta – accepted.)

"Spook you, Gene?" Norm digs. (Hard reality is best faced with friends, is the idea.)

"They're always questions that can't be answered!" Gene protests.

"What better questions are there?" Norm poses.

"Why..." Joseph wants to try one, "is there death?" (Not "what is death?" –"*why* is there death?")

"To put an end to these questions," Gene mutters much like Joseph did earlier.

"To question life by contrast," Howard thinks.

Ba-Dee has a theory: "Life is just a test. Death is the cool part."

"Maybe we created our own life..." Howard tinkers with it.

"Like Norm with that sweet Suzanne in the back seat here?" Joseph chortles and the others chuckle with him. Norm denies nothing.

Howard persists, "Maybe we sat around the hereafter one day with nothing to do and thought this place up..."

"We're gods?" Joseph isn't so sure.

"No, we're just sorta part of God and He helped us – or let us – do this...experiment, this world to experience...all this shit," Howard has to trail, remembering why they're on this back road tonight.

"So...then why were we so hard on ourselves?" Norm remounts the quest.

"So we keep trying to get it right," Ba-Dee concludes.

"No," Norm insists.

Joseph has just guzzled another beer there in the black corner. He thinks for a second more then staidly creates: "Ere the wind takes life, never more chained to strife – "

"Death is our sure way out of this!" Howard suddenly realizes. "We built in an inescapable escape!"

"From our tests and learning the hard way!" Norm understands.

"So..." (with merely that, Ba-Dee here is plainly about to resist) "Janet escaped? Seems like the hard way to go. Sure, we can imagine the guy who did it learning – unlearning something. So what was in it for her?" he asks, a little angry.

The car is quiet for a moment; the rain peppers it heavily.

"Paradise," Norm ventures, "must somehow make anything that happened here feel somehow all right..."

"Did so!" Ricky barks.

"Assholeface, it didn't!" Jack sternly rejects Ricky's claim that his hit rolled to the fence, and that's a home run. Out there leaning back on the fence, Heap Henry is still sitting on the ball in deep centerfield where he flung himself at it. All eleven others are circling at a safe distance around Rick and Jack on the pitcher's mound.

"You jus' think whatever you say is the final truth!" Ricky roars.

"You're so full of shit – "

"There! You're doin' it again!" Rick accuses.

"This ain't about me!" Jack claims. "This is about the friggin' baseball and how far it didn't go – !"

"*Did* go!" Ricky snarls.

"Henry!" Jack turns and yells out to center again. "Get your lumpy self in here!" But Heap continues to be fascinated by... blades of grass.

"So he's admittin' it!" Rick observes. "Or he'd be in here arguin' like a lizardlips like you!"

"You pricknose! He's sitting out there 'cause he's chickenshit!"

"You're the chickenshit – !"

"What?! You care to repeat that?" Jackie pushes his face close to Rick's.

"You're the one wouldn't go over to Janet's!" Rick blurts.

Some gasps escape from the rigid ring of boys.

"Go peek at girls undressing in windows?! Get reamed!" Jackie sneers.

"If we'd went, Janet would still be alive – we would've scared the jerk away!" Rick declares.

"Why didn't *you* go, pervert?"

"I wasn't going by myself – "

"Chickenshit, right?" Jackie repays him.

"Like I could've stopped the guy – "

"You didn't have to. All you'd have to do is tell us who it was – "

"Then she'd still be dead, wouldn't she, dinkhead!" Rick scores.

Jackie is momentarily caught. "Better than nothing!" is all he can come up with.

"Right!" Kenny interjects from ringside. "Least he'd be in jail right now and no one would be scared about the next one!"

"How do you know there's a next one, bucketmouth?" Jackie feels up to fighting with anyone, including his own first baseman.

"The guy's sill out there, ain't he?" Rick butts back.

Right then four boys start drifting away from the circle, upset by the subject, not the argument. Most of them have heard enough of it at home, and can't bear the feel of it for too long a time.

"Oh, shit," Jackie moans, realizing they're leaving (knowing also that it's too heavy a feeling in them for him to try to say something). "Piss on it!" he throws up his hands then bends down and picks up his glove. "I'm gone loose! Someone remember the score! Tomorrow, ten ayh-emm – the game presses onward!" he commands, striding off the field.

And shuffling up dust too, the others drag themselves back to the dugouts.

Moments later, a few gather at home plate and decide to hit the ball around, and soon they're yelling at Heap to give it up.

Henry climbs to his feet and strolls the ball in, taking forever, of course.

...

His thin, tanned features all frowning, his shaggy black hair dangling limply with the heat, Jackie leaves the park and rides his bike toward Red's variety store up main street. Buying himself a cola and some gum there, he sits outside on the store's low, wide window ledge tossing back gulps of his drink, his black eyes gathering in the whole scene of cars and people up at the stoplight. Soon, he sees Chief Cintz looking back at him from Lucy's bench, and watches as he leaves the old guy he's talking with there and walks across the street. Jackie thinks he's heading for his cop office, then realizes he's angling down this way. (Now what? he wonders.) Or maybe he's just coming to the store...

Chuck walks right past him, but holds up a finger as in "wait one minute" before he goes in. Soon back out, dangling a cold soda too, he sits beside Jackie on the sun-hot ledge, and squints at him in the midday glare.

"Hi, Jack," the Chief greets him flatly, breathing deeply and sweating a little through his light blue shirt. His expression is neutral, neither smiling nor scowling.

"Hay," the thirteen-year-old responds just as dryly, though he's not sure what he should be feeling, talking to a policeman right on the main drag where everyone can see him. (Not that he feels guilty or anything. It's mostly just uncool.)

"No game..?" Chuck trails.

"No. Well, postponed...due to immaturity."

"Oh," the Chief smiles, a finger wiping the droplets off his cold pop bottle, remembering how it was.

Jackie stares at the sidewalk, then glares back up at Chuck. "You want me for something?" (He figures he's going to hear something about his mom, direct from the Force.)

"Ah...maybe," Chuck hadn't thought how to put it. "Well...you know all the kids pretty good, don't you?"

Jackie, just noticeably, grins. Of course, officer.

Chuck then waits as a woman walks by.

"Jack, do you think about the murder very much – about Janet? I mean, does it bother you much?"

"Yeah..." Jackie reacts, and letting out only that much causes him to let loose: *"Son of a bitch!* Some son of a bitch is screwin' up this town, what he did! I wish you'd just catch him and tie him up for us on that bench..!" he seethes to a stop, eyes tensed fiercely toward Lucy's past the Chief's startled expression.

Chuck takes a drink, and has to admit, "I think everyone would like that." (Himself included.) After a cooling short silence he comes around to it: "Well, there's maybe a way you can help." His eyes shift back to meet Jack's.

Jack scowls at him.

"But one important part, a critical part, is you've got to keep it quiet – secret." (Chuck has been trying to stick to adult words.)

Jackie thinks for a few seconds, then nods. "Yeah. Sure. I can do that. I'd really like to get him..." he states firmly, with renewed forced calm.

"Okay then, Jack, you know some kids were hanging around peeking – "

"Oh, shit!" Jackie bursts, his whole body stiffening. "Some kid saw it!" he guesses, searching deep into the Chief's eyes for confirmation.

"That's it, Jack. We found fresh bubble gum, then a small footprint on the side neighbor's fence rail. It rained the night before, so some boy must have stood on it and made a new footprint that night, and watched – because it looked like something then made him trample the grass to hide behind that tree back there."

Jackie focuses on the sidewalk again, slowly shaking his head. "Shoot! We were just talking about this – "

"What's that?" Chuck asks quickly.

"Aw, nothin'. Some pervert kid just said we shoulda been there, or something. Anyway, you want me to try..?" his eyes meet Chuck's again.

"Whatever you can find out, Jack, will help narrow things down, you know?" (Chuck makes a mental note, though, about the "pervert kid".)

"Sure..."

"I'll leave it to you, Jack. Figure out what you can do. But if you're stuck for ideas, call me. Don't come in the office, though. Better you call, right?"

"Check." "Right," Jackie adds to Chuck raising his pop bottle as though in a toast.

The Chief then strolls off up the street, leaving Jackie there full of completely different thoughts than when he found him.

(N ext) "I push my hand hard on her mouth. She doesn't even try to scream but her eyes are wide. She recognizes me. I wish she was struggling, but I'm really hot anyway.

"I grab her head and pull her off the picnic table." (Here he chooses not to write that he was actually afraid he could pull her head off, he was so forceful.)

"Dragging her across the lawn now she starts fighting. I could bone her right here but I'd rather take her out where she can scream and my hands are free.

"It's really tough getting her over the fence but I heave her over so she thumps on the ground and doesn't yell, and I'm on her real quick. But in the car I have to punch her out on the back of the neck so she'll sit still and shut up and I can start feeling her up while I'm driving..."

(Again, that's as far as he has to read to relive it, and he closes the book, wipes himself off, and turns on the television.)

The late-day sun still radiates warmth through the cooling, windless air along Main Street. Tuesday as a business day is ended for most, with only Nick's Bowl, the gas station at the curve, the Dairy Cone Drive-in just past it and Red's Convenient Drugs and Milk three doors down from the police office – plus Lucy's – still open.

On the bench, Wilf sips a large coffee (his wife is inside talking with Chuck's wife and other friends) as the Chief leans back beside him, enjoying the advancing shade from the buildings across the way. No one else has showed up to sit, yet.

"The whole town's getting' touchy," Chuck starts up with a sigh, laying one outstretched leg on the other, pushing his thick fingers through his limp hair one more time. "You can't talk to anyone like you used to."

Wilf knows just what he means. "And even if the guy's caught, it won't get any better," he sort of snarls his words.

"Maybe."

"Nah, sorry, Chuck. That sounds awfully discouraging, and you know I'm really not that pessimistic. I just wish the guy was caught, so everyone wasn't on edge." Wilf takes another slow sip, then gives Chuck's feet a gentle boot, as though to snap him out of it.

"Wilf, you've done a lot for this town. And you're far from dead," Chuck grins, angling his eyes up at his life-long friend. "That Christmas stuff you do, and the ball diamond" (Wilf had almost single-handedly built the stands, screens and fences) "and everything else – you sure you don't want to be Mayor? – we'll go toss Jimmy Jimms out right now!" The Chief makes like he's getting up to go do it.

Wilf leans over and spits coffee on Chuck's shoes. "There: assaultin' a cop. Can't be Mayor with a that blemish."

Chuck laughs. "Lick that off."

"Told you, not in public, Officer Chief," Wilf frowns at him. "Take 'em off, and I'll dunk 'em inside in the toilet."

"Okay, charges dropped," Chuck smiles wide and nestles back down into the corner of the bench. Once he's comfortable again, he begins, "Well, we did get Carl's car back, already..."

"And?"

"Nothing – what did you expect, Wilf?"

"Nothing – you know, anything's possible, in this world," Wilf slumps back too, and his tiring blue eyes squint up the street, then down.

"There was lots of stuff on the floor – bits of grass and dirt and stuff – but nothing specific for us. Carl never washes that thing anyway..."

"True," Wilf grins with a kind of affection. "Anything else?" He's wondering about the teenage detective squad.

Chuck thinks for a minute, staring and blinking at the empty gray pavement. "No one else here knows this – just me – and it's likely nothing..." he pauses and meets Wilf's eyes, "but there was an inch of red thread caught on her belt..."

Wilf stares back. "Did you check it out?" is the obvious question.

"No..." the Chief sounds distant. "For some dumb reason, I'm still just thinking about it..."

Wilf sits up straight. "Well, let's go! We'll go ask if you can check her room again – you'll have to check Jennifer's, Carl's and Margaret's too – and I'll talk with Jennifer and Carl while you're doin' it." He plainly feels this could be most important.

Chuck takes a few seconds before he agrees (appreciating that Wilf's family's long friendship with Carl and his family will make it easier than if his assistant Tom was to come).

They soon excuse themselves to their wives inside and walk the two blocks down the side street to Carl's. The father welcomes them kindly, and has Jennifer come down from her room to wait with Wilf and himself in the kitchen. Chuck begins to give them a reason why he wants to search every room, but Carl stops him, saying "Whatever you have to do..."

Chuck isn't long upstairs. When he returns, he takes Carl aside and tentatively explains, then asks him about laundry (there's none) or if they have given any clothes away, and whether Margaret owns any red outfits that she took with her to her sister's. She doesn't.

With friendly good-byes, the two visitors are soon gone.

"Nothing," Chuck reveals, a few steps up the street.

"Nothing?" Wilf studies his face intently.

"Not a red thing anywhere," the Chief feels somehow a little surprised.

"And she wasn't wearing...?"

"No."

"Oh... Uh..." Wilf isn't actually ready for it, either. "So we watch for guys with red shirts..?" But he can't believe it might be anything near that simple.

"I guess..." Chuck's thoughts are spinning. "We certainly run it through all the textile tests, now... They might tell us what kind – T-shirt, or whatever."

"Sure," Wilf imagines they can.

On their way back to Lucy's, they talk about the peculiarity of things, how this little piece can feel so encouraging and might be the big clue to the puzzle. Back on Main Street, they announce their return to the boisterous bunch inside the restaurant, then sit back out on the bench, moods factually changed from an hour before. Soon, just as Mel, Bert and Shooter appear down at the curve, Sid comes out to sit, but sees the three trudging this way and spins right back inside to get chairs and coffee. Next, seven kids arrive out of nowhere on their bikes, and Ed coasts his car to a stop straight in front. Chase then shuffles out working the squeaky screen door and flops between the two on the bench. (Maybe, Wilf wonders, this town won't ever change much, after all.)

"Here comes fuckhead Bert," ol' Chase says glaring at nothing across the street as though announcing it to the peace and quiet.

Wilf glances at the pack of snickering kids. Like they haven't heard swearing before. He thinks: "And life goes on".

...

"Wait a minute!" Wilf suddenly thinks of something and stops, only a few steps from Lucy's on their way home in the glow of the streetlights. He excuses himself from Sue, leaving his wife puzzled and standing still on the curb. Walking along in front of them, Chuck stops too and turns, smiling meekly at his wife as he leaves her in the middle of the side street they're crossing. Wilf eases close, and face-to-face with Chuck on the center line, eye-to-eye asks quietly, "What do you mean, no one else knows about the red thread? Didn't you tell Tom? – you didn't tell your assistant?"

"No..." Chuck plainly replies.

Wilf stares into those soft blue eyes for a second, then just barely shakes his head. "Oh, shoot," he mutters.

Again, the sweet summer night air is warm and black and full of crickets as the stars twinkle down on the open-windowed parked car and its five beer-sippin' searchers of truth. It's Tuesday night, and it's five in a row.

"Why doesn't anyone ever use this road?" Gene suddenly realizes from behind the wheel – never having thought about it because he is rarely granted the responsibility of his father's car to go anywhere...say, like, to go park on a country road and guzzle beer. Tonight, though, his dad is in the hospital for tests, so his mother was giving.

"No one lives on it," Ba-Dee notes the obvious, feeling he should answer because he's the one who lives in the country. (Gene moved here only two years ago, and still asks these kinds of questions.)

"Oh," Gene sounds fully satisfied.

"So..." Norm begins characteristically, "if space itself is expanding...then so is everything in it. Including the space and mass and energy of atoms – "

"And so are we!" Howard exclaims.

"So, like, you're taller?" Joseph scoffs at stubby Howard's little celebration.

"It's relative," Ba-Dee notes with Einstein wisdom.

"Then time is created by the creation and expansion of the physical dimension..." Norm wrestles with his images.

"No, time is like a point," Howard thinks. "Something happens, and it immediately starts fading down 'time', a point of all existence of your moment that travels away from you."

"It fades down behind the expansion where the entire universe was an instant ago when it happened..." Norm begins to suggest.

"Neither of you are making any fuckin' sense," Joseph takes his position on it then slurps down beer.

"Crusher," Gene turns half around to his gnat-like adversary in the middle of his back seat, "shut up and hand me a beer. And lets get to why we're here. My meter's running."

"We'll have the class lists," Ba-Dee announces. "My cousin says she can copy them tomorrow, if she can get into the school."

"Which cousin – ?" Gene starts.

"Don't ask him," Howard interjects with a giggle. "Except for us four, he's related to every person in this county."

"She's okay, if that's what you're worried about," Ba-Dee informs Gene. "We're close. She doesn't ask, she just trusts me."

Joseph peeps, "We just trust you, Ba-Dee...what the fuck is a Ba-Dee, anyway?"

In response, Ba-Dee just pounds Joseph on the arm as hard as he can slug, causing Joseph to jump and the bottles to fly up out of the case on his knees and clink and clunk down across the back seat and floor. Gene almost has a seizure. Fortunately, none are broken.

"I got two kids," Ba-Dee then immediately declares. The others wait for it. "Nick's Bowl's little twins. Nick's been away for three weeks with them. Wish they'd never come back, actually. 'Til I go back to school, anyway. They're non-stop bowlers..."

"One hundred sixty-three," Gene calculates.

"Oh! My neighbor's kid was home in bed – the little shit broke his little nasty leg," Howard laughs vindictively.

"When we get the school lists tomorrow we'll scratch them off," Gene commands. "Just keep thinking of more."

"Right!" two voices obey.

"Yep-er," Ba-Dee acknowledges.

Heading off a looming moment's wordlessness, Joseph rumbles, "And Earth careens through the cosmic chaos...six billion people hold on tight."

"True." "Yup," two other voices again concur.

"Fuckin' fer-shur," Joseph climaxes, causing the car to start.

"So I unbutton her top more. Slow, because I have to turn down all these streets to get out of town. She's unconscious with her head on the seat right beside me and her hair on my leg."

(He's bored, loafing around watching television all day, and he wants to get off again, like this morning, so he reads further along. It's late; he's in his room, upstairs.)

"She's got no bra. She's small but with big nipples. They're so soft, tits are so soft.

"I whip out my dick. I wish she was awake now.

"I undo her pants button. Push down the zipper. And feel the fuzzy hair."

(And he comes again quick.)

The town sleeps.

"Bastard!" Wilf screams, piercing the country night. Joseph growls from the back seat, "Piece of shit!" "Scum!" Sid shatters the depth of darkness and the steaming caldron of the motionless car. "God damn his hollow soul..." Howard seethes. "Anti-life..." Ed moans. "Slime! Murderer!" Chuck yells – "Sleaze!" he shouts. His wife Beth mutters, "Heartless rodent..." "Swine!" Ba-Dee roars. "Satan!" Reverend Fisk scorns. "Evil scourge..." Norm groans.

Outside, clouds swiftly churn across the hot stars; the ghostly, shimmering car shudders with boiling anger.

Jackie wails, "Fucker!" "Worm!" his mother Nancy cries. "Beast!" "Slug!" "Coward!" Ricky, old Chase and Heap Henry erupt together.

"*Burn in Hell!*" Margaret and Carl screech in unison, clasping their hands over Jennifer's mouth.

Outside, the car is white hot and throbbing with hate, hysteria. It tremors the Earth.

"He killed our town!" Mayor Jimmy Jimms bellows, and lightning cracks as it flashes all around.

The wind is raging – tree limbs swirl in a vortex. Chasms rip across the fields. Rain slashes down and howling thunder deafens the night.

The wind strips the land. All the sky is webbed with lightning. The rain is a solid deluge, the car: a blinding arc of fire...

Ahead, on the road, firm, steady, Looker peers into the distance. Unquivering, he stands, feet braced against his sight, arms taut at his sides; his face, carved strong by life, is expressionless. And his eyes – his pale gray and depthless eyes, his wise, serene and burdened sight – his eyes...calmly see the storm.

"Didn't sleep well...bad night, last night..." Chuck squints at Mayor Jimms through the yellow morning sunshine emblazing the police office. Assistant Tom has just headed out across the street to pick up a round of coffee.

"Lot of people 'round here aren't too relaxed, lately," Jimmy observes with stone-face seriousness. Slipping off of Tom's desk to sit on the chair instead, he eases his tall frame down as though it's painful.

"So? This social or political?" the Chief asks exactly what he asks every time the Mayor comes in. He then rakes his fingers through his hair again and smiles his ever-friendly chubby smile, his eyes sparkling with his ever-genuine good nature.

"All the above," Mayor Jimmy selects resonantly. His slicked-back, thinning black hair glistening in the sunlight, he takes off his wire-rimmed glasses and starts hinging them in front of him with both hands. Wearing a white dress shirt and loosened tie, dark blue jeans and black boots, he looks the lanky southerner that he sounds. All he needs is the right hat. "Anything new? – people are buggin' me awful!"

"It's early, yet, this morning, Ya'onor. We just talked on the phone last night, remember?"

"Well, guess I was hopin' you maybe forgot some little thing..."

"Nope. And? So..?" Chuck lets out an impatiently prompting little sigh.

"Well, See-see...uh...there's somethin' I think I best tell you – it's been buggin' me terribly, lately – can we keep somethin' confidential, Chuck?" (He intently examines how the Chief's lips reply, "Of course".) "Well, see, it's where I came from..."

"I know," Chuck stops him cold.

"You..?" Jimmy Jimms begins but Chuck blocks him again:

"We may be kinda dense out here in the cornstalks, but those razor-sharp heads over in Elston are connected!" he divulges, eyebrows raised in faux awe his only expression... "Oh, com'on, Jim! There's no secrets in this law business. Not for most offenders, and certainly not for you murderers. Give us some credit. I knew fifteen years ago."

Mayor Jimms now eyes Chuck blankly. He crosses his legs, inhales tensely, then asks the obvious, "So why didn't you ever say..?"

"Second chance. Just about everybody deserves one, don't they?" (Jimmy nods, barely noticeable.) "But next time – we shoot 'em!" Chuck grins wide.

The Mayor chuckles hesitantly, as though unsure how relieved he really is. He listens to his own laughter trickle to an awkward silence. "I want this town to be like it was," he finally composes himself.

"Was never perfect – hey!, you should sit here for the next twenty years, Jim, then you'll see all too well what I mean. Then I'll go do all that useless shit you do."

"No way," the Mayor smirks, then is immediately solemn again. "But it's such a good town...community. This thing is draggin' – "

"Whoa! – hold on, don't say it!" Chuck is abruptly angry (though he suspected this might be His Honor's main mission, this morning). "You don't want to swing the weight of this town all over on top of me, Jimmy. There's little means to solve it, so there's no solving it quick!"

"I only wanted you to know what I'm up against, and know that I'm worried."

"You think I'm not worried? You think I'm not heartbroken!? Lord-lump-it, Jimmy! I was born here, my wife was born here – every friend I ever had is here!"

"I know, I know..."

"You just don't worry, Mayor Jimmy Jimms! You have my assurance, and you have my unwavering determination that I'll find that son-of-a-bitch – and I'll tell you what: if I don't, I swear to you I'll quit, then you can rush over here and rush through this investigation yourself and then rush that killer right up to Elston's jail, just the way you want it!"

Chuck is now rigidly standing. And Mayor Jimms is sitting wide-eyed with regret.

"No, Chuck, no! – no, I appreciate what you're up against. No, I'll leave you alone! I was wrong, I'm sorry. You just go to it, and I'll butt out – promise!"

"Well... I'm sorry, too, Jim – I'm sorry for our town, and I'm sorry I let loose on you... You know, sometimes it builds up, and then...it's like a flash – like an angry bull, or something, and all I see is red – don't ever wear red comin' in here, eh Jim?" Chuck laughs.

"Ha!" Jimmy Jimms reacts loudly with his best campaign smile. "Hate red, never wore anything red, ever..! Hey, thanks, Chuck. Thanks for everythin'. We'll see ya..."

And the Mayor catapults to his feet and strides out into the bright morning.

Right off, Jackie had wondered about one kid: Ricky's center fielder Eggie (Eddie, the egghead book reader) Ogden. As soon as the Chief had walked a few steps away from him yesterday there in front of the variety store, Jackie thought of Eggie. Why, he isn't sure.

So now, across the late-morning ball diamond's baking heat and eye-aching sunshine, Jack watches this gum-chompin', glasses-wearing, short Eggie kid. From his place in the shadowed dugout, Jack studies his moves, and follows his seemingly shifting eyes – what is Eggie watching for when he glances around like that outside the ball park? Like he's waiting for someone to come, or something... He never did that before, did he?

Jack decides to try something:

"Time!" he screams, and the game freezes in mid-motion, though the ball in the air halfway from Ricky to home plate keeps going. "Glove check!"

"*What?!*" Rick shouts with incredulity, his mitt slipping off his dangling arm to the dust of the pitcher's mound. "*What* glove check, frogeyes?!"

"Don't you ever read baseball rules, pissbreath? Gloves can only be so big," Jack explains the obvious as he steps out of his dugout, baggy T-shirt flapping with the breezes, hands braced on hips, black eyes drilling holes in Rick's.

"So yer doin' it in the middle of a bat!" Rick throws up his arms in frustration.

"Can if I want. Manager's p'rog'tive," Jack claims authoritatively, trailing little puffs of dust as he starts out for first base. All the fielders except Rick slump to the ground, impatient looking but glad also to rest in the escalating heat.

Jack holds his own glove up against Dale's the first-baseman, then strides over to second and does the same there to Kevin's. Rick is calling him names all the while. "Peckerface." "Shitbreath." "Horsenose." "Toadhead..." (Right there, Jack turns his head and frowns questionably at Rick, as though criticizing that last weak effort.)

Jackie pushes onward to third. (Seven players a side: no short-stop. Or catcher.) As he walks, he's desperately trying to think of something that will snare Eggie.

"Close," Jack snarls ominously, precisely measuring Ben's the third-baseman.

"...Snotbrain."

In left field, Danny refuses to reach for his mitt beside him on the ground and hand it up to Jack. Jack extends a fist, threatening a pounding. Danny, lying flat on his back gazing at the sky, issues an indifference raspberry. On a mission, Jack has to lean over and pick up the glove himself.

"Wormnuts!" Rick is still standing drooped and motionless on the mound.

As Jack starts out across the dried grass toward Eggie in cen-ter, he can see the little guy fidget nervously as he sits there in a cross-legged knot.

Soon Jack is close. And now he thinks what to say: "Pervert," he whispers.

Eggie springs to his feet.

Rick gets serious: "Hey, dinkless, what'd you just say to my Eggie?! Hey Eggie! Say something – talk t' me!"

Eggie won't even look up into Jack's eyes. He just gapes help-lessly at his chest.

"Pervert," Jack whispers louder, not visibly interested in Eggie's glove.

"What, Jack?! Whataya want?" ten-year-old Eggie quivers and takes a little step back. Rick starts walking out there. Eggie bends over awkwardly and picks up his glove. Jack yanks it from his grip, still staring him down.

"You know *what*, Eggman. Egg-perv," Jack growls. All the oth-ers are watching this closely, but no one can hear.

"I'm no perv..." Eggie moans, his eyes in behind his glasses shifting to the ground.

"Oh, perv's nothin'..! But witness, Egg-eyes! That's the big one: *witness!*"

Suddenly Eggie grabs back his glove, fixes a quick glare at Jack, then runs around past him to go stand behind Rick. He's clearly holding back tears.

"You dogmeat!" Rick stretches close and shoves Jack with a hand that glances his shoulder – chancing obliteration (though he's almost as big). "Whataya sayin' to my fielder, dorknose?" (Without the name calling, it could get serious.)

Jack smiles pleasantly wide. "Took him a minute to find his glove," he explains in a most compassionate tone, then he briefly leans eye-to-eye nearer to Rick before turning toward right field.

"Gobeater," Rick mutters when Jack is halfway there, then he tenderly pats Eggie's shoulder and points him back to his posi-tion. Eggie smiles weakly, gently punches the pocket of his glove, then abruptly throws up.

Heap Henry groans "Gross!" from the dugout, but they all feel sorry for Eggie Eddie. "Hang in there, Eggie man!" some-one shouts, and most everyone cheers encouragement. Eggie laughs bravely, and sidesteps along the outfield grass to a fresh position.

Attentively, Jack has glanced over his shoulder several times, and, finally finished in right field, he tromps up a curtain of dust on the way back to his dugout, duty done.

...

"I know who the kid is but no way he'll admit it so I'm not tellin' ya," Jack spits it all out to Chief Cintz on the phone when he gets home for lunch.

Chuck stays quiet on the other end.

"But I'm working on it," Jack gives him.

"Fine. Good..." The Chief waits him out.

"Well, I'm not positive, yet. I wouldn't wanna – "

"No, Jackie, don't do that. You're right," Chuck is quick to agree. "But Jack, do me a favor. Just write down the kid's name, seal it in an envelope, and give it to me on your way back to the ball field – only me, okay? And I promise I won't open it – "

"In case I get squashed by a truck..?"

"You know how serious this is, Jack..."

"Alright, alright," Jack goes along with it, rudely hanging up the phone to go find something to write on.

...

Jack delivers as agreed, and leaves wordlessly.

As tempted as he is to immediately tear the blank envelope open, Chief Chuck made a promise...for now.

"**G**ot it!" Ba-Dee beams at Norm who has just walked through the doorway of Nick's Bowl.

"Got what?" Norm crosses the black and white checkerboard floor and squats on one of the redtop counter stools.

"The list, the school list," Ba-Dee stands unmoving, where he's been standing doing nothing for hours.

"Of course...already? Where is it?" Norm scans the vacant little restaurant and five lifeless lanes beyond, as though worried someone might see it.

"Gene was in. We separated the age groups and scratched off those three names, then marked off all the girls and highlighted some of the younger boys."

"Good. So where is it?" Norm still sounds nervous.

"Gene took it. Where's your aunt's postal list?" Ba-Dee then asks as he dispenses Norm yet another free soda.

"I was just going over there to get it – I'll take it over to Gene's," Norm answers after a sigh of relief, feeling that their little project is again safely out of sight.

"This list could be slow going..." Ba-Dee circles around the end of the counter and sits three stools away from Norm.

"Well, we all wish there was something else we could do – don't we?"

"We're not the Chucker. He has the authority. He has practice at it," Ba-Dee tries to ultimately reason away guilt by inaction.

"Chuck's a good man. But that doesn't automatically mean he'll find...anything."

"No."

Norm takes a gulp of soda, and then angles his troubled eyes toward the bright window beside them, with its view of the parking lot and some of Main Street beyond. "It's scary, isn't it? – that sense around here that it'll happen again..."

"Sure is," Ba-Dee agrees sadly. "And some other poor Janet..." Lowering his head, his eyes have quickly glazed with tears. (Norm knows no one more profoundly compassionate.)

Their eyes meet again across the stools, and they both just smile weakly. Neither sees what all this will mean to them some-day, and they're each at this moment aware of that. It's as though they're somehow too young, in this town...

"It's Jimmy Jimms. Guilty." Norm submits firmly.

"It's Nick."

"It's Beverly," Norm makes one up.

Ba-Dee is almost stuck..."It's all of us: hang us all!"

"Hi, honey," Carl says softly to Jennifer standing there against the kitchen doorframe. Her dad is sitting hunched over the breakfast table, stubby fingers caressing a long-empty coffee mug. He's facing the other way, but he heard her come down the hall.

Jennifer forces a deep breath. "Hi." Her voice is faint. She's hugging herself, as though she's cold.

"That was Mom calling..." he turns his head half around, not brave enough to meet her eyes, not wanting to scare her off by looking right at her.

Jennifer responds only by not going away, like she has been lately.

"She's staying there two extra days. She'll be home Saturday... She misses you – did you want to talk to her? I'll call her right back..." he eagerly sits straighter, as though to get up.

"No...it's okay..." "I miss her, too," she adds, and new flows of tears rush down her cheeks.

"It's...difficult, for the three of us, isn't it?"

"...Yes."

"Each of us differently..." he sighs. (It's the first time they've talked directly about it.)

Jennifer sniffles, then slowly steps into the kitchen, and as she passes her father, she reaches and – so gently – touches his shoulder with fingertips.

Tears well in his eyes.

"Maybe you'll know," he continues quietly in the utter stillness of the kitchen and the house, "what a baby means to a mother... someday." (He still likes to call Janet and Jennifer "babies".)

Jennifer sits on the chair across the table – half sits, awkwardly, painfully looking, with her short, thin body leaning hard on the table.

"Your poor mom..." Carl glances up, catching his tear with quick fingers as he focuses back down at his mug.

"Poor you, Daddy..." Jennifer sobs lightly, lowering her eyes, too.

Carl smiles a small, brave smile for her, then reaches and lightly touches her hand with just one finger.

Through a silence, they try to regain some strength.

"Are you...are you afraid?" Carl asks. Though knowing she hasn't been out of the house and yard at all, and aware he's been instinctively listening for her every move, he's worried sick about her.

"Just now..." she reveals her reason for coming downstairs.

"Of..?"

"Of him... Of dying, now, sometimes..."

Carl feels all his insides sear, then an ice-cold shiver crawls up his spine. He takes half a minute to find words:

"Jennifer, I – and your mom feels the same – we would never have brought babies – you and Janet into the world if we didn't believe in...in Creation, in a Creator, to all this..." He pauses and watches her for a reaction, to see if she'll storm off out of the room, or something... She doesn't budge. "It's a big universe, honey. An amazing complexity. We'd be arrogant to claim we know what isn't real and to have all the answers, wouldn't we? There's a great

Intelligence...I feel there is. And Mom does, too... I'm sorry, I'm getting heavy, here..."

"No...thanks, Daddy. I'm glad you said that..." As their eyes meet, Jennifer leans back a bit in her chair. Then weakly, she asks, "Can we...um, go out for a drive?"

"Sure! Sure, Jennifer. Com'on! Good idea, it' so nice out. Uh, I'll call Mom, in case she calls back, an' all..." and he pushes to his feet and reaches for the phone. Looking back at his daughter as he starts to dial, he is gripped by the sight of her widest smile, and the wettest torrent of tears he has ever seen anyone cry. He continues dialing, clumsily...

And they're soon in the car easing out of the driveway.

The sun is a sphere of shimmering rose above the rich red brick of the buildings across from Lucy's. High in the deepening blue, a lacework of cloud edged in pale pink drifts slowly with the summer wind.

All business traffic is long over, and only a few cars still hold onto their spots at meters. Another comfortably warm evening, quite a number of folks are out for a walk, heading for an after-supper coffee or taking the kids for an ice cream, on their way to bowl a couple or anticipating the sweet air of a peaceful twilight.

A lazy breeze rustles the leathery green leaves of the big maples down the street. As a young couple cuddle and kiss on a bench in the small park, the nearby stoplight dutifully changes again for an intersection with no cars. A few feet up the street, little sparrows flutter to the sidewalk and curb, sociably looking for seeds.

Wilf emerges from Lucy's and stands in front of the door, the joking inside still making his lean face smile and laugh-wrinkles frame his sleepy eyes. He peers up and down the street, then sits on the bench. Leaning back, with legs stretched out and arms braced up and held by fingers locked behind his head somewhere in his long, sandy hair, he savors a deep breath.

A minute passes, then Chase, Bert, Mel and Shooter push out the squeaky screen door, each carrying their personally monogrammed Lucy's coffee mug.

"Yer wife's goin' on about you again in there, Wilf," Chase chuckles, eyeing him overtop bifocals as he sits down beside him.

"Good," Wilf grins wide. "Let her spill it all out here," his deep, gentle voice fills the quiet, "then she's calm at home."

Next, Sid steps outside with a stack of chairs; Ed follows right behind and helps spread them out. Across the street, Chief Cintz sees everyone there and decides to take a break and stroll over, leaving the office lights on and the door wide-open, as always.

Tom Addison soon parks the police car in front of the office and elects to come over, too. And up the street, Ba-Dee gets off work and starts walking to Lucy's with Norm and Howard, who were waiting for him.

Seeing the gathering, Jackie and eleven others of the fourteen baseball boys detoured their bikes on their way from the darkening diamond and circle the end zone there at the street corner of Lucy's Large Lunch. All of them are wondering if it will be worth putting off the Dairy Cone ice cream and shakes they were headed for to chance hearing something ripe. (The score is four thirty-two to four twenty-six, for Rick's side.)

Blue uniform nicely pressed, Tom leans against the parking meter nearest the hydrant on which his boss has lifted a leg. (All the jokes about that were long ago used up.) "Just saw Carl and Jennifer at the Dairy drive-in," he announces.

"Oh, good, good," Chuck reacts for everyone. "It takes time..." he trails thoughtfully, some small relief showing on his serious face.

A few seconds of concentrated silence pass.

"So what's new, Chase?" the Chief then beats the ol' boy to the question.

"Nuttin!" Chase barks from the bench, tugging down his red ball cap. (There's no guessing if that's good or bad, anymore.)

"Nothing?" Bert questions with challenge, sitting primed-straight on a chair opposite him. "You ol' mutt! You lasted another day – for someone old as you, that's some miracle. Every day still on Earth is a miracle, for some – !"

"You're older than me, you crusted-up ol' wreck!" Chase roars and smirks.

Norm, Howard and Ba-Dee have filled in the circle near the door, and now stand there smiling at the ol' boys. Some of the young boys rock their bikes, as though warming up to leave.

Scratching in his short, white beard, Bert huffs and starts "Chase, you're only as old as ya talk, and you – "

Suddenly, a car squeals around the corner up the block and screeches to a stop right in front. It's Ann McCallum. She had opened her door while still rolling, and she jumps out screaming over the roof at Chief Cintz: "It's Doug! It's Doug..!"

Chuck leaps off the curb and rushes around the car to her. She grabs both his arms. He clenches her shoulders, pushing his face close for an explanation. Ann is dazed, in shock, and can't talk. He squeezes her a little. Everyone in front of Lucy's is frozen. She finds words, but only Chuck hears her. He presses her gently down to the seat, telling her to move over so he can drive. As he holds onto the car, about to lower himself behind the wheel, he looks up and instructs a rigid Tom Addison, "Come over to Ann's – it's her brother Doug. She says it's suicide..."

Bug Doug is dead.

No one speaks. Tom runs across the street to the cruiser as Chuck speeds away with Ann around the corner. Tom is soon racing after them.

Bug Doug...they all think. But without details, without confirmation, it isn't quite real yet.

...

Everyone sits and stands still, muttering. Everyone who was inside is now out front. In fifteen minutes they hear the ambulance from Elston. Fifteen minutes after that, Chuck walks around the corner where Ann sped toward them a short while ago.

"Doug's dead," he approaches and officially reports with a heavy sigh, his eyes finding his wife's under the surreal mix of sunset and streetlight. "Bug Doug's dead..." he repeats limply, taking the space on the bench that Wilf offers.

"What happened?" Ed asks for all of them.

"In their garage. He just closed the doors, then started the truck, it seems..." They all can see the pain in his eyes. For Chuck, most everyone in town is like family. He's known Doug McCallum since he was born.

The two young lovers from the park have crossed the street, and Sid repeats Chuck's account for them. Now, for a minute, the large gathering stirs wordlessly: Chase and Bert and Mel search into the distance, as though for reason; the young boys' eyes self-consciously fix on their bikes or on the ground, each kid occasionally glancing up. Norm, Howard and Ba-Dee feel stunned, and they study beyond the concrete for an answer to why someone just a little older than them – a sort of role model, in a way – would do that. Wilf's and Chuck's wives wrap their arms tight around each other's shoulders. And Shooter starts pacing the sidewalk up the block a few yards... Reverend Fisk soon pulls onto Main Street driving from his part of town to Ann's.

Ed finally ends the silence. "Lord," is all he moans.

"Any reason? Like, any note, or anything?" Wilf has to ask.

And everyone – even most of the kids – sees what the answer might hold.

"Not yet, no..." Chuck doesn't look up. If anyone else had asked it, he likely would have resented the implication. But he knows how Wilf was as much a friend to Bug Doug as he was himself – as much as the young man would allow. "And no, he wasn't a suspect at all… Wasn't even on my list," he lies. (His hated private list of the whole town, that he and Tom had joked about days before, has not grown much shorter, and dying is not a way off.)

Bert rubs his beard and suggests, "He had a real rough bringing up – "

"I know that! Damn it, Bert! Don't tell me my territory…" Chuck tries to hold in his impatience. (Why is it always so automatic to blame the questionable characters first – and so fast?!)

"How's Ann?" Ed interjects.

"Confused."

"More than ever, now…" Howard speaks up, shaking his head while still staring at the ground. He had worked with her at the grocery store, and understood her despair over her brooding, volatile, tender brother.

Most everyone knows what Howard means.

"You should go see Julie Grant," Jackie then points out to Chief Cintz, pushing his bike forward a bit, surprising everybody just by opening his mouth. (None of the baseball boys ever talk in front of Lucy's, and Jack rarely talks to any adult, anytime.)

Chuck recognizes privileged information, knowing this one is a truth of Jack's mother Nancy (and that it would get out in the open soon enough anyway, so there's no use holding the boy back). Julie Grant lives with her toddler in a little house a half mile out of town, and she "came from the same place", he would put it, as Nancy.

"He still sweet on her?" Wilf asks Jackie with a kind smile.

"He was on her like paint…" Jack blurts, then seeing his choice of words causing some tight grins, he flushes with anger.

Right there, young Eddie Ogden backs his bike out of the circle, turns it around and rides away. Chuck glances a look at Jackie.

Because Doug's death is so new, no one is comfortable talking any more about it; because of the shock, no one feels like talking about something else. So, the boys on bikes drift away, Norm and his friends walk on, and the women file back inside. Chuck, catching himself about to cry, stands stiffly and faces Wilf with his "coming over?" look, and they both stroll tiredly across to the office. The young lovers decide to go into Lucy's. And the ol' boys, along with Ed and Sid, just sit.

...

Chuck pulls out the Sunday bottle. Wilf slumps in Tom's chair across the way. They sip whiskey slowly and talk about Doug McCallum, waiting for Tom and Reverend Fisk.

...

The next morning, nothing more is known about why. Ann had searched through Doug's things half the night, finding no clue. All the while, Reverend Fisk had talked with her to the brink of exhaustion, hearing nothing but lives streaked with pain. Chuck and Wilf have sipped away the night, and after the Reverend leaves the office at daybreak – and after three coffees from Lucy's – the Chief wearily heads out to Julie Grant's.

Julie is a mess. She's sobbing, makeup all over her pretty face, her long blond hair all tangles, her small arms and neck all sweaty from hours of pacing furiously across her wide kitchen floor. Her little two-year-old is playing in the yard just outside the door.

Chief Chuck doesn't ask her, but she knows he has to hear it:

"That wasn't it – that wasn't why," she swears, lighting yet another cigarette, still pacing. "He wasn't that way ever. Other things fucked him up, and he was angry. But he was never violent!"

Chuck nods at her from the sun-drenched doorway. She never did invite him in to sit or anything.

"Oh Jesus!" she wails, as though reality just struck her again. "He was no fucking angel!" she spins and pierces a look through the police chief. He is melted by the sight of the wash of tears across her face. "He had rough friends – real pricks! But I'll tell you right now – *and don't you ever fucking ask me again!"* she screams. "He never killed that girl, I swear it! Yeah, we'd be surprised, peoples' secrets! –but I know otherwise! 'Cause he..." and she sobs uncontrollably and runs out of the room, leaving Chuck Cintz standing there heartbroken.

"When I have a kid, I'm namin' him 'Bug'," chubby teenage Chuck Cintz says out of the blue. At the moment, the sun is gloriously setting beyond the first base line, and the last of all the other boys are wandering off toward it. Slouched at the end of the one-plank players' bench planted there in the open off the third base line, Wilf and him are savoring, and recovering from, the conquests and prideful aches and pains of their ten-hour day of baseball.

"'Bug'?" Wilf grins, leaning back on bracing arms. And he twists up his thin tanned face with curiosity as he looks at Chuck sideways with bright blue, knowing eyes. "'Bug'..."

"Yeah. It's cute," Chuck affirms, smiling at himself. Combing his dark hair with his fingers, his foot twirls the pedal of Wilf's old red bike propped at the end of the bench beside him.

"You're almost fifteen, and that's too old for cute," Wilf suggests.

"What would you name him?" Chucky cranks another grin at his lifelong friend, his soft blue eyes sparkling.

"Don't know that I'll have kids," Wilf peers into the amber sun.

"Some of these little baseball farts are like having kids," Chuck jokes, leaning over to pick up a pebble in the dust. Groaning with a tired arm, he tosses it at the third base slab of wood a few feet away.

"Maybe we're too old for this," Wilf poses, watching the stone skip away.

"You don't play half the time anyway!" Chuck flings some diamond dust at him.

"I'm sorry. It's my fault... Otherwise, you wouldn't lose every single game," Wilf beams wide at Chuck's managerial frustration.

"A better ballpark would help – "

"It's the same for both sides," Wilf reminds him how the field is rough for everyone.

"No one's done anything since that screen," Chuck flips his right thumb toward the backstop.

Wilf thinks for a moment. "Why didn't you ever ask your dad?" He means to volunteer fixing up the field. Out of all the kids who play, plus all the others around town who they talked into asking, only one father – Wilf's – said he would. But he wasn't about to start at it alone.

Chuck told him before, but this time he explains in detail: "He's too busy, I guess. He's never home anymore, traveling and meetings and things. The first thing he does after supper at night is doze off in his chair. And it's like when I asked him to help me get my bike going again he says I'm old enough to do it myself now... But what's more important is I'm saving it up to ask him to teach me to drive next year."

"Right. Then you can teach me," Wilf agrees with that strategy.

"Do you love your dad?" Chuck now poses a strange one, totally out of character.

Wilf smiles at him, not embarrassed that his true friend would actually come out with it. "Sure. He's a good guy."

Chuck nods his head a bit, then reveals, "Sid says his dad beats on him..."

"He does?!" Wilf gasps, almost tensing to his feet with alarm.

"I believe him. He showed me bruises – on his back."

"No shit..!" Wilf stares at Chuck. "Whoa...! His ol' man doesn't seem so bad, though?" he questions.

"No," Chuck scratches the dust for another stone. "Guess you never know – what some people do."

"We should do something, Chuck. We can't let him do Sid that way," Wilf slumps down again but is still wide-eyed shocked.

"I'd like to. I hate that shit."

"So, let's say something."

Chuck hesitates...but it's Wilf, "I did."

Wilf watches him, waiting.

"I told Chief Phillips..."

"Oh... So, what did he – ?"

"Can't do anything," Chuck finds another stone and throws it hard. "He said Sid or his mom have to do it – go to him. So I don't tell Sid that, but I tell him he should do something...but he says no way."

"No way?!" Wilf cries out as he stiffly stands and walks his thin frame behind the bench, leaning slowly over to pick up his bike. "He likes it, or somethin'..?" He doesn't understand.

"No. But Phillips says it's never simple, that we'd be surprised at all the stuff like that going on." Chuck stretches up too, and, with Wilf pushing his bike, they both start out, dragging themselves across the field, heading for home. Now the sun is a red arc behind a distant row of trees and the crickets are tuning up in the sweet, warm, evening air.

"Does that mean some more of these kids are..?" Wilf doesn't know the word.

"I guess... Were you?" Chuck asks directly, trying to be nonchalant by kicking up a last big cloud of infield dust into the still air.

"Never. I remember my mom slappin' my hand once. She still apologizes, and that was years ago."

"My dad slapped me once. But I deserved it, 'cause I was being really mouthy. That was years ago, too. I think he regrets it."

Wilf mulls that over for a second. Shuffling his runners through the outfield's long grass, he pictures Chuck's father and tries to imagine what his best buddy could possibly have said. He didn't know he was ever a rebel. "You wonder why people do things," he puts it to the first star he sees as he looks up into the deepening pure blue above.

"And you wonder they grow up so messed up and unhappy."

"It ain't right," Wilf insists.

"And there's a world full of it," Chuck protests to his friend and the gods looking down on them as they leave the ballpark and mystically merge with the evening shadows down a side street.

"Well, Jennifer and I know it wasn't Doug, if that means anything to you, See-see," Carl leans in and attests to the Chief, who is across the office seeming heavily weighed in his chair. As Carl is stating that, he is straddling the open doorway while anxiously glancing back at his daughter in his car at the curb a few feet away. A light rain still falling out there looks like the last squeezed drops of the brief summer downpour. Little Carl's bald spot is dripping a few drops, though his plaid shirt appears somewhat dampened.

Chuck nods his head slowly. Braced by crossed arms on his desk, he sags like he still feels overwhelmed by it all. And now adding to it, he's muddled by lack of sleep. "We certainly didn't find any evidence that he did it," he raises his voice against the traffic noise and rain behind Carl. Part of him wishes he had found proof of Doug's guilt, so that this poor man, who he knows so well, could put an end to that side of it for himself and his family. And another small part of him instead wants to tell Carl about the red thread, and that Bug Doug's whole wardrobe consisted of only one white and several black shirts.

"Jennifer says that Janet liked Doug McCallum, and that he was nice to her..."

Chuck just watches Carl find words.

"Once, she just told me, Doug gave Janet a ride on that bike of his..." he ducks down again to check Jennifer in the car, "and he told her his secret, that Julie's boy is his, but that was his last one, because that accident he had before their baby was born – remember it, Chuck, when he was run off the road and smacked the fence? – well, that ended it for him having more kids, she said..."

Chuck sits there suddenly gaping. He didn't know about the baby, and he didn't know about that part of Doug's injuries. The doctors at Elston Hospital sure can keep a secret, he sees amid his growing confusion.

"I'm glad, in a way," Chuck soon collects his thoughts. He then stands and approaches Carl. "I knew it wasn't him, but I'll get this confirmed and we can put Doug to rest, at least." He presses a hand on the father's shoulder for a second as he appears to study the rain clouds. "Carl, in another way, I wish it had been him..." He doesn't have to elaborate. And Carl smiles weakly then steps out onto the wet sidewalk toward his car and his daughter, thanking Chuck with a little wave just before he gets in.

...

The rest of that day and Friday are mostly sunny, with both the evening and morning a little cool. Chuck Cintz had taken the red thread to the Elston labs yesterday, as scheduled, and he got the call late this afternoon telling him what they could so far: basic shirt material, but an unusual color chemical dye lot believed used by only two manufacturers, one making women's clothes and the other a small-scale sports shirt company – who affix little emblems on their pockets. On red shirts, it was learned, they sew little charging bulls. The lab people will confirm that detail after factory samples are obtained and more tests are run.

Tomorrow is Bug Doug's funeral.

Up at Nick's Bowl, Ba-Dee is anxious to finish his shift and his workweek. He has just phoned Gene to have him bring the lists tonight, and before that he had called Howard to make sure he picks up a box of beer. ("Why am I coordinator?" Ba-Dee asks himself, again.) ("Because I sit around here all day doing next to nothing near this phone," he answers himself.) Norm was in around noon, and they talked about going to Doug's funeral and then the dance tomorrow night. The dance might be interesting, they felt.

Over at the library, Chase is sorting painfully slow through the twenty or more boxes full of used books that were donated this week, the first round of their annual one-month book drive. (At this rate, without more volunteer help, he will have them all catalogued by the end of the current great age of man.) He likes to open up every book, hoping to find inscriptions or margin notes (sort of like a featherweight grandpa voyeur). But then, poking around in his next box, Chase finds something peculiar: a five-decades-old hardcover math text with its middle pages replaced – someone had cut out about fifty pages and then tediously taped in blank ones. They had even dirtied up the edges, he can tell, to try to make them match. Yet, thumbing through the blanks, he is intrigued to see the first few have writing on them. It must be a diary, he muses. Goody.

He adjusts his bifocals and red ball cap, then starts reading: "The sky is black. Some shaded dirty clouds are pushing across. The wind is moaning. Leaves flap and cling. A tiny red glow brightens then dims right above the hard outline of the picnic table..." Or maybe it's just someone's attempt at a novel, Chase thinks, and he feels some disappointed. But then why would they hide it so carefully..? He reads more.

By the middle of the first page he begins to suspect, but he doesn't know what. It's neatly written initially, then soon gets rushed looking. Everyone starts out tidy, he grants...

But as Chase carefully absorbs more lines, his uneasiness builds. Further along, with burning alarm, it finally occurs to him what this could be: it could be the cold, sick account of Janet's murder! He stops and squints out the nearby window at the visible section of street, and his eyes glass over as his mind begins to accept the real possibility. "Merciful God..." he whispers. He then reads to the end...

There's no doubt. "Lord..."

Chase looks for a student's name, but finds none. Why isn't there a name in a school text...? Well, he remembers being told not to write in his – they had to be passed down... He glances around the bright library, at Elizabeth bent over her front desk, as ever, then at old Mary Higgs down the "Mystery" aisle, and then at all the cardboard boxes full of donations lined up on the long table where he's sitting... He stands slowly. The book is there closed in front of him. His hands don't want to pick it up again. He starts to think about young Janet, but shakes that off, afraid his tears will flow. Instead, he asks himself how this ended up here... Someone must have given it away by accident – unknowingly. Obviously, it's just an old textbook... When someone else finds out it's missing, he then realizes, we'll know 'cause he'll be leaving town – or he'll die of heart failure..! "Good!" he jokes aloud satisfyingly. Then, at last, the way the mind works in steps at times like this, a final realization hits him through his haze of horror, and he thinks of Chuck Cintz: he's got to get this thing right over to him! – but he has to keep it quiet!

Rushing past Elizabeth, the book behind his back, he smiles wide at her, trying not to make it look phony. But he can't come up with anything to say to her. She thinks I'm racing to the crapper, he hopes. Old folks are always doing that...

On the street he wishes he had brought a stack of books. One – *the one* – looks so conspicuous! Thankfully, he meets nobody along the sidewalk.

When he gets there, no one is in the police office, but as he turns back around in the doorway he sees Chief Cintz stepping out of Lucy's across the late-day street. He stares at him piercingly. His cap is pulled low over his eyes. Chuck almost stops in the middle of the road when he spots him standing there that way.

"Chase..."

"Can we lock this door?!" the old man asserts sternly.

Chuck studies him, then notices the math book. He jests, "Going to read me some dirty equations?" But Chase is plainly not going to laugh. He closes the door and locks it. The third time ever.

Chase has headed for the Chief's desk, and half sits on it right in front of the empty chair. He is clutching the book tightly with both hands.

Still assessing him, Chuck crosses the office and lowers onto his chair, his eyes now riveting on the book.

Chase finds the diary section's first page and turns the book right side up for Chuck, pushing it close to his face. "This came in with the book drive." His hands are shaking wildly.

Chuck peers up at the grim blue eyes behind the bifocals, then lowers his gaze and starts reading, with both hands steadying the book then gradually taking it from Chase. After a couple of pages he looks up again, his mouth beginning to droop open. Chase nods deliberately back at him.

Chuck reads the whole thing. His hands are shaking a little, too. Like Chase did, he immediately searches the front and back covers and pages for a name. "This came in today? – with the book drive?!"

"Sometime this week."

"Any idea who – when?" the Chief gawks dumbfounded at the old fellow's face.

"Uhh...nope," Chase finally breaks his stare, focusing now into the distance, remembering. "All the books came in bags or loose. We put them in boxes from the grocery – "

"Are there receipts given?! – sorry, Chase, for interrupting – this is unbelievable!" his loud exclamation echoes in the bare office.

"That's okay, uhh...no receipts or lists or anything. Lots even came in the night slot."

Chuck thinks for a second. "Then were they put in the boxes in bunches...like..?"

"I know what you mean, so the ones that came in with this one might have a name. Nope, they were all piled on one table then sorted into boxes on the other table." He watches Chuck's gears turn. "What do ya figure..?"

"I bet some wife or mom or dad cleaned off some shelves – from everyone's room in the house – and some guy has just had, or will soon have, a heart seizure."

"Exactly what I thought... Why would some young guy have an old math book in his room?"

"Why is it a young guy?" Chuck frowns at Chase. "Why not some older guy, and his wife – or his sister or his daughter – cleaned out the bookshelves?"

"'Cause it's felt pen..." But Chase then realizes that's not good enough. Next he wonders, "Why would a guy even do this – write this?" he flicks a few fingers distastefully toward the book still spread open in Chuck's hands.

"To get off on it..." Chuck starts as he glances up again, but he sees the ol' boy's expression turn puzzled. "Get off...umm...get aroused – to relive the rape."

"Goddamn fuckin' bastard!" Chase tenses to his feet. (Chuck never heard him swear like that, before.)

"We have to keep this to ourselves – for now, Chase..." He watches him start pacing, with seeming unbearable disgust, back and forth toward the door.

"Of course... But you can tell Tom and Wilf, though," Chase absently gives him permission, as if having been temporarily in possession of the book allows him. "I know how you trust Wilf – he should be the fuckin' mayor here!" he adds roughly – as though now that he's tried this angry level of swearing he likes it.

Chuck grins thinly. As he stands and follows Chase weaving to a stop at the door, his mind is a turmoil of possibilities. He raises a few fingers in thanks and see-you-later. Chase does the same and wordlessly leaves.

And Chuck Cintz still can't quite believe what he's holding in his hands.

"It's all people," Norm proclaims after the wordless moments of Howard's (mother's) car crunching to a stop on the moonless black, cornfield-walled gravel road, followed by the ripping open of the beer case and expedient yanking, uncapping and slurping of five bottles, "that make up everything you feel and everything you react to."

"You been saving that?" Gene smiles unseen in the pitch of the back seat, from where he is just able to see Norm's silhouette in the front. (Asked like: Has it been a long week, and are all its intervening important thoughts this pressing?)

Norm, undaunted, elaborates: "There's few things you feel – or react to – that have nothing to do with people...like, maybe... scenery, I guess. But tragedy, joy, disappointment, peace...they're almost always in reaction to what people do to you, or leave you with."

"True," Howard makes it official, then tangents: "Did you ever notice people talking when you can't hear them? They look so profound, when you can only imagine what they're saying – "

"But when you hear them," Joseph interjects between glugs (there, stuck in the middle of the back seat again, as though if he wants to be part of this group, that's all he gets) "it's fuckin' drivel."

A brief silence confirms that truth, too.

"Fucking," Gene then states next, from his seat right beside Joseph.

"What?" Joseph responds neutrally, as though to the air.

"With a 'gee'," Gene notes matter-of-factly.

"Oh... Fuck-*ing*," Joseph acknowledges. He then quietly considers the point a moment... Nope. I said 'fuckin'."

Gene counters loftily, "There are rules of grammar – "

"No such fuckin' thing," Joseph quickly refutes. (Howard and Norm try to see each other's eyes across the darkness in the front, to share some of this amusement.) "Languages change all the time, and whatever you say or write at that instant becomes humanly communicatively legitimate. 'Grammar correctors' are two words that can't go together in a sentence. They cancel each other out."

"You just made a corrective grammatical observation," Howard notices, chuckling.

"Crusher," Gene reverts to his superiority, "you read too much."

There's a pause.

"Caterwaul," Joseph enunciates flatly.

"What?!" Gene is thrown again.

"Good word," Joseph explains. Norm, Howard and Ba-Dee all softly snicker. (Gene doesn't.) "*Pee*-shooter..."

"You're sitting there watching tee-vee, and the fridge shuts off," Norm feels it's time to forge onward. "You weren't conscious of it, but at the instant after it shuts off, you hear – heard it humming."

"So?" Gene gives him patience, as though it's better than dealing with Joseph.

"But, if that instant that it goes off is a point in time leaving you, the humming is in the past... The question is: did your subconscious mind just remember the humming, or did your mind scoot back in time a bit to hear the humming, to qualify the instant of it shutting off?"

The other three think it over. Gene considers, "Have a long day, there, Norm? You okay, now – ?"

"Norm's right," Howard sees it.

"Who cares?" Joseph applies his supreme deduction.

"Did you just say something, Joseph?" Ba-Dee poses. "Or did our minds just scoot back somewhere?"

The others reflect. Again.

"So, a local legend gets buried tomorrow," Gene rebegins like an outsider.

Ba-Dee responds, "Yep… They were saying Chiefie Chuck is positive Bug's suicide had nothing to do with Janet…well, it might, in a way. They knew each other, slightly."

"Still could be him," Gene offers.

"I think we don't know what The Law knows," Ba-Dee defends his information.

Norm agrees. "Probably. We'll find out what, eventually, but I hear Chuck has some sort of absolute proof… Anyway, who's got the lists?" Gene stretches and rustles them in the black beside Norm's ear. "And a pen…" Gene indicates his pen and highlighter are clipped to the pages. Norm switches on the little flashlight he brought, and they begin x-ing off the few boys' names they've come up with, reducing the possibilities to one hundred and forty-nine. Next, they asterisk the few Most likely, then "N"-for- "Nah" the most unlikely of known kid personalities and question-mark all the doubtful by age. The list is soon down to just thirty-eight names, now emphasized by the yellow marker. "We'll work on these – I'll write these out and copy it – "

"No, I'll do it," Gene proposes. "My father has that copier in his study downstairs."

"Good. Whatever," Norm hands it all back.

"We'll get him eventually," Howard promises.

"The kid or the murderer?" Joseph is unclear.

"The fuck-*ing* murderer, of course," Howard makes seething sounds.

"Well, there's one less possibility being buried tomorrow," Ba-Dee returns to that.

"Is this another list?" Joseph interrupts his engorging more beer to question.

Norm reacts with a huff, "No, I think Chuck's got the one true list going – and under control. We'll just try to do our part."

Ba-Dee and Gene decide it's leak time, so they all five end up scrambling out of the car...

...The doors closed, interior lights off, the substance of night seems almost pure black. Stars glisten preciously overhead, and the halo of the town dabs the dark horizon. The air is refreshing – cooling – and powerfully sweet. And a remnant wind animates the nearby cutout of trees as it murmurs through...

"Don't touch me with that *pee*-shooter!" Howard roars with laughter where he's standing leaking too as Joseph edges threateningly near.

"Just let me piss on your foot, Howie," Joseph pleads. "I would be forever honored."

Howard waddles away bowlegged down the road, giggling uncontrollably.

"Beer time! Let's fill these bladders back up!" Gene rallies some spirit in the darkness, and Joseph u-turns instantaneously. Howard comes strolling back, and they all resettle into the car.

"Nice evening," Norm says inside the closeness again, still gazing out at the heavens.

A little reflection and rustling passes...

"It was Looker," Howard starts once more, out of nowhere.

"Mayor Jimms," says Ba-Dee.

"Bicycle Man," Joseph offers up the harmless old fellow who used to fix bikes in his garage for everyone.

"Frog Man," suggests Gene.

"Rocket Man."

"Early Man."

"Handy Man."

"Scoot Man," Ba-Dee then insists with finality. "From behind the fridge, he came from the Future..."

ug Doug's funeral was strange. As Ba-Dee, Gene, Norm, Howard and Joseph sit at a dark back-corner table at the Local Order of the Varmint Hall Saturday-night dance, they reexperience, through Norm and Ba-Dee's recall, Chief Cintz's few sensitive graveside words, Reverend Fisk's predictably deathly eulogy, Ann's depthless grief for her brother, Julie Grant's silent tears and struggle to contain her active little boy, the few quiet odds and ends townspeople, and the fifty or sixty ugly bikers. The bikers, Norm relates, wait patiently in a big, solemn bunch for Reverend Fisk to finish, then shoo everyone except Julie away: "Fuck off! Fuck off!" they coax the citizens.

"What they did next, we probably don't want to know..." Ba-Dee's mind's eye pierces the old wooden table in front of them, groping the unfathomable.

"Let's pray Doug's still in the ground," Joseph enriches the image.

The dance hall doors have been open for an hour and over two hundred people are here already (almost double the usual). Some maybe dropped in for just a little while, but more are steadily filing through the entrance. So it's jam-packed, the beer's flowing fast, the band is jumpin', and these folks just want...good company, tonight, it seems. Fortunately, the bikers had other engagements.

"We haven't pinned down much for Chuck, yet," Howard squints across the dimly lighted hall toward the Chief and all his regular group crammed around their usual front table.

"He's the one getting paid for it," Gene observes as he scans for girls at tables around the perimeter. "He can wait."

"Sure," Howard grasps that. "And maybe someone can meanwhile just take out an ad and ask the killer to wait, too."

Gene indifferently continues his mental safari.

As the moments roll along, people come and go through the main doors nearby; old friends, schoolmates, ex-flames and mixed others stop at their table for as many reasons. And four of the five friends even dance (with girls, not fantasies). Joseph, however, merely wedges deeper into the corner and takes it all in.

But then, near eleven o'clock, with the music carrying everyone away and laughter ringing off the rafters, a tussle breaks out. It's beside the front table, and just about everyone quickly squeezes around to see who it is. The band even stops playing.

Norm soon leaves his group and circles the twitching pack. "It's Sid!" he can see through a gap, turning and shouting above the roar of the masses to his buddies now approaching.

Reaching the perimeter, Howard climbs up on Ba-Dee's back to see. But several folks think they've started going at it too and begin trying to pry them apart. "Ho shit! It's Mayor Jimms!" Howard screams with his one quick glimpse before he and Ba-Dee succumb to the pushing and pulling and begin to topple, bringing down a sizable stand of people to the floor with them. Two or three of the men quickly scramble to their feet fighting, and Howard and Ba-Dee are there in the midst. Their cascade of bodies has caused a surge all around the main event, and shoving matches break out all through the mob. Several turn into new fistfights – all while someone screeches hysterically. The fists flying in the tight crowd cause elbowing and kicks, so that those who get hurt, or those compelled to avenge wives who get hurt, start throwing punches too. In a five-minute span – enough time for Sid and Mayor Jimms to wear themselves out and flop onto chairs – three-quarters of the Saturday-night gathering are flailing or restraining. Few have retreated to the walls.

Finally, several minutes later, with some bloody mouths being wiped and torn shirts tucked back in, the rumble has ended. Though there is still some grumbling as chairs and drinks are uprighted, it's apparently settled well enough.

All the while, Grover Gewh – the aging band leader and guitar player, who has been coming here Saturday nights for twenty-one years and always looks bored and rarely talks to anyone – is standing between his two accompanists at the edge of the stage grinning blissfully, as though he can't believe his entertained eyes. Without gesture, he opens his mouth and at the top of his voice shouts, "Great! 'Bout time! Drinks for everyone – on me!"

Everyone gapes at him...they hesitate...then they all laugh and applaud uproariously!

And the dance has become a party.

Soon sitting back at their table, Howard rubs his bruised jaw, sticking it out toward a fully amused Norm. "Any blood?" he asks through his teeth. Norm shakes his head, too locked up in smiling to talk.

"Who did *you* get?" Gene's eyes pop as he notices Ba-Dee's messy knuckles.

"Several," Ba-Dee beams. "Don't know who, but I got in some good ones. What fun."

"You're the one who flattened old Mrs. Weston, Ba-Dee," Joseph points an absconded beer bottle at him.

Howard starts giggling again. "No, I think I landed on her first, when we fell over. She came up swinging, I remember... In fact, I think she's the one who started the big punch-out!"

Around them the hall is still buzzing loudly with voices, and for some time longer, laughter erupts in big patches.

But the five corner-huddlers don't hear explanatory details through the usual roaming storytellers as expected, until finally, in his Saturday-night white shirt and white sneakers, Chief Cintz approaches, weaving between the faintly lighted tables, a little rumpled but smiling at everyone sort of philosophically. When he's near, Norm offers him: "Trade you what we got for what happened up there..."

"Heh!" Chuck stops in his tracks. Grabbing a chair from the next table, he slides it into their shadows and sits on it cautiously straight. "Okay. Who's first?" He pushes back his hair with the fingers of both hands as his eyes circle the group.

"Thirty-eight," Norm gives him theirs.

"As in...possible kids?" Chuck raises his grayed eyebrows.

Norm answers, "Yup."

"Gettin' there! Good going... Well..." the Chief tips back on the hard chair, hooking his thumbs on his jeans pockets. His rounded face tenses alternately along each jaw line for a moment, as though he is carefully balancing some thoughts. "Well, seems Jimmy Jimms was a little arrogant with Sid – you know how Sid's always helping people, even running in and getting coffee all the time for the ol' boys 'round Lucy's – and Jimmy really talked down to him, told him 'go fetch' something. That was in the middle of a heated discussion at their table about Bug Doug." (Chuck is right here aware of how intently all five young men are paying attention, their ten eyes glued right on him... Concerned town sons, good citizens in the making – the Chucks and Wilfs coming up, he recognizes.) "So, Sid lost it – came unsprung. I knew he had a temper, but only saw it like that once or twice before, ever."

"One of the nicest guys around," Joseph inserts emphatically (by his use of normal words), evidently from some sort of experience.

"Sure," Chuck smiles openly again at them all. "But he's nobody's doormat...we're all glad for that. And he knows he's a good guy – I mean, he'll admit he works at it, at least, at being positive. He loves his town and wants to do his part, and tries to set an example..." Chuck stops, as though to let that sink in while he takes a quick survey around the hall.

"Sounds like Sid," Ba-Dee speaks for everyone.

Norm steers back on track: "So Sid is *wild*..."

"Calls the Mayor an outsider – 'foreigner' was the word I heard," Chuck can't keep from smirking slightly, his focus appearing lost for a second in a little daydream.

Right then, the man himself happens by: "Sid!" Chuck and two others call together, one as "hello", one in surprise, and the other as an invitation to sit.

Sid pulls over chair. "Hey," he grins self-consciously, settling beside the Chief, facing the half-circle of young men. "What's up?"

"Jus' talkin' 'bout you," Chuck answers in a loud whisper out of the side of his mouth, holding his face expressionless.

Sid doesn't ever mind. "Sure. Anything good?"

"We're just wondering what else you called His Honor – besides foreigner..." Chuck sounds fully serious.

"Foreigner point of view, I said to him," Sid clarifies. In a bright yellow plaid shirt and faded jeans, he looks quickly relaxed on his chair, his plump body overhanging it somewhat. He flings back a few strands of long blond hair off his face, and his hazel eyes twinkle with his usual friendliness. "I was tellin' him that his point of view about Doug McCallum isn't the same as most of us. We grew up with Doug, I say, and know – knew him a lot better than he ever would have."

"Right..." Chuck agrees, trying to prompt the main part of the account (all five others here shifting their focus back and forth).

"So, he wasn't really lookin' at me, you know? – as I'm sayin' that. But when I finish, he looks at me cold and says that fetch thing – I don't even remember exactly what it was..." Sid apologizes to the group. "Well, that's when I blow. I call him pompous shit and...umm...ego-tripper and low-life jailbird – "

"*Whoa!*" Chuck stiffens. "What was that?!"

"Jail..." Sid starts then trails as he recognizes the Chief's restraint-above-surprise expression. He thinks for a second, then asks, "You mean..?"

"Yes, I mean," Chuck frowns at him.

Sid explains himself. "I thought everybody knew that and everybody was just politely quiet about – "

"What's *it?!*" Howard finally bursts. And the other four also fix expectant looks on Chuck.

"Too late now," Sid grins meekly at the police chief.

"...All right," Chuck unsticks his glare from Sid and shifts his relenting eyes from one to the other. "Jimms was in jail before he showed up here. No one knew about it, for a few years – "

"Few months," Sid splices in, commanding another blank look from Chuck Cintz. "I knew someone in Elston police," is all he has to explain.

"In jail for what?" Norm isn't going to forget to ask.

Chuck takes a deep breath. He futilely wishes his letting this out now won't make any difference. "Murder..."

"Shoot!", "Oh shit!" and "Wowie!" all blurt out at once, trailed by Joseph's "Fuckin' no!"

"Yep," Chuck nods as Sid nods more vigorously beside him. "Twenty years, he served time, then came here looking for a new start – a second chance..." he ends forcefully, making a plain point to the five of them.

Ba-Dee's neurons are firing overtime: "You weren't – he wasn't on your...list?"

Chuck's eyes angle toward the front, finding Jimmy Jimms having a good time again at his table. "You have to consider everybody," he gives them. "Most are quickly as good as off the list. Others... No, he's not," Chuck then concludes too flatly.

All of them notice he said "as good as" off.

"This town's really unraveling…" Norm reflects.

"No question," Chuck leans both hands on the table and pushes himself to his feet. "And some don't seem to know they have a role…a lifetime role…" he prompts as he watches them.

"To help keep it together," Ba-Dee knows. And by all appearances, his four accomplices agree.

"Won't be easy to keep doin'," Sid stands up, too. "As long as the guy's still out there…" he turns toward the Chief.

Chuck meets his eyes. "Well, maybe it's all just got to boil some more, before it spits up the scum."

The black umbrella of tree leaves above him merely rustles with the soft breezes. Eggie can see some stars between the limbs, but he mostly keeps watch on the houses ahead of him. As he steps lightly across the side neighbor's lawn, he is aware that half the town – including his own parents, amazingly – went to the dance. ("Do what your sister says, Eddie, and no sneaking out to the store to read comics!") Everyone around here has gone out, he's sure, everyone except Carl and Jennifer in their house right there. (But no one – especially girl kids, he recalls how he has noticed lately – just wander out of their homes and hang around neighborhoods, any more.) And (he now frowns at his mind's image) his parents even made his sister lock all the doors and windows tonight, and then showed her how to use Dad's old pistol..! Okay, yeah, she's an eighteen-year-old girl...and he well enough knows what happened to Janet... But I'm just a short little glasses-wearing young boy – innocent and only almost eleven!, he separates himself, and laments his totally unreal restrictions.

Now, he's only sorta sure why he's here. And it sure was a long walk from home, trying to keep out of sight in the dark. (He "borrowed" one of his sister's big, black T-shirts, having sense enough not to wear his trademark white shirt with collar, and having brains enough not to ride his unique yellow bike.) It's as though he just wants to see and feel this again, to fully know he was really here before, and saw what he saw. (Eddie reads a lot, and sometimes he's afraid that reality and fantasy might tangle up for him, a bit.)

Eggie likes the smell of the night air. It's full of freshness, he imagines. And he even likes sneaking around in the dark, sort of. Not to spy on anyone – he's decided there's nothing fun about peeking, and things. (He'd rather not have something bad he's done stuck on his mind, all the time.) He just likes being kinda invisible. But one thing about all this: he doesn't think about that night, too much, when he saw the guy carry off Janet – tried not to think about it at all, until he could sneak out here again and remember it clearly.

From behind the big tree a few feet away, he eases across to the picket fence, then sets one foot on its bottom rail and pulls himself up.

The picnic table is still there across the grass, a dark shape against the light spilling from the kitchen window in behind. He can't see anyone inside.

Eggie now forces his thoughts to go back to that night: He can picture Janet stretched out there on the table, slowly smoking that cigarette in the wind. He certainly remembers how the guy startled him, jumping over the same side fence only a few feet away. As dark as it was, he still can't believe the guy didn't see him right there. Good thing...or maybe, too bad... But he could have been killed too..! (That thought makes him shudder and look carefully again through the barely lighted yards all around.)

Alarming him, the light dims as a figure passes by the bright kitchen window. It wasn't Jennifer...her mom must back. It sure wasn't her dad.

"Good God!" he whispers, thinking about something happening to Jennifer, now. They must be scared, worrying about her. What if the killer figures she knows something..? (And again, Eggie searches the darkness in a full circle around him.) And then it hits him harder than ever – now that he fully feels the fear: What if the killer finds out about me..?!

But Eggie summons his last ounce of courage – to not run away – because he promised himself he would clear this picture in his mind, his picture of Janet being dragged toward him and, most especially, his memory of what the guy looked like. (Some part of him now knows he'll have to talk to someone about it, somehow, someday.)

He forces his brain all he can: he can see the guy's outline, a shadow against the houses. He's walking slow toward her, not bent over sneaking, or anything. He's got just a shirt on, no jacket. It's windy, but warm. Eggie can see the glow of Janet's cigarette suddenly blocked by his silhouette...he has short hair, I can tell. He remembers thinking the guy's kinda big, too, and that he was assuming the guy is just going to joke around and scare her, or something...and then sees that he actually is big when he bends over her, grabs her, and stands straight up with her wiggling. She only comes up to his chest...

Then the guy walks backwards across the lawn dragging her along. She kicks a little, but is spending most of her energy hitting him and trying to pull his arms away. Eggie now remembers how he then thought about screaming...wishes he had. Why didn't I? he now asks himself honestly, tears coming to his eyes – I coulda easily got away, my bike was just over at the street. (But, of course, he had no idea then what would become of Janet. He really had little idea what rape and murder were, let alone understand that it happens so real, and not just like on television news.)

When the guy gets her to the fence (Eggie now pictures the rest with his eyes closed) he flings her over with such ease...it really scares him. She just sails over like a beanbag – imagine what he could have done to a little fartweight like me, he grimaces remembering, hiding there behind that tree. And then – then! (here's the most important part to concentrate on) the guy looks back – grabs the top of the fence with both hands and cranks his head around – over my way – to check the other yards and houses! That's when I see his face! It's plain as can be, maybe ten or fifteen feet away... It's a young guy – sorta young, not older like Dad. (Eggie doesn't know who it is, but for an instant he feels he's seen him around.) And his hair is kinda middle color – not blond or black, but somewhere brown in between, and his shirt looks pretty much red...

Eggie pops his eyes back open. Everything is still quiet. He wonders, for the first time, if there is someone watching this spot, or if there is a camera pointed at him and the yard right now...

Well, one thing for certain, he thinks as he breathes deep again: I'll recognize him. He knew that eleven nights ago, and he's even more sure of it now.

Better go, he tells himself. As he focuses along the back of the houses one more time, he stops at Carl's and Margaret's and Jennifer's glowing kitchen window – it used to be just normal-happy inside there, he sighs, like some other houses, I guess – and then peers deep into the dark windows beside it, and then above. He knows which one was Janet's and which one is Jennifer's (details he's not proud of knowing) and doesn't question that both those windows are now equally black. But he's done what he came for and he's finished thinking about it, so, checking the part in his hair again out of habit, he quietly turns and tiptoes away.

...

140

All the while, from one of those darkened rooms, Jennifer is dreaming into the night. She hasn't seen anything...until he starts sneaking away. Her heart begins to race, then she quickly realizes it's only a little kid. "You morbid, perverted...well, little-boy perverted," she allows in her mind's words. But nothing in human nature, she feels, will ever really shock her anymore. In fact, she objectively thinks, seeing the kid there is sort of like having company, like the comfort of having any human watch over you... Except, she then shivers, if it was the guy...

"**Y**ou don't fuckin' know. You think you know, but you fuckin' don't." Joseph couldn't say it any plainer, he believes.

Gene just steams. Straight thinking doesn't come easy for him, trying to deal with Crusher.

"He's right, sorta," Howard responds instead (he's the third person there in the back seat, tonight). "Bug Doug was okay. He sure wasn't what he looked. But you can't say things like that about someone when you didn't ever talk to them," he vents a little of his own indignation at Gene for his "Doug the loser" remark.

Though all five had barely lasted out the dance (ending at 1:30 – much of that time enjoyed talking more with Sid and some of his supporters who came by and sat, too) they decided afterward to make a brief run out "the road", to sip a quick beer and talk just a bit. It's now five A.M.

Norm is driving, and he was the one who started on about Bug Doug (after hours of them going on about Sid and Jimms and Chuck). Ba-Dee, trying to keep awake beside him, is squinting at the horizon for the sunrise.

"You can't see it, can you?" Gene loftily censures Joseph beside him.

"See what? What's to see?" Joseph reacts affectedly, flicking some fingers into the black air (which Gene can just barely make out).

"Don't do that, you fucking moron!" Gene growls. "This is serious, and the serious part is how you four and everyone else around here are stuck in the emotional bog of this town!"

"What does *that* mean?!" Norm's not sure he can tolerate where this is going.

Joseph knows: "He means he understands better than all the rest of us – "

"I know what I can see, shit-for-brains! Can't *you* see this objectively?" Gene's voice is a loud groan of frustration.

"You mean it's all too plain?" Joseph says as though it's reasonable. "Innocent young local girl gets fucked then completely fucked, local young man shuts himself down – one and two is three, case closed, how can you doubt it?"

"No, it's not *that* straightforward," Gene's tone now has the feel of backing down a little. "I'm saying you can't *dismiss* – "

"You think Chuck and Tom are stupid!" Howard dangles one out there.

"Well..." Gene ignites it anew with an inert word.

"Oh!" Joseph lilts. "Of course they are! This is a hick town, isn't it?" he cranks his head around checking. "Everyone here is a turnip!"

Gene snarls, "Fuck you, Crusher – "

"That doesn't answer it," Norm persists from the front.

"Awright, awright!" Gene snorts. "Cintz is a genius! But he still makes emotion-based decisions – "

"What other kind of decisions are there?" Norm interrupts. "That matter?"

"Ohhh, I get it!" Gene roars. "Forget common sense! If someone's a good guy, just round up the usual character witnesses and then – whatever he did wrong – slap his wrists!"

"That's not it either," Norm won't be untracked.

(Ba-Dee is waking up. He realizes this noisy discussion is drifting through the open windows far off across the darkened land.)

"Oh, Jee-*sis!*" Gene grunts. "Why is everybody so thick?!"

"*Thick?!*" Joseph bellows, genuinely insulted.

"Because we take into consideration someone's character?!" Norm's getting hot, too, and is recklessly waving his half-empty beer bottle around. "And because it's decided that in no way does what happened add up to *this guy,* or that he was never *that way – ever!*"

"And," Ba-Dee's blood is flowing again, "that the Chief Chuck knows – knew him better than all of us put together?"

Then Howard inserts, "I think Chuck knows something we don't – that no one else knows."

Gene sighs, "Like fucking what?!"

"Well if Howie knew, he'd tell us fuckin' what, Gene," Joseph assures him with fatherly calm.

"Like what difference does it make, *Geeene?!*" Howard whines. "Shit, don't you trust anybody?" He leans forward to look past Joseph, as though he could actually meet his target's eyes there in the pitch-black back seat.

"I trust the facts. I trust what's obvious," Gene won't budge.

"Wait!" Norm counters. "You trust your own *conclusion.* What's obvious, and the apparent facts, are only part of it."

"Facts are facts – "

"Except when they're half-facts," Joseph cuts Gene off.

"Don't give me that shit!" Gene raises his voice again. "We're talking about murder! Sometimes there's only one thing that matters! In something this important, maybe it's the *plain, simple, unemotional facts!*"

"We're waking up the chickens..." Ba-Dee hears roosters crow in the distance.

"The point is – "

"The point is, we're doing what everybody does," Gene cuts off Howard's point. "We're making something more complex than it really is just by talking about it!"

"Well, excuse human nature!" Joseph grumbles sternly. "But, *Gene*, that's what people do, and that's how things get *fine-tuned evolved*, unraveled and sorted out! And human nature *has* to sort things out – in order to be sure of itself!"

"Exactly," Howard concurs. "We have to weigh everything carefully – "

"At the expense of victims!" Gene contests.

"No," Norm has one, "because we're not perfect: we lie and we're inaccurate."

Ba-Dee catches it: "Hey! Who said that the other day – just a few days ago?"

"Gene," Joseph scores the point.

There's a pause as that sinks in.

"Well, why isn't this Bug Doug even investigated? I mean officially brought to trial or something to get all the facts out in the end?" Gene again eases off a little.

"So all the attention can go to that and away from the actual murderer?" Howard suggests.

Norm agrees, "And investigating for the real murderer will be put on hold?"

"For months?" Joseph supports them.

"Plenty of time," Ba-Dee makes it unanimous, "for the guy to do it again?!"

"Oh, save us!" Gene sorta prays. "You all still won't consider Doug McCallum's guilt!"

"Cuz he's innocent in the ground," Joseph declares.

"Oh, God!" Gene moans again.

"Listen, Gene," Norm re-approaches sincerely. "Maybe because you're an outsider" (he says as objectively as he can) "you can't feel the feeling."

"The feeling of pushing back the truth – ?"

"The feeling of *trust!*" Norm shuts him up. "The knowledge that your feeling of caring and understanding for someone is an absolute basis – as absolute as you and everyone else in your little society of equals around you needs – to trust his innocence."

That silences the car again for a second.

"Bullshit," Gene responds.

"Oh give it a rest," Howard tries.

Now Ba-Dee thinks he sees someone trudging across the fields with a shotgun. "Here comes Farmer Fred with a bazooka."

All heads angle to where he's pointing, toward the pale glow of sunrise. "It's a tree," Norm is certain.

"You'll all see," Gene won't give it a rest. "Eventually, I say this Bug-a-Doug will be found guilty. It's just all too obvious."

"You said that already," Howard is weary.

Norm begins, "You can't fight our sense – "

"What?!" Gene flares up again. "You mean like a sixth sense? Is that what you're saying?"

"Why not," Joseph states rather than asks. "It's powerful – "

"Like vibrations in the air?!" Gene is incredulous.

Norm explains: "No, it's not an intuition, or anything. It's kind of a collective mood of how a town full of people feel – a sort of emanating feel of consensus based on years together, a– "

"Mood?!" Gene quotes as though he can't believe his ears. "You override facts with moods?"

Howard suggests, "How many societies are ruled by the feeling of the whole – like a swaying of consensus, to go the direction they *feel* is right, sometimes disregarding some hard details?"

"That doesn't make them on the right track!" Gene challenges.

"Right track for what?!" Joseph is again a little irritated. "Gene, the world is for people. Humans took over, and Earth belongs to them. Whatever direction they end up going is the right one, because that's the way they swayed. If direction was decided by perfect accuracy, we'd still be living in caves debating the correct morality of eating meat versus eating fruit or whether to go with the wheel idea because – the facts are! – someday it'll run someone over!"

"Well, the other end of that point of view works too," Gene relaxes. "We can decree too much just from feelings. It's been done, and people follow."

Norm understands: "Understood."

Howard is willing: "To a point."

Joseph flatly summarizes, too: "'Cept in this case, Gene, you're fuckin' wrong."

Ba-Dee's bleary eyes are still watching out the window – *"He's aiming it at us!"* he suddenly screams, and before anyone can verify it's a shotgun, Norm starts the car and is fishtailing it down the road – desperados of the dawn, homeward galloping from the conquests (of some common life-filled immaturities).

Only after he has dropped them all off does Norm remember that Gene was supposed to give everyone copies of the shortened list of potential witness kids.

The first daylight begins to brighten the street-scene window behind the little gathering in the police office. The fluorescents inside, though, still whiten everything mercilessly. On the two desks, several Lucy's take-out paper coffee cups sit at different levels of emptiness, long neglected.

Mayor Jimms (with a slightly cut and swollen left eye – but pride generally intact) has been mostly silent; Chuck, Wilf and Tom have been talking the night away. The kill diary, looking all the world like a math book, lies closed on the Chief's desk.

"This could put us a whole lot closer," Chuck had said to Jimmy Jimms as he handed him the book hours before. That was soon after the dance ended and Lucy's was closing, when Tom and Chuck told the Mayor to come over and see for himself their startling piece of luck.

Mayor Jimms is mostly relieved (personally) and somewhat optimistic that maybe now the town might soon get this all behind them. Wilf, by contrast, is elated.

After Chuck's repeated explanations of its discovery, then several runs through some theories of how it ended up in Chase's hands, they discussed who exactly its owner could be. And, naturally, they are still on that subject:

"He drives. He owns a blue felt pen... But what else does it really tell us?" Tom constricts it for the third time since they started. (Even though it's been a long night dragging toward the dawn, with lots of slouching, stretching and pacing around the small office, he still looks quite crisp.)

Chuck reacts with his normal patient impatience. "Like I said, Tom, you got to make some major assumptions, and the assumptions add up to a mighty close direction!"

"Then what we got," Wilf is determined to keep things clear so he reads from his little pad of notes, "is the driving, the pen, the conclusion he lives with someone – who unknowingly gave this book away, and the someone has to be older, to own a textbook this old – "

"But why couldn't it just belong to some alone young guy, passed down from parents? Or grandparents?" Tom continues his role of disbeliever.

"Young folks wouldn't keep it," Chuck assures him. "Not without something personal in it – like an inscription, or at least a name. And he wouldn't go out and buy it – too conspicuous if he's not living alone, and unnecessary if he is."

"You assume," Tom gives it only so much.

"And he's a literate kind of guy, educated enough – he writes literate enough," Wilf checks off another one.

Tom begins, "You better destroy that list before – "

"Of course he will," Chuck reacts, as neutral as he can sound.

Wilf holds back most of a grin, then continues with renewed seriousness. "He's gotta be local, to know she always smoked outside there. And you can catch him ogling young girls," he adds one of his own.

"Not any more," Chuck exhales it. "Now you can catch him conspicuously avoiding ogling young girls."

The other three each nod different degrees of agreement.

"What does that thing about 'shit in the wind' mean?" Mayor Jimms wonders, opening his mouth for the first time in an hour. (He's been sitting on the edge of Tom's desk, with his eyes glued to the floor. But now he locks his gaze straight over at Wilf and Chuck there at the other desk only a few feet away – as though he just regained stability.)

"Huh?" Wilf looks up, not sure what the Mayor is driving at.

Jimmy explains: "Well, does it mean anythin' that he'd bother to write that down – the smell of farms in the night air?"

"Probably means he's not a farm kid," Wilf suspects. "Otherwise, he wouldn't notice it."

"Why did you say kid?" Chuck picks up on Wilf's automatic choice of words.

"I don't know...doesn't it read like a kid to you? I mean, an older teenager or twenty-somethin'?" Wilf squints a bit, as though imagining him.

"Uhh...okay," Chuck wiggles his interlocked fingers set on his belly as he leans back even more in his swivel chair. "Young, driver, literate, felt-penned, mothered..." He shoots a look at Tom, as though to halt any protest over that last stretched assumption he hung out there.

"How many like that live in town?" Tom says instead of what he was going to say.

(Not another list! Chuck immediately dreads.)

"We could do that," Wilf considers. "Or we could talk to all the moms and do a list of who gave away books – "

"She estimated four hundred donors the first week," Chuck reports what Elizabeth the librarian concluded (to Chuck's asking "out of curiosity"). "A 'roaring response', she said."

"How many are moms?" Wilf speculates, pushing on his chair arms again to try to keep himself sitting up straight.

"All," Chuck suggests. "Anyway, trying to find out, we'd scare the guy off – or chance making him act again."

Mayor Jimms thinks to ask, "What about the kid – the witness kid? Anything more?"

Chuck fills him in: "Yup, we got a kid who thinks he knows who the kid is," he reveals most of it, "but he refuses to say who it is until he's certain – "

"*But the killer's still out there!*" Jimms explodes, leaping off the desk to his feet. "Can you – can *we* afford to wait for some *kid?!*"

"Yup," Chuck responds with restraint, now feeling why part of him didn't want to give him anything.

"Why?!" Jimmy needs to know, and sees he has to actually ask to get an explanation.

Chuck accommodates. "You don't think the guy's going to try something now – with his little literary climax set free out there? He sure knows where it went, and he knows there's some chance that his little story-in-a-book is now discovered, and, unless he's looking to get caught, he'll just lay low."

"But if he *is* looking to get caught, now is a perfect time to push it...he's never been more out over the edge," Jimms thinks.

"And never been more pissed off, now that he has nothin' to get off on," Wilf notes perceptively, adding to a possible picture of a maniac about to let go and rampage.

Chuck counters, "I think he's just being real careful – look at how he did up this book! He's not challenging or looking to get spanked." (All through this listening and talking he's been thinking about the red thread. He is sorry he can't be completely open with the Mayor – and his own assistant, too – but he simply feels he can't chance setting that one last fact loose – as though it's his truth-clenching hound.)

"Well, what's next?" Tom believes they have circled around every point enough for one night.

"Wonder how much that 'she recognizes me' part means?" Wilf still has some energy left.

Chuck's eyebrows rise a bit on his tired looking face. "I've thought about that. Why did it mean something to him – enough to write it down the way he did? Like the timing of it was so important…"

"You don't mean like it gave him even more of a charge?" Tom takes a few seconds to react, standing again to stretch, straighten his tie and pace some more laps.

"Will you take that fucking thing off!" Chuck smiles and points at Tom. "It's the unholy dead of night, there's no one around, you're going home to bed – and you're still straightening your fucking tie!"

Jimmy's eyes widen, amused. And Wilf grins knowingly. Tom ignores his Chief and tucks in his shirt. Again.

"Guess it might," Wilf sees Tom's theory. "More of an adrenalin blast for the guy?"

"So do we aim for her closest boy-type friends?" Tom then stops pacing and wonders.

"It's part of the picture, I guess," Chuck can imagine the diary coming from there.

Jimmy Jimms stands too, ready to go. "You know, Wilf, I think you're right, with that young guy thing. Didn't he write something like 'I was on her quick'?"

"*Real* quick," Chuck quotes. "And that sure indicates an athletic…well, maybe just boastful…wannabe."

"But I still think there's a surprising lack of detail in that thing," Tom starts roaming around again, pointing at the math text with one hand and bracing the other on his hip. "It's like he could have thrown it on the sidewalk right in front here and nobody would figure it out."

"Oh, so he gave it to the library himself!" Chuck spreads his arms wide.

"Nohh!" Tom reacts irritably. "But it could be some sort of game with him. And maybe we'll find more – or probably, he'll give us more."

"Wouldn't rule that out," Wilf can visualize it. "Hey, it's strange, too, what we were talkin' 'bout before – how the end tells us less than the beginnin'. There's really so much more description at the start..." he scratches the day-old beard along his thin jaw, then rubs the back of his stiffened neck, under that long, fair hair.

"He got his rocks off more on the chase than..." Chuck doesn't have to finish.

"Wacko," is all Tom can think to say.

"But we'll get him!" Chuck promises, rocking his weary body to his feet. "Like I said, we're getting closer... Thanks also to a town full of people who care a whole lot."

The other three agree with a "right!", a "yup!" and "true!" – each said with a spark of renewed optimism – as they file out the door into the quiet new morning.

The ballgame hasn't restarted yet. The boys are debating.

"Assholes eyes! – eat shit!" Ricky roars at Heap Henry two feet in front of him. Jackie stands firm right beside Henry.

"You eat it, jizzbrain!" Heap counters.

Rick leans closer and shouts, "*I* didn't say it, greaseball! *You* did!"

Heap Henry lunges at him, but Jack holds him back. "Turdwad!"

"And you can't take it back!" Rick tries to put the forever curse on Heap.

Since it started, Jackie has been trying to calm things down – including himself. "Heap didn't mean Looker's really your father, wormlips! He was jus' talkin'!"

"Your mother's pignipples!" Henry erupts at Rick again, pulling considerably taller Jack forward in his attempt to body check significantly taller Rick.

Rick cocks back an arm and fist, about to punch Henry out of his obnoxious consciousness. All eleven other boys, clumped to one side of this discussion at home plate, nervously take a step backward.

Jackie pulls Henry harder, enough to budge him so he can step in between. "Back off, pervertprick!" he takes over for the Heap.

Rick shoves Jack with his untensed arm. "You're the pervert one always sneakin' peaks, bigmouth!" (Now he just crossed the line: to where the insults get factual.)

"Ream yourself, jerk!" Jack swats away Rick's arm.

"The killer's your father!" Rick now reveals to Jack – as his face abruptly flushes reddest of the three. "And your mother's a whore!"

That does it. Jack leaps on him. Heap's eyes pop in horror. Jack is pounding away down at Rick in the dust. Rick is impervious, punching straight up as hard as he's being hit.

Now all the others shuffle little steps closer. Henry snaps out of his shock and yells at them: "Back off, twerpballs!" He'll take them all on...

Yet, the battle is short-lived, as though both Rick and Jack simultaneously realize who they're actually fighting. (They've often exchanged truly ugly words, but always as mere routine exclamations of their years of mutual manly respect.)

In fact, with their fifteen-second flurry now finished, they both quickly jump to their feet, brush themselves and each other off, shake hands wordlessly and embarrassedly, then begin pointing and shouting Heap Henry and all the other boys back to their positions – like it's their fault.

And the score is 506 to 491, for Jackie's team.

N orm leans into his brother Jeff's room, silently pushing the door open...

Across the way, a stream of sunlight angles through a window to the wood floor, and sky-blue curtains stir with the soothing warm wind that softly hums through the screen. That window frames a sharp, bright scene of midday summer trees, sky and clouds. An old desk at the end window is piled high with books and games, a few pens lie scattered across its bare center. Peacefully serene, the room's dark colors give it quiet strength; posters of modern music heroes give it life. Some clothes are tangled in a pile by the opened closet door.

In the corner, Jeff is stretched out on his side on top of his bed's midnight blue bedspread. In white runners, jeans and dark T-shirt, his mass of messy black hair droops down the arm that's bracing his head. He is vigorously smoking a cigarette (a fourteen-year-old ranging far afield from caring what his parents think). His thick, black eyebrows twitch a bit when he sees his older brother poke into his space. He doesn't say anything, but his brown eyes boldly stare him down.

"Hey," Norm says, quiet as the room.

Jeff blinks slowly in acknowledgement.

"You doing okay?" Norm asks, stepping wholly into the room, trying to balance his tone between stern and wimpy.

Jeff hesitates, as though figuring where it's coming from. "Sure."

Norm's mind is flashing up images from the years they used to play together in this room, when it was papered with cute little animals. Though a four-year age difference limited what they did, it was still great fun for both, through many otherwise empty hours. (It's only lately that Norm pulls rank on him, when he sees him doing the same dumb, parent-wrenching stuff he used to do.)

Now, Norm realizes what an adult-forming thing it is that Jeff is going through. "I was just...thinking – wondering if you're okay, or pissed off or something."

Jeff takes a long drag, lowering his eyes to the ashtray as he blows the smoke out forcefully. "Yeah."

Norm moves toward the chair at the desk, gesturing to it as a way of asking permission, and his brother glances up.

"Sure," Jeff answers lifelessly.

"It's just that you've been closed up in here, most of the time. It's gotta be hard..."

Jeff only nods, once, without looking up.

"There's a song," Norm thinks to say (he came here unrehearsed, hoping something would come to him) "with a line like 'life's full of loss'..."

"Oh..?"

"Well, I guess we're sorta young, still. But if you look at older people and you hear what some have gone through, losing others – look at Mom and Dad, the brothers and sisters they lost... and Grandma..."

Jeff takes another deep drag. "Yeah...that's true..." he exhales.

"You gonna be okay..?" Norm asks again, his eyes shifting to the side window with its trees in the sun.

"It's...I know what you mean..." Jeff starts, awkwardly. "I knew it's part of things...life... But it took a while, you know? – to think of it that way."

Norm sees what he means, that he knew it but never felt it before. "Well...uhh...it might be better if you tried going out a bit, maybe. Hang out with your buds...a little."

"I was thinking that... I guess you need things to help you... forget."

Norm watches him, and says nothing.

"I suppose Janet" (Jeff's voice breaks on her name, a little) "would say...like, just remember me, don't fall apart..." He has to stop, because he doesn't want to cry, anymore.

"Sure," Norm smiles openly.

"And I keep wonderin'...you know, what they say, that she's in a better place, or somethin'..."

"Just about the whole world believes that's what..." Norm doesn't have to finish.

"And you know," Jeff then pushes himself up and sits hunched over the ashtray, "I was thinkin' I used to be tough about it – that people were just weak, or somethin'. But when it happens...I had no concept what the feeling would be...how powerful it... It really pulls you down..."

"Dad told me it took him twenty years to finally accept his older brother's death...to put it behind him," Norm offers.

Jeff stares at him. That revelation could never feel more meaningful to him than it does right now. He can't speak, and his eyes fill with tears.

"But I think if you stand back – when you can stand back – and you try and see some meaning to it all, sometimes it all seems okay. Like, it's not your doing, you know, Jeff? It just happens and then that's the way it's supposed to be, and something a whole lot wiser than you and me is in charge and watching..."

Jeff has never heard anyone say anything like that without getting all bent-out-of-shape religious sounding. And it occurs to him it's time to do the right thing: "If I tell you, will you keep it to yourself – until it matters?"

Norm gives him his "of course" brotherly look.

"Someone was buggin' Janet – some guy, just stopping her on the street, you know? – and asking her to go necking and sucking, and ignorant things like that... I'm not saying his name. I will if it's sure it means something, 'cause I don't want to get the wrong guy arrested...okay?"

Though immediately bursting to shake it out of him, Norm just nods with agreement. Still, he suggests, "You've thought about it meaning something real serious?"

"Sure... But I can't believe this guy would do it – I know, don't say it." He takes another long drag, then butts out the cigarette forcefully. "Somebody did it, and we'll all be freaked when we see who it is." He now thinks for a second, and gazes out the window. "It's just that I'd like to find out something more sure, like some other thing that puts it together more..."

Norm, tactfully, now reveals his own secret. "Jeff, there was a witness. A kid."

Jeff is plainly shocked. He holds his breath as he gapes at his older brother. Norm tells him the details, explaining how the police figured it out but they don't know who it is, and then how he's trying to help by working with his friends on the kid list. Jeff doesn't blink once all the way through it, it seems.

"This kid and me need to get together..." Jeff finally reacts in a mutter.

"Right," Norm agrees, half smiling. "The problem is, we could take our time to carefully figure it out– well, for the Chief to, but like he says, the guy could do it again any day."

Jeff blinks hard, and swallows audibly. "I know, I know! But if the wrong guy gets nailed... That's worse, isn't it? The guy's still out there!"

"True," Norm can't argue that. "Well, let's keep it quiet for now, and...and maybe you can get out there and watch your guy, or something...for Janet's sake – and the next one's..."

Jeff nods his head, but still sits there motionless, bent over the ashtray, staring at his hands gripping it.

Norm stands up, gazes around out the window a few seconds more, then crosses to the door. "Seeya," he says softly.

"Yeah..." Jeff raises his wet, brown eyes. "Hey...thanks," he says just as softly as his brother.

As Looker sees the lady coming toward him on the sidewalk, she notices him. She smiles; he shows...friendliness. And above them the sun embraces warmly; around them the world is lively green, and birds chirp cheerfully. He walks on by, with an easy gait, of strong frame, just strolling.

Main Street is somewhat busy, but not as much as Saturday. It's Sunday, and traffic comes and goes to churches. People walk to Reverend Fisk's, then after they'll gather toward Lucy's. Looker might go into Lucy's – he does go there regularly, where he likes to sit and have a coffee, or take one out across the street, to the little park. (They know in there what he likes in it, from the first few times he fixed it himself, years ago. If he doesn't sit, then it's take-out. And he always has exact change, and never wants anything else with it. So they just smile, and he seems to smile back.)

Near Nick's Bowl, three boys pass by him (not baseball kids – older). They watch him, one nods; Looker watches back, appears to brighten slightly, and walks on. (They respect him. No way he's stupid, anyone can easily see.)

If only it could always be summer. (In winter he walks around some, light jacket and black leather gloves, no hat.) This ravishing blue sky and white sculptured summit clouds, the symphony of bugs, birds and wind, the green of life, the profound, delicate movements of the living, the security of heat, the pull of fragrant flowers, the unhurried feel of comfortable evenings and days...

He checks the store windows, though nothing is changed from yesterday when he walked by this way, too. He just likes to look at stuff. He has never been known to go in and buy anything, though he does go in, sometimes, and does regularly buy groceries. (He gets packages, is all his landlady says, and quite a lot of mail, from a lot of places.)

Before the police office, past the light for Road 93, is the little park, where he sees three teenaged girls sitting under the tree on the bench that he likes to rest on. So, he'll just sit on the side bench, the one up against the orange-red brick, there in the full sun. As he walks by the girls, he is clearly cool. He's steel, he's tender; they gawk at his firm frame unashamedly. They just love him. And through soft gray eyes that stay on them for an honest instant, he plainly knows them, and likes them, in return.

Looker sits straight on the bench, at first. Then he slumps down a little, spreading his strong arms along the top rail as he tilts his head back...absorbing the fiery sun, the snug wrap of warm air, freedom in the crystal blue sky, the savory wind, fellowship life in the fluttering birds nearby, and innocent sounds of passing street life – sensed with pleasure, as though never felt quite so pure before.

"Hunker," one girl declares matter-of-factly as her two friends sneak peeks at Looker. (Apparently, he's beyond giggles: he's too serious a hunk.)

From the bench, he rises slowly, warmed; he walks unhurriedly to the intersection, Highway 3, and waits. Cars roll by; he sees them, but all the while, like always, he is obviously just minding his own business.

The light changes.

Across the street he disappears into Lucy's. And a mere moment later he pushes out the screen door with his usual patient touch with things, carrying a coffee (paper cup) and – for the first time ever! – strikingly, though no one is watching, sits right there on Lucy's bench!

Looker is alone there, and he hints at an expression of quiet wonder, from seeing something in a way never imagined, a perspective unlike his, and wholly yours. Cars crisscross, folks march across his sight (all smile); the screen door squeaks beside him, a boy blinks by on a bike; and the stoplight controls the flow, of the traffic down these roads, the patterns of the highways, of commerce, of boardrooms and markets worldwide...

Opposite, up the side road 93 beside the park, Looker sees the faded asphalt, the upheaved squares of sidewalk, the stately, massive overhang of trees; and he sees kids, walking home from school – this spring. And, disturbingly, he sees Janet alone, after Ellen, Wendy, Gail, Sheila and Shelly all turned down their home streets out of sight – Janet walking rigidly along, clutching her books to her chest, and the white car keeping pace beside her. He can see her start to run a bit, but the car keeps up. She turns the corner near her house...and the car swerves the other way. Then he sees the car go by Lucy's many times, sees where it's usually parked, who drives it most, who drives it least.

And Looker sees the police car cruise by, or parked across the street; he watches Wilf and Sid go by in the truck, and Wilf and his wife ride by in their car; he sees his landlady driving around (she always sees him and waves eagerly); and he notices the five young men, in so many combinations or all together sometimes, in one of five different cars, mostly Friday and Saturdays nights, the odd time starting out from Nick's Bowl: one green car, one tan, one blue, and two white.

Now, he sips his tasty coffee. He peers through the blue above: there's galaxies. Next, he studies the sturdy brick of the buildings across the way. With the last flavorful drop of coffee, he stands and heads down Main, returning the way he came, toward the tree-lined curve, past his street and the sidewalk's end, to a country road with sandy gravel crunching underfoot, soothing waves in seas of golden wheat, spinning gulls, and the crooked laneway leading home...

Having gone home for some rest, Chuck is back in his office by noon. He slept only a few hours; he can't put the diary out of his thoughts that long. Or the red thread. Or the kid witness – with Jackie and five young men trying to pin down just who exactly the boy is.

He stands at his favorite spot at the window, its waist-high burgundy curtain drooping with age in front of him, the door beside him open. From there he can see up and down the whole street, the main street of his home.

To his right, a block away, church is letting out. He thinks of Beth, and smiles. He couldn't be more fortunate, to have a wife who says "I guess it's time for church..." and doesn't even look at him or bug him about going with her. It's purely up to him, always. She understands everything.

Across the way, some folks have gone into Lucy's, with more heading there from the service; the bench is still empty. To his left, down at the curve, he can see looker between the traffic and tree trunks, strolling the long way home. Looker, he thinks... "A delicate web of human interaction" he remembers Wilf's words. (And he and Wilf genuinely like them all.)

But now, all these people are painfully tightened up – by most outward appearances their usual selves but inwardly terrified that another young girl will die. And he hasn't, for the life of him, got a clue what to do next.

He could question kids, starting with the thirty-eight Norm and his buddies have on their list, and force his way through them to the witness... But he doesn't for a second believe he'll find him out that way. Half the young boys would be shaking and stuttering, and all their parents would be outraged... Chaos, is the word he keeps ending that image with.

Or, he could open Jackie's envelope, which he tucked safely away at home. Or at least drag him in here and lean on him heavy... But he promised the kid, and he fully believes Jack will have his proof soon.

And the diary – the gift, the possible miracle! But what to do with it next? (The textbook is in a bank safety deposit box, right now. Photocopies of the diary pages are hidden at his house and at Tom's.) He's still thinking about requesting exam papers from the high school, to compare the writing, but it could easily be someone older. And knowing his town, word of doing something like that would soon get out. (And why not? It's their town, their concern, they have the right! Then, beyond that, it's his responsibility to control any investigations, if that's what is needed.) Or, he could do the door-to-door check for book donators. (He has to see Elizabeth tomorrow with some excuse for keeping all new library donations separate, and maybe have her take a list of names. It's not likely anyone would clean out their old books twice – she could ask that, too. It would rule out some... And Chase is confident he separated all the Saturday haul.) Tracking the years the math text was used against class lists would narrow it down, but he already knows the school course records don't go back that far...

Ultimately, anything he thinks of trying has attached to it a closing scene of the murderer slipping away to do his sick stuff somewhere else, in some distant town or city or country...

Scratching his head, his mind wanders for a minute, absorbed in other thoughts about the gathering of people at Lucy's...

How, he then wonders again for the thousandth time, do I fit the diary to the red thread? – to driver, to felt pen user, to something of a stud, to somewhat literate? How do I pluck one guy out of this town, out of a thousand guys (more probably three or four or five hundred) – who is truly evil? All lists together would narrow it down to a likely two or three hundred, but what next? Get semen samples from all of them? (Yesterday, he had discreetly checked the two local stores that may have carried the red shirt: No way, they said.)

What is needed, Chuck dreams, is a bit or two more of information, or a slip-up on the murderer's part: something said or done – like wearing a red shirt with a little bull on the pocket! (Sooner or later, he's got to wear it...unless he realizes where he pulled the thread...) He would even welcome a failed new attempted abduction, as long as it doesn't go past *anything whatsoever.*

Maybe we should watch the library, like Tom said, in case the guy goes looking for his book... But then we would have to get more people in on it, or cameras, and everyone would soon know and there goes the whole idea and all the advantages of secrecy, again! So then, we could just put the thing on the shelf – Chase could, and they would have to record who took it out...but then the guy would feel exposed, them having him on record – especially if he doesn't have a library card and has to sign up – and them waiting for him to bring it back. And if his diary hasn't been discovered, the guy thinks, he would simply tear out his pages and bring it back. But if it was discovered, he's caught – just walking out the door with it...or he could tear out the pages right there... No, who would be that stupid, to take that chance? He must realize it's discovery won't necessarily reveal more than what's known – and actually might add to the game of it for him!

Of course, when Chuck takes it to Elston's lab tomorrow (he has to remind himself that this isn't all there is, that it's always "ongoing" with new potential) he might be rewarded with the tidbit he needs: a hair, a fingerprint...but he doubts it. And anyway, what can he do with that? Go house-to-house yanking hair samples and taking prints? But then, that would be far less painful than another murdered girl...there are plenty of unused pages in the diary.

Certainly, Wilf's thought about checking the dump for the torn-out math pages – mixed with identifiable household garbage – is a good one, but only if the murderer fixed the book not too long before or after he killed Janet. It's like Tom said, the guy could have prepared the diary section years ago, putting the actual deed on his wish-list: someday, eventually. Regardless, a bunch of people sifting through the garbage heap would be reported all around town before they ripped open their second bag. Besides, the killer could have burned the math pages, or flushed them...or ate them.

No, the diary is essentially proof, he concludes, usable only after the guy is caught. It's not a workable lead with any obvious potential finality, at least.

The real clue, he comes around to it again, is the kid witness. From day one – the investigation in Janet's back yard that Wednesday morning – it's been the big lead of hope: someone watched it happen – some kid out there (Chuck glances up and down the street again) has that scene of abduction playing over and over again in his mind, and has a good mental picture – but cannot be absolutely positive or he would have been here in this office by now saying the name – has a pretty good mental picture of the guy who killed Janet. Chuck realizes it's likely one of the fourteen kids who play ball all the time, for Jackie to come up with it so fast... Well, he could compare team lists with Norm's... But then he already has the right kid's name in an envelope at home, anyway, he's sure.

Chuck's thoughts then return to the end of the diary, and he wonders again that there is so little detail. The killer writes about unbuttoning her top, touching her breasts, says next to nothing about the drive to the back road, and then states plainly that he pulled her clothes off and simply "did it to her". He doesn't describe where that was, though it must have been in the car since there was no dirt or grass in her clothes, or exactly what he did (for his future "reference"). He doesn't write down that she had no underpants, how conscious she was, or why he put her clothes back on to kill her and toss her body into the rough – though in plain view – across the ditch. He certainly doesn't say why he didn't try to hide her in the bushes, or something, or if she spoke to him before she died. Before raping her, he described the night only a bit: "stars and clouds" along a "black dirt road", and near the end how he was "getting off on her soft skin". Then, beyond that, nothing...

There is little doubt, Chuck thinks, that the guy was conscious about writing too much. In that – who said it? Tom? – it's a game, a cat and mouse thing, as though part of him wants to be suspected, or at least wants his literary work discovered, so he can watch the police and whole town squirm as he feels the adrenalin of the chase...or, at least, fulfills a compulsion to live on the edge between guilt and ruin... Well, maybe he did donate the book himself... No, then what would he read on those lonely nights..?

For a few minutes more Chief Cintz stands there working through it all again in his mind, until Tom and Wilf step out of Lucy's and cross the sunlit street.

"There's rumblin'," Wilf sighs coming through the doorway. Tom enters fussing with his mustache, then straightens his tie as he angles toward his desk.

"'Bout what," Chuck reacts indignantly, with a tone of knowing that he doesn't have to ask.

"Some folks were sayin' over there that other folks are sayin' you and your force over here have some sort of information you're just not actin' on – "

"Or we're just not acting on anything, period!" Tom obstinately finishes for Wilf.

"Sure," Chuck states to the street, somewhat absently.

"And that's all you need to hear right now, isn't it?" Wilf sympathizes.

"Maybe they're right," Chuck turns his back to the window and faces Wilf, who is now sitting in the seat beside the Chief's desk. Crossing the office, hands shoved in his pockets, Chuck slumps onto his chair.

"What do they know?" Tom mutters coldly. "There's nothing more to do."

"Doesn't bother me," Chuck smiles acceptingly. "In fact, I'd be disappointed if they weren't pissed off."

For several minutes more the three of them talk about towns and citizens – until Chuck raises his eyes up away from Wilf in front of him to see, of all things on the surface of the Earth, Looker standing there gazing in the window! That's definitely him at the end of the window above the curtain... What in the world is he doing?! Chuck wonders... Yup, there's Looker, jus' lookin' 'round in here..!

Looker's eyes now meet Chuck's, and it's abruptly clear to the Chief that the man wants him for something. (Looker has never done this – or anything like this – since he came here ten years ago.)

But then Looker walks away... Hoping to appear merely restless, Chuck stands up, having decided he better not try to describe to the other two what he just saw and they didn't. Waddling casually to the window, he sees Looker across the street peering back at him. Something's definitely not right, Chuck thinks. Tom and Wilf there behind him are still talking about people and things... He has a thought:

"Tom," Chuck starts when there's an opening, "I wouldn't pull rank on you, but..." he turns his head back toward him and grins meekly, "I'm tired, and the sooner you go home and finish resting, the sooner you can come in for your evening shift..."

Obedient Tom smiles back and resonates, "Sure thing." And in a minute he's out the door walking home, whistling along.

Wilf is still talking away about something, and now Looker is coming back.

"Oh, shoot..." Chick uses an expression he has seldom, if ever, uttered.

"Beg pardon?" Wilf's face instantly freezes with concern as he studies his friend.

"It's Looker – don't move! He's coming here..." Chuck tightens nervously.

In a second, Looker is at the window again, appearing as characteristically him as ever.

"He wants us for something!" Chuck exclaims. "Let's go!" And he and Wilf are both quickly outside.

On the sidewalk, Looker just watches them.

As rational as he can sound, Chuck states, "You want us to go somewhere, don't you..." He is motionlessly face-to-face with him – another first.

Looker does not indicate otherwise.

Chief Cintz turns and strides around the police car parked there at the curb, glancing over at Looker repeatedly. He releases the back door for Wilf, who promptly dives in without expression. Looker eases himself into the front, as natural as a Sunday drive.

"To the road – where Janet was found..?" Chuck figures, having seen him walk toward there on his way home a while ago.

Looker reacts with an open stare at the Chief, then blinks slowly as he focuses back out the windshield. (Sitting so close, Chuck now notices how perfectly well groomed he really is, clearly seeing the strong features of his face and intelligent eyes.) Chuck starts the car.

In few minutes they are on the back road, Chuck and Wilf having exchanged eye contact in the rear view mirror only about five hundred times.

Chuck stops the car at the spot where Janet's body was found, at a long stretch between farmhouses, the dirt road separating corn and wheat fields. All three get out at once, two of them watching the other one.

Looker starts walking. Chuck and Wilf hold back and study each other's puzzled expressions...but are soon right behind him.

A half mile along, Looker stops and waits, facing Chuck and Wilf, thumbs hooked on his jeans pockets. He then turns toward the four-foot ditch and fence and the few bushes beyond. An old lane crosses the ditch, but a new fence now blocks the way. Looker steps up to the fence and gazes to the right, toward three little trees to one side of the bushes a few feet away.

Wilf and Chuck lean on the fence on either side of Looker. They follow his eyes to the spot. It's something blue.

"It's something about Janet..." Chuck ventures to their new friend.

Looker just meets his eyes.

Wilf watches both of them, and then thinks to peer out into the distance... "You can see over here from your place!" it strikes him.

Looker glances toward his home and then at Wilf.

"And you saw the car...that night--" Chuck begins.

"Too far away to see the car – at night," Wilf figures, "but you saw the lights stop a second time here...to turn around?"

Looker faces Wilf and again slowly blinks, as though it's an expression of relief at being understood.

"The guy stopped and threw something over there..." Chuck reaffirms absently while searching the ground around them for tire tracks or footprints – days late, he knows. There's no sign of anything on the old, packed gravel, but the weeds sprouting up through do seem like they might be recently crushed by tires. Then abruptly, he looks up. "Thanks," he says warmly to Looker, who is still leaning on the top wire of the fence. (Chuck wishes he could remember his real name – even his landlady says "Looker".) He then starts to scale the fence. Wilf stays where he is, not about to tramp all over the evidence.

As Chuck steps cautiously through the long grass on the other side, he can't see any tracks. (Why would the guy climb the fence to throw something away?) He circles the three trees. Crouching, and soon satisfied the thing just landed there, he carefully picks it up by pinching it with a leaf from a bush. There is nothing else near it or underneath it. He carries it dangling, and at the fence he hands it gingerly to Wilf while he climbs back over.

Wilf holds the clumped cloth up to eye level.

"Underpants," Chuck moans in the country quiet. "He decided against keeping souvenirs..." he trails, suffering the same pain he sees in Wilf's wide eyes. Both then turn to Looker, who has backed off onto the road, standing there rigid, hair messed by the wind, arms limp at his sides, and eyes – locked on the garment – brimming with tears. Chuck and Wilf melt at the sight, tears welling in their eyes, too. Poor, helpless, innocent Janet...

Chief Cintz then sees something inside the wadded blue fabric, and, with Wilf still solemnly holding it out, finds a little stick to probe at it. He picks another leaf to grip it and pull the thing out, and gently shakes the rain-stiffened little papery lump to open it up... It's a napkin from Lucy's – "Lucy's", they print in small but bold black letters on the corner of the plain white paper...

"Oh save us..." Wilf utters in a trance – the equivalent of saying, "It's one of us!" He and Chuck then both turn again together to see Looker walking away, with labored strides, up the road toward home...a little slumped over and staring, it seems, at the ground.

Wilf and Chuck follow his steps as far as the car. Chuck hands Wilf the napkin to hold while he digs in the trunk for plastic bags. On the hood, they drop the underpants into one bag. Placing the napkin on another, Chuck prods at it and spreads it all the way open with the twig he carried up the road. There is nothing inside, that they can see.

Chuck seals the bags. "Good chance the guy has a bunch of these napkins in his car all the time..." he speculates.

"Good thought," Wilf nods, breathing heavily with anguish. His hands are shoved tight down his back pockets; his wise blue eyes are straining hard, as though they've finally seen too much. And he thinks to add, "Guess Looker kept passing by here, and never saw it before..."

"Guess..." his friend agrees.

Back in the car, Chuck writes up every detail. Then together they sit there in the stillness and gaze once more at the ditch and down the road to the old laneway and the fence, and say nothing. Eventually, Chuck starts it up, drives along and pulls in to turn around where the killer did, hesitates, then reverses out and heads back into town.

On the way in, both men struggle with images in their minds of all the regulars passing in and out of Lucy's squeaky screen door.

...

"Was always times of crimes and things 'round here," ol' Shooter is saying to Bert, Mel, Sid and Chase at Lucy's bench as Chuck and Wilf walk across from parking the car. "No such thing as good-old-days."

Bert nods agreement as he studies the expressions of the two latest arrivals stepping up on the curb. "Sure, but there was long stretches of peace and quiet."

"That's it, ya know," Chase thinks so, too, angling down his red cap against the midday sun edging overtop the buildings behind them. "It's one of those remember-the-stretches-when-it-was-peaceful-but-you-don't-care-to-recall-the-ugly-stuff things."

"But there was never a murder here," Mel returns to his original point, his deeply wrinkled face all the authority needed for his claim.

"Not openly recorded," Chuck interjects, glancing around at each of the ol' boys, at Sid by the door and now Ed coming out and standing beside him, then at Norm, Ba-Dee and Howard clumped at one end, and at Mayor Jimmy Jimms aligned with three Sunday-suited local farmers all in a row near the curb. "Chief Phillips would tell me about the two he had, but they were both really unintentional domestic things – husband and wife and son against father."

"That's right," Mel now sorta remembers. "But them's a whole dif'rent kinda thing."

"*Truuue*...but sure was enough other awful things goin' on *heeere*," one of the retirement-aged farmers drawls distantly, as though he wouldn't to this day dream of living amidst the so-cially convoluted criminal complexity of a metropolis such as this. (Right then, the three farmers' wives emerge from Lucy's, smiling from some good fun inside. Each in an attractive flower-print dress, they are, as always, a delightful addition to their rural representation along the curb.)

"You don't think it's the same all over the world?" Bert raises his bushy white eyebrows at the well-known old out-of-towner. "There's nowhere on this here planet with no crime!" he attests. "And anything can happen anywhere tomorrow – even out there down your county road!"

"What about some of those groovy native people – in the jun-gle an' all?" Sid thinks he has the exception.

"Nah!" Chase squirms on his straight wooden chair, all eyes on him. Yanking the toothpick out of the corner of his mouth, he insists, "You'd still find nasty things going on – maybe just not as often. There's lots of stealing and jealousy and murder every-where, eventually."

(Norm, Howard and Ba-Dee are following this closely. It's subject matter for back-road nights – not the jungle people, these characters here.)

"Well, maybe there's a little ugliness in all of us," Ed ventures, his customary bit of cynicism furrowing the forehead under his ever-regressing hairline. His very thin face has tightened again with his doubts.

"No, there's a difference from what you're saying, Ed," Wilf counters, leaning on a street sign, an arm wrapped around it. "There's a clear line down what's acceptable, or forgivable, and what's not. Things that aren't, you know they aren't and they de-serve your society's punishment...whatever your society puts in their rules."

"Problem is..." Sid starts, leaning back on the window frame, trying to keep inside the narrowing shade, "is what makes folks do things in the first place. Just stickin' 'em in prison doesn't solve that."

"That's right," Chase picks up on it, too. "You can after-the-fact reasons for it right up to the noose or the gas chamber – and then forever."

Wilf takes it further: "What humanity needs is a basic change in basic character – in some values and judgments – "

"Emotional judgments," Chase thinks, interrupting. "Seems everything that goes wrong is someone's overly-emotional reaction – "

"Everything *is* emotional," Wilf is quick to steer the point straight, countering Chase. "Even the strictest calculating scien-tists get all wrapped tight in their discovered facts because of the thrill of revelation – sharing. So human nature – that's what it means: the nature of us – all that nature is always kept in motion by feelings."

"Murder is just cold and calculating," Bert begs to differ.

"But the thing is, Bert," Chuck stands there firm, hands in pockets and voice patient, "the reason behind the calculating is emotion...it's a primal push..."

(Everyone around is intent on every word. Another young couple coming from church has stopped halfway into Lucy's, catching the depth of what is being said.)

Bert doesn't disagree, saying instead, "Well, what would we be talkin' about right now if it wasn't for young Janet?"

"Something else primal," Chase attests, having sat around here half his life.

"Corn!" Ed blurts out the real truth. "T'maters."

The young couple laugh together a little at Ed's straight-faced lament, then continue through Lucy's doorway. Norm, Howard and Ba-Dee somehow wordlessly agree to go inside, too. Chuck is blinking sleepily (visualizing the hammock in the shade on his porch) as he waves a lazy arm and walks away. Wilf turns the other way, responding, "Seeya soon," as he starts out on errands before heading home to its comfort and caring wife. Mayor Jimms gestures the three farm couples onward to the municipal office, to finish hearing the complaints they raised outside church. While the ol' boys just stay and hold the front line.

The sun is setting slowly on the last half-inning of the day. Jackie's team has had their final at bat, and Rick's is down to their last out. Everything's fine. The whole day has been summer holiday heaven for boys, since the morning debacle.

Summer's too short, Jackie thinks as he waits on the mound for Rick's next kid to come to the plate. And this summer (he actually shakes his head in disbelief to himself, out there) has been one wild one so far. Standing there drooping, limp from another satisfying marathon of baseball and sun and grit, arms feeling stretched as they dangle at his sides, he shifts his eyes to the opposition's dugout and finds Eggie... Jack's thoughts churn again: What next? – how can I get this kid to spit it out? He knows – he just *knows* for sure – that Eggie is the witness. He studies all the kids on the bench, everyone still fooling around joking and wrestling (the witness included) even though they're worn-out ragged... So now he wishes it was someone else, some runt less thick. Then he thinks: Maybe I should be buds with the kid, let him hang around with me... (Not really so narrow in his devices, Jack does feel genuine concern for Eggie, and worries that the little witness peeker could split open with pressure.) Yeah, but still most important, he reminds himself again, is finding the low-life shit-sucking snake who killed Janet – for her sake and for my own sake and for everyone else in town..!

Jack sets to pitch. The batter taps the plate and waits. Jack tosses a soft one and it's looped to center, where Heap Henry easily pulls it in.

Simple as that, the game is over, for today. Some of the boys immediately start drifting wearily away, thinking only about dragging themselves home (and tomorrow will come when it comes, and maybe it'll rain, but they all really hope it doesn't).

"Who's coming with me for ice cream?" Jack then jolts them by shouting, still up there on the mound. (He doesn't often invite anyone to anything.)

Rick steps up out of his dugout groaning "Comin'" as four others moan or raise a weak hand, too. And as they all shuffle out and gather behind Rick, Jack is pleased to see Eggie is one of them.

"Five hundred twenty-two to five hundred eleven for us!" Henry thinks to scream from beyond the right field fence, turning just his head half around as he plods onward toward home alone. And in a second, he melts into the twilight shadows.

Jack strides down from the mound and off the infield out into the closing darkness, and growls loudly into the hot, still air at his pack of five boys barely keeping up behind him, "Com'on, you lazy toadeyed dogfarts!"

...

Out at the Dairy Cone Drive-In, Jack and his buds are slowly reviving with the energy of ice cream. Still, they all just sit there quietly off to the side at one of the three small outside umbrella tables in the weak spill of light from the little restaurant's few inside booths' bare bulbs, watching a car come, then a car go.

Finally, crunching up his last lump of cone, and with his shaggy black hair wildly framing his always-intense black eyes and thin face, Jackie tilts his head in dog-like observational alignment with Eggie's across the table from him. The Egg is resting his head on his ball glove propped on his one outstretched arm, and is clutching his half-eaten ice cream right in front of his se- riously-prescriptioned eyes, evidently fascinated by the cascading drips striping his cone and hand and puddling on the table as he lies there plainly too worn out to summon another lick.

"So, weenie-Eggie beannose," Jack opens sincerely, "the other day – I didn't mean to rag on you – you person'ly, you know? It could've been anybody...with the glove...you were jus' there... dork," he explains everything.

Eggie's weak eyes pop and squint. The rhythmic panting through the cute buckteeth of his sagged-open mouth stops with a little gasp: Jack is actually looking at him and being nice! (All of them know, though, that Jack doesn't ever really mean any of them any harm.)

Eggie stays horizontal on his glove. "Uh..."

"Sometimes the game...say, like this morning...uh...you know, isn't the start of a war, or anything. People jus' let loose, some- times, you know?" Philosopher Jack looks away into the night for a second. (Eggie gulps, then tries to smile agreeably.) "So, we're all buds, right, pukes?" he then grins openly around at the five of them. "Everybody is everybody's bud, the way I see it..." He leaves himself completely wide-open.

They all nod or grunt, a little warmed, though surprised. And Jack reaches across and playfully pokes only Eggie.

"They're rodents!" teenaged Chuck cries exasperated to young Sid and only slightly older Wilf sitting between them. "Every time we play anymore, these little dips whine and cry or have baby fits, or something..."

"Hey, Chuck, they're alright," is all Sid can feel to say. (He has little brothers, and knows how it works.)

"Yeah, just remember you're fifteen and they're still runts," Wilf smiles, gazing out at the dusk-tinted infield and closing-in night sky.

The three boys-becoming-men, alone in the ballpark, sit spaced evenly on the third base line players' bench, each – including Chuck himself – waiting for Chuck to cool down.

Since school let out it's been good, regardless, the three of them feel: not hot and not much daytime rain, lots of baseball, bowling at the new allies, the little swimming hole Ed discovered last year in the creek out the dirt road...and tonight (they each appreciate) as dandelion seeds soar like bug parachutes into the red sunset evening, the warm air is full of peaceful, pleasant, summer calm.

But it seems Chuck has had about enough pickup ballgames for one lifetime. He feels like he's had to drag himself to this rough old diamond, lately – as though, anymore, he's playing merely out of obligation to friends and kids. Maybe it's time to go on to other things, Wilf suggested a few days ago: a summer job, dances, parties. (Chuck knows he's right. It's just that part of him finds it hard to let go...he's not sure of what.)

"We'll look back on this," Sid dreams across the darkened diamond. Beyond, a street full of houses is bathed in the pale yellow glow of bare light bulbs set under ruffled metal shades high on telephone poles.

"And?" Chuck thinks Sid needs to finish that remark, somehow.

"What? And what?" Sid's wayward concentration is broken.

Wilf knows what: "For all that we're bound to go through in our lives, we'll look back and think this was easy – this was the good times."

Chuck contemplates it. "I guess," he realizes it's true.

"So...whatta you guys gonna be?" (Sid sounds like he's been saving that question since he was six.)

"Nothin'," Wilf's been saving his answer, too.

Chuck glares at him sideways. "You can't be nothing. You have to work somewhere."

"Oh – work!" (Wilf smiles like he knew all along.) "I only meant I've got no burnin' ambition to start on some treadmill job, just to try and go faster and faster. I just want to make a livin', and work at bein'...I guess, content."

"Good plan," Chuck nods emphatically. "Hey, Sid, it's your question. You gotta answer it, too."

"I think I'm with Wilf," Sid laughs easily. "So, what about you?" he puts it back to the Chucker.

"Mayor."

"What?!" Wilf bursts. "Did you say mayor?"

"Sure... Right in the thick of it. Helping people out. Doin' good stuff...I mean, for the town – "

"Thick of the bullshit," is Wilf's theory.

Chuck disagrees. "I don't think so. It doesn't have to be that way."

Sid says, "My dad thinks it's a rough place to be – caught in the middle of everyone and everything, he said. He wouldn't want the pressure, he said."

"Well, what's pressure for some," Wilf considers, "might be only a challenge for someone else, maybe."

"I don't think it would even be a challenge – not a hard challenge," Chuck feels, kicking at the dusty sand in front of the bench. "A job like that would just roll and flow along – it's just living, no big degree required. Just do the best you can do. As things come up."

Wilf studies his friend for a second. "Okay, Yer Honor, you got my vote... Sid?"

"Two votes, Chuck," Sid commits.

"So...Mister Mayor," Wilf then starts with a whine, "it's about this shitty ball diamond..."

"We'll get a big committee right on it. And then we withdraw millions from your bottomless tax pit and build a sports palace!" Chuck beams wide with the satisfaction of another complex crisis solved.

"You're a natural," Wilf grins as he glances from the last light of sunset to his destiny-bound buddy Chuck.

Sid smiles too, but realizes, "That would be good, though... helping people out, keeping a town decent to live..." He's not sure how to exactly express his feeling about it.

"You're right, Sid," Chuck leans across Wilf and pokes Sid's arm with playful encouragement. "You could wander all over the world looking for what's probably the most important thing you'd ever want: what we got now right here."

"Omniscient." (Joseph is doing his good word thing.)
"What!" (Gene doesn't want to know, he just wants Joseph to stop.)

Tonight, Howard drove, Ba-Dee is in the passenger front, and Gene and Norm frame Joseph in the utter blackness of the back.

"Onomatopoeia," Joseph is certain. "On. Oh. Mat. Oh. Pee. Yyy-ahh."

"Shut the fuck up," Gene suggests.

"Ootheca." Joseph is stalwart. (He's obviously recently big on the "o" pages of his dictionary.) "As in: cockroach – "

"You – !"

" – Egg."

Norm sips his beer. Ba-Dee just scrapes the label off his, balancing the bottle on his knee. Howard braces against the steering wheel and turns to see if he can get a visual on this encounter in the back. "Good one," he notes, mildly, to Joseph.

Joseph has a beer in each hand. And the half-emptied box on his lap. He absently goes to drink out of both bottles at once, and almost hurts himself.

"Good one," Gene observes.

"Testosterone."

"Joseph," Norm has an objective, "hold on for a sec. Let's do this list." (Gene has finally brought the photocopies of the kid list.)

"It's relevant," literary Joseph protests unemotionally. And he has a little story – his little voice springs from a point of singularity in the sightless pitch of infinite night: "The fuckin' no-good murdering prick piece-of-shit went out and destroyed a girl. He was full of tess-toss-terr-owen. The fucker."

"So you're saying it's chemical?" Howard doesn't quite understand Joseph.

Joseph hesitates, so Norm answers instead. "It's a compulsion."

Gene leans forward to look past Joseph, as though he could see Norm there in the other corner. "Umm..."

"I read about it, dipshit," Norm defends his innocence.

"So, everybody has them, right?" Howard asks but nobody answers so he has to step back in quick himself: "Everybody has compulsions to different degrees, like for beers or to masturbate, and things."

Three others can now safely respond: "Oh. Yeah." "Yep." "Uh-huh."

"Howard! You *m*-word?!" Joseph squeals. "Howie! Shame!"

Howard ignores him. "So, like, what makes the difference, that one nutbar's compulsions end up going that far? I mean, as humans, we're all the same, but some are animals..."

"If they had the answer to that," Norm believes, "they could probably prevent it."

Joseph angles back in. "Well, then what do you fantasize...uh... Howard," he picks him at random, "about...let's say you've got this gorgeous young blond in a cabin in the woods and somehow you can do anything you want with her without thought of consequence or retribution – "

"Is this your fantasy, Crusher?" Gene scoffs loudly beside him.

"Sure...Gene," Joseph doesn't care.

A silence dignifies the hypothetical, enough that Howard is compelled to answer. "Uh, I don't know, just do it to her..."

"No good!" Joseph pipes. "Next: Norm?"

Gene begins, "What the fuck do you – "

"It's all right," Norm thinks this is fascinating. "He's got a good point."

"So, Norm?" Howard is intrigued, too.

"Uh..." Norm finds he can't answer.

Joseph has thought this through: "Too personal? Too private?"

"Maybe he isn't sicko," Gene huffs.

"Too private, Gene?" Joseph counters. "What goes through your mind? When I suggested the cabin and the blond and anything goes – what went through your mind?" (Mercifully, he doesn't want a vocal answer. He just wants them to see his point.) "Or anyone? Does everyone have loopy fantasies..?" He leaves that one hanging.

"The point is, why do the eventual social criminal types follow through," Ba-Dee sheds some caution on the point. "Doesn't matter that Joseph or Gene have warped thoughts. The question is what causes someone to go ahead and play them out."

"Thanks," Gene moans.

"Not so, Ba-Dee," Joseph disagrees. "It's precisely the point: that at its primal base, human nature is loopy. Thoughts jump in and out of your head. You wonder about weird stuff – not that you'd do it, but you imagine you in that position: murderer, rapist fantasies..."

"So," Norm can only think, "how can we change that?"

"Fucked if I know," Joseph reaches his limit.

Evidently too near the precipice, Norm swings this conversation away and brings up the list again, and they all get copies beneath the soft glow of the car's interior light. Factoring in relevant pieces of town life that were gathered by four of them, the thirty-eight boy list is reduced to twenty-nine. Eleven of them, it's observed, play in the endless baseball game. Past that, no further conclusions can be made.

"So...Norm," Howard then starts up next amid the close quiet of the car and the country night, "you get anything more from Jeff?"

Norm takes a deep breath. "This morning..." he stops himself. (He is still deciding how much to give them from his talk with his brother.)

"Is he okay?" Ba-Dee asks kindly.

"Yeah... I think so," Norm sighs out his open window. The black outline of the fields and trees darken the depthless night. "Janet was his best friend...at least."

Howard prompts, "Uhh..."

"Turns out..." (Norm knows what they want to know, and feels he can't be less than honest with his friends.) "Turns out – hey, all of you realize this is serious stuff – you get that – for him to handle, I mean. He really seems caught in the middle, and he didn't want to tell me and I shouldn't say a thing – it may not be important in the end or sound like a huge thing now, but to him it is. So you gotta keep it to yourselves – yeah, of course, we just want to end all this... *God! Why does all this have to happen?* ...This *fucking* world is so *fucking* imperfect!" His voice has sadness beyond frustration.

"You don't have to say..." Ba-Dee responds softly, talking out his open window, too.

"No, I think the more that's out there, the better the chance things come together and the guy gets caught," Norm states firmly back into the car. "You know, I wish he would just go tell Cintz and not worry how much it means or doesn't mean – it's too critical a thing, this guy running around free..." He pauses for just a second, then says it: "Someone was bugging Janet – stopping her on the street, talking at her and trying to put moves on her...well, more than moves..."

The car and the back road are deathly silent.

"Like...nasty stuff?" Howard cautiously asks, head lowered over the steering wheel.

"Yeah, I guess dirty stuff. Real mouthy, you know? She was scared, he said. That's how bad it was."

"Whuh," Joseph utters in disbelief, then has to ask, "Did he say..?"

Norm is breathing easier, and he exhales, "No. And I'm glad he didn't. Oh, he knows – no question – who it is, but the problem is the outcome of saying it, so I don't want to know either if – "

"What do you mean?" Gene asks flatly.

"Well, if I know, I'll go crazy with it – every time I see the guy. But I can't say anything because Jeff will just deny it, then – "

"What's that mean, outcome of saying it?" It's Howard's turn to interrupt Norm.

Joseph knows: "Jeff's afraid of sending an innocent sleaze-brain to the gallows. Better a guilty sleaze-brain."

Norm purposely sloshes down a long glug of beer, indicating agreement.

"Get him to tell you who it is," Ba-Dee strongly suggests with rare hate in his easy voice, "and we'll go beat the living shit out of the guy. Literally. Right now."

Joseph is willing: "Good plan, Ba-Dee. Just for being a low-life! – murderer or not!"

"Exactly," Howard's tone is equally stern. "Even if he's not the guy, it's guys like him that lead to...to..." He can't pin it down through his anger.

"Contribute to the mass insanity," Joseph helps him out.

"Well," Norm feels better now, full of friendship, "Jeff is deciding. It's not as though he refuses to think about it, or anything. My guess is he'll say something soon."

Howard has an ugly thought: "Hope he doesn't decide to act on his own..."

"Like try to get his own revenge," Ba-Dee is right with him.

"No, he won't," Norm is sure. "He knows he's...uhh, too young, or something."

"But what if he bumps into the guy on the street?" Joseph can imagine himself in Jeff's position.

"I think he'll just watch the guy, and try and clear his head about it," Norm believes his suggestion to his brother will stick.

They each consider that through a short silence.

"What if – what if..." Howard raises his voice on the second what if, as though in a rapidly crystallizing revelation, "there's other pieces just like this one out there? Like, a bunch of people have all these fuzzy pieces to this murder puzzle, and they just haven't got together?"

"I still think Chief Chuck has a secret bunch of fuzzies," Ba-Dee reiterates.

Howard is still visualizing his theory. "You wonder if you got everyone in town together in a big room and got them to say any little thing they know – "

"Everyone would spit up countless little meaningless fuzzies," Ba-Dee laughs at his own mind's irreproducible image.

"Except one guy," Joseph notes. "And in Gene's perfect world where no one can lie, that one guy would open his mouth and the mystery would be over... Then we hang the prick."

"It's no perfect world," Gene assures them once more.

They all fall silent again for a moment.

"Why isn't it?" Howard is still full of questions.

"Why isn't it perfect?" Norm asks the asker.

"We just did this," Ba-Dee reminds them about their raising this issue a few nights ago.

"Not quite," Howard qualifies his objective. "Now I mean from the point of view of everything – "

"Like what everything?" Norm goes for it.

"Like not just life – what we were saying – but the physical world, even. Like things that don't work, don't fit. Discoveries that are so hard to come by – why don't all possible discoveries just *exist?* And why aren't we made sorta physically perfect..?"

"Gives us something to do, Howie," Ba-Dee thinks. "Shoot for perfection."

"Nohhhhh!" Howard reacts with his irritated half-laugh. "If we didn't have all these imperfections to struggle with, we could concentrate on the important things – "

"Like what?" Joseph sounds like he's smiling broadly.

"Yeah, what?" Norm wants to know what that could possibly be, too.

"Well..." Howard intends to explain. "It's like this book on reincarnation I read that says there's seven levels of spirit life, or something – like, seven levels! So, even the first-level folks have no physical imperfections to deal with, so what do they do with all their spare time? Let alone everyone on the seventh floor?!"

"You're assuming it's true," Gene notes a flaw in the thought process.

"No, fuckface!" Howard doesn't like his conjectures invalidated. "My point is that here, on Earth – why is there even an Earth? Why can't we be beings somewhere where there isn't...isn't..."

"Coat hangers!" Joseph reaches a pinnacle. "I hate those fuckin' things – "

"Plastic packaging!" Ba-Dee has one, too. "Why do they have to encase everything you buy – "

"Maybe there isn't," Norm tries to stay with Howard.

"Isn't what?" Howard perks up from a brief disgust.

"Earth," Norm announces.

No one moves. As though realized, Earth might right now evaporate.

Norm elaborates: "Maybe Earth is all just our own and God's or whoever's imagination – sort of. Maybe it's not as physical as we think."

"Yeah!" Howard is happy again. "Maybe it's like they say about time: it's kind of an invention by consciousness– linear time. Maybe Earth's an illusion, too."

"Not a complete illusion," Joseph has an angle. "Maybe physical stuff just isn't as real as we were made to interpret it."

"Right!" Norm sees. "Our physical limitations limit our ability to see how narrow the range of our concept of physical reality is!"

"Jeeez-us!" Gene groans loudly. "What the fuck difference does it make?! None of it's true! None of it makes sense! We're accidents in a universe that's one big accident. There's no spirit shit. We live our little span, then snuff: nothing-blackness! Death! By definition!"

That shuts them up a half-second.

"You finished?" Joseph now turns his head so he's nose-to-nose with Gene. "We're trying to celebrate life here, Gene. Have a beer. Loosen up."

"Eat shit, Crusher," Gene replies listlessly, his wrath now spent.

"Oh, my..." Joseph evenly reacts.

"Don't worry, Joseph!" Norm suddenly offers to rescue him.

"What?!" Joseph now chimes cheerfully.

Norm explains: "Eat away! Shit – like Earth – isn't real anyway!"

"But then..!" Joseph has a horrible thought.

"Then what?" Howard lilts.

"This beer isn't real – so what's the point? And none of you are real! And this car and this talk – !"

"But *sooo..!*" Norm roars with profound realization, "neither are humanity's problems! We have absolutely no problems!"

"No problems! No problems!" the chant now immediately reverberates out from the car – across the fields of grain and into the holy night, in waves of liberation around the troubled globe and through all the depths of infinite cosmos beyond...

Only when Chuck Cintz leaves his town does he see it as clearly as he wants.

It's Monday. First thing this morning he talked with Elizabeth at the library. (He decided the thing to do was take her into his confidence and tell her about the diary. Swearing her to secrecy – he actually had her raise her right hand and promise it "for the official record" – he then asked her to keep new book donations separate and to just quietly write down those folks' names after they leave. She was aghast, all the while very serious, and more than eager to help.)

Now, out along this gently rolling road to Elston City, he questions the point of it, whether having those few names recorded can possibly contribute. (Elizabeth told him how the first week of previous book drives "generally yielded eighty percent of the averaged donations.")

And, as he visualizes the town as a whole, a cluster of lives there behind him settled amid the fields, he can feel their one and only focus – held in place by a range of moods, from the secret delight of morbid curiosity to barely restrained impatient rage – a focus and search among themselves for a single – lurking – evil presence.

Beside him on the seat is a beat-up old briefcase, the honored icon of past administrations. Inside it are the math book with it's dark core, the bag with the "Lucy's" napkin, and the bag with the undergarment – an awkward, private, shocking rag of blue cloth, so recently worn by a living girl...

This morning, saying good-bye to his wife on their porch, Chuck felt the pull of impatience himself. He almost decided to walk back in the house and open Jack's envelope with the name inside and immediately go drag that mystery kid into the office and squeeze what he could right out of him...

And out here away from it, he questions again why he is waiting, and imagines everyone back there in town watching him drive along just thinking and thinking...

Over the next couple of days, Jackie eases closer to Eggie, talking with him a little here and there, acknowledging him on the ball field, and joking with him at the Dairy Cone Drive-in. And though Jack is still on his mission to get the kid to talk, now he realizes he feels for him, too. (Actually, he finds he kinda likes Eggie – "Eddie", and admires his intelligence.)

Tuesday, walking out of the ballpark together for their lunch break, Eggie talks with Jack about reading, suggesting some books he feels are fun. Jack is pleased that anyone could think he is capable of being a reader, and he offers Eggie sincere appreciation: "Yeah thanks." (It isn't as though they will ever be inseparable buds. Still, both are learning to be more open about a different character of person.)

At times, Jack even thinks he should maybe tell the kid about what he's been up to from the start, but stops at the thought of undoing the part of this that feels good. And, anymore, he can see Eggie as someone needing help for what he must be going through, maybe as much as someone in Janet's family. What Chief Cintz needs is still most important, but Jackie wants – more and more – to do right by Eggie.

So, he'll wait it out, hope for Eggie to open up, persuading but not pushing him to talk. (He is now sure Eggie doesn't know what to do with what he knows.) Yet Jack struggles with how exactly to go about it – as in what exactly to say when the time comes. He is fully aware that Eggie spends all his waking hours either at the ballpark, at the library (lunches), once in a while a few minutes at the Dairy Cone, or else snug at home, and does not seem at all concerned about looking around town – for the guy, that is... Which means he must be sure of who he saw that night, Jack thinks, and does not need – or want – to see him again. But what would be worth trying, Jack decides, is somehow have Eggie spend time with him hanging around Lucy's. The guy just might show up there and, face-to-face, in the middle of everyone, maybe the Egg will feel safe enough to let it out.

...

And during the next few days, since his comforting older-brother talk with Norm, Jeff sees Janet's creep several more times.

He watches him drive by twice on Monday afternoon, as he sits in the little park across from Lucy's.

Monday evening, he comes almost face-to-face with him in Red's Convenient Drugs & Milk, where the guy is buying...milk. (Milk, Jeff thinks. How wholesome.)

Tuesday, he doesn't see him. But Wednesday afternoon he watches with thumping heart as the guy turns onto 93 opposite Lucy's, where, up a block and a half, on her own, Janet's friend Wendy is strolling home. His car seems to slow down. He definitely checks Wendy out, head cranked around so far it must hurt. But he doesn't stop. (Wendy, Jeff notices, keeps her eyes fixed on the white car as he drives away down a side street. Jeff wonders if she knows what Janet had confided in him – he thought she told only him.)

Wednesday evening, from lying flat on his bed thinking about what he had seen that day and the too-real possibility of "it" happening again – that maybe he had watched how it begins, how the compulsion first builds – he almost turns and steps into the police office after jumping up and walking quickly downtown...

But he still can't be sure what that scary little scene with Wendy means, in regards to murder. There's all kinds of that type of guy, he has begun to figure out. Guys get their rats rigid over all kinds of freak stuff – Janet told him some, saying she had heard of "lots more". (From that angle, the odds are good that reporting what he saw would nail just a routine freak and not a one-in-however-many-freaks murderer.) Then, he inevitably gets back down to what he has to always remember – where he knew to stop with Norm: his fear that the damage he could do someone who is actually relatively innocent could be really severe.

...

And, no one but Wilf and Chuck notice that Looker hasn't been around much lately. Chuck does see him Tuesday around noon getting a coffee at Lucy's, but after drinking it uncharacteristically fast sitting there on his favorite bench in the little corner park, Looker springs to his feet and, intently, heads straight back toward home. Yet that isn't really very unusual, Chuck reminds Wilf as they talk about it later. Looker is never at all consistent in his downtown appearances, he says, and often it seems he is walking around preoccupied. Or then other times it's like he is out of sight for a week or two at a stretch. "But one thing for sure," Wilf notes in turn, "anytime you see him walkin' around, you can never tell by studying the man's face whether he's happy or hurtin'."

...

Also, in a couple of cautious afternoon sessions at Nick's Bowl, Ba-Dee, Norm and Howard manage to reduce the kid list to just seventeen. It's reported by Joseph that his little brother's little friends happened to talk about a few kids who were away the week of Janet's murder on a school program camping trip. Joseph persuaded his brother to get their names (undertaken with sworn secrecy or suffer excruciating death!). Meanwhile, Norm and Howard had uncovered information that delisted two others. Gene, however, has been too busy lately to contribute, having been enlisted to help his mother paint and paper the entire inside of their home.

The whispered conversations at Ba-Dee's lunch counter station, though, are not driven by optimism. The three of them can't figure out how to narrow the list any more, without talking to the kids directly. Then they generally conclude they might have to take what they have to the Chief, to let him figure it out, or maybe have him help them somehow go further.

As well, though he doesn't say anything to his friends, Norm has another talk with Jeff late Wednesday night. Though hesitant, Jeff does tell his older brother what he has seen lately (less the guy's name and car description, and Wendy's name, of course) though he doesn't mention how he almost stormed into the police office. (Jeff senses it's what Norm really wants him to do.) Norm, of course, is horrified. Even though he is always well aware that the guy is still out there – a potential new murder in the head of one cross-wired guy still stalking through these streets – hearing Jeff describe Janet's friend's encounter sends shivers down his spine. (If there was a way to get it out of Jeff, he would try. But years of bribing or threatening him, squealing on him and even actual arm twisting, have never once breached Jeff's cast-iron-thick stubbornness.) What he himself would immediately choose to do, Norm tells Jeff, is watch the guy and his car twenty-four hours a day, with the hope of preventing another attack – adding (said in that context) that it (he) would need Howard, Joseph, Gene and Ba-Dee's help, too. Jeff reacts with an angry *"No way!"*

Their talk, in Norm's bedroom, is left dangling right there as Jeff walks out. And with that, Norm quickly realizes the only thing for him to do next is try to watch his little brother watching the guy, and starting Thursday morning he keeps track of where Jeff is, always.

...

From Elston's labs, the red thread little-charging-bull-on-a-pocket shirt connection is confirmed. Sitting alone in his office, Chief Chuck just nods to himself slowly as he reads the confidential hand-delivered report (all the while aware of how he now notices every man's shirt before looking at his face – even in passing cars and newspaper pictures).

In addition, lab documents are enclosed detailing Janet's body examination, the attacker's semen analysis, and the scouring of Carl's car (Chuck doesn't even read that one), which finalize all the initial test results.

And included in the thick envelope too are preliminary findings about Janet's underpants and the Lucy's napkin: nothing they didn't expect.

The diary, however, is still being examined. Clearly, a memo about it in the package states, the guy is right-handed, the felt pen is one of several best-selling sub-brands made by one company, the text pages were likely cut out with a standard razor knife, no hairs but some skin specks were found – they are yet to be tested – and all pre-library fingerprints are blotched out – except one partial. (It's quite likely the guy usually wore gloves when he handled it or at least painstakingly wiped it clean of prints with dish soap, the expert says in his notes...especially meaningful considering the theory that he may have all along wanted it found – just for fun.)

Chuck relays some of this to Tom as they change shifts Wednesday night, telling him he's taking the reports home to think on them some more, and that he'll phone the details of them over to the ever-anxious Mayor Jimmy Jimms.

The thing that sticks in Chuck's mind, as he sits on his big porch tonight enjoying the summer sunset air, is the gloves point. Rubber gloves, he wonders? Like a surgeon's? Or maybe that cheap, general-purpose kind they sell at the hardware store..? But then, people buy those things all the time (he even uses them around the house sometimes, and so does Beth for her occasional creative bursts of abstract painting). When his wife comes out to sit with him on the swing, he tells her everything new. As they have for many nights lately – as though they can't rest until they feel they've thought through it as fully as they can – they pick at the significance of each detail over and over again.

...

At Janet's, Margaret and Carl and Jennifer have been hanging around the kitchen a lot, eating meals there instead of in the dining room or in the living room in front of the television, like they used to. In the evenings, Marg and Carl usually play cards at the kitchen table for a while, and Jennifer likes to sit there too and be part of the conversation. And they talk openly about Janet, without feeling self-conscious anymore when one of them, or all three of them, start crying again.

Tuesday, Jennifer spends a few hours at a friend's, and returns noticeably cheerful. On the weekend, she'll stay two nights with the friend at her family cottage.

And what all three have discovered about each other, aside from some fundamentally similar deep beliefs about death and an afterlife, is an almost equal abhorrence for what the murderer did to Janet and to them – not a bitter hatred for the man, but for what he did, and that it happens in human nature at all. Once they know who he is (they are sure he'll be caught, but are unsure if it will have to be after more attacks) they believe they can forgive him – though not what he did...yet only if he is locked away in prison to live the rest of his life feeling only his guilt.

On his porch balcony at the back of his rooms on the second floor, Looker sits in a ragged old armchair and studies the world.

Never, never, did a day feel so long.

Below, sunshine creeps over a broken countryside, baking Earth dry.

Out there, he feels the aimless wind, that shoves clouds, that stain the blue; he sees wayward birds, lowly bugs, trees prisoners of the gruesome, pulling, glutinous ground.

He senses: Stillness, as a timeless void lurking in each day, in the night, without explanation, willingly, treacherously, taking faith, fear, and every breath...

Then: Depravity.

Human divinity...forsaken – on impulse.

As if irreversible, the clinging outrage of human cruelty rules hearts, so that everyone living – the unborn – are touched, stricken, hollowed, saddened; made forlorn, melancholy, mournful, wretched – are violated, brutalized, made cold, indifferent; become bitter, hard, evolve murderous, cruel.

It makes us feel: Abandoned by God.

A cross town and out a country road, miles away and facing the opposite sky from Looker's, Julie Grant sits on her back step and watches her handsome two-year-old boy play in the gentle sunshine. In everything the little blond rascal does, she sees Doug McCallum.

"L'le Bug!" she calls to him, just to hug him again. (She never called his father "Bug", but she likes to use the nickname now, when no one is around.)

Out here, she still loves the warm summer days and caressing winds, as much as ever. There is no sound here, except the rustle of cornstalks, the flutter of leaves in the tall trees all around the yard, and her son chirping sweet musical nonsense. And she loves the comforting heat of the radiant sun – to simply sit there, sipping tea, enjoying having only this to do...

Julie misses Doug, and the way he would just appear in the yard, from nowhere, never calling ahead. She misses how he adored their son, and played with him so patiently, tenderly. (But she doesn't mind being alone – she always preferred to live alone.) She just misses the sight, the anticipation – and the never before felt trust of a family kind of stability and contentment – whenever Bug Doug McCallum rode that old bike up her country lane.

"He doesn't often jump into things," Wilf understates it to Sue as he steps back out onto their darkened porch (his turn to refill their coffee mugs). Though his wife hadn't directly criticized, he feels he should draw that one boundary about Chuck's performance ability (before she can observe again "how slowly things sometimes move").

"Better that he doesn't," Sue smiles. As she looks up at him, Wilf notices yet again how attractive she is – how the lamplight through the window behind them sculpts her silken cheeks and highlights the twirls and curls of her pinned-up honey hair.

Setting her mug down on the armrest of her wooden chair, his perceptive gaze stays on her big brown gentle eyes for a moment, as though in a friendly challenge. She grins wider. (There is nothing more warming than a human smile, he thinks. And hers is still the prettiest.)

"Chuck has clues," he reminds her, "but he isn't about to go thrashin' through the whole town just to pull in some iffy suspects."

"Most everyone feels he's doing exactly the right thing," Sue claims evenly as she takes a small sip of her coffee. She raises her eyes up from her mug to see his look of appreciation, then peers out across the streetlight-flooded lawn. Though the long day is winding down, their neighborhood is still lively, with people watering their lawns and flowers or talking with others. Up and down the street, kids are riding bikes or playing tag – but only on the brightly lighted sidewalks. (She loves their town and home as much as her dear husband does, she has said openly, and Wilf and Chuck Cintz have always had their place at the community heart.)

"But you're right, what you said," Wilf gets back to her remark from sometime before he went inside. "It's like living with plutonium. You can't see it, but..."

"I meant that it's impossible to live with – to live with that tangible apprehension. It...it's like it has this grip on everything I do...and probably everyone else living here feels the same, Wilf," she explains calmly. "But I do realize the only real terror is for the next victim."

"That's it exactly. So it's – so *he* is ruinin' a good, secure feel, here, the feel of belongin' – maybe ruinin' it forever... There aren't many places as good as this town, are there?"

Sue smiles, and nods.

"Now, half the guys I see every day, I wonder..." Wilf sighs, slowly spinning his mug on the arm of his chair.

Studying his thought-creased brow, his lean yet healthy face, she again feels her life-long dedication to this man, and all the ways she loves him (as many ways, it warms her heart, as he loves her). For the first time, it crosses her mind that she would like to know his deepest thought about it: "Do you actually have some-one in mind, Wilf?"

He glances at her. "You tell me yours then I'll tell you mine," he quips...solemnly.

"I don't even have possibilities." Mindful, Sue reaches over and squeezes his arm, glad she doesn't have one of those hus-bands who gets all offended when asked to repeat some of his secret man-talk.

Wilf pats her hand gently, and thinks. He takes a deep breath of the sweet night air, full of the freshness of a living summer. At the end of the cross street a couple of houses over, he can just see a piece of Main Street, a section of buildings a block from Lucy's.

"Before you asked that," Wilf wants to tell her first, "I was thinkin' about what we were saying, that now we're sorta glad we didn't have kids." He rubs his temple a couple of times, as though trying to stimulate the truest words. "Chuck was just tellin' me they chose not to have kids partly because of this kind of thing. He said along with all the trouble Beth went through as a kid – the molestin' and that – it definitely was one point in their reasons, and they feel it again now. Her health problems were the main thing, we knew that. But I was surprised to hear him say they're glad they don't have a daughter right now... God! What is this world comin' to!" he raises an arm to his town, not the planet.

"Oh, no, Wilf! Don't think that!" Sue sighs heavily. "Then you and Chuck will start talking about not driving a car because of all the accidents others cause or flying in airplanes – and even walking down the street!"

"The reality is, the feelin' exists," Wilf reacts. "People here now are more than disillusioned. And it gets down to where they'd rather avoid those big worries about havin' kids."

"Oh, I agree it's reality, but I don't believe it's a choice that's realistic," Sue debates. "You have to decide if there's hope for the world, and whether you're going to do all you can to make it better. I think lots of people have perfectly happy lives, if they're brave, at all."

Wilf can't dispute her objectivity. "True enough, hon. Then I guess maybe it's both a reality and a choice. And I suppose if we had kids, we'd feel all right about it – I mean we'd be up to all the challenges... But you know when this is over, it'll all feel different again."

"It may never be over," Sue suggests, scowling with her own negative thought as she takes repeated sips of coffee... "What if he's never caught – that happens all the time, doesn't it?"

"Not in our l'le paradise, stranger!" he half-heartedly jokes. Yet both know that is exactly how social "paradise" should work: The closer people feel in a community, the more assured it is that, together, they will insist on – and connect with – solutions.

They sit in silence for a moment, waving at some passing neighbors and smiling at the little kids next door disputing that it's time to go inside.

"Well?" Sue hasn't forgotten. "Who do you think?"

Wilf wanders around town in his head a few seconds. "There's lots I'm sure it isn't, and some it might be."

"Just the maybes," she pokes him in the arm.

"Ben Schnider's always worried me," he begins, watching her eyebrows rise at the name of the car mechanic virtually no one likes. "Okay, well, him aside, you'd think it has to be someone nasty, and that's why the kid witness isn't talking, right?"

"Sure... Who else? No holding back, now," she insists.

"Well...Mayor Jimms – "

"Whoa – !"

"He's not completely ruled out," he reminds her. "He has a housekeeper who could've cleaned off some bookshelves..."

"True," Sue barely allows, holding back comment. "Go on."

"Tom Addison – "

"You're kidding!" she abruptly sits up on the edge of her chair.

"No – hey, you've got to keep an open mind, here. It's kind of suspect-until-proven-otherwise thing. It's that, or end up rulin' out the killer because he's such a nice guy or he's just one of the boys, or somethin'."

It takes her a minute, but she does agree, and settles back in her chair again.

"Tom was on duty," she recalls.

"So?" Wilf is quick to counter. "He has a wife who can clear out old books. And he patrols sometimes in his own car, just like Chuck – they get gas money, remember? And he hangs around

Lucy's..." (He hasn't told her yet that Chuck secretly checked Tom's car for Lucy's napkins, but found none – though there is often a bunch in the police car.) "He probably owns a felt pen..."

"It sure would explain why the kid won't – ohhh!, what am I saying?! No way in the world it's Tom!" she groans.

"You're doin' the one-of-the-boys thing."

"Alright!" she quickly relents.

"Then," he continues slowly, "there's Buddy Simpson – you know, that creepy guy who drives cab back and forth from Elston?" (She nods.) "And, um...oh!, that bunch of young guys I told you are tryin' to help Chuck find the witness kid?"

"Sure," Sue knows.

"They all make me wonder..." his soft voice trails a little deeper. (Though now that he said it, he realizes his reasoning is plainly weak.)

"Why?" she wants to hear it, even though she doesn't know any of them.

"Well...they're just wanderin' around all the time – more than any of those others – altogether, or individually. They're always drinkin' out along that deserted dirt road – "

"How do you know that?"

"They're always buyin' beer, they're always slippin' around most nights, then they disappear. And they don't show up anywhere else," Wilf explains. "It's kinda obvious."

"Even more so when one is aware that's where you and Chuck and a few of your other friends used to go – "

"And you and me," Wilf notes, too.

"We didn't do much beer drinking, my sweet."

"Well, maybe they're just communicatin', and so were we – sorta," Wilf smirks.

Sue laughs openly, then continues, "So, which one?"

"Don't know... Nah, sounds stupid, doesn't it? I just thought it could maybe be one of 'em, as much as anyone." Wilf now scratches vigorously in through the long hair behind his ear and up across his head, then gulps down his coffee and announces, "Walk time! Once around the block, sumptuous Sue?"

And a minute later, they're hand-in-hand strolling along their street, enjoying the stillness of the night and glimpses of twinkling stars through the silent trees.

As Wilf and Sue approach the intersection at Main Street, heading back from their walk, they are passed by Eggie racing through the darkness on his bike. He is speeding home from the ballpark, then the Dairy Cone, and now, ahead up Sideroad 93, a quick detour past Janet's house. (Eggie's been riding by her place the last several nights, since sneaking over there Saturday night – when he started worrying even more about what he knows.)

"I'm the only one in the world that knows who the murderer is!" he's started saying aloud to himself when he's alone, like in the shower and right now – but only when he's real sure he can't be heard. And lately – with time passing by so quick! – he's beginning to think it will be entirely his fault when another girl dies...

Each time he goes by Janet's, he slows to a crawl right in front of the house, peeping in all the windows to be sure – he believes – he isn't seen. (Though it's quite dark right in front of Carl and Margaret's place, there is probably just enough streetlight to recognize a gawking young boy.)

Down along the right side of the house, he tries to see the fence and the neighbor's big tree, and to imagine from this angle how the guy looked that night as he climbed over the pickets and crept across the grass. Then, after Eggie coasts beyond the front, he cranks it around the block to try to see it happening again from between the back neighbors' houses. And tonight, from there on their front walk, he can plainly picture the guy half dragging, half carrying Janet to the street, out this same dark driveway he used himself. From behind the big tree that night, where he stood scared frozen until he saw the car ease away (he realizes the guy must have left it running, because he doesn't remember hearing it start – loud as the wind was, he probably would have heard it), she looked like she was somewhat conscious, not like she was limp and unconscious.

Now, like every other night this week, he relives that scene, and ends by fixing in his mind that one clear look at the guy's face scanning around before he leaps back over the fence...and like every time before, he feels chills at the thought of seeing him again – even if it's in the daytime in the middle of a crowded street...

"I'm the only one that knows!" he had whispered to himself again a few minutes ago (once he was well past Wilf and Sue on the sidewalk). And now, he tries to grasp it fully one more time: "I'm the only person anywhere who can stop it happening again!"

Then why doesn't he decide? – it's so simple! Go tell the police: problem solved..!

But (he stops that thought where he did every other time) then they'll know I snuck out to peek at girls! And Dad will beat on me again, like before. (His dad told him he better not ever find out he was still doing that, after the police came around to his work complaining about all the kids peeking – and after shouting that, he still got so mad he hit Eggie then squeezed his hand so hard he broke a finger and told Mom, "Your stupid son fell out of the tree house!") No, he realizes as he remembers how it hurt, I sure don't want that again...

And what would the police do? he fears as he peddles hard home, peering into the distant blackness where the sidewalk fades away. They might only make fun of me! And push me around because they think I'm making it up – I don't even know the guys name..! And Dad will get mad not believing me – and kill me if the police don't believe me either!

And, lastly, he comes down again to the big one: What if the guy isn't immediately locked up, because there's not enough evidence or something, and he knows it was me telling on him? But the guy knows I'm right, so he'll have to kill me to shut me up..!

But then, close to home, Eggie has to put all his confusion aside because he's worried, as always, if Dad's home yet from his regular evening "Goin' out for a drink!" – he hopes he isn't, so he can get up to his room and maybe fall asleep quick without having to see him.

"You've never gone through anything even close to this," Beth observes, sidetracked on her way through the kitchen to come stand behind Chuck and comb back his wavy gray hair with her fingers. It's soon after sunup, Friday morning, and Chuck tiptoed downstairs a few minutes ago to put on the coffee. Now, as he sits at the breakfast table waiting for it to brew, his dear wife, wrapped in her yellow summer robe, has come down to join him. "And proof of it is, you haven't been up and dressed this early since you were first appointed," she laughs lightly and starts scratching his head furiously.

Chuck leans back and relishes the massage, hands spread open on the wooden table, legs crossed and stretched up onto the opposite chair. (Today, his official uniform of short-sleeved blue shirt and midnight blue pants is complemented by comfortable white sneakers.) Across the kitchen, yellow sunshine is angling in through the little window over the sink, setting the flowered wallpaper in front of them ablaze. The compelling aroma of brewing coffee fills the whole morning.

"Never anything like it before in this town," he finally responds, as steadily as he can as Beth kneads on.

Beside them, their aged mutt Quadruped is extended flat-out on the cool tile floor, whimpering meekly, as though anxious for a few rubs, too.

"Quad-roo-ped," Chuck shifts his half-closed eyes down toward his long-haired, black and white ol' buddy, and the dog's eyes roll back and forth even faster between Master and the scratching lady. His shaggy tail wags one rotation just above the floor. "You want some itchin', bud? Eh, bud? So why don't you come with me anymore? Can't you see I need your help, Quad-sie? Quads are *so* quicker than bipeds!"

"He can barely rise for lunch, anymore," Beth smiles, her brilliant green eyes full of gentle sympathy. Making comforting kissing sounds at their pet as she passes him, she crosses to the counter to fill the two big coffee mugs waiting there, then turns and sets them on the table as she sits opposite her weary police-chief husband.

"Remember how he used to wanna ride on the hood?" Chuck recalls, then grins down at his dog. "Couldn't grasp the car concept, eh, Quad?"

Quad wiggles just the white tip of his tail this time, his head now resting on his two front paws, waiting for someone to take him seriously.

"Take him with you. Maybe he could sniff the goddamned bastard out!" Beth suggests with characteristic fire, as redheaded in temperament as she looks.

"And carry Quad around cradled like a baby? I wouldn't embarrass ol' Four-on-the-floor like that – would I, brown-eyes?" Chuck leans over and pets him.

"So...Chief!" Beth then boldly scowls straight across the table at her husband. "Did you open Jackie's envelope this morning?" (The way he was talking last night, so frustrated that nothing concrete was coming together, she felt sure he was going to tear it open before he came to bed.)

"No... Didn't even dig it out," Chuck grins emptily back at her (though, as always, he's appreciative of her spirited approach to his often depressing work.).

"Fine." She's with him all the way.

"But I'm thinking about pinning him down today. He's taking way too long, considering what's at stake."

"We assume there's good reasons. Jackie probably knows the reasons better than we ever could," Beth imagines. Testing her hot coffee, her eyes stay fixed on Chuck's.

"Probably," he understands. But then slouching and laying his head back on the top of his chair, he lets out a deep breath before adding with a bit of a groan, "There's always the same dilemma: too many possibilities still out there, not quite enough clues..."

"Then add in a whole lot of sensitive people in a close-knit town," she recognizes how such a positive quality of community can be simultaneously negative. (But he knows she's just stating a fact, not a frustration. She grew up here too, and wouldn't have it any other way.)

They sit there silently for a moment, staring – full of thought – into each other's eyes.

"But then what's your alternative?" Beth soon narrows it, concerned for her town and husband. "We've speculated so much about forcing something – like searching every closet in town for a red shirt or locking up Jackie's kid witness until he talks...well, if he can even identify the man – or grilling everyone in town for any little tidbits... So then, Chuck, what happens if we do nothing? Is that really an alternative? – that we just keep our eyes open and hope?"

"We're not responsible for this thing, Beth!" Chuck reacts angrily (though he understands her need to express it, and is aware she always talks about town problems as "ours" and not "his"). "Me and you and everyone except one person in this town are not to blame – did not commit the act!" he exclaims, sitting up straight and pushing a pointing finger down hard on the table. "And if he acts again, it's *still* not our doing! Oh, sure, maybe if we'd been luckier or if we'd been outright brutal going around gathering facts – or if human nature was just a little more observant or perceptive or something – we'd be past all this shit by now! But we aren't, so we aren't! And the wishing-it-so of three thousand people is *not* going to collectively affect the wonky brainwaves of a sicko predator!"

"Agreed, my little round biped," Beth's words concur but she's staring him down. "You, however, are the one who's beginning to tear apart with self-blame over it. So then you can't fully believe what you just said – or you wouldn't be up at sunrise over it! But you know all too well that a murder is everyone's to try and solve, and everyone's to try and prevent."

Chuck breathes deep, and decidedly relaxes. "You couldn't be more right, there..." But then he simultaneously frowns and smiles at her, countering, "So what, my sweet red-hot-curly-top wife, is your best suggestion?"

(Quad is still down there resting his head on his paws, but his eyes got tired of following their voices back and forth, so he went to sleep.)

"I think you should open the envelope – I thought you should've opened it the instant Jackie handed it to you – "

"You don't know him – "

"No, it's you I'm still talking about. It's the biggest thing hanging around your neck right now: feeling ineffective – with that information in your hand – "

"I'm not the problem! Jackie's not the problem! It's the kid himself," Chuck reminds her again. "There's something abnormal going on with that kid, or he would've come in the office by now – or he would've immediately told his parents – and we would've had it all solved that night! So either he's unsure – like he doesn't think he can identify the guy – or he's scared shitless!"

"I think it's the scared shitless," Beth chooses as she leans back, giving up trying to force self-concern on her husband. "So how do we overcome that?"

"We just wait for it... Something has to happen – eventually – doesn't it?"

Beth thinks it over. Though she rejects the thought of standing still, she feels no alternative whatsoever. And so, bluntly, she states the next obvious point (in the now familiar sequence): "But the worst thing fate can do to us – like we deserve another clue – is another rape and murder..."

Chuck feels numb again at the thought of it. "The hard reality is, we could have nothing more until then." Through a wordless moment, he gazes longingly at Quad, then sighs, "Some of us peds got it easy."

"But no thumbs," Beth states after a few seconds of studying the half-asleep dog, too.

"So what? So he can't hitchhike – ?"

"Can't open dog food – "

"Oh-oh. Or grab a beer – darn! Hey, I'm sorry, Quad buddy. I didn't realize..."

Quad the dog opens one eye a crack at the mention of his name.

"Yep, us higher beings get all the fun," Beth notes sort of philosophically.

"Well," Chuck decides, standing up cautiously so he doesn't startle the Quad, "I'd better go get some more good times at the office. See what's going on, anyway...if anything."

"Chuck..." Beth pushes to her feet in front of him and sets both hands firmly on his shoulders (Quad strains to his four feet, too). "You're the best. I just love you..." She rubs her soft, pink cheek against his chubby clean-shaved jaw. "I just don't want you hurt by this, you know?"

Chuck holds her carefully. "You're always good to me, Beth. I always appreciate that, and love you always."

After a reassuring embrace, they separate smiling. And Quad vigorously wags his whole tail, consuming a whole morning's energy reserve at once.

"Something good will happen – soon," Chuck assures her, stepping into the hallway. He then turns half around and smiles at her, adding, "We all deserve it."

Beth beams a positive look back at him from the middle of the bright kitchen, green eyes sparkling.

"Com'on, Quad-legs!" Chuck pats his side encouragingly at the sight of his old pal standing there beside Beth. "You can ride on the hood..!"

But Quadruped sinks to the floor again, exhausted by the very thought of it.

The noon sun bathes the thickened air above the ball diamond dust with unrelenting heat.

"Hotter the better," Jackie rejects Eggie's apprehension (about everyone melting) as they sit in the shade of the brick dugout. All the others have gone home for some lunch, but Eggie had made himself a stack of peanut butter sandwiches, and he offered Jack one and a half in exchange for a lemon-lime soda...two of which Jack has just peddled back from the store buying. Though they're sitting at opposite ends, reclined against the walls with feet up lengthwise on the bench, the windless day is so densely quiet they could hear each other even if they whispered.

"But it's hard playing in it all day," Eggie notes with a mouthful, wide eyes behind his glasses blinking back and forth from the field to Jack.

"Yeah," the more experienced player agrees, squinting out into the intense brightness, "but I still like it. I just like being outside all the time. But not when it's cold, as much."

"Wish it could be like this all year long," Eggie does feel the same as him about being outside (and he's eager to discover some more real things they have in common).

"Wish for a lot of things..." Jack's deeper voice trails, his one-bite-notched sandwich dangling from his hand draped over a raised knee. His moody black eyes are peering, appropriately, somewhere out in left field.

For the next half-minute or so, Eggie just quietly watches Jack repeatedly push back his long, sweat-dampened black hair. He thinks he knows what he means – the way growing up can go from okay parts to crappy parts... Anyway, he hopes Jack likes his plain peanut butter sandwich, even though now he's stopped eating it.

"Like, one wish is I wish I'd quit hearing from everybody around here about my no-good father – wherever the fuck he is..." Jack offers his revealing example more absently than angrily. He then takes another big bite of his sandwich, thinks again for a second, and adds, "I mean, I wish he'd just completely disappear altogether – like he never existed. Some people blame my mom, I guess – don't ask me why. But she's still around, and he's..."

On top of the unexpected openness, Eggie is shocked to see tears abruptly glisten in Jack's dark eyes. He then realizes tears are about to overflow his own eyes, too. "Did you ever know him?" he questions cautiously.

"I guess," Jack answers oddly, still staring into the distance. "I mean, he hung around until I was three, or something, then completely abandoned us, Mom says. But I don't remember him at all...the asshole..."

Before he thinks, Eggie blurts, "You can have mine..."

Jack's mind snaps back to the dugout. His eyes shift straight to Eggie – with a look so full of revelation he doesn't have to say anything for the Egg to feel suddenly understood.

"He's a prick..." Eggie now calmly proclaims for the first time in his life. And because he has just admitted it to himself for the first time ever, too – and out loud, even – his tears quickly over-flow and make trails down his cheeks. (He also surprised himself with his bluntly conclusive way of finally saying it.)

"I thought..." Jack stumbles, "I thought, you know, that your family was all...normal..."

"We are...except for my dad," Eggie qualifies it, as though catching a small inaccuracy.

"Does he...is he rough, or something?"

"Yeah," Eggie sighs hesitatingly (though he's not at all clear yet just how profoundly unburdened he now feels). With eyes glazed open wide, he begins going through the motions of munching his sandwich again.

"What does your mom say...do?" Jack tries to put himself in that situation (Eggie having two parents, rather than depending wholly on – or dealing with – just a mother). And as though cued, he begins nibbling again too, trying not to stare at Eggie hunched there with his big eyes searching the ball diamond – though the little guy is now clearly somewhere in a world of images way beyond the outfield.

"Nothing... She gets mad, too, sometimes. But not so much..." Eggie responds wistfully.

"Then she's not normal – either..!" Jack defiantly begins, but stops as he watches Eggie drop his sandwich on the dirt floor and gape at him. (His mother, Jack can see immediately, is an angel of mercy – no matter how angry she gets – compared to his father.) "Oh, God..."

"What..?" Eggie moans as though wounded.

"Egg Man," Jack feels he better spit it right out, "if your ol' man's tough on you, it doesn't make it all right for your mom to be mean – even without wackin' you, or something. She should be stopping what your dad does, not doing it to you, too!" He then glares the poor kid down, trying to demonstrate, along with his wise words, how strong and serious his point is.

Eggie sits frozen for a few seconds. He looks as though his last friend – his own mom! – has just betrayed him.

"Eddie," Jack calls him, for the first time ever, "it ain't right, you know, if your dad hits you. Shit, it ain't right if he even just talks mean to you all the time! You're innocent – what did you ever do to deserve it? Did you ask for it? Are you evil, or something?!" Eddie's face is now flooded with a cascade of tears. He's softly sobbing, but still wide-eyed facing Jack. He's slumped and helpless on the bench. And Jack, amid his own tirade of indignant anger, is heartbroken. "You hafta know that, Eddie! It's fucking wrong! – those two people are wrong! You're just being all you can be – *and nothing about it is your fucking fault!*"

Eddie just stares forlornly at Jack, tears dripping freely off his face. And every tender fiber in his youthful being feels he has just heard the most profound personal truth he'll ever hear.

With their eyes locked in deep understanding (that's much too experienced for their age) they sit motionless for another timeless moment. Finally, Jack can't stand it anymore, and his gaze lowers to Eddie's crumpled brown-paper lunch bag on the bench down there in front of the kid. "Com'on," he pretends hardness, "give me my other half, and let's go..." Sniffling, Eddie reaches and picks up the bag, pulls out a half sandwich, and walks it down the dugout to Jack, raising little puffs of dust with his smudged white runners. He then stands there and digs out another half, and clutches it to his mouth and wet face. Jack stands up too, chomping a huge bite.

Though he doesn't say where they're going, Jack starts out across the diamond – with Eddie keeping up right there beside him. Jack soon explains, "We need ice cream – I'm buying."

As they shuffle purposefully off the field, eating thoughtfully and trailing long clouds of dust, Jack briefly wraps a caring arm tightly around Eddie's shoulders.

As the afternoon wears on, Chief Cintz has to handle three difficult new encounters with questioning citizens. The first was a long hot-air theory from an anonymous caller (Chuck knew who she was from word one) followed by two separate in-person men "just dropping by". (He's had only one previous over-anxious caller since the day of Janet's murder, and can't figure out why these people have all hit him at once today. Maybe they play cards together Thursday nights, he imagines.) Only one man – this last one in – is really angry. He's old Harold Hall, the aloof yet well-enough respected storeowner, who happens to have seven granddaughters (five live elsewhere). So, sympathetically, Chuck tries to act like he genuinely feels just how a concerned grandfather feels, but the miserable old fellow doesn't buy it. What gramps wants is action! Chuck explains some of the situation, but community-conscious ol' Mister Harold Hall says while whirling about to leave – with his unique pragmatism – "I pay my fucking taxes and I'm owed a fucking arrest! Goodbye!"

Tom has been sitting wordlessly through all of this last stand-off, watching without expression from his desk. "Never ever seen anything like that before!" he exclaims with a clear overtone of derision as soon as the old fellow is gone.

"You don't really blame him, do you?" Chuck counters from the doorway where he just defended himself. And slowly crossing back toward his chair, he now feels frustrated and a little angry – though his question to Tom was asked calmly.

Without flinching or hesitating, the junior police officer firmly answers, "He has every right – "

"No, no, com'on! What do you *feel* about it, Tom?"

Tom twirls his pen on his desk. He glances once across the office at Chuck, then, focusing again on his rotating pen, concludes, "We're still nowhere – "

"So then what do you propose to do?" Chuck challenges him with growing impatience.

"Hell, I've got no – "

"You know, it would be nice to get some professional support, here, Officer Tom," the Chief, now stern and cold, right here decides to get something cleared up. "You have this thing, it seems, about looking the part – dressed professionally and talking professionally, then going out driving around in neat patrols and things – there's nothing wrong with any of that, but it feels sometimes that's about all you do!" Chuck lets it out. (He is still mostly cool and collected, and doesn't much care that his assistant is turning beet red.) "You better think again about just what your role is here, Tom. It's certainly true that there's never much going on in a small town like this – not that there isn't an important role for us at any and all times! – but when something does happen – something serious like this – it's time to stop going through the motions and start really thinking! As in: professionally!"

Tom glances up, as though checking if the Chief is about finished. (He isn't.)

"You've been steady at it for a long while here, Tom, but this isn't the first time – and now's when I really need it, isn't it! – that you weren't much of an official support at all...or even much of a friend through things...come to think of it..."

Tom raises his voice just a little. "You know I'm not a good thinker about these things like you are!" he protests.

"You don't even try – that's my whole point! The question here is why don't you get your head involved here and not just your uniformed body!" Chuck snarls back.

Tom doesn't answer. He just stares at Chuck.

"Well, it's just a job to you, isn't it?" Chuck now poses with a lilt and a smirk, finally lowering into his chair. "You're just acting out the part here – just going through the motions making a living! So then I wonder: how much *do* you care about this town – about all these people? Or then maybe you've got something to hide in all this..?" Chuck surprises himself by coming out with it (but he's glad he finally did).

"You and Wilf – "

"Wait a second! Don't start that way! Me and Wilf are simply the same as everyone else here in town, and every single one of us cares enough to openly hate what's happened – twenty-four hours a day since it did! So we're all coming from just one direction here, you see, Tom? – the whole entire town!"

"Well I just don't think it's anything that...unusual. It happens all the time all over the country, and you people act like it's the end of the – "

"' You people'?! Does that mean you not only feel different, but you don't want to be part of us, too?" Chuck is now wondering why he never saw Tom this clearly before.

Tom compulsively pats down his mustache once more, then argues, "I'm not that worried! If the killer hits again, or again after that, we'll get him eventually. We can't stop something happening we don't know anything about!"

"Now you're making it sound like you don't care about another life – another little girl! Someone you know! And what about any one of our friends who might suffer that kind of devastating loss?"

"Sure I care. Just like everyone. But life's rough! Things happen. All we can do is solve what we can solve. We can do some solving only when it's plain there's something to work with," Tom insists, hard eyes locked on Chuck's.

"I've worked with you three years and I'm just hearing this now?!" As he asks that, Chuck pushes to his feet and deliberately walks the six steps across the office and stands over – and almost toe-to-toe with – Tom down there in his chair.

"I'm just more realistic than I used to be," Tom tries to defend himself, stroking his mustache and straightening his tie again as he glares up at Chuck. "If I was working in Elston or somewhere, this killing would be taken in stride – "

"In *stride?!*"

"Sure! And the public there wouldn't expect us professionals to get all worked up, because everybody knows the ugly people are out there and none of us in authority twist their arms to go do what they do, but even if all of them want to go around robbing and killing each other – it's their society!"

Tom's positioning – to this degree – is news to Chuck, and the look on the man's face, as he sits stiffly at his desk down there in front of him, is new to him, too. But Chuck right here recalls that he said something similar to his wife this morning – similar to what Tom just said –and only now sees, in this instance, how different people can state the same reality from such wide-apart personal motives and ideals.

"Are you saying you'd be more...comfortable working somewhere more...impersonal – is that the right word, Tom?" Chuck leans over-top his assistant a little, his normally soft blue eyes now piercing.

Again, Tom chooses not to answer. Instead, he stands, face-to-face with his police chief.

"Well, Tom, let's just think about all this some more. And specifically, maybe you should think about your place here – in this town..." With that, Chuck turns away and strolls toward the window... "Because, Tom, I think a city attitude like you're saying doesn't fit well in a tight-knit town like this..." – he pauses to be certain about it: "and I'm not sure I ever want to face this kind of thing again working with someone holding your particular point of view."

With those last icy words, Chuck turns his head and stares straight back at the defiantly narrowed eyes of the younger man. In reaction, letting out a little huff, Tom scoops up his pen and walks out the door, ending his shift.

"Shit!" Chuck fumes aloud in his empty office. What have I done now? he wonders, squinting out at the busy street and Tom walking away. Or was that really anything at all to do with me?

But as the minutes pass, Chuck comes to understand what their confrontation means – what he wishes he was clear about all along: A community works only if its people care enough (he's always known), but if those who oversee its structure – oversee the caring, in a way – if they don't have their hearts in it, how can they ever do it any good? (Let alone not sink to doing it harm!)

What he said to Beth this morning was the other side of the spectrum (of the same light of logic) from what Tom feels: nasty stuff happens. But it's what we do about it, or don't do – or even feel about it – that means everything. So, if everyone took the neutral approach like Tom, then when the going gets seriously ugly no one would have to bother about reactions because there wouldn't be communities worth feeling anything about anyway!

After standing there another half hour going over in his mind what was said, trying to determine if Tom, deep down, has been this way all along and never had cause to show it – or (it suddenly occurs to him how Tom didn't react at all to his "something to hide" taunt) is it only lately he's had some dark reason to back so far off from working on this killing..?

Soon, putting off deciding whether to act on it officially or leave the next move up to Tom, Chuck lets himself think about the murder again...

Out along the street, the very people who he claimed to Tom are caring community members are walking and riding by. And he can feel very plainly that they do care – about themselves and others and how their lives together here are of a quality that results from their very own attitudes...and he likes what he sees and knows he was right. But old Harold with the granddaughters was essentially right, too, about action leading to results, and Chuck here says a silent little prayer asking – for his sake and their sake, for every single caring one of them – that he and they soon find the means to solve this wrenching crime.

Finally, Chuck tells himself to let go of it for the time being, and he strolls out across the bright street for the heartfelt comfort of the unconditional togetherness (expressed with or without words) of whatever good folks are right then hanging around Lucy's home-away- from-home.

C huck has been back in his office for a couple of hours. Since his reaffirming reconnecting with the incidental gathering of loafers over at Lucy's, all his thoughts this afternoon have circled around the blank pages in the killer's diary. Standing at his favorite spot at the window looking out, what he can't think past now is whether the guy may have actually intended to fill them all up.

So, he reasons once more, if the murderer does ache to do it again, will the fear that his own handwritten proof of guilt is possibly discovered really cause him to hold off? And, if he had felt invincible before (considering also it wasn't necessarily his first attack or murder if he happens to be originally from out of town or he travels out of town, Chuck of course realizes) how does he feel now – with this identifying piece of him exposed – about his personal power? Well then, what if all the known facts and clues about him were made public? Would that simply scare him into never doing it again? Or scare him right out of town? Or instead, would it challenge him to dare do his evil thing again? – like he's never been challenged before...

Inevitably, Chuck forces himself across to his desk to wade through some paperwork (with the ghostly image of Tom, there at that other desk, entering and reentering his thoughts just to irritate him). But after only a few minutes, he is surprised to look up and see Jackie standing in the ever-open doorway, leaning against the frame, ball glove hooked by fingers of a hand hooked by its thumb on a belt loop. The late-afternoon sunshine behind him is bright on the buildings and clouds, but in Jack's silhouette the Chief can readily make out the pain of forced teenage patience in the two ebony eyes amid the thin dark face and reckless black hair.

"Com'on in…" Chuck urges, barely audibly, not hiding his positive surprise as he tilts back in his chair. (He is wondering, like everyone does at times, if this is one of those surreal coincidence or psychic things, having decided only this morning to finally confront this kid today.)

"No," Jack says.

Chuck understands. His expression doesn't change at all as he silently studies the young man. Then raking his hair with his fingers once, he tosses down his pen, rocks to his feet and eases over close to him. (This "boy" is almost as tall as he is, he realizes.) He stands in front of him, hands in pockets, leaning a little toward him. "You okay, Jack?" he asks firmly.

"He's scared of everything," Jackie lets loose his rehearsed line. "I want the envelope back."

Somehow expecting something like that, the Chief asks, "You still think he's the kid?"

Jack shows that look of someone wary of being cornered and backs away a few inches.

"That's not the whole reason you're standing here now, is it?" Chuck gambles. "I think there's another large part of you that wants to give it all over to me right now, because in your confusion you hate that this murder isn't getting solved and can't stand that it's still hanging over this town – just as much as any good person here hates it… Am I close?"

Jack nods honestly. Then snarls, "But you don't know what things are like, for some…"

Chuck gets it right off: Jack empathizes with the mystery kid, because there's some added foul thing dragging down both of them. Understanding that now, Chuck's blue eyes soften even more. "Don't you think, me doing this job for so many years, that I haven't seen and heard all the pathetic and sick and tragic sides of all these people of our little town?"

The thirteen-year-old just stares back at him – with normal teenage suspicion.

"And do you think I'd still be doing it if I didn't really care about everyone?" (Right then Chuck silently hopes this young citizen never hears the full story about the three years of tax-payers' contributions to merely life-support Tom Addison.) "And that I'd still have the confidence of this whole town if I had a big mouth?"

Jack hesitates, then moves the few inches back inside. By the expression on his face, he is capable of conceding if he hears the truth: "He's the kid. He didn't tell me yet, but I'm even more sure."

"But you certainly don't want him hurt...more than he already is," Chuck makes the next correct assumption.

"Yeah," Jack grunts.

Chuck thinks a second, openly eyeing Jack up and down. "Let's keep in mind what the hard possibility is, which is that more good people like Carl and Marg and Jennifer are likely to be hurt, and that some poor young girl – your age..." He doesn't have to finish. He can see by the mix of anger and fear in Jack's expression that his point is already well understood.

"I'm real close," Jack assures him.

"But you're struggling with how it should come out in the open without your new little friend getting the worst of it."

Again, Jackie doesn't answer, indicating agreement.

"And it'll mean everything if it comes straight from him – instead of through you or from me twisting it out of him," the Chief patiently suggests.

Nodding once, Jack clearly understands that. "But it's after he says who it is…"

Instantly, Chuck has two boys in mind. (Tom also flashes through his thoughts, in that if he was here right now he could say to him, "There you go!" – that, if you care, you do end up knowing everything that happens in town that's right to know.)

"I can help there. It's easy," Chief Cintz guarantees him so casually Jack's face reacts with relief.

"He needs it," is all Jack wants to say.

"Then we'll do that – either way it comes out. But the best help for him right now is for you to just be his true friend – which will help me a lot, too."

Jack nods again, and involuntarily smiles a little.

Chuck thinks to ask, "Does your mom know?"

"No…"

"It wouldn't hurt to tell her, Jack. She's a real good woman…I respect her, you know. And talking with her about this whole thing would make it easier for you…to think this through."

Jack is impressed. He never believed anyone in town ever understood his mom, much – even the police chief (who, matter-of-fact, he always wondered was just going through the motions, paid to put on a show like half the world he's seen so far). He doesn't answer, but by the light in his eyes he plainly likes the thought.

"I'm here," Chuck ends, still sternly eyeing Jack, though his sincere easy smile starts to show. "And you know where I live if I'm not here, remember…"

Jack blinks, grins faintly too, then abruptly turns and is gone.

And somehow, Chuck feels, the reassurance of Jack's commitment to help solve the murder is less powerful to him at this moment than the pull to help save another life – or at least the quality of life – of some innocent, scared young boy.

He has to give Jack just a bit more time.

"My mother asked me if it was me who killed Janet," Joseph blurts. (The car had been intensely quiet since it stopped a few minutes ago amid the country blackness, with only the crisp sounds of their yanking out and opening five beer bottles so far initiating tonight's enactment of the late-night rite.)

"What was that noise...did you just say something, Crusher?" Gene taunts, several seconds after his nemesis vocally broke the membrane of darkness. (He's sitting beside Joseph in the back seat again, and his voice already has that "what-did-I-ever-do-to-deserve-this" tone.)

It's Friday night, however, and as has happened before, their youthful intensity plus some likely further neo-adult outrage and wonder have been held unspoken for days. Building up pressure.

"My mother asked me if it was me – "

"He heard you, Joseph," Norm tries to start anew from the driver's seat.

"She what?!" Gene now chooses to accommodate and issues the prescribed response.

"My mother asked me if – "

"I bet," Howard stops him this time by observing, "every mom is thinking that question – and every girlfriend and wife in town, too... So then, Joseph, what was your answer?" he prompts earnestly from the utter pitch of the other back corner (with a mix of disbelief, amusement and suspicion in his voice).

"I told her *you* did it...uh..." Joseph hesitates ominously, "...*Ba-Dee!*"

Ba-Dee, attentive and sippin' away there in the front passenger seat, just burps.

Joseph is quick to react: "No use protesting your innocence up there, Ba...ba...so like, what the fuck is a Ba-Dee, anyway?!" he asks as though asking himself.

"Joseph isn't man enough to do half that much to a girl," Gene suggests nastily.

"I may be warped," Joseph openly allows, "but I'm not ill, depraved, inhuman, evil, contemptible, vile, wicked, bestial, malevolent, satanic – "

"We get it, Crusher," Gene finally stops him.

Outside, a giant sphere has just cleared the black horizon, aglow with the fire of our Sun, tinged amber with the edge of Earth...

"Green cheese," Joseph starts a new one. "Did some of our ancestral stock – adults even! – actually believe the Moon is made of green cheese? Norm?" he queries the one he knows knows.

"Never green cheese," Norm attests. "Because, throughout civilized times, it's been plain to learned persons that our Moon is a remnant of the creation of Earth, a by-product – a gradationally detached lobe of primal planet matter... It's a turd. An Earth turd."

"The Moon is fascinating enough," Howard reflects as he daydreams out the windshield at it, "but what's really unreal is what's beyond it and around it, what we're hangin' in the middle of ... We're on a little ball in the middle of endless space, the infinite..." he leaves it for Joseph because he knows it's gotta be one of his favorite words:

"Abyss..." Joseph sighs deeply, then glugs down a whole beer.

Norm then poses, "Imagine how many people are looking up at the Moon right now, too..."

"Like the witness kid," Howard visualizes someone mysterious, "gazing up there, searching for an answer from the heavens... and the moonlight connects us...we can almost see his image bouncing off it – see who he is..."

"And! – gawkin' at it too, right now! – wherever his is," Joseph adds even more melodramatically, "is the killer! So, drive a little closer to it, Norm, so we can make out the reflection of his heinous face! – bouncing off it from amid all the vast cosmos – from somewhere so very near to us here on Earth..!"

Realistically, Ba-Dee then questions, "You wonder what it all means sometimes – going from people killing people to the real meaning of the huge universe."

"You wonder," Norm seems full of the same curiosity. "And sometimes it feels we're just meaningless little specks, and other times it's like our thoughts – our feeling about a thing, fills all existence..."

"So...why is that?" Joseph asks, as though he's on the brink of learning a Secret of Creation.

Clearly unanswerable, Howard steers away from it and ventures "What I wanna know is, like in the big scheme of things, how much control over another human being should we have been ideally individually given...originally?"

"Like to do what?" Ba-Dee needs an example.

Howard suggests, "Like murder. Why is it allowed – in the scheme of things? Why is it possible to do that? Is it another lesson? And suicide? What cosmic thing does that accomplish?"

"Or why is suicide illegal in some places?" Norm goes further sideways. "Why does a society – a majority of people – believe they have the right to direct someone's life at all, let alone the most personal choices?"

Joseph knows: "The people of Earth have a right to enhance any quality of their world and neighborhoods and lives."

"But then," Howard thinks, "they get pushy, and start imposing their particular beliefs, and then they become territorial, and then start wars over it."

"Wars start over real things," Gene qualifies that.

"Same point," Norm counters. "People make conclusions – that what they do or want is the right thing. Some do it for the sake of everyone, including themselves, some just for their own selfish materialism – the real things, you call them – and they'll fight to the death for it."

"Buut!" Howard whines, "in the big scheme of things, why is there an option in our nature that allows us to even try to control – in fact, compulsively *causes* some people to build fortresses and start wars? Or causes others to jump on someone else and *start fucking and killing them!*"

Joseph mutters, "Good question..."

Norm poses one, too: "If there's other worlds with scholarly, wise beer-sippers out there, and they're sitting in their cars right now under their stars shootin' their particular shit, just what are they talking about? Do they even have war? Or murder?"

"They don't got cars!" Joseph ridicules. "They just walk around carrying their box of beer under their...arms."

"So if they don't have war and murder," Howard inquires while giggling at Joseph, "why do we?"

"Maybe we want it," Ba-Dee offers one of his profound quick observations.

"That's it!" Joseph realizes. "We choose it, even though we're autonomous, undirected partners with a loving God, we can't get wise enough on our own to finally decide that murder is not an Official-Plan-sanctioned death, and that nature's natural horror is not a pattern we have to force ourselves to follow and invent new ways to do – "

"And that maybe we want it," Howard contributes, "because we're bored without conflict – "

"What?!" Gene contests as he tries to draw the line.

"He's right," Norm believes. "Even if it's just in their heads, life has no thrill if there isn't confrontation, for some."

There's a short silence.

"I miss Bug Doug," Joseph confesses.

"What's that got to do with ..?" Gene sounds more confused than impatient.

"He had the ultimate confrontation: his own demons," Joseph sort of explains.

"And," Norm adds, "a society that couldn't fit him in."

"It's more complicated than that," Howard feels, halting in mid-slurp to get in his point. "He had a lifetime of complexities – like everybody, but it overwhelmed him and caved him in. Then because he wanted to be noble and not hurt anyone, he directed it all back into himself – whereas someone else might just simply go out and shoot someone, or maybe start a feud or war...or, he could just *jump on some innocent young person and stab her with his prick and kill her!*"

"Jeez, Howie," Joseph says kindly, "you're really pissed about this – "

"It's just part of the sickness!" Howard rages on. "It's a world race of so many sick attitudes – of territories and religious intolerance! And racism and ego and hate!"

"Attitudes!" Joseph picks up on another good word. "I heard that the leading cause of driving deaths is attitude: people get in their cars with an attitude that they can do anything they want, because it's their little piece of rolling territory, and they certainly know how to handle their own territory! So they speed, or fumble for the cigarette that fell on the floor, and they say, 'I'm fuckin' comin' through! *You* watch out for *me,* or else I might just *accidentally* fuckin' *cream* you!'"

"It's the same thing Howard's saying, then," Norm tries. "The built-in ability to choose extreme individuality."

"And sick is the right word, too," Ba-Dee acknowledges Howard, also. "It's like anything that's counter-happiness and counter-healthy to society is in some small or large degree sick."

"But what degrees of what behaviors are acceptable? And then forgivable?" Norm attempts to pin it down more.

"Not murder," Howard snarls.

"Well, someday there may be a nothing-counter-healthy-society," Norm now projects (and like Ba-Dee, he's unable to find the single word that says it all).

"Someday," Joseph then concludes optimistically, "every individual in our world society may never do anything that needs any degree of forgiveness..."

And for a moment, they all sit in silence imagining heaven.

I t's Saturday morning. Last evening, Chuck and his ol' bud Wilf spent a few hours willingly sacrificing brain cells to beer at the hotel bar, where traditionally, on occasional Friday nights (and lately more frequently) they try to dilute their problems and celebrate their joys.

Patiently waiting out others who kept leaning on the bar beside and between them to just have a few words, or those who kept clumping around to try to engage them in their own drunken good time, they eventually talked about Jackie. Then Tom.

Jackie, Wilf reacted (after some emotional adjectives of both outrage and compassion for the kid and now the considerably less faceless poor witness kid) is the easier one to figure: trust him – however he can still help – he agreed with Chuck. Tom Addison, however, is the real dilemma. It would certainly be understandable, Wilf told his good friend, if the official solution has to end up being dismissal (or at least officially convince Tom to imagine how much happier he'd be elsewhere). Wilf admitted he had always been mostly okay with Tom, but he sure could see some limitations in him over the years, too. Yet he was a little surprised when he heard Tom's latest words of such cold indifference – which made him even more suspicious of the guy, still (and impatient that Tom should "make up his mind about what he really wants to be in life, if anything," he added).

Chuck was not quite so condemning, but he didn't dismiss any possibility, either: "There's nothing to guarantee Tom's innocence," he concluded, a little strangely. ("It's supposed to be innocent until proven guilty," Wilf did remind him.)

Now this morning, having just come in the office ten minutes ago, Chuck has been sitting across from Tom trying not to study him. His assistant is shuffling papers, too, and doesn't seem to be at all self-conscious about yesterday's confrontation. When he's finished his shift later this morning, he will be off for a couple of days (leaving Chuck on duty and on call). The Chief believes he remembers Tom saying he is heading out of town tonight, or maybe tomorrow...

And today is the day Chuck will absolutely open Jackie's envelope – sometime. And late yesterday, the killer's diary came back from Elston's lab, no new clues discovered. (Right now, it's locked in the safe at the bank.)

A few minutes pass by, and Chuck catches himself daydreaming about opening the envelope and reading the witness kid's name, or hearing it from Jack...and soon after, he has the boy finally sitting right there in that chair beside his desk, plainly saying who he saw that night. Chuck then sees himself walking out that door to go arrest the killer (the guy is wearing the little-bull red shirt)...the murderer confesses, he rushes him to Elston City jail, and just that abruptly – with immense relief! – it's all over..!

Equally possible, he reminds himself, is a call any minute of any morning, as likely today as tomorrow, that begins with some frantic words about a missing daughter...

A little while later, from a typical crisis of a barking dog that required a brief investigation two blocks away, and then someone's concern about an unfamiliar parked car on their street (people take that chance, having visitors stay overnight, in these times), Tom returns and writes them up. He then completely clears off his desk, as usual, and stands to leave. But instead of walking out, he moves slowly toward Chuck – who is deep in thought at his desk with his gaze penetrating the papers in his hands.

Hovering tensed-lipped over his boss for a moment, Tom finally speaks. "I was thinking about what you said, and I guess I see what you mean, Chief." Except for his hands clenched behind his back, he's almost standing at attention. His face is stern, his eyes steady, his mustache stiffly trimmed...but now somehow amused, he begins leaking a little smile. "I guess I see where I'm... somehow different. Still, though, I do care, but I suppose not the way I should – or should express, the way it's done in a town like this..."

Chuck stays hunched over his desk, eyebrows raised, watching Tom's blank eyes.

"So, like I said, you're probably right. But that's the way I am, and can't see changing – how can you change your basic character?" At that, Tom grins fully, as though most amused that someone might expect him to apologize for who he is or isn't. "I'm still thinking it over, but I'm leaning toward moving on... applying in Elston, actually, maybe..."

Chuck smiles weakly back, feeling a twinge of friendship (and great sudden relief from twenty-four or so hours of this tension). "I understand," is all he says.

Tom adds, "I'll let you know Monday, something definite... But I'll understand if you decide I'd better go."

"Thanks, Tom," Chuck responds, now leaning back and openly studying him. "Give me until Monday, too," he adds frankly.

"Chuck," Tom then begins again loudly, shifting his weight a bit where he stands, his gaze lowering to the floor, "I heard you were searching my car – my neighbor saw you...I guess these blue uniforms are easy to recognize against a white car, in the middle of the night..." he laughs nervously with that, as though to ease the moment's choking tightness. "Were you...did you really...uh... *suspect* me?"

Chuck doesn't flinch. He stares at Tom while he thinks. Eye-to-eye, he answers, "Yes, I do..."

Tom does not look surprised. Or hurt. He just lets the smile fade from his face, then turns and steps toward the door, straightening his tie as he walks briskly out and along the street.

Immersed in some subsequent sharply reflective thoughts, spent pacing the floor between the two desks (all the while pushing his fingers through his hair over and over as though to stimulate conclusions) Chuck does happen to notice Wilf across the way peering into Lucy's window. A second later, he sees him turn and cross through the heavy Saturday traffic of Main Street, heading for the police office.

Halfway through the doorway, Wilf stops to evaluate his friend treading around. "Exercise period? Or can't find your desk?"

"Come in, dipshit," Chuck says hospitably, taking one more half-threatening step toward him. "Don't stand there in between like you're an intelligent citizen, or something."

"You're just worried how people out here are talkin' – that none of us sane ones ever dare be seen goin' completely inside this here gerbil wheel." Finally getting a smile from Chuck with that one, Wilf strides to the chair beside the Chief's desk and announces as he sits that Beth and Sue are bringing over lunch. "So be good."

"Good," Chuck reacts, and then taking just a few minutes, he fills him in about Tom (ending by reminding him about Jack's envelope – that he'll open it before Tom leaves tonight).

"Good," Wilf concludes.

"Yep, good!" Chuck stands there and spreads his arms a little. "Then objectively I guess it's really been a pretty *good* morning so far. Hope it keeps up..."

nother perfectly warm summer morning, with blue sky blazing and unthreatening clumps of white cloud lazing overhead, this is one of those days kids dream of all winter, the kind they wish could go on forever, when they do finally come.

At the moment, Rick's entire team is wearily spread out in the shade along their bench. Jack and his six players have bunched right in front of their dugout, their dust puffs drifting off in the sunshine. It's close enough to noon to break for lunch (they can go home anytime Saturdays and find someone there to feed them) and Jack's and Rick's taunting and joking around as they came off the field (over which side is more supremely talented) has drawn them all together here before they leave.

Honorably, Jack does relent to a sensible inquiry about the uncertain score, at least: "We couldn't be any fuckin' closer – what is it, Heap?" he asks his snarly center fielder, who is standing slouched barely upright to his left.

"Six-o-*one* to six-o-*two* – for *us!*" Henry shouts it with a scowl and a grin, pleased it's a tough fight at least as much as he is about being still in the lead.

Jack smiles too, and with camaraderie, leans his right elbow up on his first-baseman Kenny's shoulder. He then beams wider at sagging Eddie down there along on the bench. And the Egg

Man smiles back. "So, all you pork-lip petunias," he puts it to Rick and his team, "just 'cause you're always losin', don't give up, okay? 'Cause it's great for us, playin' such dog-butt-sniffin', inferior – "

Over and above the eruption of "cow-nose" and "turd-head" and a few unintelligible rebuttals, a more dignified Rick speaks for his team as he courageously laughs, "Ha! There's lots of summer left, Miss Wiener!"

"No *ka-ka* chance!" Heap Henry leans back roaring, his long and wet blond hair hanging like cooked spaghetti. "We're in permanent control for a day now, and you dildo-dork, scum-eyed anuses are permanent losers!"

Impressed, Jack proudly pats Henry on the back of his once-white shirt – releasing into the air around them a morning full of reckless slides into every dusty base.

But then Rick defiantly declares as he quickly jumps up on the bench amid his boys, "From here on in, *they're* the losers! The loser twinkies – today we overtake the twinkies!" All his players rise, too, and brandishing their gloves high then wagging them in the faces of their lowly rivals in front of them, they begin chanting, "O-vur-take the twink-kies! O-vur-take the twink-kies!"

Leading them in their spirited new battle cry, Rick leaps off the bench and bounces barbarian-like onto and across the diamond, his six hardy lads bobbing and screeching in a line behind him.

Jack and his team stay in front of the dugout watching them, laughing hilariously in the warm noonday sun.

As the tribal war dance ebbs at the rim of the infield, Jack's bunch starts to catch up. In the right-field corner, everyone files out the gate opening, chattering and cursing joyfully.

Boys dissipate in every possible direction, some individually, some in pairs. Jack, Rick and Eddie have clustered in lively conversation, and they make their way, in spurts of bent-over laughter and surges of walking, to Jack's house for lunch.

...

On Main Street, people are strolling up and down, shopping and talking. It's a purely beautiful day, noontime Saturday, with a midsummer sky, soft breezes, and relaxed, easy feel of nothing much to do other than savor the moments. Folks roam unhurried, with storekeepers as small-town as can be: glad to be friendly and joke, at length, with everyone. Little kids clutch weekend-waited small paper bags of gooey candies and chocolate; moms and dads hold their hands and smile, connecting affection. Bigger kids on bikes drink red or orange sodas as they roll along, or hazard the delicious chaos of a sun-dripped ice-cream cone as they ride the wind.

On the pavement, cars ease slowly through the downtown, their drivers not rushed to turn off toward home or head out the highway. It's as though along here is the place to be, to park and get out and walk, with people to bump into and fun things to do and look forward to – a get-together tonight, or tomorrow – and to anticipate...the rest of the week or the rest of summer.

And elderly ladies wear old-favorite flower-print dresses; young women: ragged-cut jeans shorts above sunshine-tanned legs. Old men with canes inch along sidewalks, smiling benevolently and lovingly at everyone – especially at the women with great legs. Young men embrace hardware store bags full of project supplies and longed-for tools, and greet others who played cards with them last night, or who are coming over soon today for the big barbeque – before they all step out to the dance tonight, around sundown. Many of these folks will walk home around Main Street's corners, but will likely be back once or twice more for something they forgot or just for second helpings of the sidewalk summer day.

In front of Lucy's Large Lunch, Julie Grant drifts along slowly in her comfortable old blue jeans and best black T-shirt, proudly pushing her cherished little boy ahead of her in his stroller. He's wearing his huge, white, wide-brim summer hat, and is chirping and flirting at the world delightfully.

On Lucy's bench, Bert, Chase, Shooter and Mel, with Sid and Ed on chairs right across from them near the curb, all grin wide and make dumb faces and wiggle their fingers waving at the cheerful little tyke as he passes. Julie laughs, and is openly spilling over with joy.

"This is my favorite time of all," husky ol' Shooter declares happily as he leans back again on the bench. Watching Julie walk away, and glancing at all the other folks streaming by along the shaded sidewalk, he reasons, "We got this nice day, we got only people watching to do – *that's* ultimately important..." he adds with a dry sort of self-amused undertone. "Daydream, sip good coffee – hey, new round here, somebody..!" he exclaims, peering deep into his empty paper cup before glaring challengingly around at everyone.

"Mel's turn," Bert mutters as he avoids everybody's eyes and starts scratching his frosty beard.

"Bert's," responds frail little Mel.

"My turn," Ed admits unusually quick and calmly good-natured, then pushes his thin frame up and into the restaurant to order the next round.

"Sid!" Chase then erupts, followed by his characteristic wordless pause (calculated, some speculate, to irritate) during which he uses both hands to carefully nestle his years-worn, best red ball cap squarely back onto his thick gray hair. "When you gonna run for mayor!" he states, rather than asks.

"Yeah!" Bert whole-heartedly agrees, his head cranking back and forth watching the world go by. "That jumpy Jimmy Jimms bin at it *way* too long. Time for someone full o' real give-a-shit!"

No one has ever suggested anything even close to this before, so Sid almost falls off his chair. He is especially honored having it come from these wise – though near-petrified – coots. "Uh..."

"Right! Elicited like a master politician, Sid!" Chase recognizes. "Dazzle 'em with your thought processes." (He winks at Sid with assurance he doesn't really mean him.)

"Hey Sid, why don't you go right over there across the street and get signed on with Chuck. He could really use a new gun-slinger," Shooter seriously suggests in his rumbling deep voice. "That stiff-as-a-dick Tom-turkey guy sure never buys us coffee..."

"I already got a job," Sid protests with a grin, his whole pudgy face blushing.

Raising his thick eyebrows, Bert points out, "And everyone knows you don't like it. You're not like Wilf, where you can just love doin' that telephone technical shit. You're a people man, boy! Go see Chuck. We'll all back ya up!"

"There goes any hope there," Sid smirks with resignation, adjusting his well-rounded body on his chair.

"They should let all us old peckers choose the mayor and things," Bert believes. "We've been around here long enough to pick who's best for what."

"You know," Chase then has to say, "you look around here, and you see just how nice a town this really is, all these good folks, tryin' to do their best for themselves and everyone else, too. And it's just too bad there's this one, single, putrid little mind – one person out of all these good ones who's ruinin' it – "

"Oh, it's not ruinin' anything, Chase!" Shooter cautions. "It'll be near the same again – still is, most ways. It's just one of those real nasty dips in the road that a lot of families or communities go through."

"Right," Sid feels the same. "It's not the end of everything, at all..."

Ed comes back out with a tray full of coffees. "What'd I miss?" he asks as he sits on his chair, holding out the tray for the others, some in-between folks walking by.

Sid fills him in: "Some dynamite seventy-year-olds walked by – these here dinosaurs are resetting their pacemakers – "

"We elected a new mayor," Chase corrects him.

"Or hired a new police officer," Shooter adds, nodding respectfully at Sid.

"Him?!" Ed grins, raising his free arm to extend a thumbs-up. "He should actually be made king – Your Roundness, your coffee..."

"Well, 'bout time, low-life!" Sid regally accepts the brimming-hot, brown-liquid offering.

"Let's us coots take over!" Chase then fully envisions Bert's seniority approach to government to a clear conclusion. "We'll rule the town!"

"And shower gold and honey o'er all our good citizens!" (Mel has leanings toward the theatric.) "Then, we purge the evil little murderous *shitball* from our midst!"

"Purge the shitball!" four old guys suddenly chant loudly and straight-faced together, causing several pedestrians to hesitate walking past.

"We'll be pure once more!" Chase proclaims. "We'll be back to a perfect life, with perfect coffee, perfect people – !"

"And guarantee our own particular perfectly ridiculous self-righteous way to live a life!" Sid concludes triumphantly.

And they all rise to their feet and stand tall, saluting their Lucy's mugs and paper cups to the promise of a perfect future!

...

Over in the parking lot beside Nick's Bowl, Howard, Norm and Joseph are dropping Ba-Dee off at work, after a late-morning get-together to help Norm's cousin move. Ba-Dee has a rare six-hour Saturday afternoon shift looming ahead of him (summer weekends are busy – he will have to actually flip some burgers).

All four of them are well settled into the hot seats of the motionless car exactly like they are many Friday and Saturday nights (though now the view out the windows isn't black and there's no background serenade of croonin' crickets). Today, Howard is driving, Ba-Dee is beside him, and Norm and Joseph are in the back. They're waiting for Ba-Dee's starting time, just keeping him company until he has to go in.

"I hear deputy Tom of The Force over there is leaving," Howard reveals.

"He is?!" Norm jolts with disbelief, glancing in the direction of the obscured police office. "How do you know that?"

"He lives upstairs from my neighbor's friend at work, and his wife and Tom's wife are good friends," Howard verifies his sources.

"Hey! – did word get around yet: I had a two-turd shit this morning!" Joseph acknowledges once again the amazingly efficient grapevine of their town.

Grinning wide, Ba-Dee turns half around to observe Joseph while determining, "That's it then: killer-rapist Tom – "

Norm interrupts, "You can't say – "

"He's leaving because," Howard interrupts to fill in details, "the Chucker thinks his brass balls don't connect to his brain – or that, unlike a man, he has none."

"But he's so professional!" Joseph attests. "He's the vanguard who awarded me my littering ticket! Which I – "

"I guess it's something about Tom not being enthusiastic enough." Howard tries to remember exactly how it was said.

"He just doesn't give a damn," Norm figures it. "You can tell – easy! Like when he's over at Lucy's and everyone's talking, you can see he's not interested in what they're saying about anyone around town – or anything at all that affects things here."

"So? Who cares?" Joseph passively recognizes the right of indifference.

"Not in that job!" Norm frowns at Joseph beside him. "In a small town? Where everybody knows everybody else so well?"

"Oh," Joseph sees... "So then he *did* do it, didn't he – *killer-cop Tom – !*"

"Nohh..!" Norm reacts with a moan (though he can't help picture how his anxious fourteen-year-old brother Jeff would be understandably holding back saying the name of a well-enough respected policeman – with a gun).

Joseph crisply hardens his stand: "Why not?"

No one has a ready reason. Or comes up with one.

"Then he's the worst of the fuckin' worst," Howard has to conclude with disgust, glowering out his open window at the visible piece of downtown.

"Wait. No way," Norm now tries to stop mad speculation, and Ba-Dee can't see it either: "Absolutely no way."

"So, we hold off until he's gone and see what happens?" Howard wonders what to do next.

As that image plays out in their minds, all four are briefly speechless...

"It's Looker," Joseph now reestablishes.

"Mel," Norm submits weakly.

"It's Gene," Howard picks on the one member of their group who isn't there.

"Gene's been more of a prick than Officer Tom, lately," Joseph points out.

(And as Joseph is saying that, a tremble of realization shakes Norm: the killer still could be any one of these friends! The thing they have joked about more than once during their back-road nights loosened up with beer may very well be true. And, he connects with icy logic, it could sure be a strong reason why Jeff refuses to tell him what he knows... Norm now feels a little faint.)

"It's that guy out the highway with the cucumbers," Ba-Dee offers another.

"Kuke Duke?" Howard actually says the name of the world-famous, record-setting local cucumber grower, the brand name every easily embarrassed young adult in town despises.

"Yeah... Don't say that name!" Ba-Dee cringes. "No sane person would go on national television and call himself that."

"Or paint his silo to look like a giant cucumber erection!" Joseph roars hardily, as he does whenever it's mentioned or every time he sees it.

"Definitely not the guy. Too much to lose," Norm observes (equilibrium recovered).

"Sure has..." Ba-Dee concludes that one. "Well, time to go work."

With Ba-Dee about to leave, they make their arrangements for tonight, with all five of them to meet as usual at Lucy's after supper, then off to the dance, and then, of course, another night's vigil on the back road: to assure a new dawn.

As Ba-Dee gets out and starts walking away, Joseph mutters from his window at him, "Happy hamburgering."

"Flip fetid farm flesh forthrightly," Howard adds, equally emotionless.

Walking along hearing that, Ba-Dee turns his head back toward them and grins...but then suddenly stops in his tracks. Purposefully, he returns to the car. Leaning through the open window into the passenger front where he was just sitting, he focuses squarely and earnestly at Norm in back, then at Joseph, and then at Howard behind the wheel. Sincerely, gravely, he states, "It wasn't me. I didn't kill her."

A strange, dense reality warps the four dimensions of the car. Three emotion-charged pairs of eyes stare back at Ba-Dee.

"That's right..." Norm acknowledges softly. "We know that, Ba-Dee..." And then he confesses too: "And it wasn't me."

"Wasn't me either." Joseph swears plainly. And the others look directly at him, too, like they did with Norm. It's true, they know.

"Not me either," Howard whispers last, as deathly serious as the others, at this oddest of moments in their lives...

And four names erase off the unwritten master list.

...

All afternoon the ol' boys pilot Lucy's bench through the heart of town...as folks stream in and out via the squeaky screen door beside them...a few stopping and hovering near to hear outrage, or maybe some earthy words of mirth.

Meanwhile, Chief Cintz strolls around the sunny and lively street, wandering into stores just to say hello and talk, then passes by Lucy's bench to threaten multiple arrests. Later, he takes the patrol car for a slow cruise through some back streets, waving at lawn cutters and basketball dribblers alike.

Up the street, Nick's bowl is busy, with all five lanes rumbling plus all twelve stools almost constantly occupied with moms and kids and dads (and Ba-Dee behind the counter searing cow patties furiously). At the edge of town, the Dairy Cone drive-in has been steadily packed with cars. On the ball diamond, the game is raging on, while a block away the school's two small diamonds are alive with clusters of younger players: the larger group, the littlest sluggers, encouraged energetically by two dozen parents, and the older kids in the other game hoping to make it to the big time: to Jack's or Rick's team.

Not far away, a half block out along the street that angles off from the curve on Main, there in the Local Order of the Varmint Hall, the two Saturday night dance employees are setting up the bar, the tables around the hall perimeter, and the three chairs on the stage for Grover Gewh and the members of his nameless band. The doors open at eight.

In his church up past Lucy's on Main Street, Reverend Fisk sits in the closed-in silence of his tiny office, struggling with his sermon. (It's an effort every time, because he tries his best to always follow official church guidelines – to invoke the truths of the Bible – but not make it sound like preaching.) As it is, he inevitably has a good-sized congregation because he makes a point of dedicating much of every Sunday service, sitting at floor level in his favorite old armchair up there in front of everyone, to "shootin' the breeze" – objectively discussing nonpolitical issues of the town, the world, his own, or anyone present. He avoids gossip religiously – things said maliciously or not based on facts – and everyone finds his sessions comforting, fun, inspiring (when he manages to incorporate a timely Bible wisdom) and fitting to the reasons they all like living in a small town.

Toward suppertime, most storeowners are preparing to close at six, and as they roll sale merchandise back inside and crank up awnings, the volume of cars and people along the street is noticeably less. The four old fellows are still holding down Lucy's bench, though each has gone away and come back for one reason or another. (Their Saturday night long-standing tradition is to eat at Lucy's, so the three wives – Chase never married – will be along soon.) Sid is still there, too (his favorite place to be) and Ed has just walked back with his wife from dinner at home (she continues straight inside to talk with all their dance-night friends).

Soon, Wilf and Sue stroll up, dressed for the dance. Both head inside, and Wilf immediately reemerges with a coffee, dragging a wooden chair behind him. "So?" he questions the group with his usual resonant softness. After he sits, he peels the lid off the cup and sips, his easygoing, wise blue eyes blinking from one man to the next as though looking for his answer. In his upscale white T-shirt, faded best jeans and fancy carved boots, he's as casual as you can get, all dressed up. He slowly lowers the paper cup away from his tanned, lean, and patiently-waiting-for-an-answer face.

"So *what?*" Chase responds when their eyes meet.

"So you tail-sniffin' farm dogs been gawkin' at ol' girls all day here, makin' fuckin' nuisances of your lecherous selves... What've you got to say about that?" Wilf asks in their language.

"We're completely in control of everything!" Chase now readily opens up, and they proceed to tell Wilf about their newfound power and official appointments.

A little while later, when most stores are closed and the street is quieter still, Chuck and Beth pull up across the way in the police car. They both head directly over into Lucy's. After a short time inside, Chuck reappears with coffee, steps across to stand beside Wilf at the curb, and with a forced sour look on his face, demands:

"Well?"

Bert reacts: "What is this, information central?" Yet they once again eagerly run through the achievements of their day for the Chief. In recognition, Chuck leans over, shakes Sid's hand and mumbles without expression, "Welcome to the Conglomerate."

Soon, Reverend Fisk wanders down, taking a break from sermon writing, accompanied, as he often is, by Mayor Jimmy. They stand near the end of the bench by the door, hands jammed in sports-jacket pockets – plaid shirts, open collars, no ties...friendly grins.

Up across the street, Howard and Joseph walk through the now nearly empty Nick's Bowl parking lot and stop outside the door, waiting for Ba-Dee to finish work.

Then minutes later, back down at Lucy's bench, everyone is surprised and pleased to see Carl and Margaret driving up. They park across the road and walk straight toward Lucy's, dressed, it seems, for the dance. Marg smiles warmly at all the courteous boys, then slips inside to be with her always-supportive friends. Welcomed with a little flurry of sincere "Hey, Carl" plus friendly nods, Carl joins the circle, but stands a half step behind the Reverend, just quietly listening to everyone else. He looks worn, but at ease.

"Arrest all of us for loitering!" a stern Shooter now surrenders to Chuck.

Eyebrows raised with a glimpse of opportunity, Chuck suggests, "Maybe some of you sorry ol' decrepits would be better off shot..."

The jabs and taunts continue in earnest, and a short while later, Howard, Joseph and Ba-Dee amble down to wait for Norm and Gene. All three file inside for coffee, and file right back out carrying brimming paper cups. They expand the circle near the door.

Though the sun is still gently warm as it lowers close above the buildings across the way, the air feels temperatureless, as ideal as it gets, with a pleasant caress of breezes. In both directions that the main highway wanders, summit clouds majestically tower into the deepening, sightless, breathless blue. Some gulls try to scale them, and the winds press them slowly on...

Still shading the street down the way, the big maples now gradually turn darker green. Sparrows spurt in and out of them, and flutter daringly to the sidewalk below, always in little flocks, then instantly sweep up, as though they're one creature, off to other worries.

Here where the two main roads meet at the light, there is a tantalizing aroma of cooking drifting out of Lucy's, so that even those who have eaten feel a little hungry again, if they're anywhere near. From inside each of the few cars that coast by or stop for the light, people gaze out at the gathering on the sidewalk and wave, or just smile friendly smiles.

Soon, Norm walks around the corner beside Lucy's, coming from home with his brother Jeff. Norm crosses through the circle to stand with Ba-Dee, Howard and Joseph, where all four will wait a few minutes more for Gene, tonight's driver. Jeff, on his way to Nick's Bowl to meet friends, stays at the opposite side of the still growing ring of people.

Just then, down at the curve in the highway at the end of the business section, Looker appears. Norm and a couple of others see him, but think nothing of it at all.

Looker is walking his usual steady pace, fit as ever, in his snug T-shirt and light-blue jeans. From a distance, the strength in his face is easily visible, and noticeable too: his dignified stride. As always, you can see he focuses on things around him as though fascinated, and with no apparent concern that he's approaching a sidewalk full of folks straight ahead.

When Chuck follows the others' glances down along the walk, he's glad to see Looker out again. He's noticed him around only once (briefly, Tuesday) since they discovered that newest evidence last Sunday along the back road... He would dearly like to buy Looker a coffee – at least.

A minute later, as Looker reaches the far end of the next block, Jackie rolls fast around the corner that Norm and Jeff just appeared, and slams on the brakes of his beat-up bike, squealing to a hard stop. (The ballgame often ends early Saturday evenings, with some parents going out to the dance.) As always, Jack looks mean, characteristically. He inches in closer to the group so he can hear, holding up right beside Jeff. Chuck studies his black eyes briefly...then is stunned to see – seconds behind Jack – young Eddie Ogden zip around the corner, too – alone – and Eddie pulls his bike up straight beside Jack, and Jack doesn't object – not a single curse or sour facial expression whatsoever... The Chief just stands there gaping...though he does think to check the Ogden kid's shoe size...looks just right...

"Being in charge," Chase and his ol' buddies are still administrating their kingdom, "we declare more Saturdays in the week."

"And more summer!" Bert adds authoritatively. "We need more fuckin' summer!"

Doing his dark side thing, Ed grumbles, "You'd just get spoiled ugly."

"They aren't already?" Wilf huffs. "These nothing-but-free-time crustaceans have it too good as it is! If they ran the place – "

"They do," Mayor Jimms moans (with a wide grin).

"Then shoot 'em, Chuck!" Ed flings his hands in the air like it's just entirely hopeless.

But Chuck is only barely listening (though he catches Ed's skillful anguish and laughs along with the others). The one he's watching...is Looker – who has now slowed his pace just as he is about to cross 93 Sideroad and reach the gathering. What Chuck has noticed is Looker's gray eyes – which are fixed with unusual rigidity on something up Main Street the other way. Chuck turns...and sees a white car easing out from the next street up... and it's heading this way...then seems to slow as though intending to pull up here in front of Lucy's.

Then as the car does brake to a stop right in front of them, Chuck takes a glimpse at Looker again – and sees he is wide-eyed and clearly alarmed! – and has come to a standstill there between Jeff and Jack...

Most in the group stare puzzled at Looker – who is now actually present among them..! The two or three others standing there not quite so amazed are trying to see, over the car roof or through its sun-glinted windshield, who is about to get out...

But while the car sits there still idling for a second, Chuck – involuntarily – gasps. What he has just noticed, through the passenger-side window right below him, is a little stack of restaurant napkins on the seat – "Lucy's" printed boldly on the corners...

The car shuts off.

Coffee cup now dangling at his side, standing stiffly straight from leaning on the back of Wilf's chair, Chuck angles a brief glare of foreboding down at his friend – and Wilf readily catches the intensity in his eyes.

In the next instant, as he hears the car door open, Chuck just glimpses Jeff stumbling back toward the bench, bumping into Mel. Jeff's eyes are wide and frozen on the driver, too...

And Eddie, Chuck sees in the same quick glance, is suddenly pale white and whispering – quivering – to Jack...

Then it explodes:

"It's him!" Jack screams. *"It's the guy – the killer!"* He drops his bike and lunges to grab hold of Chuck.

Eddie bursts too – now that it's out: *"It's him! It's him!"* His finger stabs the air over and over, pointing frantically at the car.

As Chuck twists back around toward the street and the driver standing there, his eyes lock first – with heart-stopping shock – on the red shirt...with a pocket...and its small crest: a charging bull!

But unlike Eddie and Jack, it takes a fraction of a second – once his eyes rise to the face above the red shirt – a face now drained of color and terrified, too – for any words to come to Chuck's lips...to find the name that fits the face and force it out of his mouth...

Finally, fatefully, conclusively, he does:

"Gene..!"

EPILOGUE

U nable to bear all the memories, Carl, Margaret and Jennifer decided, near the end of summer, to move to Elston City. They return often to visit friends.

Also at the end of summer, Ba-Dee broke a leg and some ribs in a serious accident (while running an errand for Nick in his "Fast Lanes" truck, one Saturday) and was lucky he survived at all. The crash wasn't his fault. Mercifully, he lost his job.

And Tom Addison left town for a junior patrol position in Elston. He offered no parting apologies to anyone, and no one apologized to him. About two months later, Chuck went out of his way to visit him on duty there, and was (for the most part) glad he did. It was friendly.

At Lucy's bench, the town meetings continued faithfully – and peaked to reassuring new heights of outrageousness (with everyone feeling suddenly so much more positive). Comfortingly, the same reliable faces appeared there over and over (though they began transplanting their sit-fests more and more inside, like always, since cooler weather intruded). As it turned out, neither Bert, Mel, Shooter or Chase – or even Sid – became king.

In early fall, Julie Grant won a few thousand dollars in a lottery. She did not buy L'le Bug a chopper. She did, however, have his dad's favorite old black leather jacket repaired and relined for him (for someday) and had the silver studs that spelled "Doug" on the pocket flap changed to "Bug Doug".

And as the days passed, Jack and Eddie stayed friends. It took some time, but Chuck (in a manner of speaking) persuaded Eddie's hopelessly abusive father to permanently leave town, and then found help for his (relieved) mother to learn to be a better parent. It wasn't perfect; others besides Jack helped. Yet, relatively, Eddie became deliriously happy. Which made Jack proud, and happy, too.

In the fall municipal election, to everyone's surprise, Mayor Jimmy Jimms stepped aside. Though he retired, he still works hard with Reverend Fisk on all kinds of new church projects. Even more sensational (as in the "wonderful" meaning of the word) Wilf's wife Sue was elected as the new mayor – by a landslide!

And Sid, as envisioned, soon quit his job to become Chuck's assistant. Chuck couldn't be more pleased with his new officer; Sid couldn't be more content.

Of course, the Saturday night dances continued. (The one on the night of Gene's unmasking was a real our-town-is-saved, tension-bust blast!) Grover Gewh, however, has yet to buy another round.

Sadly, Beth and Chuck's old dog Quadruped died. That same cool and quiet night, in the darkest of early morning hours, alone in the police car, Chief Chuck drove slowly down the length of Main Street with ol' Quad laid out flat on the hood. Smiling, Chuck cried. Next morning, when he told Beth what he had done – "carried out Quad's last wish" – she just melted. A week later, someone gave them a puppy.

In the end, though Rick's boys had been basking in the lead for more than a week, Heap Henry won the summer-long game for Jack's team with a grand-slam home run on the very last day before school. (Looker watched.) Henry subsequently bought everyone ice cream. The next evening, right after school, the post-season game began in earnest.

And, one warm and relaxed autumn weekday, as he sat alone in his office, Chuck was surprised to glance up from his paperwork to see Looker coming right inside the door! He walked straight across to the front of his desk – perceptibly smiled! – then placed a rather thick hardcover book down on the papers in front of the Chief. And of all possible things (Chuck was so thrilled to see!) it was *his* book – Looker's first published book of poems! –written, it said on the cover, by "Looker" (Chuck laughed) and was dedicated simply to "My town"...

Since then, Looker has become a huge local hero, and was the next nominee for king.

...

On an air-sweet cool weekend night, the last before they all leave for college, Norm, Ba-Dee, Howard and Joseph are parked at their accustomed place along the blackened country road. Beers have popped open. The windshield has fogged a little. And out the side windows the stars glimmer brilliantly down on them from all around our profound cosmos.

"Dungwad fucker," Howard at the wheel vents yet again at the thought of Janet's murderer sitting right here in the back seat of his car – sitting there lying through his teeth and playing his insanely sick role of someone with a speck of genuine concern...

"Why didn't we see it?!" Ba-Dee laments for the fifth session in a row, said trying to reposition his leg and its plaster cast in the front seat.

"*Gene..!*" Norm sighs with enough ongoing disbelief for everyone.

And Joseph beside him in the back burps repulsively.

After their recurring feelings of outrage over their ex-friend Gene settles, Howard announces:

"I'm coming back."

"As a woman?" Joseph thinks reincarnation.

"To live in this town...asshole-face..." Howard groans, though smiling.

"Here? This place?!" Joseph struggles with the concept. Then glugs lots of beer. (They've never really talked much about life after college...evidently, Joseph believes in the outside world more.)

"Not this *place*. These *people*," Howard corrects. "A town is *people!*"

"This one produced a murderer," Ba-Dee cautions.

Howard reminds them, "No it didn't. Gene moved here a few years ago – "

"Hah! He's moved out now!" Joseph huffs with a bottle tipped at his lips – spraying beer all over his legs – recalling the parade of police cars and the prison van that came to help Gene on moving day.

"Where's better?" Howard now poses. "The city? The tundra?"

"Lookerville!" Joseph exclaims. "Here at the heart of the country!"

"Nohhh!" Howard whines another rejection. "It's *your* heart that matters, not what appears inviting or where the opportunities seem to be. The big thing is where *you* feel at home...with people. To make a life...and do some good together, or something..."

"It's really something," Norm interjects, "how everyone was there that night – like Jeff, him knowing it was Gene bothering girls on the street..."

"And that Ogden kid!" Ba-Dee laughs with unending delight. "The clincher kid!"

Then Howard recalls, "Remember what Gene said about humans lying? – that our world is so complicated because of our ability to lie, like it's God's big mistake with us, or something!"

"How ironic..." Joseph sums that one up.

And Howard still can't understand: "Why the fuck did he wear that red shirt?"

"Didn't know he snagged that thread," Norm insists why.

"And the diary! What an idiot!" Howard giggles with utter dislike. "Like he didn't see his mother was going to clear stuff out to paint the whole place!"

Ba-Dee then summarizes: "Well, everything sure came together in the end, thankfully."

"That's what he means," Joseph observes.

"What?" Howard reacts (not at all indignant like Gene used to get).

"That's what you mean, Howie: The town fixed itself. And that's what you like about it."

Yet with keen comprehension, Ba-Dee all-inclusively grasps, "But that's gotta be possible anywhere – or in any neighborhood... you would think..."

I t's another back-road night, some time later.

"So..." (here comes Norm, again) "if God is the energy of every atom – and there's billions of atoms in, uh...say, in this beer, alone – and I read one physicist estimated ten to the eighty-ninth atoms in the known universe – what we can see so far – "

"What's your fuckin' point?" Joseph can't stand the suspense.

"And that's just the physical stuff – "

"Let alone the untold energy of universal consciousness and emotions," Howard carries it for a bit. (He and Norm must have run through this one before.)

"So what exactly-the-fuck is the point..?!"

"That God," Norm theorizes, "is not some bearded human guy with big neurons. God – *God's not a he!* – God is the energy of every concept and action including intelligence...except that maybe our own self-motivated aspect of intelligence is the one force we're sort of allowed to completely...self-direct – so *God* is the intelligence of everything..."

"Intelligence of *things?*" Wilf contests from the back corner.

"Yeah. Like how do atoms know how to act – behave – so exactly for eons?" Norm explains with a question to one of their two highly honored guests.

"But they decay," Chuck knows some elementary physics. (Squeezed into the other back corner, he awkwardly takes another sip of beer.)

"Decay into other particles or energies – infinitely," Norm steers clear.

"But why..?" Howard now wants answers.

"Why does anything change?" Ba-Dee jumps in. "Why do we? Life changes constantly...then death..."

"Terminally passing time," Joseph rumbles his grim view.

"But that's it!" Howard glimpses (skipping over Joseph). "It's the evolving thing! Nothing would evolve – intelligence and learning – if it wasn't for change and...and..."

"Built-in expiration?" Wilf suggests.

"Right..! So..." Norm starts a conclusion, "how does Janet's birth and short life then death fit into the huge – *expansive* complexity of the immense universe and its vast energies and knowledge – ?"

Joseph stops him again: "We get it, Norm. There's no human adjectives for what you're raving about."

There's a pause.

Which Chuck ends: "Every moment of every life is profound..."

"And every moment of any form of life," Wilf adds, "is...maybe on some cosmic, sitting-in-the-car-having-a-beer-and-talking-with-God level...infinitely meaningful."

Howard agrees: "Right. So then everything is all right in everything that happens...because it just 'is'..."

"Right," Chuck follows. "And our lives and moments and people in our town are doing exactly okay,"

"Right," Ba-Dee rides the consensus.

"And – as Chuck and us wise old dogs finish our turns first, then you warped young mutts get your chance – we just simply keep continually going on from here," Wilf sees.

"As best we can," Ba-Dee understands.

"To be better all the time," Joseph hopes.

"Maybe," Norm adds, "to make a better overall humanity, too."

"I guess so our lives might have real meaning, then," Howard feels.

And it's Chuck who finalizes: "And so we can see some meaning for us in Janet's life – as if, in a way, she lived and died for our sake, too."

Looker

Commonality II

"**F**ucker..!"

No one heard. The restaurant is quiet, but no one heard Mike's muttered condemnation. He sits and glares – challenging him: the compelling tranquility, the inviting years-layered mystery of this calm and comfortable interior.

Beside him, the soft glow pressing through the pleated silk shade of the little sconce warms the booth, and illuminates his scowl. The wall fixture's deep brass glimmers elegantly in its own light, and the polished grains of the rich wood panels and mold-ings at his shoulder...absorb his mid-teens heat.

He's the only one sitting in the side booths, this afternoon. Two of the five back ones, though, hold one person each – both businesswomen, each sipping coffee and reading, unaware.

With its pleasantly dimmed light, this large room is embracing, peaceful, an attractive blend of the deep-green fabric of its plush benches, carved wood posts between, and topping the backrests: glass panels etched with arrays of frosty vines and fruits. Over-head, silhouetted against a preserved tin ceiling (a pale peach now, coating a hammered pattern with character), twin rows of dark-stained paddle fans silently, gently, propel the air. The side and back walls are papered with images of lacey wildflowers and meadow grass, all seeming to nod with breezes; a thick fiber carpet spans the open floor to the old waxed hardwood. And all along those slats, the long counter stands braced by twenty-five stools – ornate brass and moss-hued fabric cushions... Two are occupied: ol' Bert and equally-so Mel sit side-by-side on the first and second ones nearest the white marble cashier's counter.

Behind the lustrous, thick oak bar and that long, precisely anchored row of high swivel stools – behind the burnished aged surface and its uniformly spaced clusters of old glass saltshakers and handmade napkin holders (full of white paper folds monogrammed with simple yet bold black letters on their corners) is a dazzling exhibit of glimmering decanters, vintage bottles, and curious antique kitchen and restaurant gadgets arrayed all across the crafted brass and wood wall of shelves. And amid a few adjacent segments that display some compelling framed sketches and simple paintings by locals (hobbyists), a special small section at their midpoint has been recently (last year) cleared for the much-praised creative work by the current local legend: "My Town" – a first-work book of poetry by the always enigmatic yet so-well-admired town son of eleven years – the otherwise nameless, the ever-silent and (clearly) astutely observant guy-hunk everyone has always just called: Looker. This copy, Looker's gift (still unautographed) – burgundy hardcover with simple, silvered lettering – reclines propped open at the title poem.

Suspended over the bar, a disciplined row of eight pastel-glass pendant light fixtures – not Tiffany reproductions, but domes of delicate flowing shapes and colors (designed by regional artisans, craftsmen) – softly brightens the countertop. Across the front, extending from the double-door entrance foyer: a dark green café curtain on a thick black rod and its crisp, bright window and its Wednesday afternoon, early summer sunshine-flooded Main Street. Beyond is the little park across the way, plus the town's only stoplight, and as well, still here on the sidewalk just under this window is the original wooden bench set in place on opening day, thirty-some years ago. And fastened flat on the brick high above it, in plain white with bold black letters, the sign declaring this as the one and only true location of the county-wide favorite: LUCY'S LARGE LUNCH.

Back inside, behind the counter, standing on duty alone (for the moment, at this traditionally quiet time of a weekday afternoon) with arms crossed below a wide grin, and joking with the two senior patron-friends, is the innkeeper of this town's contentment – the globe-traveled native child come back home so long ago (to spice this rurality with world culinary fare) – the admired, the enjoyed, the profoundly hospitable, wise and generous Lucy. He's like a father.

Lucy has glanced repeatedly at Mike back there, and with his ever-smiling blue eyes has noticed the young man's moving lips and angry stare (a glare hot enough to make that glass of cola in front of him boil, Lucy thinks). But, drying his strong hands on his spotless green waist apron as he half-listens to ol' Mel and Bert, he knows to think little of it – because, through all the years of standing here watching, or serving tables for one or twelve, or sitting down over coffee talking with a single patron or any group of them – all kinds of folks, in this town – his only customers who have ever sat here alone muttering to themselves, he well recalls, have been teenagers.

U p the street, Nick's Bowl is deserted. Except for Ba-Dee. And his buds.

And right now, Joseph is once again about to respond with a question to his truly-miserable-working-here-again husky friend's grumbling there behind the bowling alley's twelve-stool lunch counter:

"Ba-Dee...who fucking cares?"

"Not you, obviously," full-faced Ba-Dee quantifies Joseph's repeating position of indifference (though plainly, Joseph has not the pluck to not really care, and has not yet been able to summon that rigid back-away-from-caring fortitude ever since he quit his journalism courses at midterm and came crawling home to waste his days away steaming in failure). All Ba-Dee had hoped to hear – unlike Joseph's latest attempted broad determination – was some genuine sympathy for his own mindlessness at agreeing to take this "hamburger-flippin', milk-shake mixin' bowling-ball-thunderin' fuckin' job" again this year – "I'm a total idiot."

Beside Joseph, two stools away, Norm sits thinking about something else. And on the other side of Joseph, three stools down, hunches Howard, thinking about something else altogether. (It's like, just returned from scraping through another year at school, they're back on safe ground and free to feel the shock of everything out there.)

"What if there's nothing..?" Howard begins one, asking only the air he's staring at.

"Who cares?"

"What if there's just nothing? Only black emptiness – less than sleep?! You live all your life, then: *zero!* Isn't this all pretty fucking pointless then?! *What's the fucking point?!*" (Howard's locked eyeballs are now glassed over, and his pointed face has turned red with real rage.) "Then what difference does *anything* make – ?!"

"Howie, snap out of it," Ba-Dee has to wearily tell him for the third time this afternoon. "Drop philosophy next year."

"Oh. Okay," Howard does get a grip. "Hee," he adds one monotone syllable of self-deprecating laughter.

"You care," Norm in turn also returns to this reality and confronts Joseph.

"No I don't."

Ba-Dee poses, "You wouldn't even be sitting here if you didn't."

"That's different," Joseph argues.

"Different than what?" Norm questions.

"Than that."

"Than who cares?" Howard tries.

"Precisely..." Joseph trails.

"Precisely what?" Norm probes.

"Precisely who cares?" Joseph reestablishes. (He couldn't be more serious.)

"Oh! Maybe he means who in general cares about anything..." Ba-Dee theorizes about Joseph much better by pretending Joseph isn't there. (It would be nice, so early in this summer, to find a solution to Joseph's incessant infantile riddle.)

"So what's gonna happen this summer?" Norm now wants to talk about something else besides the great big questions.

"Last summer was too much," Howard moans, recalling the rape and murder of poor young Janet and all the climactic focus of guilt put on their (born and raised elsewhere) very own ex-friend Gene – now permanently locked out of their circle.

"Not a single thing happened here all winter," Joseph attests. "No one died, was born, got married, opened a business, went bankrupt, flew a kite, shit a brick – "

"Okay, okay, dork-o! We hear you," Howard pleads.

"Does anything have to happen?" (Norm has had enough happenings, with his younger brother Jeff still suffering the defiling and death of his girlfriend Janet and he himself still reliving the trauma of a murderer in their midst all those black nights braved with beer down their sharpened-consciousness country road.) "Let's go for just good times – the dances, those mellow few beers, jus' shootin' the shit like before... Isn't that enough – ?"

"Something's gonna happen," Joseph interrupts to cryptically announce in his deepest ominous tone, stroking his scrubby mustache with a big finger.

"Why?" little Howard spins on his stool, his expression challenging the ridiculous. "Because you want it to, O Master of Gloom?"

"Or," Ba-Dee scowls, thick arms bracing the counter in front of Joseph, "because you're gonna cause it!"

"No...because..." Joseph's fuzzy gaze behind black-rimmed thick glasses narrows with warning, "because the time is right – it's the perfect time for it...it's least expected – at this time..."

"This time?" someone queries.

"This perfect time!" Joseph rumbles.

"*Perfect* time?" Howard bites.

"When nobody cares!"

On the street, traffic is thick, and every parking place along the three-block business section is taken. (Shoppers have responded enthusiastically to the yanking out of all parking meters. And so have the businesses, which now maintain profits and of course pay taxes and are that much less likely to go under and turn this into a ghost town with everyone driving to the malls in Elston City ten miles away! – thanks to the sensible quick work of Sue Granger, with a little help from husband Wilf, new mayor as of last year.) Up and down the sidewalks on both sides, quite a few people wander in and out of the stores and, in turn, the late afternoon warm June sunshine.

Standing there at his favorite spot at his police office window, Chief Chuck Cintz watches up and down the street. Up the way, he sees Reverend Fisk trimming the shrubs around his church; almost straight across, Ben Williams Jr. has been out front of his hardware store talking to Mrs. Gant for an hour (though they're next-door-neighbors on Mill Street). And one building down from them, with only a slight angling of Chuck's eyes to his left, he sees no one sitting on Lucy's bench. Yet.

Further down toward the curve at the end of the business section, Chief Chuck half expects to see Looker pacing along on one of his random excursions...but he isn't there. Yet. He does spot Jack and Rick with Eddie Ogden racing away on their bikes, ball gloves flapping on handlebars, on their way to the old ball diamond and their pre-season after-school weeks-long game – spring training for their annual summer-long game.

Seeing Eddie, the events of last summer now roll through Chuck's thoughts again – Gene the murderer identified right over there in front of Lucy's by young Eddie Ogden and Norm's brother Jeff – and even by Looker's expression. And Gene wearing that incriminating red shirt, and almost not needing to confess his guilt five minutes later in the police office after nearly fainting with doom's realization there by his car at that curb..!

And not long after that all ended: Looker revealed as the local poet – suddenly renowned! "Ha! Looker!" Chuck now blurts aloud with delight (only afterward aware that his new assistant Sid isn't sitting there on duty at his desk behind him). Looker... the surprising town mystery, now *the* illustrious young man of words...

Gazing back up the bright, busy street, he sees his senior-teen new buds (from last year) Norm and Howard walking slowly along, discussing some deep college thing, he supposes, as they head for Lucy's. That other one – that Ba-Dee – must have started his summer job today at Nick's, he assumes... And here he asks himself again: Just what in the name of normalcy is a "Ba-Dee", anyway? Also, conspicuously – worrisomely – absent is that tall, cantankerous, hangin-'round-town-all-winter guy, Joseph Welt.

...

Norm and Howard choose a back booth. Lucy is cheerfully pouring the coffee they requested as they greeted him at the cash counter. Bert and Mel had nodded hello (their clique always acknowledges everyone they see, sometimes merrily, sometimes offensively) and got nodded back. Sixteen-year-old Mike in that side booth, however, kept glaring at the core of the Earth.

"Hey, Mike," Howard turns and tries to budge him with a little friendliness before he takes a seat facing away. But twenty feet across the uncluttered carpet, the strong-featured teenager with the zipped blond hair remains rigidly self-gripped...He fails to respond.

Howard blankly eyes Norm as he sits. He then leans out of their booth, twists around and tries again: *"Hey fuckhead Mike Watson right there..!"* he practically shouts. (Lucy looks, his muscular short frame and little potbelly tightening a bit with concern, forgetting for the moment that the two women who were sitting back there both left.)

Now Mike forces his eyeballs around without turning his head, but they won't rotate back the needed one hundred and forty degrees.

"What's this?" Norm sits pointing gun-like at Mike as he queries the air, puzzled by such unfriendliness. (Not that Mike's a bud, or anything. It's just that every person in town knows everyone else and everybody speaks to anyone. Plus Mike is a sometimes-friend of Norm's brother Jeff, so they've talked.)

Mike is now back to melting the ice in his cola with his stare, and his right hand relentlessly clutches the tall glass of black liquid. His charcoal T-shirt seems a little damp at the pits. His jaw muscles flex repeatedly, just visibly in this light.

"Maybe him and Joseph are teaming up?" Howard poses an indifference insurrection theory.

Norm shrugs. "Could be...let's talk to him."

"No way!" Howard reacts, feeling slighted by the kid. Instead, he morbidly resurrects his contemplations of death's anguish begun an hour ago at Nick's Bowl – which was ultimately ended by Ba-Dee whacking him with a burger flipper to get him to shut up or leave.

So as Howard rattles on with his deep soliloquy, Norm studies Mike. The boy looks seized, he thinks. He sees the tension in his whole body, and the only thing he's noticed moving – except for the odd spasm – are his twitching lips. (What puzzles Norm even more is that his own brother Jeff has never mentioned any peculiarities about Mike or his friends or the Watson family, something Jeff would be quick to spill because he always likes to share how he finds people so hilarious.) His dirty, beat-up sneakers are flat on the floor, and his legs in those worn jeans are spread wide, as though bracing for the upcoming blastoff. Mike's thin, white arms aren't flexing, either, and his brown-specked eyes don't blink.

Lucy serves their coffee, and talks with them a minute about college – somewhat uplifting Howard's spirit with a mere few positive words. (Lucy has an upbeat way with everyone, being so considerate and understanding.) When Lucy returns to his counter, Howard starts off on some long anti-argument to his own vision of gloom. When they finish their coffee fifteen minutes later, Norm decides to stay and talk with Mike – Howard has things to do, anyway.

Mike Watson, in the meanwhile, still hasn't budged. His ice is melted (and Norm wonders if cola, when irradiated, turns sour). As Norm sits tight, alone in his booth, he considers whether he really wants to talk with Mike. He feels kind of obligated, because he knows him a bit, but also feels he is about to be pulled into something – as in something as heavy as last summer's too-human tangle of feelings for murderer and victim. Spinning his empty white coffee mug with both hands, his eyes shift back and forth from it to Mike. He frowns his high forehead, and forcefully combs his fingers through his thin brown hair. In the dim light, his hazel eyes strain with his observing – with indecision – and his long fingers keep twirling the mug faster... Then abruptly, impulsively, he stands, noiselessly crosses the carpet, and plops opposite Mike.

Who still doesn't crack.

"So, Mike...what's up?" Norm tries the direct tact.

"Fucker..." Mike re-alleges.

Norm quickly now, at least, grasps that it's something *out there,* and obviously it's a who. "You okay?" he genuinely sympathizes. And in the beams from the little wall fixture, he can see the red strain around Mike's eyes – whether from crying or seething, it means the same.

Mike's thin lips are still shut tight, his fierce glare still locked on images in his mind (their meaning he so clearly needs to re-solve) when suddenly – like an Earth-shattering quake in the midst of such rigidity – his eyes flick straight up at Norm's as he releases his grip on the cola glass in order to form a very tight fist to emphasize: *"I'll get him – !"*

Instantly, Joseph is standing beside the booth. As tall and solid as he is, he had entered silently and lumbered unnoticed back here to stop right beside Norm. Across a span of Joseph's forehead, just above a thick eyeglass lens, is a distinct pink welt, one side of it a straight edge.

"Ba-Dee whacked me with his burger flipper," Joseph testifies clearly, as though to the investigating officer.

"You wouldn't shut up about who cares," Norm can readily guess, peering up at his sorely persecuted friend, trying not to grin – easier to do after this frustrating interruption right here at the brink of hearing who Mike is gonna "get".

"Well, it was an accident," Joseph flatly admits the truth about the assault (Ba-Dee's grip slipped) as his eyes fix on the bare sec-tion of seat beside Norm...

Norm relents and slides over. Joseph sits with a thud. Poking back his glasses, he then pushes up the sleeves of his green spring jacket as he fixes on the teenaged pillar of rage four feet across the table.

"So...Mike!" Joseph sternly puts it to him right off with that tone of admonishing older brother (though he barely knows him – though they're close neighbors): *"Who cares?!"*

Of course Mike springs to his feet and leaves, neglecting to pay Lucy as he forcefully strides his five-foot-six body speedily out the squeaky screen door.

"Waytago, dipshit," Norm eyes Joseph, sliding his cold coffee mug and himself more into the corner...conscious that he's now one of two guys sharing one bench of a booth.

"I started a story," Joseph doesn't care, "about scientists who discovered how to control time, so all Earth voted to have time stand still..." (Norm has heard many of literary Joseph's false starts at serious writing.) "The problem was, it isolated Earth from everything else outside. So with the last frontier closed off – space exploration and even all types of astronomy were naturally closed off now – people lost their fascination with life – lost their sense of discovery, their hope in their search for answers, answers to profound human-nature questions, like..." (He doesn't have to say it. Norm now sees where his big question came from.) "So, what's *his* problem?" he then without gesture promptly jumps to Mike's quandary instead.

Without repeating what the mid-teen said, Norm just pushes Joseph out off the seat to go sit on the other side, then waves at Lucy to please bring over two mugs of coffee before responding, "Dink! We may never know, now!" (Adding to himself: "Until 'it' happens".)

...

Sometime after Chief Chuck Cintz saw young Mike Watson pace briskly away from Lucy's across the street, he watches old Bert and Mel swing open the restaurant screen door then sit in the bright sunshine of the bench, each senior precariously balancing a brimming "Lucy's" monogrammed white mug of steaming coffee. Moments later (still standing at his office window surveying his town, like he has been for the last half hour) he sees his shaggy-blond-haired assistant Officer Sid Seed appear around that same opposite corner (arriving for his shift two hours early, as he often does) then slip into Lucy's, and then step right back out to plop his hefty blue-uniformed (no tie) body onto the remaining bare stretch of bench the ol' boys allowed.

Chuck rakes his fingers once through his ever-graying hair... thinking only about how peaceful his community jurisdiction has been this year, with all these good people seeing to it. A few minutes later, slim Ed Donald stops his little car in front and effortlessly eases himself out to join the group, followed soon after by ol' Chase strolling up, and then by Reverend Fisk with ex-mayor Jimmy Jimms, out for a bit of a walk down Main Street together.

And Chuck can't resist. Heading out through his always-opened office doorway into the warm sunshine of a cloud-patched sky, the Police Chief wades through the softly rolling traffic of the street, steps inside Lucy's for a coffee plus wooden chair, and reemerges to park his own blue-uniformed (no tie) and slightly plump self at the curb, filling in the gathering.

"Individualism," Ed is saying, also there by the curb, his lean face and dark eyes adding to his dramatic point, "leads to the ruin of every ruined society."

"That's Commie shit!" Bert huffs, tugging fretfully on his snow-white beard as he raises high both equally white eyebrows above his glare at Ed.

"That's not what I mean..." Ed frowns down at the sidewalk, rattled at being called such a thing as a Communist. His rail of an arm raises his paper cup to his lips, and he furrows all his forehead up to his thinning scalp as though desperately lost for corrective words.

Sid edges in. "He means greed – with money being...that thing about evil," he blushes, again, as always, a little self-conscious.

Reverend Fisk forcefully suggests, "It's the blind pursuit that's the root of negative –"

"Yeah!" Ed brightens. "I meant pursuing – when people pursue things full-force or...you know..."

"Obsessively. With an agenda," Chuck suggests a couple of characteristics.

"Right," Ed agrees, smiling weakly at passing pedestrians and then at Chuck beside him at the curb. "Agenda's a good one. Like when someone has a game plan – I mean a heartless game plan for their life...say, like, to obsessively be a millionaire..."

"There's nothing wrong with financial success," Reverend Fisk is quick to adjust the course of this. "Prosperity is healthy – it can help the whole world."

"But," Chuck leans his chair back a bit, questioning gaze circling the little group, "it's how you balance it that makes you human or inhuman."

"Balance?" Sid questions his boss, innocent as ever.

"Yeah, like if getting your success is all self-centered and hurts others, as opposed to doing your fair share for your community and helping friends in need."

"You don't even have to do anything," Chase pushes up his old red ball cap and taps back his bifocals in one motion. "You don't have to give it all away to charity, or anything. The only important thing is how you treat people."

"Right!" Ed now feels understood. "So if you're too individual, you're hurtful to others..."

"Or indifferent," adds little frail Mel.

"Or greedy – at others' expense," Sid sees.

Reverend Fisk pokes tall Jimmy Jimms, as though instinctively knowing Jimmy has something he needs to say here:

"Which can't possibly be the real purpose of life," Jimmy contributes. "Material things can't be more important than people...in life." (Said as a kind of confession, Jimmy Jimms here again feels his own murderous guilt of just that, from twenty-some years ago in a distant but never-forgotten former life.)

Though hesitant to bring it up, Chuck decides to say it anyway: "It's attitude. It's the same self-serving attitude of...of 'me above everything' that drove that *Gene*...that drove him to kill Janet last year."

Sid sits straighter with comprehension (though humbly not realizing he is a local example of just the opposite of what Chuck is describing). "Right! And everyone can choose it, too. Exactly what they wanna be."

"Or *not* want to be," Ed emphasizes.

"Imagine," the Reverend wields his livelihood again, "if everyone was just *aware* that life's *real* purpose is treating yourself and everyone else with loving care – without an agenda..."

And it's Sid who concludes, "Even in the simplest little day-to-day things."

Now, Mike Watson is only languishing along, having reached the slowly heaved sidewalk that leads past his home. In the shading canopy above...tall maples have spaced their hundred thousand collectors in an efficient lacework to soak up the energetic sunshine, letting only a few beams of radiance angle through to the ground. And the lawns all around are lush green, with myriad spring blades still surging faster than any mowers can tame. ...Here, this back stretch of Fuller Street always seems so quiet to him, only three blocks off Main – though straight ahead a big pack of grade-school kids, huddled together over some awesome secret or maybe a new summer game, crowds the next corner. And, all around, the streets are still.

The homes over here on Mike's street are modest, mostly. Some are small brick cubes; others: siding-cloaked bungalows in a range of pale colors. His house – just ahead on the left – is one of the few two-story originals.

Mike almost stops walking. So close to home, temper forced to cool, all he can think about is his mother there inside – father working, year-older brother Frank at some after-school activity thing, and six-years-older brother Ray out somewhere, too... (Mike wonders where Bill would be right now, if he was still alive.) He slowed his pace because his mom, he feels here again, doesn't deserve his anger – ever. She's tried too hard, did so well raising four boys...and, only one short year ago, losing one...Bill, second oldest – lost to the insane unending carnage on the highways... Mike can't be giving her his problems. She needs only his strength, his independence, like Dad.

Here, he does stop, as though wary of stepping onto his own family's property. He looks around, fixes on the fading gray of the asphalt driveway stained with drops of oil from the succession of worn cars and bleached in patches by years of car-wash suds...and there toward the back where it ends at the single-car wood-slat garage jammed with derelict bicycles and junk... Over here, it paves the way to the lopsided screen door that leads up to the kitchen, and past that, edges the plain back yard – the weed-choked unused lawn surrounded by big pines...and two twenty-foot maples spaced in the bare middle, planted as seedlings years ago by ever-hopeful and eager young Bill. Up front, spanning the house, with screened ends and a glass-paned face, shaded beneath Fuller Street's big trees, is a wide white-framed porch. All around, sky-blue siding layers up past the windows to brace the black roof.

It's the only home Mike has ever known.

Mike takes a deep breath, then heads in. Up the few steps and into the kitchen, he listens for Mom... She rounds the corner right in front of him, and he pulls the stairway door shut behind him.

"Hello there," she uses her practiced positive tone (though Mike can clearly hear her precision concern in her voice – he knows she senses almost everything that's going on with her sons, and deeper inside, he cherishes that). Such a small woman, dark hair and face, almost fifty now, and Mike has not yet considered, in his young life, how she generated the power to be homemaker for five males.

He glimpses into her loving brown eyes. "Hi," he manages, heading for the refrigerator.

Mom smiles a weak one, but she's plainly aware of Mike's rage. He's the youngest, and is burdened with sixteen years of being the youngest, she fears. And like her (and her husband and Mike's closest brother Frank, and even – though he's so hard to read – her oldest boy Ray) she knows he misses Bill...terribly. And she still, after a year, has no idea how to get herself past her loss, let alone help the father and the three remaining brother-sons.

"Mike..." Mom hesitates.

She sees his anger, he's sure. "It's okay..."

"I know it's been – "

"No, it's okay, Mom! You just take care of yourself."

"You can tell me, Mike..."

"It's just...things, Mom, y'know?"

But she's afraid it's a whole lot deeper. "We haven't talked at all, yet...about Bill..." she begins, but quickly spills over with a flow of tears. She crosses weakly to the table and slides out a chair. Mike watches her brace to sit, like someone years older. She soon finds some control, and wipes her eyes. "Your dad and I have done some talking about it – he's so sad, since it happened, you know – "

"I know," Mike reacts softly, pouring a small glass of milk. He tells her, "Mom, that's not it," believing fully it's not. (Part of him wants to let loose the real reason, but only to sidetrack this unending anguish of a mother outliving her child.) Now he sits across from her at the round wooden table.

"Everything was so good for us, before..." she chokes. "Well, looking back, it seems..."

"Mom! It's just stuff, y'know? School bugs me...and I'll get a summer job and it'll be better – like Frank," he desperately tries to set her back to normal.

"I know, Mike, I know..." And she wipes away her tears again, for this son's sake.

"Maybe I'll go up and do my homework now," he tries to please her that way, and he throws back the last gulp of milk.

(Though he currently in his life has no intention of ever doing homework again.)

"Okay, Mike, that's good," Mom sniffles, proud of his show of strength. And she reaches across to pat his hand, but pulls up just short, once more.

Mike pushes to his feet, allowing a little smile for his mother. Turning and setting his glass in the sink, he then heads out through the dining room and leaves her there alone. (She soon gets up to fix supper.) Into the front hallway, he climbs the stairs, taking two at a time. At the oval upper hall, he stops...the bedroom straight across is Mom's and Dad's: he never thinks about it. To the left, at the end, is the bathroom; on its left: Bill's room – not, to this day, untouched, but since he died, un-slept. On the other side: his own room (and since Ray recently came home again to stay "for a while", it's Mike's and Frank's room, splitting the bunk beds like when they were little). And lastly, just here to the right at the top of the stairs where he paused – in front of him like some stranger's whole world, like the Forbidden Territory (of some older brothers) – no one in there right now but the door shut tight anyway in the middle of the day – is Ray's room. Ray's room...that Mike now briefly pictures as he sneers at the door – the quickest of scenes in his head – in which Mike envisions during the deepest depths of night with everyone else snug safe in their beds – a fantastic glimpse of the darkest of nights instantaneously ablaze with only this room behind this door exploding away from the house into oblivion! – in a fireball of death..!

"There's Crusher – *again!*" thirteen-year-old Heap Henry impolitely shouts – well within Crusher's (murderer Gene's intolerant nickname for Joseph – ironically) hearing range – from his position in center field (although since last summer Heap has stretched about eight inches and doesn't look heaped anymore, though his long blond hair is still ratty and he spits, chomps gum and sweats disgustingly, as always, and curses and diamond-dusts his customary white T-shirt with the same outstanding abandon). He points like a statue at Crusher Joseph Welt sitting crossed-legged out there right behind him deep in the tall weeds twenty feet past the fence.

Suddenly, the late-Wednesday sun glints off something in that underbrush. "He's guzzlin' again!" Henry adds, and Jack turns from his set position on the mound to look – causing the two base runners plus Rick and his three other players in their dugout to simultaneously scream *"Balk!"*(Little eleven-year-old Keven at bat is the only one who doesn't yell it out, because he has no idea what a balk is.)

"Eat it, buzzard-beaks!" Jack scans them all with his black and brooding eyes. (At fourteen, he's the oldest, though other-team captain Rick shot up an inch or two taller than him since the fall.) "It's time-out! Obstruction on the field!"

"He's way out there in the wilderness, puke-breath!" Rick disputes.

Henry horks an angry gob onto the outfield grass and bellows, "He's still a turgid 'struction!" ("Turgid" being his choice for today, maintaining a word-a-day-from-the-dictionary discipline – as though it's one possible way to help fill in the long blanks between his characteristic sparse talking... Perhaps this is why literary Joseph chooses to squat where he does, close by in the centerfield rough.)

"Up your turgid, Heapie!" thin Rick cranks his glare toward the outfield.

Manny at third turns with drooping glove to query Rick in the dugout. Never speaking much, either, his expression says, "I don't get it".

"What, Manny-maggot?!" Rick erupts. "Turgid! *Turgid!*"

"Obstruction, dorks! Friggin' obstruction!" Jack on the hill loudly rules officially to both teams.

"Never-the-fuck mind!" Rick now gives up, trying to look indifferent.

"Suck piss anyway," Jack had one ready and has to use it. But as he returns to the set position he's thinking about Crusher Joseph sippin' booze out there again (about the tenth time he's been here this spring). And since Joseph lives just down the street from him, Jack has seen him a lot this year heading out to wander around – and at night, especially, Joseph makes little effort to hide that regularly quick-tipping flask. Yet Jack sort of empathizes with him, coming from the same rougher part of town. But he also envies him his father (Jack's took off), his respectable mother (Jack's used to be a whore) and his house joyously crammed with little brothers and sisters (Jack has none). With all that going on, he feels, you wouldn't have to think about just yourself, all the time.

"Bean-balls!" Eddie (formerly Eggie the Egghead) Ogden proudly devises a pun one from the bench. "Throw it!"

Jack stares at the spectacled kid, grins (whereas, prior to last year, he would have glowered death rays), then pitches...

Swing 'n' miss, strike two.

As Kevin picks it up and tosses it back to him (seven per side: no catcher, no shortstop), Jack wonders again what's up with Joseph Welt. He knows he quit college, he knows he just wanders around because he feels lost. But what's he so *deep* about? Is life so unjust? Did he run out of all possible opportunity..? As Jack rubs the ball, he turns and peers once more through the chain-link and tangle of weeds out there...and finds the two sparkling eyeglass lenses beneath the high round forehead and stringy hair... Where others have called Joseph's recent actions weird, now Jack can only conclude – pushing back his own long, black hair and rubbing the chest of his plain black T-shirt – that the guy's just trying to find, somewhere in town – without persecution – his own life.

"**W**hu'd you say to her?!"

Mike doesn't answer. He won't even look at Ray leaning in at him.

"Why're you so goddamn *dumb?!*" Ray barks, stiffly encroaching two jerks further into Mike's room. Though Ray is now inches shorter than recently sprouting Mike, the fact that he's six years older makes the younger brother quake at his every word – and every twitch closer.

"You *ever* gonna grow up?!" Ray growls coldly at Mike's silence.

Mike stays rigid, at his little desk. He wants to jump up and run out – to go live somewhere else...though he can't begin to think why. Burning inside, he cannot define what's causing it. Someone watching this could quickly theorize something, but the real causes are years in the making. All Mike knows, in those clear times he's away from this house, is that life could be –

"Mom cries non-stop all through supper and you're the *dummy* that was here all alone with her before!" Ray still wants a response – or an excuse. (Black, curly hair cut brutally short, and tight little body tense, for an instant it seems to Mike that his small-featured face is made of stone.) "*Whatever* you said to her...*if you ever go 'n' say it again..!*" Ray ends his threat with another few seconds of merciless staring.

And though Mike is trying to reason just how he had upset his mother (what did he say that was so insensitive?) he reacts – not technically mindful of his oldest brother now strutting away down the hall – right here he lets out, with lips barely moving, in the faintest possible mutter:

"Fucker..."

eing late spring, with evenings still cooling off some, all the men who had gathered out around Lucy's bench tonight have come inside, into this subtly magical aura of well-being. And Lucy is there behind the counter slicing a few wedges of his renowned homemade pie and pouring his exquisite coffee by the bucket. (It's too early yet for beer or drinks, which no one here cares much for on weeknights, anyway.)

Ed, spurred on by his near-parallel-thinking wife on the next stool, has staked his challenge to the epidemic of Individualism, and has the attention of all the restaurant – about seventy or eighty folks:

"That's who makes 'em self-centered in the first place," Ed concludes his theory of misguided parenting to everyone looking back at him from every other stool, from the arrangements of padded wooden armchairs and wingchairs opposite, the eleven side and back booths, and from the few folks standing around in clumps. (The typically soft quiet of the comfortable restaurant interior is otherwise broken only by Lucy and his evening helpers – timid old Jerry and little Rebecca – cautiously handling dishes.)

"But if those self-centered ones are allowed to do it at all," adds Wilf from a back booth (dear wife Mayor Sue beside him and best friends Chuck and Beth opposite them), "then they'll just keep on doin' it to you."

Sue wants her husband's point qualified: "You mean it's the victims of greed and inconsideration who are at fault – for not standing up against...'them'?" she gestures toward Ed's phantom individuals.

"Partly," Wilf thinks.

"Who else is gonna stop 'em?" old Chase agrees from his counter stool, buddies Bert and Mel on either side of him leaning back facing the room with arms crossed in front of them, too. "It's like victims are askin' for it, sometimes...just by takin' it."

(Deep in a corner booth, Norm, Ba-Dee and Howard are merely observing all of this – they're here having a coffee while waiting for Joseph to probably show, as agreed, so they can decide what to do tonight.)

"Well, ambition is a strong human motivation," Chief Chuck has turned himself outward, elbows on knees, facing the open floor between the side and back booths. "But it's like there's a fine line between what's healthy self-determination and what's hurtful..."

"That's why there's laws," Ed joins back in from the middle of the counter, caressing his empty white mug, his wife embracing his arm.

"You can't legislate kindness – or even consideration," Wilf is quick to react, his wise and tired eyes set firmly on Ed twenty-some feet away across the soft light. And a few emphatic words of agreement percolate from the gathering.

"No," Ed allows. "Well...it is a sort of legislation – will of the people, everyone getting together to help against someone's destructive behavior."

With that image, all concur, everybody demonstrating solidarity by voicing some rousing words of agreement all at once.

And, in this atmosphere so much livened by their usual community concern, the discussion keeps on rolling, as often happens here in Lucy's (as though these coffee-swills are unscheduled yet open on-going unofficial most-provocative town meetings).

...

But as that forum bounces along, Joseph is not about to arrive quite yet. As a matter of fact, he's across the street from Lucy's, three buildings down from the police office, inside the recently rented office above Red's Convenient Drugs & Milk ("Red" being a reformed black-haired hippie-commune Communist, long-saved by the life-reality of self-worth capitalism). And this isn't the first time he's been up here during the last few weeks. It's the tenth. What he's doing is trying to land a job by use of nuisance: he won't quit coming around here bugging John Sing until he gives him a shot at it – "it", it's now very clear to John, is a trial run at reporting. (Joseph wants to test his skills in John's newly started weekly paper, The Town Talk. Fresh from only a few scrambling months of journalistic experience in Elston, John feels scared enough without Joseph Welt.)

"I've got a hundred stories already," Joseph says as he sits across the flimsy table from the precarious new editor. Around them, the stark white walls shimmer beneath the banks of fluorescents, with the original dark wood trim and brown tile floor adding further austere feel to this thrifty enterprise.

"That's what I'm afraid of," John beholds him straight in the eye, gripping his crossed leg and not grinning in the least. (A gentle Asian, he's a little concerned what this twenty-year-old ape might do if laconically rejected.)

"Why don't you just let me bring in some of the ones I wrote?" Joseph still can't understand why John won't allow him that much – he's had two years of journalism courses, after all.

"I told you. It implies a door is open." And John snugs up his wire-rimmed glasses with one brisk hand motion.

"What's so wrong with that?"

"Okay, I'll tell you what's so wrong – only because I'm in the honesty business," John now gives in an inch, confessing with a conscious smile: "You scare me."

"Good!" Joseph pokes back his glasses with a flick of a finger. "If I didn't, I wouldn't have potential for controversy, would I?"

Editor John just scrutinizes him.

"Tell you what I really came here tonight with," Joseph pulls himself up straight in the hard chair, seeming about to be honest, too, but truthfully about to try one last desperate angle: "I'll work for praise."

"Beg pardon?"

Joseph is sort of smiling, his crooked teeth like an opened box of flat noodles. (He's smiling because he's actually proposing this.) But his arms are folded determinedly tight above his bulbous belly as his ego pushes his words: "I'll decide the pieces, you just print 'em. Pay me ten dollars per positive or piqued reaction – call-in or letters."

John Sing's thin black eyebrows rise just perceptibly. Thinking a moment, and realizing this odd looking young man is admirably determined to break into the field, he counters: "And debit ten bucks for every outraged reaction." (He chose "outraged" intentionally over "negative".)

"No, because you can blue-line the whole outrageous piece, if you want. You wouldn't put dangerous shit in your paper in the first place."

"Valid one," John admits openly, then silently ponders this a few seconds more... "Okay, give me a couple of test runs –"

"Oh no," Joseph has points on the board, now. "John! Commitment! I can't do a real one without promise of publication – short of it being an outrage, of course."

Expecting that, John is still willing to gamble. "Fine. But no responses, no dollars. Less than five responses average a week for five weeks, end of handshake."

"Sounds fair," Joseph smiles the smile of the newly employed, and for ten minutes more they discuss it. On his way out the door, Joseph promises his first submission by next week's deadline to a now somehow rather stunned-countenanced Editor John Sing.

...

By the time Joseph Welt the reporter walks into Lucy's, the issue has changed to the subject of spring weed spraying, and Norm, Howard and Ba-Dee are amid deciding to leave without him. When Joseph tells them his good news (in limited detail), he also offers up his stashed case of beer, which entices their heading for a few cool ones out along their favorite country road, not once all the while posing his dilemma of nobody caring.

rank Watson gazes with complete understanding at his year-younger brother Mike. (Right here, it occurs to Mike that seventeen-year-old Frank does – he supposes – look classically handsome – having heard it from everyone around school often enough – with his night-black hair and strong brown eyes, like Mom.) They're sitting in Dad's car at the Dairy Cone Drive-in, having a shake after supper, just the two of them. (Each with their own group of friends, they don't often do this now, and are long past doing everything together. But once in a while they will, even if it's just an errand to get out of the house.) Mike has just told Frank about their brother Ray coming down on him only an hour or so ago.

Frank finally reacts, and it's all he can think to say: "Dark Presence..."

"*What?!*" Mike is shocked – not sure what Frank means but it's obviously grim.

"That's what Ray always felt like to me around home."

"Are you serious?" Mike asks, dumbfounded.

"Yeah." Frank is not kidding. "He feels like this threatening, black cloud..."

"I always thought you sorta got along with him better – "

"No fuckin' way." Frank couldn't be more emphatic. "He's never in any way treated me better – now that you ask."

"Whuh!" Mike huffs. "My thing, he was always just kinda not there, to me…like, I can remember maybe two or three times him ever being around, all the time we were growing up." (He was thinking only of positive moments, saying that.)

"Dark Presence," Frank firmly assures him of the real truth again, pointing the straw in his milkshake at him. Then, leaning an inch toward Mike from behind the steering wheel, he intently waits, with expectant stare, for true comprehension…

The setting sun is blazing Mike's face, adding fire to his astonished look. He pokes his straw at some bubbles deep in his tall paper cup, thinking about what this means. "So I'm not wrong," he gathers.

"Less than not wrong," Frank comforts him.

After another pause, Mike asks (avoiding his cherished brother's eyes by watching the cute carhops), "So, what do we do about him?" (He avoids looking at Frank because of what he has felt like doing to Ray, lately – and suddenly now with his unexpected equal in misery, what he feels frighteningly – decidedly – on the brink of actually doing.)

"Nothing," Frank has already figured it out, as usual a few steps ahead in clear thinking. "He'll move back out, someday."

"Yeah *when?!*" Mike cries spontaneously. "We thought he was permanently gone already!"

"He's just between jobs. He'll find something."

"He's not *looking!*" Mike reminds him with panic (though that other part of his mind flashes a glorious alternative image of Ray laid-out dead and ultimately gone).

Frank has no idea how near the edge Mike is. "Just wait it out," he advises calmly.

Mike settles back in his seat. With a deep breath, he fights the hysteria impulse to conscript Frank into helping him do something more final, more permanent – right now! "Right…" he allows, with a no-guarantee overtone.

"It feels better, doesn't it?" Frank starts the car.

"What?" Mike looks at him, unsure.

"Knowing it's not your fault."

Mike thinks that over. Ultimately, he has to come back to it:

"It doesn't undo anything," he snarls.

C ool black space leaks pinpoints of shimmering light through its infinity all above the shadowy outline of the parked car. Ahead, the moonless gravel road disappears a few feet out into the pitch of night. And two beacon glows on the horizon – not yet walled off by not-yet towering corn in the adjacent fields – reassure the four young men in the car that there is civilization in this unimaginably boundless universe.

"Ripe with festering life," Joseph sternly re-attests from the back corner seat, following his own pause punctuated by gurgling beer. "Heck, on my street alone – right there on my block of Fuller Street! – there's *at least* a hundred stories of human depravity, anguish, defilement, consternation – "

"Joseph!" (Norm knows to stop him, because once started on his good-word expedition, Joseph can go on indefinitely.) "One real one, if you can," he challenges. With Howard contributing support at the wheel and Ba-Dee in the other back corner "yup"-ing regular concurrence, Norm in the passenger front has been poking through the utter thickness of Black at Joseph's boastful monster of over-confident journalistic attitude. They're still on their first beer.

"Are you three all comatose?" Joseph's heavy voice questions from a point of nothingness in the sightlessness. "Don't you talk to your neighbors? Don't you communicate with your fellow community-ites? Don't you listen..?"

"We don't have an output file – just input only," Howard insightfully differentiates. "We listen, but we don't have a use for their stories of woe – I mean, we don't at the moment have thoughts about writing their stories down for the world to know."

"Oh," Joseph is gripped by such truth. As though he thought everyone's brain worked like his.

"Give us just one real one, Joseph," Norm is insistent.

Joseph searches his head for something relevant... "There's ten installments alone from this very back road chronicling Innocence-fucker Killer Gene!"

"Great. So then someone can come after us four like we were this back-road cult thing scheming with him!" Howard whines, sitting up and turning from slumping at the wheel to try to glare down Joseph in back.

"Oh." Joseph is neutralized again. "Bad example?"

"*Yeah!*" Ba-Dee threatens with noticeable amusement. "Leave us out of your examples of humanity!"

"Or else, you're dead – slumped lifeless on your qwerty!" Norm draws a picture.

Joseph brightens. "Good item! I'll make that my very first piece: NEW COLUMNIST IMMEDIATELY THREATENED BY APPARENT FRIENDS." He retaliates in capitals. With a guffaw.

"You know what we mean," Norm compromises, searching outward through the windshield for Reason in the night. "There's gotta be more human interest stories in this town than just Killer Gene and us four – if that's what you're talking about doing."

"Myriad multitudes," Joseph believes fully, and, pausing for effect as he distinctly in the silence drains the last foaming liquid from his upended bottle, he then dramatically adds the poser of the evening: "Undoubtedly with stories of Earth-trembling portent materializing at this very moment!"

...

318

At that very moment Mike Watson is perched on the topmost bench of the darkened ballpark's third-base-side bleachers beneath the same feeble stars, wishing he smoked cigarettes or had a flask to sip like that Joseph Welt guy.

Inside, Mike feels so hollow, drained empty of worth or love or meaningful promise for the life he was born into...those very purposes that some small and almost forgotten part of him once felt. Someone, it seems, took them away from him.

Out there, he imagines, through the street-light-straight neighborhoods, a town full of all kinds of people sleeps, putting today in the past and dozing off. (What young Mike can't comprehend is that there could be many others around him– his age or not – with the same defeated mood as his.)

So what (he questions once again) exactly did he do to end up feeling so bad? God!, I must be something evil, it grips him for the first time. He must have this contemptible part of him – that he was born with, has to live and suffer with. Keep doing things so wrong – pissing people off... I must be so self-centered! Said and did all the selfish wrong things when Bill died – poor Mom...and Dad. Should have been stronger for them, should have thought harder to say the right things. (Tears now brim Mike's eyes, and overflow.) Yet what he can't see is how he could be better – change myself, he laments, so that everyone would appreciate me for my...strength...the good things I do and say – so Mom might forget, and Ray stops being so...

Then, wrapping his arms around himself against the cooling spring night, Mike has another thought pop into his head: he recalls how none of them (the four sons) have ever expressed their specific personal hopes and dreams to Mom and Dad (though he has no basis for comparison when it comes down to just how little his family talks openly). But next, as he wonders what Bill's life dreams were, he does remember one such revelation (other than Frank's modestly spoken "probably medicine" leanings) from a few years ago: he can still see Ray – the oldest, the strongest – proclaiming to Dad at the supper table one night – Frank and Bill, Mom and me just sitting there quietly eating – Ray promises him flat-out and firm: "Someday I'll be a millionaire."

Someday I'll be a millionaire... Mike echoes those words and that scene a few times through his mind. But so far already Ray has failed three times...well, he says it's because he couldn't stand his employers' "backward stupid thinking" – three times. I guess, Mike allows, it's part of the process, of getting ahead and making your first million. It's about being tough...it's having an agenda (he uses Frank's term for some people's careers). But thinking of Frank makes him question what that means, because Frank's "agenda" to work toward medical school doesn't make him in any way like Ray – Frank, in fact, agenda and all, is the friendliest, most helpful guy he knows...

"Shit..." Mike mutters, realizing now that coming here in the middle of the night to try and think about things freely has just made him even more confused. And with that confusion, his rage impulse returns – a reaction to hopelessness, feeling cornered – in that now *he's* the rat he once cornered with a shovel – the rat that, to his astonishment but immediate respect – seeing no escape, turned on him hissing – weak little rodent against this huge creature with a deadly shovel...determined with all its meager strength to take me on – *to try and kill me rather than give in and die..!*

As he stands to go home, Mike has one more uninvited impulse flash through his head: a wish that the big hunting knife in his jacket pocked was a gun.

I t's nine in the evening, the next day. Soon about to leave for Nick's Bowl (to meet Ba-Dee – who got sucked into working late, tonight – and then, around eleven, to head across to join up with Norm and Howard at Lucy's) Joseph is sitting at his little desk (stacked with dozens of paperback novels on and around it – he was once witnessed with nine of them spread open in mid-read) at the narrow window of his and his next-youngest brother's tiny room. He is fluently forging his first feature.

Outside, a few houses down the block, he can see Chief Cintz's patrol car sitting idling, flashers blazing, and he imagines another story in the works. Actually, picturing it is easy: it's the Schumanns. No, particularly, it's Albert Schumann beating the shit out his two little boys again, and probably his wife, too. It's been out in the open for just a few weeks, and though he doesn't do more than bruises – well, matter of fact, he's only once on record – he is pathetically repentant afterward – Albert the lush (Joseph believes drinking is no excuse and is therefore irrelevant, here) is despicable and has to be stopped soon. And Joseph hopes to soon say exactly that, in print. To the whole county.

...

Meanwhile, at Nick's Bowl and squeaky-clean luncheonette, Ba-Dee is standing behind the counter doing absolutely nothing except grit his teeth. Nick's twin boys (age about ten, Ba-Dee figures, though it's hard to tell because most of their life's growth seems to have been width rather than height) are bowling. They've been bowling since three-thirty this afternoon. Ba-Dee has made each of them three hamburgers and two orders of fries. He has delivered innumerable colas to their five lanes (they're using every lane because Thursday is no-league night and it's usually very quiet). He's asked them what's on television right now, but they don't seem to care. Then he found out from Papa Nick that their bedtime is the same as his quitting time tonight... So, consequently, Ba-Dee has since silently swore to never be persuaded to work outside his regular weekday afternoon shift again, to never, after this summer, work here again, and to never have kids.

...

Norm, contrastingly, is eased back on a blanket beside the secluded swimming hole amid its tranquil river glade off a back road two miles out of town. Birds are singing joyfully, the sparkling creek trickles down a little rapids into the clear pool, and the radiating setting sun warms through the swaying boughs of the encircling green trees as he gazes up into the sky's blue depths completely naked – with Suzanne similarly undressed close beside him. The tricky part is: conversation, now that they've detached again from tender, caring, passion. What's so awkward is Suzanne's frightening mix of feelings about sex: she's open and wild and eager, but often she claims she abhors it. She was abused. As brilliant as she is, she can't outsmart her feelings. They just come back, sometimes, and Norm has learned by mistake to now try with all he has to not say the wrong thing. "This is paradise, isn't it?" he smiles, his embracing hazel eyes close to hers. "It's heaven," she agrees softly, long dark curls of hair blanketing his shoulder where she rests her head. A gentle little breeze titillates their bare skin, again. A little fish gurgles the tranquil surface of the pond. "Want to try swimming again?" Norm grins.

(Upon arrival, they had skinny-dipped briefly, shivering up to their necks – providing, at least, some slipperiness to make their hungry hugging more fun.) "No!" she quietly chuckles, big brown eyes bright with pleasure. Then she forces a small frown. "You don't have to pick your words," she reminds him about the few serious talks they've had lately. Norm cannot find any to respond. She insists, "You have never been anything but wonderful to me. You're innocent. Some other man made me feel those...negative things." Norm wants to hold her and comfort her, but that vague last part about her father pushes him back powerfully. "Hold me," she feels, cuddling tight. Kissing his chest, she adds, "I can separate you, you know! At no time do I lose consciousness of who you are, and why you're doing to me what you're doing..." "Thanks," he sighs, "for saying that." And scurrying up on top of him, she smothers him with playful kisses, and he chuckles under the onslaught. And only then does he manage to bury, in the back of his mind, his horrible male guilt for his ex-friend Gene raping and killing that poor fourteen-year-old female, Janet.

...

At the Watson house, Mike is enduring his self-imposed exile in his room pretending to read. Frank is out with friends, Dad is at one of his almost-nightly meetings, and Mom is downstairs as usual, vacantly watching her undemanding television friends. And Bill...Mike can't keep the thought from recurring...is dead. Dead, he shudders... What if Bill was still around? Living in his apartment downtown he used to come by home often, to talk cheerfully with Mom, to wash his car, and often to take an hour before meeting up with all his many friends to toss a ball around with Mike, or to drive him and Frank out to the Dairy Cone and buy them a shake... Sometimes Mike thinks Ray moved to Elston back then only because Bill got an apartment so close – as though Ray couldn't stand how well everyone at home got along when

Bill was in their midst... And with that thought, before the tears can build to a cascade, Mike springs up from his desk and grabs his jacket, striding out into the hallway – *Ray is right there!* Mike almost slams into him – nearly touches his wiry little body. Ray just stares up at him. (He must have been heading for Mike's room.) Mike steps back a bit. "Where *you* goin'?!" Ray growls. Mike slips on his jacket, but doesn't speak. He slides one hand into a bulging pocket. Ray barks, "Out runnin' around all night again?" (Ray gave him shit for staying out so late last night, even though Mom had gone to bed without knowing and Dad came home later...who knows when.) But Mike, for maybe the third time ever in his life, right now feels he has an option: he doesn't have to take this. The Dark Presence doesn't have to win. And he thinks: all the years of taking this fucking shit – since I was little, since my earliest memories of this oppressive home! – I don't have to carry it around with me all my life! – I could leave right now! Or I could take control (his blood races hot inside him) and put an end to this right now..! But something causes Mike to merely avoid Ray's tight eyes, as he steps around him to head down the stairs outside.

"**N**EUROSIS NEIGHBORHOODS," Joseph responds. Howard moans as Norm chokes on beer as Ba-Dee gasps.

"Com'on!" Joseph objects to their sound-effects objections to his first column's subject headline. "You think this town is pristine? Proper? Puritanical? Norm! – wake up! It's full of humans! *Humans!* Howie! – depraved, idiosyncratic, individualistic meat-beaters!" Joseph's booming voice carries out the open car windows into the sacred peace of black countryside midnight. (They all met at Lucy's: Ba-Dee after work, Howard after puttering around home, Joseph after climaxing his article, and Norm after his climactic date with Suzanne. But they always find they can't talk as freely there at Lucy's, even if it's late and it's only noble Lucy within hearing range of their sordid talk.)

"Alright, Joseph," Howard gives in first from the back. 'Flush it out – so to speak."

"Fuck off, Howard," Joseph begins from the passenger front as he turns toward Norm at the wheel for respect, instead. "It's about human nature, that's all. How the quaintest little town is still just a gathering of people, and people have characters. Some characters are mostly the good kind, some others are full of lotsa bad shit – but all have negativity. Everyone has guilt. And most of it is over mistreating someone else. Some, however, feel guilt for mistreating themselves – or for being greedy or indifferent. Or whacking-off their wieners raw – "

"You didn't submit that!" Norm believes Joseph actually could have turned in that last part to the rather dignified, well-respected Editor John Sing.

"Of course not!" Joseph roars, sipping one of the limited remaining beers from last night. "I'm just saying – "

"You're gonna embarrass all of us right out of town," Ba-Dee suddenly foresees.

Joseph, however, sees an opening: "Why, Ba-Dee? How many times did you jerk your jellybean today? Can I quote you..?" He waits for the number in silence. But adds, "My record's nine times...in one day."

"Way to go!" Howard giggles uncontrollably at Joseph's penchant for confession. "Another timely article, there!"

(Norm here keeps self-consciously quiet, after his indulgent date today.)

"So, Joseph," Howard tries again, "are you exposing or condemning all the lowlifes?"

"You don't get it, Howard," Joseph stands firm. "What it says is that everyone is just human, and that realizing it should make people more accepting of others' faults – "

"People will just judge people even more, if they knew some more dirt to judge them about," Ba-Dee keenly observes from the lightless back seat.

"Then that's their shortcoming all over again," Joseph assures his three friends. "People who want to do the right thing will do the right thing and accept that there's frailty in everyone – including themselves..."

"I can do it ten times," Howard suddenly yet flatly declares, like King Cock of the Roost.

"Eleven," Ba-Dee challenges.

"Eighteen!" Joseph himself doubles his best output.

"Wonder how much come you spurt in your lifetime," Norm says Joseph-like.

"Would it fill up a bathtub?" Joseph must have wondered about it, too.

"What about nose-dirt?" Howard has another one. "What if all living humans throughout history were to have flicked their none-dirt in a pile, how big would it – "

"'Nose-dirt'?" Joseph peeps in the abyss of night. "Howie! Doo-doo! Ka-ka – !"

"Yeah: Ka-ka mountain!" Ba-Dee also finds one. "If all humans throughout history – "

"They say," Norm now tries to stop their adolescent regression, "that atoms get recycled, so that you may right now be breathing in an atom that was part of some dead guy's brain that dissolved in a river in Africa ten thousand years ago..."

"Norm?" Joseph tries to stop Norm.

"Yes?"

"We're spiritual. Atoms and come and ka-ka have little to do with life," Joseph instructs Norm for a change. "Life is energy, not matter."

"Yeah," Howard can see that. "And life is what you do, how you act with others – "

"Then there sure are lots of greedy people around who don't get it," Ba-Dee observes.

"Who are shitheads with agendas!" Howard notes also.

"Who consider themselves above the humanness of shitting! Who despise the common man!" Joseph attacks the mighty.

"Having been afflicted by inhaling lots of evil-mind atoms!" seems the only way Norm can explain the logical biophysics of it all.

1t's Monday afternoon and Mike is home from school (final week before summer break). No one else is here except Mom, and she's upstairs, having a nap. Mike is soon gingerly transporting a stack of cookies, a big glass of lemonade, and the latest edition of the relatively new local paper out to the screened-in front porch.

Easing precariously down onto the wooden rocker, he sets his drink on the floor, piles cookies on both knees, and unfolds the thin newspaper: The Town Talk. (He has thoroughly read every issue since it's been out. Like everyone, he appreciates how it reports what's going on, without dirt.) And today, amid the sprinkling of new ads and expanded Letters page is something unexpected and unique, this column headed:

WELTS
(JOSEPH'S)
THIS WEEK'S SUBJECT:
HUMBLY HUMAN

(Joseph had abandoned "NEUROTIC NEIGHBORHOODS" in favor of a less antagonistic alliteration. It reads:)

Who are we? – that an outsider might point and ask: These three thousand, two hundred and forty people – just another town full of folks, right?

The answer is: No, it's an exactly equivalent number of individuals, each distinctly human.

For example, one local woman I know about is a widow, husband long ago run off, to a suicidal end. She still cries forlornly, when you get her talking about her life's true love.

Another human, on a different street right here in our town, is a long-sober alcoholic, with a grim story about scraping to stay alive mired in the absolute bottom sustainable film of life, prickling my skin when I heard details of his horrors living a lifestyle worse than death.

I know of someone else who years ago confessed to sexually abusing his little sister – well, bragged is a more accurate verb.

As well, a man I met is a war veteran, with unspeakable guilt for killing people. Now, he feels unbearably shocked by the ongoing savagery of humans.

And a friend swears his neighbor walks around the back yard late at night in a bra, heels and panties... The guy looks ravishing, he claims.

Yet, when these five citizens step out their front doors onto our sidewalks, they look...perfectly normal!

So, the obvious question is: How many people with such a story do you know? – yes, you there reading this! With hers and his and everyone else's all-too-human example thrown into the personality pot, it seems very likely to me that, in the end, we could strain it out and total exactly three thousand, two hundred and forty all-too-human beings (minus, probably, a couple of perfectly as-yet pure days-old infants). Meaning you and I are in there too, of course, by way of someone else's opinion.

MY POINT: My point (no, it's not that we're all loopy) has to do with: Acceptance – compassion, understanding, sympathy, empathy, forgiveness, second chances. But acceptance is something we choose to do. As opposed to choosing: condemnation – belittlement, rejection, denigration, and general writing-off.

And the best acceptance, I believe, is *not* just that usual everyday 'accepting someone even though they're different' thing. True acceptance is seeing that:

WE'RE ALL THE SAME

It's that (excluding the inhuman things some people sometimes do) no one is humanly worse or better – no one is very much closer to perfect than the next person. And that we are at our best, as a community and as a race, when we know our common failings and go on from there, to first try to live a better life ourselves, and then, with acceptance, work to live beyond our problems together.

So, try something: From here on in, when you see people around town, try to think this first, before negatives take over your thoughts:

Try to picture the infant innocence, then the life tragedies, of the mistakes of natural imperfect thinking and the small or large burdens of guilt from the inner conflicts of primal drives that are surely in there behind that face. Then forgive them their simple humanness.

And hope they're allowing you the same.

Mike reads it three times. Joseph Welt lives four houses up the block, says hi to him once in a while. Mike feels as though he has a new friend.

He never thought about people that way – no one's normal, no one's *so* bad – except some. And my problems, he now wonders, maybe are just common –anger: common, the problems of my family: everyday stuff. And this Joseph guy understands – not me, specifically – but things people suffer through.

Gulping the last of his lemonade, Mike stands and heads straight for the phone and calls John Sing at the paper – the sort of thing he's never done in his life. All he says is, "My name's Mike and I think Joseph Welt understands problems people can have better than anyone I've ever known and I'm gonna read him every week, for sure," then hangs up before John can say a word.

Next, Mike slips out the side door and peers across the back yards, to see if there's any sign of Joseph four houses away. There isn't. So he walks up the driveway then along their street to the Welts' front door, and knocks. Mrs. Welt recognizes him, and responds to his inquiry about Joseph by letting him in, then watches him, with curiosity, as he bounds up the stairs to Joseph's room, where the young columnist is writing.

Mike Watson, Mrs. Welt readily notes, comes back downstairs and leaves two hours later.

As the yellow evening sun cools to orange above the opposite buildings, the conversation centered at the bench in front of Lucy's Large Lunch still reverberates with the impact of today's paper's topically raised community welt. (Joseph's.)

Ol' Bert repeats, "He's a twerp kid," a caution against intrinsic immaturity.

"He's still got a good point," Chief Chuck sticks to his only comment about Joseph so far, rocking back on his chair at the curb. Wise and firm-eyed Wilf beside him has agreed adamantly.

Ed, however, has his usual doubt: "Human nature can't be changed that easy. People just react automatically – "

"The point is to *try* to change how you react," Wilf quickly counters Ed again.

Ol' Chase, beside Bert on the bench, tugs his ball cap another notch lower on his thick tufts, angling it against the rays of the still warm sunshine. "What's he after, anyway? Everyone here gets along!"

"Yeah!" Sid and little Mel both react at once, and Sid adds, "We don't have gang wars or fistfights – or even many bad arguments!" (Blue uniform shirt and pants, same as his Chief across the sidewalk, could make that remark sound like a complaint of professional boredom, said by someone somewhere else.)

"I think," Chuck now ventures, "he also means that people can make their own lives miserable by believing they're surrounded by nothing but lesser-lifes."

"We are," Chase notes. "Look't Bert, here...Mel..."

"And I'm darn proud of it!" Bert acknowledges, holding in a grin. "Why, it's all you do-good, big-brained, nose-pokin' hard-ons who keep changin' things!" (Right here, Jack, Eddie, Rick and four other kids coast around the corner on their bikes, detouring on the way home from their school-night, early-ending ball game.) "By the time these here little peckers take over," Bert jerks a thumb toward them without looking away from Chuck and Wilf, "everything will be jus' fuckin' perfect."

"You're saying you're more a believer in degeneration?" Ed grins down along the bench at him, "You sour ol' sacka shit?"

"Just keep up with us," Chase too speaks on behalf of all the aged, "and we'll ease you down to a nice level of inactivity."

"Peacefully, perfectly inert!" Bert boasts.

"We slow the madness down to a sensible crawl," frail little Mel adds, mid-bench.

"Then," Bert comes back around to the point, "you'll have sufficient time in your day to belittle everybody properly, strip 'em of all that uppity shit and see the real mess of lowly humanity 'round here!"

As the kids all giggle and grin at that, inching back and forth on their bikes, Chuck smiles pleasurably and suggests, "Maybe all you ol' purified men could start a workshop, or teach – "

"Sounds like a damn improvement thing to me!" Chase blocks the thought.

Bert is right there cautioning, too. "It's not something you can just take on. If you haven't got it in you, you can't get miserable simply by trying harder."

"Precisely!" Chase is with him. "Fortunately, most people got it in them – like that young Joseph Welt is saying. It just takes some long years of practice before it comes out right."

"Like you three?" Wilf frowns, amused.

"Like us!" Bert replies. "And Shooter, too." (The fourth coot usually manning the post with them hasn't arrived, yet.)

"So," Chuck is beginning to see how it works, "if we sit around this bench long enough, we'll get the right feeling for running people down and stripping away – from a safe distance – all their remaining little patches of dignity?"

"If you're lucky," Chase allows.

Bert now suggests, "Imagine the whole town all exactly like us ol' polished gems..."

"You mean the entire length of this here street lined with three thousand decrepitly wrinkled-up shit-filled bags of skin?" Ed can imagine it.

"Exactly!" Chase beams. "Picture everyone in town just like us seasoned veterans – the whole street solid with ripe opinions and properly slanted intolerances!"

"Then," Bert wraps it up for the underbelly movement, "everyone's right down at the bottom and none of what was in that column ever possibly happens!"

...

An hour later, Joseph is across the table from Norm in a back booth of the crowded Lucy's interior. Wearing his worn-thin dark blue denim shirt, his scraggly fine hair tops off his vagrant look. He has repeatedly poked his dark-rimmed glasses back up the flat stub of his nose, and his fibrous, gangling body seems to take issue, by way of restlessness, with the plush comfort of the seat. Norm, in light gray t-shirt and plain jeans, avoids aligning his sharp, hazel eyes with his friend's blurry blue ones – as he tends to do when sensing it coming...

"So, Norm!" Joseph rebegins yet again after a break in their small talk. "You're the science dork – "

"Yep – "

"A truck hits a bunny and instantly knocks the life out of it..." Joseph pauses, as though he said something provocative.

"Nice story. You gonna submit it?" Norm wonders.

"Knocks-the-life-out-of-it," the journalist spells it out.

"Oh!" Norm sees... "No, I don't see..."

"The energy of life went flying out of it. All that's left is a suddenly uninspired and directionless mass of atoms."

"Ahhh!" Norm feigns fascination.

"Norm! Life's an energy – we've established that – after many beers!" Joseph prompts, unblinking eyes wide with enthusiasm.

"So?"

"So, life's energy can be entirely knocked right out of us, fatally. Question is, can it also be sapped out of us in lesser amounts – like when someone's living under oppression does the victim give up some bits of his life energy to the master? Or the laborer to the sweatshop? Or a child to his flawed family?"

"Give me an – "

"Mike Watson."

Norm abruptly ceases breathing. He recalls his since-lapsed concern for Mike the other day sitting there in that side booth emitting indeterminate curses, and remembers also that Mike lives four doors away from Joseph. "What about him?" he tries to not sound responsible.

"The Watson household is a human bog," Joseph attests.

"How's that? – how do you know?"

"He came over for a couple of hours."

Norm's eyebrows rise. "You talked with Mike for two hours?"

"Mike's life energy is half sucked out of him."

Norm stares.

"It's involved..." Joseph is trying to keep it straight in his mind. "And it feels like I've been exalted as the great new understanding voice of the people too fuckin' quick."

"So?" Norm responds with an air of 'what did you expect and what more could you possibly want'?

"True," Joseph chuckles lightly, aware of life's ironies. "Anyway, Mike's seized up. It sounds like, with their old man forever out or out of it, with Mom blocked up tight over the loss of number two son – seems Bill was her most cherished – and senior brother Ray no real help," (right here it's plain that Mike didn't identify Ray as his family's one true dark demon) "sounds like Mike has only brother Frank to really communicate with. But the problem with that is, they were brought up to be reserved...independent...dignified." Joseph isn't sure yet which one is his word of choice.

"Meaning?"

"Not that there's a piece there," Joseph says professionally. "Unless I tie it to my first one, in that life's energy is diminished by repellent environments or self-chosen misanthropic mindsets that resulted in our town full of monumentally warped neighbors."

"Good one," Norm says.

"But," Joseph slumps against the backrest and sips his long-cooled coffee, gazing straight at Norm through those thick lenses, "I don't know where it'll lead."

Norm squints. "The column or Mike's life?"

"Norm!" Joseph huffs. "You think I'm just mercenary? I've got a conscience! I'm worried about Mike's life! And if I start poking around in there" (he wiggles one finger slightly) "inside his brain, I might short it right out – "

"Short it out?! What's that supposed to mean? That you think he's on the edge or something?"

"Simmering," Joseph quickly qualifies. "Best as I can pedestrianly read..." Then he leans forward on the table, big fingers interlocked around his mug. "So I told him I can't help him – that I'm a raw professional writer, not a raw family therapist."

"Good sidestep. And you'll have to do that little dance at least several hundred thousand times in your hack career."

"But Norm," Joseph now laments with grave seriousness, "can't you see how backing away from people that way opposes the good intentions of my get-along-with-everybody inaugural fucking column?!"

"Uhh..." Norm didn't stop to consider that. "But you have to stay neutral – "

"Indifferent – consciously!"

Joseph shouts out his own horrible self-incriminating definition, turning every head in the restaurant (lowering his general esteem one notch as folks assume he's professionally buckling under already).

"Neutral!" Norm yells back, insisting it's the right word and the right course.

"Norrmmm!" Joseph now rebukes through clenched teeth, trying to simmer down. "I'm a traitor to my own cause! Neutral is what all the community do-nothings call themselves!"

"But your alternative is getting involved in their lives – to take part in Mike's life," Norm cools a little, too.

"And that's not reporting! That's *creating* the story as you go along!"

"Then why can't you just write about him?" Norm tries. "Factually. As is?"

"And piss the whole family off? Can you imagine how people will judge the whole Watson family for their weaknesses? However I say it? And especially Mike for blabbering?"

Norm leans back, studying his trapped friend. "Yeah, I guess," he has to agree. "So, what do you do?"

"Nothing!" Joseph promises, coming full circle to his only conclusion and the source of his anguish.

"Nothing?"

"If he comes over just to talk, I can talk with him – to a point. I really don't want to," he adds, glancing around the restaurant as though to find some other volunteer. "But Mike Watson has to live his own life – I can't guide him or expose him or anticipate him!"

Norm nods. "You should just let him find his own way, then – "

"Right. Let him figure out his own head," Joseph now abruptly stands, looking all-over itchy to walk away from this. "And as indifferent or chicken-shit neutral as it sounds, let him do what he has to do..."

The next day, Tuesday, is classically quiet throughout the town.

It's Wednesday that Ray Watson is found stabbed.

Chief Cintz raced over to Fuller Street as soon as he got the call at home. Assistant Sid bolted from the office when Chuck phoned from his car...

Mrs. Watson was hysterical, without making a sound. She sat shaking and gasping on the living room sofa, eyes focused blankly at mid-air, her anguished husband on one knee beside her helplessly trying to comfort her. She was the one who found Ray upstairs in his room on his bed, everything under the blanket she lifted soaked brilliantly red. The ugly hunting knife handle was protruding from his side below his ribs. His eyes were shut tight and her instantaneous eruption of screeching did not rouse him. She believed he was dead.

She had phoned Dad at the office, and when he forcefully got her to speak clear enough for him to understand, he immediately hung up and dialed the local paramedics – who were there bringing Ray out when he arrived, tires squealing. Seconds later, set to speed away, the attendants assured him Ray was still hanging on.

Now Dad is waiting for a second ambulance from Elston City for Mom – she looks deathly close to some sort of seizure – and for Frank to be brought from school and for Chuck and Sid, who left as soon as Ray was rushed away, to try to find Mike – who was almost certainly not in class this morning.

Frank soon hurries in, huddles with his father at the sofa. Dad and Frank talk in spurts, but there's nothing they can do.

Neighbors who had gathered on the sidewalk are now in the front porch and hall, trying to figure out how to help (it's too early). Reverend Fisk soon weaves business-like through them, summoned by Chief Cintz.

But surprisingly, for such a small town, it takes an hour and a half to finally track down the one immediately obvious suspect – as he sits mouthing swear words in a back booth inside nearly deserted Lucy's. By this time, Mom is admitted to the same Elston hospital where Ray is being operated on, with Frank and Dad pacing its waiting room floor agonizing over both (as word has passed the thirty-three percent of the population news-travels-fast level throughout their community).

...

Chuck and Sid walk Mike Watson across Main Street and into the police office. Mike is hunched over, his eyes tensed and glassy. He is not handcuffed. His hands, in fact, are clenched in his jacket pockets, and he pulls his right one out repeatedly...to push at his cropped blond hair, as though it's still long. Sid and Chuck don't need to hold his arms to direct or secure him. The few people on the street have stopped walking, and watch wordlessly.

Inside, the Chief gestures to his desk, and Mike crosses the narrow office to the plain chair beside it. The blue from the fluorescents drains the last color from the cold face. Once he sits, elbows on armrests and leaning forward, he sets his stare on the gray tile floor.

Sid eases onto his chair. He balances on its front edge. His nervous eyes – reacting to the unaccustomed silence in the office – blink back and forth from his boss at a file cabinet beside him, to the strangely motionless teenager in the chair, ten feet away. Chuck's searching for some sort of official form.

"He may live," the chief soon declares, finally finding the needed papers (said instead of "He may die"). Turning, he examines Mike, and slowly, noiselessly slides the file drawer shut.

Chuck rotates his chair around, strokes his fingers through his wavy hair and sits, four feet from Mike. He switches on the recorder in his opened desk drawer and leans back, carefully eyeing him. Trying to imagine the extent of this adolescent's anger, he guesses too at how terrified he must be over what could happen to him next. What he can't begin to know is whether or not Mike wants his brother to live.

Sid is still rapidly switching his distressed eyes from the unspeaking adult to the speechless boy and back again. And bent far over, elbows on his knees, rounded chest heaving deeply, Sid sees it through his usual few strands of dangling hair. (The longer nothing is said by his chief, the more he struggles to find the right words he might say himself – if he had to.)

Chuck focuses on Sid for a moment, forcing a humorless grin, barely shaking his head. Finally, he tries:

"Ray must be impossible to live with..." his voice gentle, and calm.

Mike blinks, seeming puzzled getting sympathy, and not blasted. After another unexpected gap of nothing more said, he nods his head just an inch. (And with that first admission, his frozen eyes brim with tears.)

"Eventually..." Chuck now leans an elbow on his desk, pivoting sideways a little closer to Mike but holding his tone soft, "eventually you'll have to tell us about it..."

Mike inhales deep, but doesn't let it out like a sigh. He's still straining forward, glare piercing the floor.

"And Mike, I know this started long before this morning," Chuck prompts.

The teen nods again, whispers, rasping, "Yeah, right."

Chuck digs in: "It seems there's a victim in all this who's been suffering for a long time before today – "

"He never lets up!" Mike tenses.

"Then maybe you're *not* so guilty!" the Chief counters.

"Yeah, *maybe..!*"

"Definitely not," Chuck assures him flatly.

"I don't *care* what happens to him!"

"He didn't care how he hurt you – I'll bet for years – "

"Fucking years!" Mike explodes, his body wrenching in the chair. Then a muffled, gasping sob slips out, and he squeezes his chair armrests for control.

Chuck lets Mike feel his way through that. (He peers over to see Sid gaping, wide-eyed.) He says, "All right, Mike, all right. There's no question you were cornered – provoked, I get it... Maybe it would help here if you could tell me what it was like – "

"What?!" Mike is rattled, as though expected to describe what knifing his older brother was like. (His eyes are still searching the floor.)

"No, not that," Chuck raises a halting hand, still no emotion in his face. "Just tell us a little about what it's like living with... what's life with your family – "

"Everything's fine!" Mike tightens again, defensively. "Everyone in my family's really good to–"

"Except Ray," Chuck interjects.

Mike squirms...exhales: "Except fucker Ray... I'm really okay about them – I really like my family...not him..."

(Chief Cintz right here is not about to openly question the roles of Mike's mother and father. He senses that their youngest son has had little or no help from them dealing with his now surfaced traumas: one loved brother dead and a hated one still living. And beyond this painful family drama unfolding, Chuck is in no way about to coldly moralize Mike's desperate choice of solutions.)

The police chief now simply asks again, "What else was it like?"

Mike sighs heavily, feeling some trust that he's being understood. "I don't know, you know?" (It just hit him that if it's a healthy kind of family he's in, why is he sitting here now?) "I always thought we were okay and...normal – we are, mostly. It was that accident that made things so bad..."

"Bill's?" Chuck makes sure.

"Yeah...that really made things tighten up, I guess. Mom got so upset – she hasn't been good...isn't the same. And Dad...I guess I don't ever know how he's doing..." He thinks about that a moment before adding, "But it's fucking Ray..!" And Mike bursts from reflective composure into tears, connecting Bill's loss with being stuck with Ray.

"It's okay, Mike," Chuck says earnestly, seeing the young man's self-consciousness (and verging on tears himself). "Let it happen – don't be embarrassed. Lots of people let loose here – guys, too."

"It's all criticism..." Sniffling, Mike relaxes a little, biting his lip. "All the time. And Frank gets it, too." (His cherished brother's disturbing "Dark Presence" definition comes to mind, but he doesn't want to say it – that Frank in any way may have pushed him to do something.) "It was okay when Ray was away working. It was real quiet...we didn't hold back...we got along."

"Sounds like Ray can spoil your peace and quiet from anywhere in the house," Chuck sympathizes.

"Yeah...mostly," Mike now fixes his reddened eyes on this cop for the first time. "Just him being around, he...he's just *there,* you know? *He doesn't have to say nothin'!*"

Chuck can hear Mike focusing all his life's frustration on his one true antagonist, and he needs to bring that to the present: "Why now, Mike? After taking it for so long, why fight back now?"

The question changes Mike's temperament, yet again. Sitting straight and leaning boldly across, he pierces Chuck Cintz's gaze.

"I got a right," he states, though his squinting makes it seem like a question. "It's like there's all these different people here in town, and everyone has their own bad problems so what everyone else should do is help them out and understand them."

Joseph Welt, Chuck immediately thinks. Monday's column. "You mean you were angry no one would help – "

"*No*, it's only that I got a right to be just human and people should understand I was so pissed off..."

"You want the town to forgive you?"

Mike pictures that. "Yeah, I guess." (He's a long way from putting it all together in his head and heart – so soon after.)

"And your family, too?"

Mike angles his eyes to the floor again, unable to put into words (what Chuck already knows) how his family is the true part of him, and that everyone out there needs to look at him and his family as one, in characteristics and actions.

Nodding at Sid, with a quick point to his assistant's phone to have him call the hospital, Chuck answers for Mike: "So this morning you had this feeling that you had a right – as if everyone else in town has something about us to forgive, and then your family and everyone should understand your predicament and understand that what you felt was...what? – that this was your only way out?"

"I guess, now you've said it," Mike tentatively replies. "But I wasn't thinking that..."

"This morning," Chuck finishes the awkward part for him.

"Yeah... Hey, don't ever think I feel sorry for him!" Mike now seethes again, wide eyes locking with Chuck's. "I still don't fucking care... When I did it, I was glad...when I finally took that pillow off his face and when he looked dead, I just felt good! – *nothing but good!*"

Chuck, confession heard, eases back in his chair. After a charged silence, he tells him firmly, "I can understand, Mike. It's not anything simple, the way it might look. But you know this will end up in court, and you'll have to tell the whole story – all of what you were...reacting to, today – "

"Yeah..?"

"Mike, did Ray ever hit you?" Chuck now leads. "For any reason – even when you were bad, early on?"

Mike never thought much about the hitting, before. "It was the same as the yelling," he answers indifferently.

"Did he hit you hard? – very often?"

"Yeah, a bit. But I didn't mind that, so much. It's his words that make me so mad. And the hitting, that was more when I was small – smaller than him. Then he'd just shake me a lot, and kick my butt, or something. Sometimes – once or twice – he slapped me hard..."

"What was he like otherwise?"

"Otherwise?!" Mike huffs with a sour laugh. "Hey, I was telling Frank how I don't even remember Ray around, ever. All those years, and I can't even picture him in the house...'cept when he was after me..."

"Does your mom or dad know Ray was rough with you?"

"No, I never told... They heard the yelling, is all I know."

"Your mom ever say anything to him?"

"Yeah, she said something to him, once or twice."

"And then she talked it over with you..." Chuck assumes.

Again Mike raises his hardened eyes at him, doesn't get what the Chief is making sound so normal. "No."

"Or Frank – well, never mind that," Chuck holds off on that. Instead, he asks, "So I guess your dad was mostly out somewhere?"

"Yeah. He doesn't say much, anyway. Sometimes he just blows up a bit."

Chuck looks across at Sid, nervously listening to all this, waiting on the phone. And here Chief Cintz wonders when it will hit Mike how much he has just hurt his family, rather than helping anything. Finally, he concludes, "Mike, while Ray stays okay, we can release you to your family, when they get home – because you're only sixteen. You'll be with one of us until they get back, and we'll talk some more, later. I think things could go easy for you, if Ray comes out okay."

"And if he doesn't?" Mike shows his first concern for his own fate.

"We'll see, Mike. It's been rough on you, but different things can happen, so let's wait... Anything else you want to say now?"

Mike sits motionless for a few seconds, thinking, then bursts into tears. He's sorry, now, obviously. Maybe not for Ray, but for causing this crisis. And Chuck leans across his desk and holds Mike's shoulder tight with one steady hand. Mike, with that touch, just cries harder.

Joseph sits on a Nick's Bowl stool looking confused. It's the late afternoon of...The Day of the Stabbing. Since Sid's morning phone call to the Elston hospital, through several checks in between, to the last one that Joseph minutes ago overheard in the police office before coming here, Ray Watson is still "critical". That's all: "critical" – no details. He may live; he could just as determinedly die. And now Joseph manages to recall some of the expressions he saw Monday afternoon on Mike's face when he came over, and tries to recognize in them, in his mind's eye, some telling nervous twitch, some revealing blink, of underlying murder.

"*I* never liked Ray Watson," Ba-Dee throws out matter-of-factly as he tosses his unstained apron on the counter, another slow afternoon shift finally ended.

"Huh?" Joseph is compelled partway back to this reality.

Ba-Dee explains sharply: "He's been in here bowling. He's too phony-friendly. I think he's self-serving – to a level that's painful to watch."

"He is?" Joseph is still dazed. "I've only ever bumped into the... the..."

"Sawed-off little shit," Ba-Dee suggests a comprehensive characterization.

"Ba-Dee! He's at mid-death! Have some compassion!" Joseph takes the humanitarian tract. But not very convincingly.

"Yeah, right. You and everybody else think he probably deserved it, Joseph Welt. And isn't that what always comes out in the end with these things?"

"Yes..." Joseph sorta grins, as though caught in the act.

"Well?"

"If it smartens him up, fine. He shouldn't have to die for it."

Ba-Dee humphs, "A little puncture is gonna change someone's character?!"

And Joseph feels caught again, seeing all too clearly the wide plane of conflict where human nature fights it out.

"Right!" Ba-Dee wins when Joseph can't answer. "And I'm goin' home. Seeya tomorrow." And he heads out the door.

Joseph leaves, too...but has nowhere to go. (Today, Howard drove back to college for some reason, and tonight Norm has another date with Suzanne.)

...

Down the opposite side of the street, a couple of blocks along at the stoplight corner, a big late-afternoon crowd has gathered at Lucy's bench. Bert, Mel, Shooter and Chase anchor the prime seat, with Ed, Sid, Chuck, Wilf and some other regulars sitting close by. And also standing all around pressing in are a least a dozen more "irregulars" (Joseph can't help brand them that, despite his preaching, as he soon passes through their midst). Of course, they're deeply into discussing the communal criticality of Ray Watson.

Many eyes follow Joseph as he pulls open Lucy's squeaky screen door – most are sympathetically reading his self-consciousness. (Only Joseph actually attaches guilt to his newspaper article, and only Sid and Chuck here know – since he detailed it all to them this afternoon – about his pre-stabbing contact with Mike.)

But Joseph is disappearing inside simply because he does not want to wade into their time-honored discussion pit (especially if anyone should choose to treat him as an authority). As it is, he believes he already knows everything they're saying out there. (They're just re-doing the facts, plus trying to figure out how it could possibly happen in their little town – they do it with everything, and it couldn't be healthier, he feels.) Still, he is most sorry for any turmoil he may have contributed to...but is also clearly and strongly grounded in the fact that he didn't create the Watson family nucleate of seized feelings, and he certainly didn't paint that knife-seeking bulls-eye of retribution on Nasty Ray's abdomen.

As Joseph takes a seat on the only empty stool at the far end of the counter, the buzz of voices all around does not focus into words for him. It's a blur.

He orders a coffee from kind old Jerry, and stares at the countertop.

Lucy, working the cash register at the other end, has noticed him. In a minute, when he's caught up, he wanders down...

Joseph gazes up at the body in front of him that isn't moving. "Lucy!" he greets him, without expression, above all the talking.

"How-dee," Lucy replies, equally blank.

"So, *Lucy*...give it up! You're a guy! Try...Luke, or...Ludwick, or something."

Lucy just looks at him.

"Okay, okay, what's with the 'Lucy', anyway?" Joseph now smiles broadly, trying the history-of-it approach.

"If you tell me what a 'Ba-Dee' is," Lucy counters, though not smiling.

"I don't fucking know! How should I know? I just know the guy, I didn't invent him!" Joseph laughs hardily.

"Come here," Lucy now smiles a bit, curling a finger at Joseph as he starts toward the back, at the same time nodding at Jerry to take over the cash register.

"You gonna beat the shit out of me, Lucy? – wait! I'm sorry! Lucy's a good name! I like it..." Joseph pleads as he stands up, gulping his paid-for coffee. "Or have you got a good story for me back here – about the rat community fighting off the cockroach hordes for control of your storeroom..?"

Lucy chuckles, graciously holding the storeroom door open for the taller, younger man.

In the dark little space, behind neat racks of shelves, are two worn stools tucked into a corner. Lucy points to them, and as Joseph half sits, half leans on one, the restaurant owner opens the door of the first in a row of three dinky refrigerators and takes out two demonstrably ice-cold cans of frosty beer.

"Here," Lucy beams, extending one towards his puzzled looking guest. His friendly blue eyes are sparkling as he settles his sturdy squat body upright on the other stool. Popping his can's tab, he admits in his compelling raspy voice, "This is the hideout, once in a while...guess you can see I genuinely like most everybody in town, but sometimes I've about heard enough, so it's back here, chug one down."

"Heh, of course..." Also, Joseph now thinks he's beginning to get a feel for why he's here.

"Tell you, believe wholeheartedly in what you're doing, Joseph! All the years I've been here, and even from the outside looking back, I never saw anyone here try to help others your way. It's a generous town when someone's sick or poor, but then all our silently suffering, lonely..." he trails, warm eyes matching his sad, open smile.

Joseph guesses, "Bet you've seen them all, then?"

"Lots," Lucy sips beer and sighs. "Trouble is, so many don't get help...or even understanding."

"So many?" Joseph catches how he didn't say "none".

"Okay... Ever notice how we don't have any of those charity organizations here in town? – oh, some work with them in Elston, but we never got any going here – "

"We?" Joseph notes another one.

Lucy forces a stern (as tough as he can manage) stare at Joseph. "There's a group here, of sorts – that we keep quiet. Reverend Fisk and Jimmy Jimms do most of it, and Chuck Cintz and Wilf and me and some of the wives – "

"Lucy! Spit it out! Do you rob the rich and – "

"No, no!" the older man laughs lightly. "We just...help people – ones we hear about. Mostly it's money, from the twenty or so of us businesses involved, and some of the church donations, of course. And part of it is just talking – we'll get together with someone in trouble, up at the church. Others, we arrange professional help in the city..."

Joseph is reasonably stunned. He had no idea. Uncharacteristically, it takes a few seconds for his next thought to click: "Oh! So then what am I doing here in this free-beer honor seat?" His eyebrows rise in anticipation of almost anything.

"Well, you looked kind of beat up, sitting out there," Lucy ventures.

"Beat up I am, by raging responsibility and double-fisted doubt," Joseph bemoans.

"It's that we – well, just me and Chuck and Rev Fisk, so far, we don't want you to give up...we certainly don't think you helped cause anything. And we want you to be part of our – "

"Whoa!" Joseph roars. "Hold on here, Luce! You want me to join your band of merry men so I can ignite everyone in town to rampage and carnage?! Oh, no! I've learned my lesson already, with this. I can't help anybody with anything. I simply want to raise a point here and there, and tell the occasional nice little story!"

"Of course," Lucy reaches over and pats Joseph's arm once to soothe him. "It's not a thing like riding around on black stallions at midnight saving young ladies in peril – "

"Hey, that sounds pretty good – "

"So, all we're asking is to hear about them – maybe someone's contacted you or you've found out something about someone... and you could have them...well, no, at most maybe get their permission to let us help – you know, help from the community. That's all we'd want from you."

Joseph studies Lucy for a moment. "You're a blood-drinking, baby-snatching cult, aren't you, Lucy-*fer?!*"

The restaurateur smiles wide again. "Some weekends," he nods. "Then it's back to being self-righteous pompous snots."

"Yuck! Snots! And you handle everyone's food!" Joseph now grimaces.

Lucy laughs, and gestures that he'd better get back out front. "Then give it some thought, alright Joseph? Especially the part about sticking with your columns. Everyone can see from your first one that it's a healthy...well, you know." And he stands and leaves him sitting there.

Minutes later at the ballpark, Heap Henry is chasing a long fly ball out to the center field fence when he looks up from scooping it off the grass to see the sunset glisten Joseph Welt's eyeglasses and flask as it silhouettes his sitting-crossed-legged bulk deep in the tall weeds beyond.

"Kiss me here," Suzanne sensually asks, offering her silky neck. "And here," she next suggests the soft swell of her rounded breast, opening her blouse for Norm to oblige. Outside the open windows, the last embers of sunset fade on the far horizon (it's the same section of the never-used back road where Norm and his friends come to talk and sip suds) and the cooling breeze stimulates their senses with spring freshness as it passes through the parked car.

Norm hums indulgently, and brushes his fingertips gently over the ripe rise of her nipples. She slips a hand under his shirt, tingling the bare skin of his chest...

A moment later, they're tightly locked and writhing through the closest intensities of lovemaking...

And many minutes after that, they're breathing deep, satiated sighs, accented by limp strokes of reassurance.

"Good one," Suzanne whispers in the tranquil night.

"Good," Norm smiles unseen, though she can tell he is.

"So then, isn't this better than sitting out here in the wilderness with a bunch of gossiping friends?" she playfully asks.

"It's a – wait, we don't gossip!" Norm defends their beer-guzzling slitherings through the base traits of humanity.

"Well, I guess judging from that article of Joseph's, you're not always degenerate," she laughs, still holding him tight.

"Don't hold us all accountable for some inanely positive outlook Joseph dreams up."

"That's what was so good about it: he was actually positive!" Suzanne sits up with eagerness. "Everybody we know – everybody our age can be so cynical and pessimistic! Sometimes everything we talk about condemns all authority or ridicules all the older generations."

"You sure sound positive about being positive," Norm observes.

"Well, I am – I want to be, at least, you know... Norm, if you choose to go on living, doesn't it seem intelligent to *choose* a positive philosophy? Wouldn't you rather be happy most of the time?"

"Wallowing in misery is mighty fulfilling too, sometimes," he jokes, but he's thinking something else.

"You're thinking something else, funny-guy Norm, and I can tell what it is: in all seriousness, you don't understand me wanting to be positive, do you?" she challenges.

"Umm...you haven't had it easy – "

"But you have no concept how I've felt – what happened to me with the incest, do you?"

"I have one brother," he says. "I can't begin to understand a young woman's feelings about a lot of things – let alone an incest victim's."

"You've had it pretty smooth – no, sorry, that's not true with anybody..." now Suzanne weakens (and in the darkness Norm imagines her eyes, then the sadness there that often retakes her). "All I meant was, I wonder what it's like sometimes, growing up like you did...and everyone – without it spoiled... I'm sorry."

"It's okay," Norm says, but it's not. In his mind, he doesn't see how to trust in her, and in that way can't see how to stay close. (In his image of people heading through life on different but parallel tracks, hers will always have the potential to veer off, into the unshareable distance.)

Suzanne really wants to get away from this feeling, but as though it's unfinished business, she can't: "Do you think Mike Watson was..?"

Norm exhales a deep breath in the blackness, and leans away against the door. Arm draped over the steering wheel, he peers out the windshield at the evening stars. Though she hasn't heard a single detail, he believes she knows just how Mike feels. "Ray? Sexual abuse?" (She "Mmm's" yes.) "I guess it's possible...we'll probably find out – "

"Do you feel like you're Ray sometimes – to Jeff?" she asks, surprising him with a point of view about his being an older brother that he never considered before. But now that she's said it, it jumps right to the surface:

"Don't know, actually. I guess, maybe. I'm not cruel, or anything – it must have been something really serious like that for Mike to do that to his own brother... But maybe I could worry about how Jeff sees me..."

"I'm not trying to make you feel bad here, you know," she wants to be sure he understands her. "But if you do, then to me it gets down to what has to be done – what most of us have to do – and that's put things in the past...do all the mature things... now – always," she returns to her positive stand.

"You and Joseph could be best buds," Norm chuckles a bit, though he's feeling on the outside of her healthy approach.

"Well, he is a little weird," Suzanne laughs lightly, too. "But we're not the only ones in the world with enthusiasm for living."

Both pause and think that one over for a second or two...

"Speaking of enthusiasm," he connects, now leaning back close to her...

Suzanne simultaneously does the same. Embracing tight for a comforting minute, she then whispers in his ear, "Slurp me like a bottle of beer..."

He giggles. "Make fizzing sounds."

She does, and, gurgling in his ear, presents another picture: "Lick me like a lollipop."

"Take off your wrapper," he moans. Then, nibbling her neck, he suggests, "I'll delight in your honey..."

She sensuously sighs, "Taste my milk buds thirstily..."

And as the silence holds them securely, as the gentle night entices – she aches, "Aren't you hungry? – I'm hungry. I want pizza."

"Oh, me too!" he realizes he's starving. "Yum – pizza! Let's go!"

And he breaks loose and starts the car, u-turns on the gravel and streaks through the summer night toward the alluring city glow, sweet Suzanne close at his side.

Wilf has just pointed out "Ray ain't dead yet" to his lifelong friend Chuck Cintz (in reaction to the police officer's lamenting over their town losing its peace and quiet again this morning after only one short year). They're sitting in the evening's deep shadows on Chuck's open front porch, their wives left frolicking at Lucy's on Main Street, two blocks over.

Beside Chuck on the floor is the police mobile phone, a powerfully silent potential for good or bad news about Ray Watson, as well as an instant link to Sid, who volunteered to keep young Mike "company" over at the presently still-otherwise-empty Watson house a couple of streets across from Main.

"Murder. Attempted murder." Chuck groans, fingering his drained coffee mug on the little table between them. "Either one don't sound so good on our town resume."

"And you're personally taking the blame," Wilf admonishes him. He then points his mug at Chuck with one hand as he braces a crossed leg and boot on his knee with the other, and reminds him, "Besides, you said it last year that the domestic ones don't count."

Chuck strains his pale blue eyes through the spilled interior light to try to read the expression in his friend's. "Maybe you're right," he soon begrudgingly allows him, as though he would really rather just stew in some guilt for a spell.

"And he ain't dead yet."

"It doesn't look good."

"It might be just fine."

"Through all the years we've been friends, Wilf, you're pissin' me off most right now," Chuck says for the thousandth time in their lives.

"Because right now I'm more right than ever."

"Well," Chuck does relent a little, "I guess no one can help everybody live their lives – to prevent this kind of thing happening."

"Exactly."

"And it can happen again next week, and we can't do a thing about it," Chuck closes his tired eyes and sighs with resignation.

"*You* can't stop it, Chuck. But if everybody in town was more like that Welt kid wrote, the chances would sure be lower."

As the police chief thinks that over (the part that means – same as waiting for Ray's outcome – he can only react to what time has in store) he feels compelled to do the dutiful thing and check how Mike is with Sid. He picks up the phone and calls.

...

As the phone rings in the Watson living room, young Mike is upstairs standing at the open door of his bedroom. He's been there for an hour. His stare keeps drifting from one room's doorway to the next, all around the oval hallway. (The telephone rang only once, and he can hear by how Sid is talking down there that the call is not about Ray.)

Mike is much more amazed than worried. The worry he feels is not for Ray and his life, but for poor Mom – and Dad, too – if their oldest son should die. The amazement is for how different the house feels ('the house', his mind's words, not 'our home'). It's that he really likes this emptiness a lot... Yet, studying his parents' bedroom doorway again, he genuinely feels they're always okay to have around...and sorta wishes they were home, now, where they belong. And he pictures Frank coming up those stairs, as he's seen him do hundreds of times before, and wishes he was here too, right now, to talk with. And straight across, past the bathroom: Bill's old room... Well, if Bill had been here, none of this... Anyway, what he's realized – so amazingly – is how that room down there – Ray's, at the front – is the one that's so different being empty – momentarily vacant, guaranteed. And he surprises himself actually thinking it (merely touching on the only source of any young life's pain – never from inside, always external): it would feel so good if it just stayed empty forever.

NELSON NELSON

aby Nelson Nelson, three months old, noiselessly followed the barely perceptible swayings of the bright-colored mobile dangling high out of his reach.

Back then, he was years away from questioning the oddity of his being there in his crib in his room wide-awake alone and unattended in the middle of the day. Besides, he had no way to complain, anyway. And also because of his age, there was no reasoning, yet, why his mother and father – Karen and Arthur – chose his last name for his first name, and why he had no middle names at all. And again, even if he could have thought it out and concluded that it was somewhat shortsighted and thoughtless of them, he was born without a voice, and had yet to – and would never in his life – utter a peep of complaint. ('Nelson', Mother and Father felt, was good enough, saving who-knows-how-much nuisance sorting through lists...or whatever people do to find acceptable names for offspring. And besides, 'Nelson Nelson' had an amusing sort of ring to it, sure to be humorous at untold dinner parties to come.)

As it was, the alternative to bearing him (short of abortion – it just wasn't done!) and having to name him was adoption. And if Karen's parents – the doting ones of the two sets of then prospective grandparents (Arthur's were too busy traveling to get involved, and Arthur's many brothers and sisters had ten or twelve grandchildren already, anyway) – if they hadn't voiced some strong objections to that alternative, Nelson would have been simply a John or James right then at that three-month-old moment, and would instead be silently gazing up from loving arms into the joyful eyes of some thankful, barren young woman.

Not that baby Nelson Nelson wasn't generally content. He never was seen to fuss, regardless... Or maybe he just somehow knew not to expect too much.

As the healthy little guy grew older, his temperament remained quite steady. And oddly, his greatest pastime was not toys (though he had heaps of them), his big passion was: observing. He would patiently, studiously, earnestly and calmly "look". He also loved books, and would sit motionless forever, wide-eyed involved in a picture book; he didn't seem to really care if someone (the rare time) chose to read him the words. Or, equally enthralling for him was television: he would stand still and peer into the magic worlds of television, equally fascinated whether the sound was off or on. (Mommy habitually turned on all four large sets, seldom bothering to shut any of them off until her bedtime.) Otherwise, Nelson toddled around their big house getting observationally caught up in just about anything – the cook cutting carrots, the yard man endlessly riding the big mower past all the many windows, the rain pouring down, or even the wallpaper patterns suggesting...who knows, to him. He was simply fascinated by – actively absorbed in – images.

Growing older, though, got tougher. When Nelson was four, they were forced to move to a smaller house. And two of the television sets disappeared, and one of the three cars, too. But the hurtful part for Nelson – rougher than being alone so much – was the impatience. Instead of being another mere distraction in the house who the cook or yardman or babysitters always handled for them, with their busy lives, and all, Karen and Arthur suddenly had to feed him and wash him and dress him themselves. And they hated it. Things were trying enough, without having to worry about another person's life on top of their own...things. So they pushed him to move faster, sometimes. (He understood everything and every word, but his not responding made him seem 'slow'.) Or often they apparently found it less damaging to yell at him rather than at each other, when tension was high. At other times, for hours and days on end, they were coldly and steadily indifferent, bullying him to his room to play, or, wordless as him, pulling him by the arm out to the fenced-in back yard where he could do whatever he did there, out of their hair.

But overall, time proved, Nelson was too intelligent to believe the problem was him. He seemed to invariably sense and conclude that his mother and father were seriously lacking in... something. He couldn't say exactly what, even if he had been able to talk. (Nelson did learn to write quite eloquently, yet he rarely chose to express anything they might see, and never wrote a word about them.)

Through all this, however, during those boyhood years, he did have one loyal adult friend: his (father's side) Uncle Admiral. (For generations, such humor resurfaced in the Nelson family, at the expense, too often, of the unsuspecting unborn.)

Admiral didn't come around much (a bachelor, he lived on the other side of the country), but when he did, he blatantly spent more time with Nelson than he did with his own brother Arthur (or less still, the boy's mother). He openly preferred Nelson's company. And little Peepers, as his Uncle Admiral liked to call his wide-eyed-bright young nephew, plainly cared for him most, too.

And what they liked to do more than anything, uncle and nephew, was walk or drive around. Yet arriving somewhere specific was not the best part for them; they simply enjoyed wandering all over observing the world, and everyone in it. They would go sit on beaches, in restaurants, on park benches, on hillsides, in city cafes and on riverside docks. And Admiral would talk a lot, about anything that came to mind, and Peepers would listen as intently as he watched.

...

When Nelson grew older, into his teens, Admiral came less often. (Nelson kept asking his parents, in the simplest of recycled notes, if he could go visit him, but it seemed there was never enough time to arrange it, or, ultimately, enough money to afford it.) So, instead, he began to rely more and more on his best local friend Sally, who lived three houses away and was a grade behind him at school. And until their mid-teens, they were close, often talking (writing – Nelson never learned much sign language) intimately. He would tell her all about his parents' tough times, and she would talk about how good-hearted her parents were (they were so loving to their three children, and volunteered for almost anything that had to do with the poor and needy). And of course they dreamed about traveling or careers. Then she would tell him all her deepest hopes for a beautiful family of her own, someday – often trying to talk Nelson into planning for a wife and kids, too. (He had "no heart for it" he would always write in response.) Eventually, then, they drifted apart, Sally soon finding boyfriends with good potential, in her intelligent young pursuit of solid father material.

In his late teens, Nelson matured dynamically handsome. He kept fit by running races on school track teams, and built a strong body by working summers on a produce farm. So, high school girls adored him. And though he easily made friends with many of them, he always chose to stay a bit distant – same with the guys at school he was friends with. (It was as though, to his thinking, if they got too close they would be witness to his troubled and disturbing home life.)

Then, at seventeen, the dilemma of Nelson's life: Graduated from high school, Uncle Admiral offered to pay his college tuition expenses (with limits). And, if he wanted, his nephew could stay with him until he graduated.

Unaccountably, Nelson's parents declined.

Nelson, of course, had nothing much to work with in understanding why, and in the most awkward of fights, firmly argued his needs while Mother and Father endlessly raged their refusal – without true explanation. (Their son in time reasoned that his parents could not get past their shame over – having once been wealthier than Admiral – the thought of taking his help.)

So, one morning, without any display of bitterness (which Admiral always would have understood but, to his liking, never found in his nephew's letters), Nelson packed one small bag of clothes, pocketed the money his uncle had sent, and left home for good. Feeling no anger or self-pity – with only a very clear conclusion of simple dislike – he had chosen to never see his parents again.

...

But Nelson took a year to reach his uncle's. He wrote him weekly, from all over the country: he was having the time of his life, observing far-reaching realms of nature and humanity he had only ever seen in pictures. He worked simple jobs, now and then, and at times slept penniless under the stars – once, beneath the mass of a snow-capped mountain, once in a hollowed rock amid a lifeless silent desert, more than once on a bench in a city park (in bench dormitories of newly-befriended vagrants) and several times on ocean and lakeside beaches. He made many lifelong-memorable, deepest of hours-only friends. He had loves and intimacies that lasted as long as days, or as little as one night. Yet most of all, most deliberately, he studied the trees, and their forests, and rushing water and the flavored wind; and he stopped his wanderings gladly for an hour or a day to watch some wild animal live some of its life. Of course, during those mountain or desert nights, alone or with friends, he would lay back and observe the mysterious heavens – the sanctity of space, the secretive – by distance – stars. And in his journals, and often in his letters to his uncle, he expressed boundless awe, fascination, spirituality and reverence for, and unconditional belonging to, this infinite and eternal Creation.

And only then, feeling part of the caring universe, did Nelson sense the sadness of his family. It was sad, he felt, that his mother and father believed in the lives they had chosen to live, instead of the caring way so natural to life, He couldn't condemn them, they just couldn't see. Accepting that, he then wondered if he had been born with a voice, would he also have grown up less able to see...

Ten months after leaving home, during only his second phone call to Admiral (a friendly waitress asked the few questions he wrote down, while ear-to-ear they held the receiver) Nelson heard that his father was trying to track him down. His mother, Admiral reported, had suffered some undisclosed ailment, and they wanted Nelson home to help take care of her. (Admiral had to be honest, telling his nephew that he had recently seen her and she still looked perfectly capable of taking care of herself.) Also, they had pressed Admiral to make Nelson stop sending him letters, and strangest of all, ordered him to tell Nelson to quit writing journals and "mail what he's written right home". (Only Nelson understood how much his parents were afraid he would document his life story and condemn them.) Also, Nelson's father had demanded he return home to "his responsibility to his parents" – to help them work their long-failing business, and hinted to Admiral that, if Nelson didn't come home, they were considering involving the police, suggesting that their "silent, brooding son" was mentally incapable of a "loner" lifestyle and might have to be "professionally cared for" (committed).

Uncle Admiral, to his nephew's gratitude, suggested to Nelson that he should disappear thoroughly, and, if Nelson wanted, he would no longer volunteer to his brother and sister-in-law any knowledge of their son's whereabouts. As for Nelson's college education, Admiral still wanted to sponsor him, only now he would support him at any college in the country he chose to attend. Nelson was overjoyed and enthusiastic, and promised to visit him and plan something out within two or three months.

During those few weeks, Nelson explored the remaining nooks of the nation he had wanted to see, and finished up, lastly, at the planned end of his trail: on his home street.

...

It was soon after sunup, and the August air was temperature-less sweet. Birds were singing joyfully, celebrating the daylight, and the new, blazing sun was slowly climbing toward a hot-summer peak.

Nelson turned the corner onto his familiar childhood street. No one in the neighborhood was awake yet, it seemed. He walked easily and steadily down the sidewalk opposite his parents' house, and stopped straight across. He had no intention of going in.

All he wanted to do was be sure his memories, and feelings of separation, were true. The thought of talking to his mother and father did not scare or repulse him; it just held no hope for anything positive. He was there for himself, and he got the assurance he wanted: after only ten minutes, he smiled a tiny smile of a whole childhood full of fond and hopeful dreams, then walked along to the end of the block, starting out for his Uncle Admiral's, several days away.

...

Nelson was in college that fall, immersed in the crosscurrents of how others define the world. He thoroughly enjoyed it. Through his four years there, he leaned toward literature. (Uncle Admiral had persuaded him that a formal dedicated plan was not all-important, and that, with his own recent greatly escalating success and wealth from his restaurant chain, he could continue to support him as long as he wanted. Then, as it turned out, others in the family – another uncle plus grandparents – contributed to Nelson's welfare, as well, in an ongoing statement of understanding of his difficult upbringing.) Admiral also suggested, and Nelson felt it, too (all the way back to childhood), a goal someplace in the realms of writing. So they agreed, tentatively, to that life plan.

And Nelson's college years were continuous good times – though less riotous than some others. He had a few (quiet) friends... as he explored the academic realms and lives of brilliant people (some, right there around him on campus) with fascination.

Also through that time, his one apprehension materialized when his parents contacted the police to have him found and brought home. But Admiral began persuading them that their son was safe, that he was looking after his welfare, and that Nelson very plainly wanted a life without them – and was not a threat to them. Karen and Arthur, after months of Admiral arguing and convincing, finally relented. The authorities were called off, and all was settled, for now. Admiral, however, started being careful and distant in conversations with his brother.

In time, when he felt satisfied with his college work, Nelson finished his credits (his grades were near the top all along) then packed up and left. In a few days he was back at Admiral's.

...

What the young man wanted next surprised his uncle. He explained that, to have assurance of continued detachment from his parents, he wanted to settle in some quiet town, anonymously. He intended to keep in contact with family members he had communicated with all along, and would continue corresponding with good friends as always. But he wanted to isolate himself – to just write, he thought... Eventually. Alone.

Admiral would not question that decision (despite visions of Nelson growing old utterly lonely and bitter, the consequence of choosing a reclusive life right then). So, together, they set out across the country on maps, listing possible towns.

Finally, after several weeks of exploring, they came across a town that looked most promising – which Admiral happened to know something about, knew someone there, actually (who he had taken cooking lessons from years ago, and, the last he heard from him, was still in business there).

They made the trip together, and easily found Admiral's old friend. And with that friend's help, they found a comfortable apartment for Nelson, and he quietly moved in.

That was eleven year ago.

...

As Nelson walks around the curve where the business section begins, he admires the picturesque old downtown warming in the late-morning, early-summer sunshine. The joyous blue above is splattered with ragged random cloud, and overhead, too, the sheltering maples stretching for light radiate green to the yellow day.

Nelson decides to have a coffee (as he often does on these excursions). With that thought, his eyes fix on the corner restaurant ahead at the stoplight and its worn bench out front (empty, at the moment) under the plain black-on-white sign: LUCY'S LARGE LUNCH. And he thinks of his friend Lucy, who helped him (discreetly) settle here, and sometimes – unknown to almost everyone – still drives him to the city to shop.

And today, as Nelson takes in his town, he is mindful of his new status here since his book of poetry was published last year (with just that capitalized title: "MY TOWN", a copy displayed in a place of honor there in Lucy's, its simple cover proclaiming its author: "Looker"...which he keeps meaning to sign). Still, what's been bothering him the last few weeks, what he's been mulling over, is his isolation – not from old friends or family, but all these people here. Since moving in, he has yet to talk (write, communicate) much with anyone except Lucy. It's what he wanted – to work on himself, his "life's work", as Uncle Admiral respectfully called it at first. But now that his poetry is published, he feels he has accomplished that intention (though he's currently amassing a big novel). So maybe he should simply interact: make friends, be part of the community – more than a walking body who writes down what he sees. (He has pretty much decided to live out his life here.) And though his friendships throughout his younger years were always characteristically easily sincere (but just as readily put aside) he now feels that he would like some closeness with people, on a permanent, open commitment basis...

...

Inside Lucy's, Looker takes a stool near the cash counter. It's Thursday morning, before lunch, and only two booths are occupied. Plus, Joseph Welt is poised on the last stool at the far end of the counter, twenty away from him.

Lucy nods at Looker and soon brings him his usual (cream, no sugar). Looker, as always, remains extensively expressionless, turned away watching the passing traffic outside the window. Then, when he takes his first sip of coffee, he glances over at Joseph – and sees he's absorbed in Lucy's copy of My Town, borrowed from its place of honor on the wall of shelves.

Looker contemplates, a few seconds...then stands and walks on down to Joseph. Fingering a pencil stub from his shirt pocket, he reaches for the thin, burgundy hardcover in Joseph's hands. Untidy and sloppily dressed, long-haired and scruffy-mustached Joseph Welt merely stares at him, yet holds out the book to the well-groomed and handsome, neatly but simply-dressed author. Who opens and signs it, handing it back with a hint of a smile.

Joseph reads it: "Nelson Nelson ('Looker')".

Joseph thinks: We finally know who he is.

It's Thursday evening and Ray Watson is not yet dead. Chief Chuck Cintz is tilting back on his chair at the curb in front of Lucy's. Wilf, beside him, has never seen him so moody.

Old Bert, older Mel, oldest Shooter, and somewhere-in-the-middle Chase have been hogging the bench since suppertime. The sun still shines from overtop the opposite buildings onto their aged faces. Sid, Ed and Reverend Fisk are sitting on chairs at the end by the door. Wives (Chase never married; the Rev, not yet) are inside, routinely laughing it up.

"Wilf, tell him," Sid asks for help at improving his chief's humor.

"I did," Wilf replies.

"Tell the man there's nothing he could've done even if he'd seen it coming," Chase suggests it as though Chuck is not right there among them.

Chuck sneers. "I knew there was nothin' I could've done about it as soon as I knew about it."

"But now you think this town's all screwed up for all time to come, don't you?" Chase stares down Chuck the youngster.

"No. Not in the least," Chuck focuses piercingly back at him.

"It's just a sign of the times!" little Mel trembles. "Violence fixing everything!"

"You think this new generation just now discovered violence?" Wilf contests. "People been whackin' and guttin' each other since God said go."

"Well..." Bert pulls strands of his cotton-white beard, and wisely observes, "it's not only that a small town like this is supposed to be more sane, it's also that this town's been pretty good at it. Even that murder last year was done by someone not benefiting from the wholesomeness of growing up here."

"So then what wholesome part did young Mike not get?" Ed again dutifully rises to his challenger's destiny.

"Instead of being against Mike Watson," Wilf has a thought, "maybe we should be sayin' stuff against Ray Watson."

"You mean Ray deserved to be punctured? – have some life let out of him? – let some of that *evil energy* out?" Shooter's deep voice joins in.

"We're talking in circles," Chuck observes.

Ed holds up a hand to stop everything and counterbalances: "There's no conclusion we can make, anyway."

"Has to live or die, first," thinks Bert.

"No hurrying that up," notes Chase.

"Well, everybody just slow down your thinking to the same rate as reality," Reverend Fisk tries a rare piece of order giving.

"That's it!" Chuck exclaims, with little emotion. "That's what drags me down, how your head gets way ahead of things imagining solutions and outcomes, but reality is still there dragging you back!"

"But that's how we work, Chuck," Wilf theorizes. "People can't handle all the shock of a tragedy all at once, so your head goes elsewhere."

And Chuck concludes with a forced sigh, "And every time you look back at what happened, it hits you again – like it didn't fuckin' penetrate the first time! – like when I saw Ray Watson lying there yesterday in half his blood, it all didn't have enough fuckin' reality to it to make me believe it...!"

S ince Sid drove off an hour or so ago, leaving Mike here in the care of his parents, no one in the Watson home has said a word.

The thirty-some hour vigil Mom and Dad kept at their drifting-in-and-out firstborn's intensive care bedside was forced to pause by doctors worried about the parents' health. (By the time Mom was brought in by ambulance yesterday, she was mostly recovered. With a mild sedative, she was soon allowed to be with Ray.) And because Elston Hospital is only ten miles from their house (Frank drove back last night), they were told to "go home, get some rest, and come see how things are tomorrow morning".

Mike has spent almost every minute upstairs – since Chuck brought him home yesterday and parked Sid downstairs to watch him – sitting at his desk or stretched out on his bed or pacing the floor of his room. (What spurred him to walk the floor was this surreal shock of a previously numbed realization that Ray's bedsheets right here up the hall are still red with his gushed blood.)

Right now, on his back on his own bed, Mike is aware that Mom is rocking in her recliner in the living room (if the television is on, the sound is set low) and that Dad is in the kitchen noisily making sandwiches or cleaning up dishes. (Mike automatically assumes that his father is irritated at having to be home for an evening, and that the several quick shots of rye whisky he downed as soon as they got back – Mike heard the cabinet door shut a few times – helped only a little.) Also, by the sound of water still splattering on the asphalt drive, he knows Frank is still outside trying to avoid being inside by washing the car meticulously.

Mike now wishes Frank was upstairs here, and that they were just talking like they usually do – used to do – as brothers, and that everything was all okay...though he understands that something still has to happen or not happen, and that time has to pass before things can be all right. Still, right now (he manages to focus squarely) it's all about happen...or not... But the struggle in his feelings is that the part of him that wishes Ray would be pronounced "recovering fully" is being involuntarily and repeatedly overlaid by his intense need to have the phone harshly ring and a cold voice from the hospital fatally pronounce, "Ray's dead."

It's as if he hasn't, through normal remorse and guilt, suppressed his determination and motive for stabbing his oldest brother in the first place...but it's not as though he's sure he would do it again – if Ray was right now down the hall asleep in his bed and a knife in hand felt powerfully huge with solution – and so then again all the stress would be suddenly dead..!

Well, maybe he would...

But then now he can clearly see how Mom is hurt all over again for having boys...and how, with this new tragedy, the family is that much less of a family all over again, too.

Yet his next thought is: I don't fucking care! Is Ray now some kind of a saint or something? Was Ray ever – *once in my life!* – anything but an all-out prick to me?! Or to Frank? – Ray, the fucking Dark fucking Presence?!

And Mike lays an arm across his eyes and lightly cries, once again, as he turns those thoughts over – cries not for himself or for Ray or for anyone else living...but for Bill...Bill. If Bill was still here, this wouldn't have happened at all, he's now sure. And though he could not put it into words, he somehow knows inside himself that his brother Bill's death one long year ago did not, as you would expect, bring his family closer together. In fact, it's plain, it made things worse...

Right then the phone rings loudly. Mike hears his mom gasp with surprise at just the sound of it. He simultaneously hears Frank drop the hose to rush inside. Dad answers it...

Dead. Alive. Dead...alive... Mike tries to figure out which one from the intensity of his father's muffled voice... He can't tell. So he could simply get up and go downstairs...but then – either way – he's the one who caused it...

But he can't just lie here...

His socks sliding silently on the hallway's bare hardwood floor, Mike crosses diagonally to the top of the stairs, and listens. His father hangs up.

"He apparently stirred a little, but otherwise they say no change," Dad immediately reports to Mom and Frank in the living room. Mom faintly moans, Frank stirs – probably to go comfort Mom – while Dad clomps back to the kitchen and starts banging things around some more before making another trek to the liquor cabinet.

A moment later, as Frank is coming upstairs to fill him in, Mike flops back down on his bed again, and sighs.

O f all the stories Joseph already thought he would like to write, the most distant from his reach, before today, had seemed Looker's – Nelson Nelson's. At one story per week, and a life's story in every person in town, he would run out at age seventy-two, he had estimated while mapping his career. Looker's, he had imagined, would be last.

Still hanging around Lucy's (now waiting for Norm, Howard and Ba-Dee) he hours ago moved from that historical stool to a back booth, and at present is hogging it all to himself amid the busy Thursday evening crowd. Shut title-up in front of him on the table is Lucy's copy of MY TOWN, newly autographed by Looker Nelson. And, as of moments ago, Joseph has studied every poem. And more times than once, he has angled his wide eyes at the loose little slip of paper, now folded up beside the book, on which Looker wrote his address.

Piecing together a vision of his life from his poetry, journalist Joseph next tries to mentally create a picture of what Looker's place might be like, plus what's in his refrigerator (as in: beer?) and then what, for goodness sake, they are going to talk about tomorrow afternoon when he visits over there. (The only thing that was communicated this morning, besides the address, was on another piece of paper with which his apparent new friend declared, "I liked your column. Good point!" To which Joseph replied orally, "I like your poems. Good words!")

Maybe, Joseph now thinks, he wants me to write his life story. Or maybe Looker put together the timing of Ray Watson's stabbing with my column..."Like I did," he utters to himself – then flicks his gaze to see if Lucy is watching him, like he probably watched Mike Watson sitting muttering in that booth over there a few days ago. But, whatever the reason, Joseph ultimately knows it will be more than curious just being alone in the same room with the one and only Looker...

All three of his buds enter Lucy's together, and they head straight for Joseph and his back booth. (He's decided to hold off mentioning to them his earthshaking meeting of realities with Looker.)

"Is Ray dead yet?" Howard tries to sound as insensitive as he can, glaring sideways at Joseph as he sits beside him.

"Got nothing else to wish for in your desperate little life?" Joseph answers with a question.

"Yeah, right, Joseph," Ba-Dee scoffs, sliding in straight across from him. "Everyone in here at this very moment has Howie's question circling around inside their skull."

"But only *Howie* here can't wait 'til the guy ceases!" Joseph chuckles, intrigued by ghouls.

"No, not so," Howard rejects that. "The mere stabbing was exhilarating enough!"

Norm well knows they're not at all serious, but has to get serious, anyway: "Jeff told me something," he begins, referring to his talk today with his younger brother. "He said Mike told him a few days ago he hated Ray enough to run away – "

"*Run away?!*" Joseph flusters. In his two-hour conversation with that sixteen-year-old, he barely heard Ray's name, let alone any inclination to escape or end him. "He made it sound to me only like he wasn't sure about his family...well, he said Frank is good to him, sure, but can't really give solutions...guess... Anyway – Norm! – running away is a diametrical action to stabbing a brother!"

"So then it wasn't the whole family messing him up after all, was it?" Howard observes.

"Don't be so sure," Ba-Dee cautions.

So Howard questions, "You mean that all Mike's frustrations over his whole family ended up sticking in Ray?"

"That's too easy to say," Joseph now thinks. "It still could've been just Ray coming down so hard on him..."

"Well then," Ba-Dee has a summating thought, "the family created Ray the monster, then on top of it, the family wasn't any use supporting Mike..."

And here all four naturally pause to once again examine in their own minds just how well balanced their own families feel.

School's out. At ten this morning a breakaway splinter from the report-card-clutching horde spilling out the exits biked straight over here to the baseball field.

Brilliantly blue sky with barely a cloud in it holds the warm sun in place above the rough old diamond. It's officially summer now, to these boys, and the dusty infield has been slowly baking to readiness through the warm spring.

The embracing fresh air welcomes the assembly of sixteen young players (captains Rick and Jackie each drafted one new recruit from the school diamonds teams to start today – though both have been sitting in the stands through every single spring after-school inning). All are eager and healthy and excited that the annual summer-long game is about to commence.

"Peckerface," Jack asserts, centering the teams gathered at home plate, "we flipped for it last year, remember? Anus-lips!"

Rick isn't so sure: "Shit-for-snot, we didn't!"

"I won, we choose: field first!" Jack leans toward him, long black hair dancing and black eyes piercing. "Or would you rather have a big fuckin' blade up your guts, scrotum-nose?"

Several of the boys' eyes pop.

"Maybe a few air holes in you would let out some of that bullshit-for-blood!" lean and long-faced Rick suggests.

The other team leader responds, "Yeah maybe you'd be more of an opponent with a bunch of switchblade handles sticking out of your–"

"Despiteous dorks!" Heap Henry impatiently interjects, utilizing his dictionary power-word for today, all thirteen other pairs of noncombatants' eyes shifting toward his eyes somewhere behind his wild blond hair dangling down. "Let's finish warming up so we can play, okay?"

Immediately the others' gaping gazes split back between obstinate pillars Rick and Jack, again...

"Okay," Jack agrees, abruptly good-natured. And Rick nods too, thoughtful yet willing.

With the two new kids blinking uncontrollably, they all separate by teams. Rick's boys clump into their dugout to get ready to bat (there really was no doubt that Jack was right) as the others fan out onto the field.

This year, there will be catchers.

"Maybe Ray hurt him," Jack reflects, halting his shuffling preparations on the pitcher's mound to peer into the dugout shadows at his good friend Rick. (Both know pretty much what that means, having heard all about that kind of thing from last year's new best friend, murder witness and abuse victim Eddie Ogden, sitting right there a few feet away on Rick's bench.)

All the other kids stop in mid-motion again.

"Maybe," Rick replies cautiously from the shade, picturing that remark suddenly boiling personal feelings in untold numbers of these boys all around.

"Yeah maybe Ray Watson is just another testicle-eyed, vomit-faced pus-brained lowly scum-rotten shit-lickin' no-good fuckin' mean bastard dog-ass-sniffin' prick," Jack expressionlessly states, rather than asks.

"Could be," Rick can see it. (If Jack weren't perfectly serious, Rick would be obliged to offer praise for that fine string of slurs.)

"Or maybe Mike's jus' loopy," he tries to be fair, bending over to pick up his favorite of their three beat-up bats.

"Possible," the almost-fifteen-year-old on the mound allows, finally giving up the ball for his infielders to warm up.

"Bet it hurt," Simon, Jack's little ten-year-old rookie player peeps from behind home plate through his clumsy huge mask atop wads of equipment draped all over him. (New players have to catch – new rule.)

Jack cringes at the thought of a big knife blade shoved in under his own ribs. "Yeah, bet," he groans.

"If he dies," Manny, his usually wordless third baseman asks, "does Mike get the electric chair?"

Jack sneers across at him through the bright sunlight and starts, "No, they don't do that to younger – "

"Mike gets a huge medal!" Eddie Ogden shouts out a fitting interjection from the dark dugout. "And a hundred thousand dollar reward – for erasing another scary sawed-off little shit from the face of the Earth!"

After a few seconds of silence – a sensitive moment of inner amusement plus formative affiliation – slowly, pensively, the proceedings of baseball finally crank into motion.

Skirting right past the ballpark late Friday afternoon in his roundabout route, Joseph Welt paces unwaveringly onward toward Looker's. (Catching sight of him walking by on the adjacent street, Heap Henry reflexively spins around in center field and checks the tall weeds beyond the fence, as though there could suddenly somehow be two of him.)

At the end of Looker's street, a humble old two-story, white-siding house sits squarely up close to the sidewalk. A few feet past its tree shaded yard, the road ends at a ditch; picking up where asphalt and cement leave off is a sunny field of precision young cornstalks.

Joseph takes the ninety-degree turn up the narrower of two walks, the one that leads to the separate entrance at the side. Climbing the dark-wood enclosed stairway, he finally arrives at the green-painted solid door to Looker's – Nelson's – apartment. Without hesitating, he knocks...

Nelson swings open the door.

"Looker!" Joseph greets him with a wide grin, feeling the moment. Nelson actually smiles back, slightly but naturally, brightening his handsome face. (He's wearing his usual pocket T-shirt – dark green, today – and jeans.) Now he flings the door open wide, sidestepping with it to let Joseph pass...

The entrance is the kitchen, and at first sight Joseph can see it's as tidy as Looker: Plain white cupboards span the upper halves of two walls overtop worn-pale and uncluttered counters. A spotless white porcelain sink sections the long one, and a four-paned window above it is bright with daylight (no curtains). At the center of the aged but gleaming hardwood floor, a bare oval table is closely bracketed by three simple chairs. It looks as though they're never used.

His demeanor calm, Nelson tilts his head a bit, inviting Joseph to go sit.

They step into the comfortable living room. Three stout, classic, conservatively upholstered easy chairs, a tasteful oriental rug, three attractive antique floor lamps and several traditional, well-framed prints on the walls, plus (for some reason Joseph is a little surprised to see) a huge television set, furnish the plain white room. Straight across, curtained glass paneled double doors are iridescent with pre-evening sunshine.

Looker crosses the carpet and opens the glowing doors, leading Joseph out. (Before passing through, Joseph has a glimpse into the bedroom on the left: its visible walls are all shelves, with every segment solid with books.)

They are now on the roofed porch that fronts the sun-soaked side of the second floor (layered over a similar one that spans underneath). A steaming coffee pot sits on a squat wicker table against the wall, two thick white mugs waiting beside it. A pint carton of cream unpretentiously completes the set. On either side of the table are wooden rocking chairs with thick, flower-patterned seat and back cushions. Near the far end of the balcony, another well-worn armchair faces the farmlands. In front of it, on a little metal table on wheels, is a straightforward looking old computer. Joseph can see that it's turned on.

Nelson leaves Joseph standing there while he strides over to his computer. He wheels it back and parks it in front of a chair, indicating to his guest, with a little wave of extended fingers (somehow it's obvious), to sit here. He then picks up the keyboard, unravels some of its long cord, and settles onto the other chair with it on his lap. He gestures again, this time toward the coffee (still expressionless – out of habit) and the visitor openly grins and helps himself.

Joseph slurps a sip, smacking his lips in appreciation of its quality flavor. Then, rather than Looker's mysterious gray eyes, he gapes at the blank computer screen and its blinking cursor directly in front of him...and says:

"Okay, Looker. I see how you do it – so spit it out."

"Ha-ha," quickly types on the screen.

Joseph angles his stare at his host. (Looker is actually smirking.)

"Nelson Nelson, eh? Very humorous," Joseph smiles in his friendly-mocking way.

"Family history of disturbed humor," Looker keys.

Joseph again can't help eyeing him (because this is such an odd way to converse plus he can't keep locked onto the reality that he is actually here with this man – this legend!)

"You're a legend, Nelson!" Joseph says what he feels.

Nelson responds, "Maybe you can tell me about that... You can call me Looker – I won't call you Crusher, though."

Joseph laughs, realizing it more every second that, aside from his profound literary skills, this individual is the most astute of observers. "So, Looker...nice spot you have here."

The cursor deposits: "Good place to soar..." And Joseph raises his eyes and gazes out onto a gently heaving sea of checkerboard fields – square shades of green edged by scruff or lonesome trees, farm houses in yards of barns and sheds that center the disciplined acres. Charging in the distance, foaming thunderheads push high into the blinding blue, halfway to the silver sun...

"See what you mean," Joseph says.

Saving the other writer the awkwardness of composing careful words to ask, Nelson then spontaneously bangs out his encapsulated life story (about five screens full) including, even, his boyhood nickname "Peepers" (as though an option to "Looker"), adding fond memories like his childhood friendship with Sally, then enough disturbing details about his parents to give Joseph all he needs to grasp what degree of family warp he's coming from. Responding next to a next-obvious-question look from the columnist, Nelson spells out just how he came to settle here in town, crediting Lucy fully. (Joseph's respect for Lucy's positive influence is expanding steadily.)

When the lines stop forming on the screen, Joseph asks, "Is this why I'm here – so you can explain yourself?"

"Uh...partly, I suppose," Nelson slowly answers. "No, wait. Don't think that it's my first motivation. It's mostly because I'm finished that work – working on myself, I guess," he admits, "and I want to rejoin the living."

"I empathize."

"And from your article, I like your noble philosophy..." Nelson trails with three dots.

"Fuckin' poets!" Joseph mutters with a grin.

And Looker, to his new friend's delight, silently chuckles, heaving shoulders and all, while clicking: "As you know, a thought doesn't materialize the same in print as it does by voice," he qualifies his being caught in the middle. He then insists, "You were right, though – in your column: It would be a better world."

"Some people always keep trying," Joseph believes. "But then again, it seems there'll always be wads in society who never see it...or refuse to do it."

"Like Ray Watson?" Nelson types.

"I imagine. And you wonder why it is that some people do life a few degrees different, like that."

"My parents..." Looker attests his complete understanding. Then, with Joseph eyeing admiration at him, he questions, "What about you? Who you blaming?"

Joseph reads it and laughs. "That's part of my point, isn't it: You can choose to direct your own life and avoid spending all your energies running around pinning victimizer on everyone you've ever dealt with." And he proceeds to give Nelson his three-minute rave-slash-rant on life growing up here.

"It's a fascinating town, here – " Nelson then next begins.

"People are fascinating everywhere," Joseph talks overtop the illuminating words.

" – And a lot of stories for you, I guess?"

Joseph just smiles forcefully at Looker.

"Sure!" Nelson laughs again in response. "I'm simply another citizen, and you're the media mouth. Smear me all into the news-print, if you have to."

"Ha! Likely down the road, some," Joseph layaways his new bud's concern, then proposes, "I have a thought: If I'm over here again sometime, why don't we search out your old friend Sally – if you're so into true friendship right now?"

"Good idea. Never thought of it that way – like it wasn't legal, or something."

"I think contact with friends will always be ethical," Joseph assures him.

After they drain the pot of coffee, Looker totes out a tub of ice-nested bottles of beer...and he and Joseph amble into a fulfilling evening of rambling, gut spilling and jabs, all in full view of the quieting summer dusk. They share belief in Chuck's assistant Sid (Joseph hears things – lately, from Lucy – about Sid's hard-ass father, open stuff but unpleasant to repeat, that he could never have imagined happening to the easygoing, non-violent native son). Then, an objective exploration of Mike Watson and family, voicing every possible theory they could imagine for the stabbing.

Leaving late in the sun-setting evening, Joseph thanks Looker kindly, points out that they'll of course see each other around town, and that he would sincerely like to get together again –

promising next time he won't be so in awe of The Legend. And, lastly, tells him to watch his local listings for The Welt's next exposing column – "It could be you, Peepers the Poet!"

Nelson smiles delightedly once more, and Joseph clomps down the stairs. Nelson appreciates the younger man's openness, and humor.

And feels good to be reconnected with life.

...

Ten minutes later, in the last draining colors past sunset, a substantially eased and overwhelmed Joseph Welt makes eye contact overtop his flask through the weeds and fence with wary Heap Henry's right there leaving center field...and laughs out loud.

Also, earlier today, Mom and Dad and Frank Watson woke up to find Mike missing. They checked every room, plus the attic, basement and back yard, but he was gone. Though they knew Chief Cintz wouldn't be so casual about it, they were sure maybe Mike simply couldn't sleep and went out for a late-night...or sunrise...walk.

Then, while Dad was on the phone to the hospital and Mom was getting ready to go, Frank, cleaning up in the kitchen, noticed something else: the wooden block on the counter, slotted for seven big knives, held only six... The knife set had been there for years, and tidy as Mom always was... At that moment the missing one stood out more missing than if it was still in there shooting out flames. Frank then searched every drawer, and even out on the porch and all around downstairs... Couldn't find it. He slipped quietly upstairs and checked Mike's room and bed, and even Ray's room (Dad steeled himself last night to change the bedding). No knife, anywhere.

When Mom and Dad were ready to leave, Frank insisted (though trying hard not to be dramatic) that he should stay home and wait for Mike. The last thing they needed to hear right then, he thought, was that their youngest son...no, he couldn't begin to guess where Mike was or what he was doing.

As soon as his parents drove off, Frank phoned Chief Cintz.

...

Mike stirs, and wakes up halfway in another world. He doesn't quite recognize where he is: he's on his back on a bed of musty old lawn chair cushions, and beside him, stuck standing straight up in the rough wood flooring, is a big knife.

As he blinks at the knife, clearing his focus, the anesthetic of sleep slowly dissipates. Last night (he replays his own movements in his mind) he couldn't doze off, again. Feeling jumpy, he went down to the kitchen... Why did he leave the house? – he felt he just couldn't stand it, that's why. Some dark sort of feeling came over him, and he had to get outside. He headed down for the front door – Mom and Dad were sleeping, he could tell when he passed their bedroom door...and there was Frank, asleep on the well-worn pullout sofa on the porch, barely visible in the light from the street. So, he crept back through the downstairs rooms to the kitchen – impulsively grabbing the knife as he passed – then eased out the side door.

It was the dead of night. Must have been about three o'clock. He wandered aimlessly for an hour, all around town (avoiding the section of Main Street with the bright window of the police office) clutching the knife... Strolling back toward home, finally feeling a little tired, he stopped walking, still a block away, in front of the Bennetts'. Their house was dark – they already left weeks ago for their cottage up north, he knew, them going away every summer for ten years now, ever since Mister Bennett retired. Right then (in the most impulsive of decisions that can change the course of a life) Mike turned and walked toward the leaning old garage at the back of their yard – he knows where the key is. (Like half the kids on this street, he earned spending money cutting their lawn and keeping the flowerbeds clean while they were gone.)

Mike reached under the rear steps of the house and found the nail with its key – they never move it. In the blackness of that side-street back yard, he unlocked the garage side door and eased in, cautiously shutting it behind him...and he thought: Instead of going home, to all that shit, I can just stay here...

At the rear wall of the nearly lightless garage, past the clutter of derelict bicycles and mowers and junk, is a rickety set of wooden steps leading up to a small loft. Without much thought, Mike climbed up, and settled down.

Now it's morning. What time is it, he wonders... He squints out the opaque-with-crud little four-pane window beside him. "Wonder if Ray died?" – those exact words form in his head. Still lying back, in the dust and dim light, his eyes turn to the knife, again. If I go home now, he realizes, I'm in deeper shit than ever...

So he stays right there.

Through the day, Mike thinks about everything he's thought about for the last few days – same routine, sitting around day-dreaming. Only now he's on the outside. In some ways, this feels better: no dread of anyone saying anything at all to him. In other ways, it's worse: isolated – maybe forever – from the good feelings he does have for his family.

Eventually, Mike faces the dilemma here that he can't see a thing going on outside. I could crack open those two front doors, he visualizes as he sits up and squints down through the soft stillness at them –

Suddenly a lawnmower starts! Sounds like it's right out front...

After a minute, he figures it's next door – but then it hits him that he has the garage key and that some kid (he tries to think who's doing it this year) will be looking for it to get in here for this mower! So now he tries to remember when the Bennetts' lawn was last cut, or how long the grass looked last night... He can't.

He could take a chance and just go out and put the key back – when they're finished next door... Well, it's Friday, school's out, so the kid might hold off cutting... He decides to chance hanging onto this key – but realizes he'll have to break into the house to hopefully find another one if he's going to stay here for a few days... He could look for some food in there, though. And even sleep inside, too – no, the police might search the house looking for him knowing there's no one home – but then they'll check the garage, too..! He has to think this out... No, wait: I don't need the key to lock it and get out – only to get in – I just unlock it, put the key back, then come in, close the door and flip the knob lock – idiot! (He now worries he's losing brainpower – maybe it's all the worrying.) But I still have to eat – fuck! What am I doing? Now I'm staying here forever?! (And he considers going home again, for the hundredth new reason – then for the same old single haunting reason, decides to hold off some more.) Maybe after dark I'll break into the house and just go snooping around a bit...

Mike next thinks about poking around the garage, to kill some time – but then I'll rub off dust from stuff, leave fingerprints and maybe footprints. So he looks down below again, trying to picture if he can hide up here well enough if someone comes in... Yeah, maybe...

Sometime later, as the sun lowers and shines broken-beamed through the trees out back and the dirty panes beside him, Mike starts to doze off. And he startles awake just once, when he dreams an image of his mother – poor, innocent Mom, hurt by him all over again, this time by his running away...

...

It's pitch black when Mike wakes up. And eerily quiet. Whatever time it is (he sits up thinking) I gotta get out of here for a while. He inches to the stairs (aware of where the knife stands, exactly – untouched) then silently down and through the side door.

The warm fresh air is delicious. The yard is not as dark as late last night, with inside lights still spilling from houses beside and behind. Too early to slip around town, he sees, so he sits on the back door steps to wait... Might as well try the doorknob here, too...nothing; try the key..."Whoa, shit!" he whispers as the key turns the lock and the door swings open. (Never told us kids about that, did they!)

So, he snoops through the whole house in the dark, with only the neighborhood light coming through the windows to see by. He doesn't even think why he's doing this. (Now I'm a thief!) Back in the kitchen, he looks for food: there's nothing whatsoever – not even a can of anything. He lets the tap water run cool, then takes a long drink from his cupped hands, and dries off the sink with a paper towel – which he stuffs in his pocket. "Maybe I'm totally loony," he mumbles loudly, as though vocally defying his own caution. He then wanders to the living room and sits on the sofa right under the front picture window, and watches the shadowed empty street... It takes about an hour to feel right at home.

After sitting there hours more doing nothing but thinking round and round the same circles, Mike impulsively stands and leaves. Noiselessly stepping out the back door, he returns the key to its hiding place before strolling up the driveway. (In his gray spring jacket and blue jeans, he imagines he's blending with the night.)

Not about to strut along the sidewalk, he keeps close to the houses, easing in behind trees to scan around and listen. He then cuts through yards the two blocks over to Main Street, and oozes out into the back of the Nick's Bowl empty parking lot. He creeps along the building right up to the street...deserted, perfectly still. Even the police office down the way looks dark.

Mike doubles back behind Nick's to an open washroom window – it's a foot over his head. He finds a bucket to stand on. Prying away the screen, he slithers in.

At the lunch counter, everything is bright with streetlight angling in through the big side window. The cavern of bowling lanes beyond is almost black. He heads straight to the refrigerator beside the grill and, opening it just enough, grabs three wrapped sandwiches and a cola (they work two shifts here, he knows, so no one will notice and miss them). He rounds the counter end and sits on a middle stool. And gazes out on his empty looking town, gulping down food.

Soon, sipping soda and no longer starving, Mike realizes he feels kinda good. In control – of how he spends all his time. And smart, that he can manage all alone if he has to. He certainly feels he's a better person than Ray ever was, right now... But then, is Ray still alive? He wonders how he can find out... As okay as my parents are, he thinks, I have my own life to live – so I have a right to take off and live it! (He doesn't forget for a second that he's an attempted murderer – at the very least.)

Mike continues to sit, pondering. Soon, the police car coasts by, toward the stoplight. His dreamy thoughts collapse at the sight of it: they're looking for me, he knows. They cruise around all night, sometimes, he's aware, but now they're watching out for me, mostly.

Ten minutes later the patrol car comes back – and pulls right into Nick's lot! Mike ducks and scurries behind the counter – no way they can see inside here, he thinks. But as the cruiser turns around, it slows to a crawl, and then stops with its headlights bright in the side window and door twenty feet away from him. He jams up tight and low against the inside of the counter.

Mike then startles when he hears the side door clunk a little: the cop's checking that it's locked, he guesses...heart thumping, now. But in a minute the lights swing away, and he peeks over the counter... The car is still there, shut off at the front of the lot facing the street. The policeman gets out again – it's Sid, he can see – and starts down the sidewalk, trying doors.

Less tense now, Mike also feels that much more confident. The police wouldn't have keys to search inside every house or store, he reasons. And with only one cruiser, he can easily keep track of where they are. (He's not oblivious to the possibility that Nick could be so restless tonight that he decides to come over here to bowl it off, for a while. But that's unlikely – he believes in the odds.) So he pulls up the tall counter-worker's stool to sit and watch out the window, and begins to imagine what he can do next...

I could steal money right now...but he pictures Nick calling Chief Cintz when he misses it and then it's an easy guess who took it. Even if I leave town, he determines, I can't let them know where I've been – they probably already think I've walked to Elston, or something. For tomorrow (Saturday), anyway, I'll go back to the garage. To get more food, he considers next, I can try the two grocery stores or the variety store. The grocery stores wouldn't miss anything...

Then he wonders about Ray again, remembering that the Town Talk doesn't come out again until Monday – if they even print anything about his condition in it... One way to be sure how it all ends up, he momentarily smiles to himself, is sneak over to Elston Hospital with that knife...

A few minutes later it occurs to Mike that all he has to do is call – pretend he's Frank phoning from home: he can't sleep, worrying, and he's just asking how his brother is doing now. So, waiting a half hour for Sid to drive off, then finding some change in the tip jar and looking up the number in the streetlamp-spill on the payphone by the door, he calls the hospital.

"Unchanged," is all the nurse replies. (Mike doesn't want to bug her with questions, in that she'd remember and give Frank a hard time when she sees him.)

So...Ray's still alive...

Not sure what time the sun rises...Mike checks the clock and decides to scurry back to the garage. But first, seeing two trays full of hamburger buns under the counter, he grabs one package... and a few shingles of cheese from the fridge. And another cola. And two chocolate bars.

Twenty minutes later Mike is up in Bennetts' garage loft, struggling in the dark and dust to make his bed of cushions more comfortable for his second day of utter freedom.

"The nurse thought it had to be Mike calling because he didn't ask about his mother – like Frank would've," Sid explains to Chuck.

The police chief nods, standing at their office window. It's soon after sunrise, Saturday. (Sid had thought it best to call his boss in right away). Chuck can see how all the nurses would have soon known about Mrs. Watson collapsing on the floor beside Ray's bed last evening when she heard Mike was still missing. (She was already distraught to exhaustion, and with the added torment of the new dread that her youngest had run off somewhere and maybe even killed himself...they admitted her.)

"You still don't think Mike's got a friend hiding him?" Sid asks, standing tensed at his desk, blue-shirted belly almost resting on it (as though he wouldn't be quite as ready to act if he was sitting down). His hazel eyes glare with concern.

"Then it would be hard to imagine why he'd have to wait until five in the morning to phone the hospital for open information, I guess," Chuck reasons. And raking his fingers once through his hair, his pale blue eyes turn intent on something across the street... (Sid soon recognizes he's just waiting for the official wave from Lucy signaling the day's first pot of coffee.)

"True," Sid sees. "So, he could be anywhere in Elston – or even in town here, somewhere, considering it's a local call." (Soon after Sid woke him this morning, Chuck had the phone company check if the alleged Mike call was long distance.)

"Sid..?" Chuck now rebegins, and his assistant leans even more alertly forward. "Remember...I hope this doesn't upset you...we're friends for life, right?"

"Of course," Sid instantly and sincerely beams.

"Remember you telling us years ago about your father being so mean, and things?" Chuck turns, catches him blinking rapidly. "You ended up a good guy, is all I'm saying. But what I wonder about is someone like that Eddie Ogden kid – after all he went through with that no-good son-of-a-bitch father he used to have." (Chuck helped persuade Eddie's dad that he was not really into fathering and to therefore move away, for the long while – at least.) "Then I could understand Eddie someday wanting to give him a few lumps, or something... Isn't that a natural reaction to have? After taking it for so long?"

"I'd never stab anyone!" Sid is quick to put his perspective on it.

"Not everyone can see the right thing to do, so easily," Chuck praises.

"Yeah, guess," Sid now relaxes a bit, wide eyes fixed on his messy desk. "I suppose it's natural when you're hurt, to hurt back."

"True. Well, I had an interesting talk with Frank Watson yesterday, over there. He painted a pretty dark picture..." Chuck pauses to watch Sid, again.

"You mean because of Ray, not their dad," Sid meets his eyes.

"Right. And now I think Ray was real tough on Frank and Mike – especially Mike. But I don't think Ray did any one specific thing to him...it just built up."

"You think it was anything sexual?" Sid poses.

Chuck is caught off balance. He tries not to show it, but the idea that Sid was sexually abused – for him to now so readily consider it – unnerves him...he never imagined. "Uh...can't rule it out, I guess," he replies.

"That's the most powerful thing, sometimes – to mess somebody up," Sid believes.

"Well, regardless, that whole Watson family is pretty reserved. I don't think there was any help for Mike when his brother Bill died, or any help for him in dealing with Ray, either. Whereas Frank seems a step or two better at handling it."

Sid thinks for a few seconds. "It's better if it's out in the open, I know. My mom knew about everything, and she kept it in the open and talked a lot with me about it. So I saw that it wasn't something wrong with me, then even when Dad got rough it seemed easier to take."

"Did you ever...hit back?"

"That's what made him stop – when I got big enough to fight back."

Chuck mulls that over and says, "Well then that's just what Mike did, it seems. Only unfortunately, he chose to do permanent damage."

"I was wondering if he's run off for good, now," Sid can see. "Like he's really messed up – in a real way, instead of any sort of nothing thing Ray could blame him for."

"Yeah, could be," Chuck exhales heavily, then sees Lucy's wave. "Com'on, let's go get a gallon."

On their way across the still-deserted main street, Chuck adds, "And with a family that's so little help, you can understand him not so much running away as trying to run toward something...in his life."

"Yup. But if Ray lives or not, we gotta try and pin Mike down anyway, right?" Sid asks as though, either way, he would rather just let him go.

"We start searching house-to-house today, Sid. And put his picture out around the county, for beginners."

Following his chief inside Lucy's, Sid sighs, concluding: "It looks like somehow the wrong guy ended up at odds with the law."

"Like a lifetime's worth in exchange for an instant's payback, isn't it? Then it's worse than ever," Chuck laments, climbing onto a stool.

And Sid beside him, and Lucy behind his counter, nod with resignation.

The weekly Local Order of the Varmint Hall Saturday night dance is just underway with one hundred and thirty fancy-footed fools already present here tonight (somewhat more than the usual one hundred and ten or so). Noticeably absent, so far, are Chief Chuck Cintz and Assistant Officer Sid Seed.

Though it's barely after eight and still sunset outside, the hall is mostly dark, with only the indirect glow from the stage and, to the right, the bit of spill from the open kitchen door (the bar) providing light. The stackable chairs scattered around the perimeter are half occupied by shadowy figures sucking at beer bottles or simple mixed drinks or soda pop; most are gaping out toward the middle as they whoop it up with friends sitting all around. The missing half from the empty chairs are out on the dance floor bobbin' and weavin' like pigeons.

On stage, Grover Gewh humorlessly and gyrationlessly wails mean ol' rock 'n' roll guitar at the lead of his hard-cookin', nameless three-piece band, tonight extending his Saturday night iron-man performance record to an unbroken twenty-two years and sixteen weeks of scheduled dance night appearances. (He has rarely ever said a word, and only once – warmed with delight – bought everyone in the place a round of drinks: last year after everyone in the place got into The Big Punch-out.)

And there, in the deepest, darkest corner off to one side of the double set of double entrance doors, sit Howard, Norm, Ba-Dee and journalist Joseph, huddled tight together, talking forcefully above the noise, about Mike Watson:

"SON ON THE RUN!" Joseph tries another headline on his buds. "Or how'bout: IS HE DEAD YET AND CAN I COME HOME NOW?"

"Asshole," Howard has a suitable critique for Joseph.

"He's in Asia," Ba-Dee imagines.

"I think he's somewhere here in town," Norm disagrees.

"That's him impersonating Grover Gewh," Howard squints at the scrawny little fifty-year-old legend on the stage.

"So where in town, Norm?" Joseph prompts the only one with a real idea.

Howard butts in, "*You* talked with Mike, Joe-the-Welt! Where would *you* look for him?'

"Under Ray's hospital bed. With that big knife he took," Joseph answers.

"*What knife?!*" Norm blurts the surprise all three of them suddenly show.

"Oh! You didn't hear? – 'cause I forgot to tell you, obviously: Sid told me they believe a big carving knife went missing with Mike – "

"Yikes!" Howard grimaces as he squeals. "He's gonna slice us all up in the night!"

"I think it was an impulse thing – picking up that knife," Joseph has his own theory. "He doesn't hate the whole world. Only Dark Presence Ray."

"Dark *what?!*" Norm is first to react again.

Joseph explains, "That's Frank Watson's nickname for Ray."

"Whoa! That says a lot!" Howard feels.

"Says most of it. But the rest remains wholly untold," Joseph elaborates, full of thought.

"By who?" asks Ba-Dee.

"Ma and Pa Watson," Joseph summarizes, initiating a contemplative moment of silence around the table...

Next topic, Ba-Dee suggests: "Joseph, why don't you write up your new friend Looker?" (Earlier, Joseph stunned them reporting his visit with Nelson, but gave no details.)

"Too soon," he says. "I actually threatened him with that, but he spoiled it by being okay with it... Anyway, now it's MIKE ON A HIKE – or else one of you three dicks..."

And, for some time more, they talk, and are regularly visited by various passing friends, are even momentarily interrupted with quick questions from scouring-through Chuck and Sid...but are, soon enough and more and more, drawn by the beguiling serenade lofting in from the diabolical box of beer out there chilling on a bag of ice in the trunk of Ba-Dee's new older-model car... So, right here, when they've had just about enough of Grover Gewh's twenty-two-year-old spectacle (and realizing they are far past any inclination to dance with anyone, anyway) – precisely then at that instant when they can each no longer bear the call and lure of that peaceful universality of the silent back road and are about ready to stand and go:

Looker walks in.

No one stares. In fact, many of those who see him standing there smile easy little smiles. It's as though everyone is thinking simply "good".

Scanning around, Looker's ever-calm but inquisitive eyes find Joseph. Joseph doesn't motion, but his pleased expression plainly says, com'on over.

Looker goes over.

As if assured by Joseph how Looker is really a regular guy (though ten or so years older), Howard, Norm and Ba-Dee readily shift around so the newcomer can also sit with his back to the wall...like, welcome to the wallflower club.

Right away, Looker slips out a pencil stub and little square of paper from his inevitable (though tonight, colorful logo-emblazed) pocket T-shirt: "Curious what this one was like," he scrawls, and expressionlessly hands it to Joseph – who reads it aloud.

"You've been dancing?" Howard asks openly (though he's working hard at keeping his eyes from popping).

Looker flicks up eighteen fingers, as in: back then when I was younger. He then yanks out another slip and writes, "Which one of you four ugly babes wants to dance?"

Joseph reads it and they all chuckle (the other three fully re-laxing, now that they hear for themselves that he does have a personality and sense of humor).

Joseph reacts as he points to the dance floor: "No, no, Nelson! Us boys do it with those long-haired better-shaped humans."

Looker smiles a bit, but scribbles another one: "Do I still have a chance with them – once they see me sitting here with the most dangerous minds in town?"

'No," Ba-Dee assures him. "But the girls will back away in awe from you for more than just your body, now."

"Then the whole primal point of bringing our urges here is lost," Nelson quickly writes.

And Howard observes, eyeing the knowing expression on Joseph's face, "Oh-oh...he's one of us!"

They sit there for another hour (Nelson mostly listening, yet appearing nicely entertained) until word spreads around – creat-ing a mighty stir that challenges Grover Gewh's boogaloo buzz – that Ray Watson has regained consciousness. No other details spread with it.

"Let's go find Mike!" Howard proposes with sudden hope.

"Let's go plan how to go find Mike!" Joseph puts it more per-tinent to their own methodology.

And they all four stand and turn to leave toward the box of beer with the car around it – and then all automatically all at once turn their heads back to a placid-looking Looker as Norm opens his mouth and most naturally insists, "Hey, Nelson, com'on!"

And Nelson Looker Nelson is plainly pleased to rise and go with them.

L ate Saturday evening, Mrs. Watson is pushed in a wheelchair up from her room to right beside her son Ray's hospital bed.

"That little shit Mike!" Ray slurs first thing, seeing her pained expression through his semiconscious haze.

"Ray, Mike's run away..." Mom starts to admonish him, but Mister Watson standing beside her presses a firm hand on her shoulder, as though telling her to hold back from upsetting Ray.

"Good!" Ray snarls weakly. "After doin' this to me! And what he's done now to youse two – we're all better off!"

(Frank is standing at the middle of the other side of the bed. Though he would never, ever do it, he has an impulse right here to poke his oldest brother really hard right in his stab wound.)

Mrs. Watson just slumps back low in her wheelchair, still as faint and pale and half-lifeless as Ray.

Then Ray looks suddenly empty, and drifts off again.

...

As the three Watson visitors in the hospital room are at that moment again left worrying about their yet-again unconscious family member – worrying as woefully as they have been about their physically missing one – Mike himself is a mere block away from their home slithering out through Bennetts' little garage window (that he managed to force open with almost no noise) and is clutching at the roof edge in the cool darkness trying to lift a leg up on it. He is clenching his package of hamburger buns in his teeth, with a soft drink and cheese slices stuffed in his jacket pockets. He's venturing out for a picnic.

Slipping and sliding on the years-layered leaves and twigs, he manages to pull himself up to the peak. He tiptoes softly back into to the open air, out from under the jungle of low tree branches...

Above, the moonless black depths are silvered with glittering stars; all traces of sunset are gone, and the breeze is gently warm. Mike squats on the slant of shingles.

Houses up and down the yards spill lively light from different windows. He even sees glimpses of someone moving in the kitchen of the first house to the left. (He is sure no one can see him even if they happened to look up here. In behind, trees hide him from every direction.)

If Ray's dead now, the heavens here force him to wonder, is he looking down on me from up there right now? (I'm in deep trouble with God if he is, the concept flashes those words through his mind.) So then, maybe Bill is actually out there somewhere? he questions Creation... Wish I knew – wish I could see him...he breathes deep, dry eyes humbly searching the cosmos...

Breaking out the buns, he builds a six-strata-of-cheese sandwich, and munches it slowly. (He had a two-chocolate-bar breakfast when he woke up at suppertime.) But tonight he'll go out shopping, hopefully in one of the grocery stores. Besides some real food (he's been visualizing one of those bacteria-farm chickens that are always endlessly spinning in a roaster by the meat counter), he needs something to read. That stretch between waking up and sunset is just way too boring. (He doesn't recognize yet how his thinking is so solidly permanent in regards to his newly independent lifestyle.)

Also, needing to feel clean again, Mike is seriously tempted to sleep in the Bennetts' house tomorrow – he'll do another prowl tonight to see how it feels. And then next, from being out here exposed to the outside world, he starts thinking hard about what he can do long-term.

What he can picture – as he spots the police cruiser cross a gap between houses one street over...it seems to be stopping, its lights still on – are alternating scenes of the biggest city he knows and television images of remote little desert towns. He tries to balance which one appeals to him most with which one would better hide him...and for some reason he thinks of Looker...well, maybe because the guy's hiding from something too, Mike supposes – but now that book of poems he did will find its way back to where he ran from and then they'll just come track him down..! Well, anyway, wonder what he did...

And there's always other countries – when I get older, he considers sensibly. Then he recalls photos of street kids in cities – images he's seen so many of at school or in magazines... I'm sixteen!, he then steams. If all of them can get by, why can't I? Lots my age just take off and start a new life – and never go home again... Home...the word goes funny on him, like words do when said over and over and start sounding silly. But the meaning of it also feels curious to him, now, and for the very first time he's sure it means something different to him than it does to most others...

Mike finishes his sandwich. He cautiously angles his slide down to the back corner of the roof, to the small tree sprouted close to the garage – it's barely near or big enough. With every move made so slowly, he takes some time to reach the ground, Crouching through the shadows to the back steps, he finds the key, unlocks the door, replaces the key and lets himself in. He searches all the rooms again – this time checking every single drawer and closet. (Mike has this idea now, after concentrating on his long-range future, that if he found a big wad of cash he'd maybe take it. And what better place to take it from – where it won't be missed for months?)

He finds nothing good, and ends up sitting on the living room sofa again, thinking dreamily about his entire life some more, for hours.

Then, around two in the morning – though several cars have rolled by – this one stops up the block right after turning that next corner. With its headlights on, Mike can't quite see who it is... He watches and waits.

In a few minutes the headlights shut off – it's the police car! He can see Chief Cintz rise up out of it and aim for the first house on the other side. It appears there's someone still awake inside, so Chuck taps on the door...he's invited in...and steps back out ten minutes later. The house next door is dark; there's a car in the driveway so he skips it. The next one – to the left and straight across – looks vacant, with a "For Sale" sign planted in the lawn. The Chief checks that house all around, shining his big flashlight into every corner of the yard and in through every window... Mike figures it's time to sneak back to the garage...

But instead of heading on down that side of the street, Chuck quickly starts over here to the Bennetts' – like now he's decided to do only empty ones!

Mike instantly starts sweating. I'll never make it to the garage, now – not without some noise if I'm scrambling... He ducks below window level. Why was I so *fucking brave!* He scampers through the darkness on hands and knees into the kitchen – and stops to listen for the footsteps on the front porch... Nothing. Then seconds later he hears the back door – Chuck's unlocking it! They must have shown him where the key is!

Half resigned to being caught, Mike stands and strides fast and quiet back to the front room. He slides the sofa out a foot, then slips down behind. The policeman steps into the kitchen, switching on the bright overhead light.

Walking softly through the living room, Chuck next...skips the hall closet – he's going upstairs, Mike figures (as he wonders how the man can't hear his heart pounding from behind this sofa).

When Chief Cintz reaches the top of the stairs, Mike eases out and glides into the kitchen – eyeing the sink as he passes to make sure it's dry. He's at the back door – it's open a crack, with the key still in the lock (Mike praises himself for returning it to its hiding place with such discipline) – and outside again. He jumps the right-side fence then the next low picket fence into the second yard away...it's dark there with all the overhanging trees, so he decides to squat behind the pickets and wait.

A few minutes pass. He watches the glow from Bennetts' kitchen light blink off, and Chuck appears on the back door steps – actually, only his flashlight beam is visible in the black-ness. The Chief crosses the yard and unlocks the garage side door...follows his light inside – the knife! Shit! Shit! Mike silently cringes. I left the stupid knife stuck in the floor up there!

Wide-eyed, anxious, Mike soon sees some flashes through the leaves above the garage: the beam from the flashlight slanting up through the little window (and Mike is at least glad he both-ered to kick it shut when he climbed out). He waits for the light to shine downward – meaning Chuck is up on the loft pointing it around...but that doesn't happen. (Mike's hope is, the loft be-ing so low, Chuck didn't bother going up there, that he could search it well enough from below. And the knife, far to the front, is probably under his line of sight.)

Mike begins to think he'll get away with this – that his new home will be safer, now that it's searched and ruled out – and that (not too unreasonably) he is maybe pretty good at this! So instead of feeling the grimness of this way of life, he can see it as accomplishment! Independence – challenging! And, barely aloud, he adds to himself, "And a fuck of a lot better than living stuck in the same miserable house with a sawed-off little prick like Ray..!"

In five minutes the Chief is gone, and Mike is more or less following him downtown.

Three hours later, Mike is back snuggled on his cushions up in his loft, four plastic grocery bags beside him full of buns, bananas, magazines, doughnuts, soup cans and a can opener, chocolate bars, toilet paper (so he doesn't use up the Bennetts'), deodorant and soap. And a toothbrush and toothpaste. And colas. And milk.

And, finally, here again in his solitude, using both hands, Mike clenches tight against his face a whole, hot, bacteria-barbequed spun-for-days roasted chicken.

John Sing stands at Chuck' favorite spot at the police office window, in one hand a tall, white paper cup (LUCY'S printed lengthwise in plain black on two sides) still half full of warm coffee; in his other, a steadied little cut-crystal glass and its inch of Sunday-noon whiskey. He's thinking over what the police chief told him a minute ago, that Ray Watson was rushed to an operating room early this morning with internal bleeding. The prognosis is back to exactly where it was at the start.

"So, John, guess you probably had your piece about him regaining consciousness all written up already?" Wilf asks. He's sitting at Sid's desk leaning back, long legs crossed, slowly twirling his shot glass on the one uncluttered patch of the blotter. (Though he's wearing his best Sunday plaid shirt and almost-new jeans, he decided to let his wife Sue go on ahead to church this morning so he could come talk with his worn-out looking police-chief friend.)

Sunk in his chair at his desk, Chuck Cintz sleepily studies The Town Talk editor's every movement. (Regardless that he likes and respects John, and trusts him to try to forever be responsible, Chuck can't help feel, as always, that anyone who hasn't grown up here can potentially misunderstand anyone who has.)

"Not too late to change it," John replies, his astute black eyes behind wire-rimmed glasses staying focused on the street's

Sunday flow. "Hey," he now brightens slightly, "I can see why you stand here perpetually, Chuck Cintz. You can watch everything going on of any possible significance..." Then reestablishing his frown, he sips some liquor, chasing it with coffee.

"Chuck calls it work," Wilf smirks. "Funny how work to some is voyeurism to others."

John chuckles and Chuck grins.

"Well, I guess I gotta ask you, John," Chuck finally lets out what's bothering him, "to not write anything about Mike Watson just yet – where he might be, or even that he's officially missing. And maybe tell that Welt phenomenon to stay clear, too...as good as he'd probably do it up..."

"Sure," John glances a look at the Chief. "Pretty touchy family?"

"Not folks who could stand much more...turmoil – same as all of us," Chuck explains.

"Okay. Will do," John understands. "But around here, I see how everything gets known within seconds, anyway."

"Well, still, more than anyone here you see the power of print, John," Chuck persuades. "Just look at that first one of Welt's. Really got people thinking twice, once they saw it in words."

"You know it," John frowns with his own disbelief. "So, it's one sad sounding story, the Watsons. One of those family tragedy things that down the road seems to lead to crisis after crisis..."

"Instead of..?" Chuck wants to hear how a professional observer might theorize it.

John half turns to face him. "It's sort of what Joseph wrote, I think," he starts, then takes another double sip. "The worse things get for some, the more they need people around them to be less self-absorbed and help them live normal."

Wilf points out, "Mike's at the tail end of a home-help unit with no scraps of help left for him."

(Here, Sid walks in for his day shift, and stops wordlessly beside John by the door.)

"Oh, Ray had plenty of energy to spend trying to fix Mike," Chuck qualifies his friend's observation.

"That's it, then," John slowly shakes his head. "What his mother and father didn't have for Mike, Ray pushed even further into the negative by being nothing but critical."

"So Mike's wholly innocent – with no one to teach him how to handle someone like Ray?" Wilf suggests.

Chuck turns that one over in his thoughts. "Well, that's the dilemma of our system. Objectively, Mike's old enough – he should really know better. But if you were to live with someone all their life and you could see the whole story..."

"Tell me something," John Sing now has a question. "Do you think if someone's family is lacking, can a community like this one take over and do it?"

Chuck smiles faintly, thinking that through, too – Joseph's column coming to mind again. Gulping the last little puddle of his bedtime drink, he rises wearily to leave for home. Watching Sid nod his opinion there beside John, he answers, "If it can, I'm afraid this time we let Mike Watson slip out of our grip."

Coiling gulls play the warm winds pushing clouds, and the clouds mount power to feed the world...

Tree-ragged folded horizon; beyond: people we once knew, around our tumbling home...

Tumbling lawfully through chaos cosmos – grains of life, we can comprehend all...

Comprehend, and drench every thing and being in Creation with human emotion...

Watching from up here, from the secure comfort of his balcony, keyboard in hand, Looker has for years followed...the silent surging wheat and battalions' thrust of ranks of corn there in the squared-ends fields; around them, the firm and anchored trees wait willfully to breathe breezes, wait for the gentle beat of clear downpour rain, for energetic sunshine to power life...

Life, Nelson stops to think...the mystery of why, physical complexities, and rampaging feelings.

He recalls all the moments with his friends – Joseph and the others – in the car last night: slurping beer, the hilarity, the questions, and the low pull of tragedies...everyone on Earth feeling just about the same.

And, they asked, where is Mike Watson? Where, exactly, is Ray? And how is it everyone in a community focuses such ongoing concern on one life or two?

Mike, Nelson believes, is still in town. He has seen Mike around so much, before, with his friends or in the car with Frank and a few times in Lucy's. (He wonders how Lucy might be able to help Mike, the same as he helped him.) Looker has noticed him often, and has thought about him some, as he has most everyone.

What Mike needs, Nelson is sure, is where he is running from: the real love of his parents, of Frank, and of Bill. Though the way Mike can find it most certainly, when he returns, is through Bill – Bill's way. Because Bill had learned to open up to love, where Mike has learned – and was taught – to close...

And Nelson does believe Mike will return – someday. He hopes Mike chooses that fulfilling way to live. Maybe a few of us can help him, he imagines.

Aware he is sidetracked, and that it could carry him away for hours, Nelson now sighs, sips a little coffee from the mug on his armrest, and looks out onto Existence again for words.

"**Y**ou can choose to walk away from things so you never have to deal with them again," Howard restates how he believes Mike probably did the right thing by running. He's inclined on the grassy bank of the ol' swimming hole out the back road where a lot of people came as kids and where some still come to...indulge. He's drying off again (for the third time) out there in the open, drenching himself in the hot midday sun – where he will soon be soaked in sweat again and will then have to leap back into the pond to cool off. His wiggly toes are dangling in the water.

Norm is a few feet away on his towel under the huge willow, swigging at the multi-quart bottle of soda he brought (sitting geographically close to, yet trying not to think about, the spot he and Suzanne so recently made memorable).

Ba-Dee is face down out there in the water, big butt buoyed up by a lifebelt, snorkel tube sticking up beside his half-dunked head. (His ears are mostly above water, and he has heard everything said so far.)

And Joseph's bulk – some of it in an enormous neon-green swimsuit – bobs around mid-pond on an old inner tube, rotating with the soothing stream... "Turtles!" he suddenly declares, squinting through his sun-glared, water-streaked glasses toward Howard.

"What?!" Howard indignantly reacts, as though "turtles" is somehow a response to his "walk away" conclusion.

"That's how you catch snapping turtles, Howie! With your toes – oh, don't fuckin' get your head huge! Your point about Mike registered."

"His point is a good one," Norm notes from across the water and above the faint flutterings of birds and leaves – the only sounds amid this wandering creek's green oasis. "Some people are impossible to deal with – so don't!"

"Run away, Norm?" Joseph counters as he paddles a hand to stay facing him. "Would you run if you were Mike?"

"Sure...well, what else?" Norm stands firm.

Ba-Dee's goggled face sloshes above the waterline a few feet from Joseph. "Run from your own rightful home?" he also counters, then returns half his attention to the deep.

"Oh. I see," Norm now sees.

"But," Howard waggles his toes again, watching them for turtle nibbles, "if Mike would've ran – or escaped or whatever – one day sooner, Ray Watson wouldn't be connected by a thread right now."

"Then right!" Norm reasserts the original viewpoint. "Sometimes the best thing is separation. You can't fight and make things worse if you're miles apart."

Joseph thinks a second, then concedes, "For some, maybe. But it shouldn't end up that someone like Mike has to be the one to start a new life – "

"Start a new life?" Howard questions.

"Sure," Joseph has a conclusion: "Mike ain't comin' home no more."

"Think so?" Norm stands and wades in up to his ankles, studying Joseph. (All three others believe Joseph knows more than he has ever said, having talked with Mike for two hours two days before he stabbed Ray, after all.)

"Whuh," Howard grunts. "That's serious. But then we can't ever empathize with how bad he had it at home..."

Joseph now inserts plainly: "Nelson can."

Ba-Dee surges out of the water, Norm's eyes lock, and Howard ceases obsessing over his toes. "Beg pardon?" Ba-Dee is the one to say it.

Joseph sees he has a community story he's obliged to orally tell here, and swooshes the few feet into shore to do so. Ba-Dee is flopping through the current right behind him.

And gathered at the water's edge, Joseph this time relates all known details of the life history of their new friend Looker Nelson, taking twenty minutes and fifty questions to adequately explain.

"Bitter shit," Howard sums up, shaking his head sadly.

"Families," Ba-Dee observes. "They can ruin your life."

Norm wonders, "Well, if everything happens for a reason, what's Looker's life lesson?"

Joseph frowns, and starts hand-oaring back through paradise, posing, "Maybe the same as Mike's..."

It's an hour after sunset and it's the boldest thing Mike could possibly think to do. He is folded like a fetus inside the big wicker chest that sits unadorned in a corner of his home living room.

He's clutching a folded blanket – to cover his face in case he has to sneeze. He even took a quick, pitch-dark shower at the Bennetts' before he snuck over here...in case he stunk. (After vaulting over fences, he merely watched his own house from the gray-black shadows of his very familiar back yard, then, once he was sure that Mom and Dad and Frank were still with Ray at the hospital, he walked right in and picked his hiding place.)

This isn't because he misses home, his being here. It's because this may be the only way he can find out for sure if he's a murderer or not. (He grasps the fact that there's no one home means he's likely not.) Plus he's now almost positive that tomorrow's Town Talk won't print the latest Ray update – so not to scare off the fugitive, you'd think.)

And accomplished at sneaking around now, Mike plans to wait until everyone is in bed then he'll simply slip away from home...once again. (His only worry is someone placing something on top of this chest – like Mom sometimes does with flowers. As in: hospital flowers. Otherwise, there's only some old linens and blankets under him, which haven't been used in years.)

He waits there an hour. When his family finally shuffles in the side door and up to the kitchen, Mike first hears Frank get something from the fridge (he well knows the sounds of his brother's routines) before forcing a solemn "Good night" as he thumps up the stairs. Mom and Dad, it seems, stay in the kitchen. (Wearily drooped on a chair there, Mom was released from the hospital today. Mike, of course, has no idea she was admitted in the first place.)

A few minutes of dish rattling pass before his parents talk, Dad bluntly grumbling, "If everything ends up right, they'll *never* live in this house together again – "

"How can you say that now!" Mom blocks in her always-tender voice. "You don't even know if Ray will live! You don't even know if Mike is still alive... How can you add something so negative as that on top of..." And she chokes back years of sobs.

"Ray's going to make it – "

"Why in God's name is it always Ray first?! Don't you have any feelings at all for your own youngest son?" she attacks her husband for the first time all through this.

Dad responds with a huff, "Mike stabbed Ray! What did Ray ever do – "

"We've talked about this a hundred times!" she counters, on the verge of screaming. "Why can't you understand that Mike had to be acting against something – you know how Ray was always yelling at him!"

"Listen," Dad won't give in, and Mike hears him detour to the liquor cabinet, not far from the whicker chest, "Ray's always trying to do the right thing. He tries to help you handle things – which includes handling Mike!" He pauses to pour an obvious sounding stiff one, then fades back into the kitchen. "But Mike – who knows what Mike's ever thinking? He's so damn moody – I can't ever get through to him!"

"You never talk with him!" Mom now hits him hard. "You talked little enough with Ray, and even less with Bill and Frank. So then with Mike, you barely ever tried to be his friend! And so you just let Ray go on and try to father him – "

Dad explodes: "Why the *hell* is this my fault again?! They've got minds of their own! They're not infants! I've always provided for them – what *else* am I supposed to *do?!*"

She sees he doesn't get it. (And Mike, too, in his sick hiding place, also feels so strongly how Dad doesn't get it. But at this stage, he could never express what "it" means.) So Mom collects her thoughts and tries another angle:

"What would you say then if they're both already dead..." And she bursts open with sobs.

Mike's heart breaks. He's really hurt her (and the dark cloud looms low over him: the voice and presence of Ray condemning). Damn! Couldn't have done anything more drastic and painful to Mom...and he silently moans. Then I did it again by taking off... should've just left before it came down to stickin' him.

By the sound of it, Dad pulls up a chair and sits close to Mom. "It won't come to that, Honey. It'll be fine, wait and see." (He rarely calls her "Honey", and Mike feels the stark contrast in tone.)

Mom sniffles a bit, then composed again allows, "I pray that's true... But I'll tell you, even if our little Mike didn't do...something drastic to himself..." she says haltingly, to try to stay clear, "I don't think we'll ever see him here again..."

...

It's an hour later when Mike feels it's quiet enough to go. Though he got what he came for – Ray's status – he's sneaking off this time with a load of remorse, guilt, heartache and bitterness – which he had no idea he'd carry so heavily. And his parting thought, right before pushing up the lid of the chest to leave: Maybe because now I'm on the outside looking in.

He cautiously creeps into the darkened kitchen, and eases open the door to the side entrance. Down the steps to the latched screen door (it's hook is in the eye, so he'll have to leave it unlocked, hoping whoever did it won't remember – we seldom lock it, anyway), he is out across the driveway then skulking his way overtop fences to the Bennetts' back yard. One minute later he's at his usual spot on their living room sofa, dreaming into the streetlight-barred darkness of their picture window.

Now, it has finally become clear to Mike that he won't begin to feel free to...move on? – take off, disappear – until Ray is definitely dead or alive. (He actually is that blankly indifferent about Ray, most of the time – for Ray's life alone – and is suffering some impatience that the fucker should hurry up and do one thing or the other.) But that's okay, he thinks. I'm doing fine, I feel good. And though he's lonely for his friends, it's no total thing – it's worth it, to be free and out from under all the thick emotional layers. Before long (he has confidence in this, too, most of the time) I'll be somewhere else, with new friends and no rules about how to be me, and no school timetables or anything...

His thoughts jump to the present: So, what's the pre-dawn adventure tonight? (What he just went through at his old home was more of a mission.) The grocery store? – could use some more stuff, but don't really need it, tonight. (And he automatically thinks of Mom, feeding him so regularly. Now he's eating whenever it's convenient for him.) Or Red's Variety? What's in there that I can't get at the grocery store? (And it occurs to him that the more places he breaks into, the greater the chances of someone noticing.) How about the newspaper..? No, for now I found out about Ray. Or the police office? – to see what they got me down for... I could wait for Sid or Chuck to go for a cruise, then walk in and snoop around for my name..! Well, it's an idea... Then he thinks of something even more tempting: the dance hall – The Local Order of the Varmint Hall. They have beer and booze in there...wonder what it's like to really get sloshed... (Mike has had a beer or two in his life, but at sixteen the opportunities are limited.) That's it, he decides. At least see if I can get inside.

Mike waits until just one in the morning (being Sunday night, the town quiets down early). He noiselessly closes and locks the Bennetts' back door, replaces the key, then stops at the front corner of the house to plan his route. (The dance hall is on the opposite side of Main Street, right there along the side street that angles off at the curve.) – Dogs! it right here occurs to him. He knows there's none kept outside anywhere in his neighborhood. (Actually, over the years there were two or three that howled, until Ray went around threatening the owners.) But through those blocks on the other side he remembers at least two mean ones...so, better go right down the main drag.

He takes his familiar portage through to Nick's Bowl and is soon leaning against the front corner of the building, searching the streetlight shadows and listening. The downtown is utterly quiet; even Lucy's is dark. Though he's on the same side, it looks as though the police office is closed up, too. But he knows to wait for the cruiser to appear.

Fifteen long minutes later the police car appears from up the highway, rolling slowly toward the center of town. Mike drops to the ground behind a little shrub, resisting the urge to peek over-top. It passes, and he watches around the corner of the building as it crawls through the main intersection and disappears down beyond the curve...

Mike stands and starts walking. He remembers at least two gaps breaking up the row of stores between Nick's and the main intersection. He'll hide in one until the cruiser passes again... But as he breezes by the darkened storefronts, he gains confidence and strolls right on past the police office and around its corner into the little park. There, he crouches behind the bench set end-on to the street against the brick wall. In ten minutes the cruiser reappears, stopping for the red light a stone's throw from him. (He wonders, frowning at the cop through the iron armrest, why doesn't he just run it? – there's no traffic for miles! And where did he go cruising to all that time? Out stargazing, or what?)

The police car is soon accelerating, so Mike hugs the building out to its front to watch the taillights blink out of sight beyond the little rise at the upper edge of town...then struts right out and along the streetlight-bright sidewalk down to the curve and there crosses over to the angled side street...

The old Varmint Hall squats in darkness, only a few feet off the sidewalk. On its left is a lifeless looking house, with tangled shrubs and tall grass in between; on the other side, lighted by one weak streetlight, is the broad parking lot. Which Mike strolls through headed for the back of the building.

In the dim light he can see that the two rear ground level windows are long ago painted shut, and that the single metal door is bolted from the inside. He moves along to the far corner and scales a wobbly pile of pallets up to the extension's low roof. On top there, he discovers a little window set high above the back of the stage. Though it's locked too, its putty is so ancient he easily breaks it all off around one pane, pries out the glass, and reaches in for the latch. The window sticks, but he keeps working it up and down until it's high enough for him to fit through.

Looking down, he guesses he's eight or ten feet up, so Mike wriggles through, twists, and dangles from its ledge...and drops – in the darkness, not at all sure where the floor is...(just before letting go he reminds himself to pick up a small flashlight, next time he's at the store). Rolling, he lands smoothly, and immediately finds a ladder glinting in the grayness and sets it up so he can leave the same way and close the window.

A minute later, he's squinting into the glare of an open fridge door, gawking at a hundred cold bottles of beer. He helps himself.

Sitting on the edge of the stage, the black and silent dance floor feels haunted. All the chairs and tables around the walls are visible only in his imagination (he's been here at the Saturday night dances several times in the last year). He quickly drains his first beer, then goes for another, this time leaving the fridge door open to allow some light to spill out – and because he noticed that's what they do here, he patiently finds the right brand among the cases at the back of the kitchen to deposit his empty.

Three beers downed and Mike is feeling considerably more at ease. The perimeter of chairs, visible now in the appliance twilight, no longer looks spooky – they look like empty chairs. And he finds that he presently cares much less about where he has come from all his life and is instead dreaming loftily about where he can travel...

An hour later, after two more drained ones, he wants adventure right now.

So, back in the kitchen, he tucks a cold bottle into each jacket pocket...then wonders about booze... The cabinets are crammed with new and variously used-up liquor bottles. But (he is still lucid enough to reason) if I take a full one they'll probably miss it. Sooo... he fills up an empty beer bottle with whisky, recaps it best he can. He then smears his fingerprints off the booze bottle...oh yeah, and the fridge handle. (He already did his empties, one by one.)

Scaling the ladder to the window, he smiles then giggles a little, thinking: This is so easy! Gingerly carrying the whiskey-filled one, he sets it and the other two bottles out on the roof and squirms through the window opening... Now he wonders about the ladder... Ahh, no one's gonna know it was moved, he tells himself. There's ten thousand volunteers messing around here all the time, he knows. So he slams the window shut – snickering with his carelessness – then resets the pane into its frame... hoping gravity is on his side and it won't fall back out. ...Should have a big ol' wad of gum to hold it, he muses – or a big fat clot of Ray's blood – ha ha! – then shakes his head for thinking such a weird thought.

Mike is soon back on the ground. He uncaps a beer and re-opens the liquor-filled bottle, taking a sip of it first (gagging) then a swallow of beer before weaving out into the stark parking lot. By the time he reaches the street, he's decided it's time to sit down, so he aims for the ballpark a block away – sure he's careful as always about being one with the shadows.

The sky spreads open above the ball field, with no trees any-where near. A three-quarter moon dangles behind its edge-sil-vered clumpy clouds...and the night world is silent...and the fresh air smells so sweet, now...wow! So he chokes down another dou-ble sip.

Shuffling across the dry diamond, Mike swerves toward the low bleachers on the third-base side (furthest from any cop headlight beams turning around in the lot behind first base). He thumps down on the bottom bench. He sighs with relief...and feels just so relaxed, indifferent, self-righteous... He takes another two sips, sets the bottles on the planks, one on either side of him, and leans back on his elbows. He peers dreamily through the mesh screen at the star and moon-lit infield (he played some baseball at school) and soon raises his eyes straight up to...the sparkling heavens, to the self-luminous moon and the outlined gray clouds in the black-filled sky, then turns his gaze behind him to where the clouds are wandering –

Joseph Welt – whoa! -- right there on the top row!

Mike almost screams. Though only a silhouette blotch, it's plainly Joseph Welt with his lunar-gleaming glasses.

"You'll feel like a turd in the morning, Mike," Joseph remarks from eight rows up straight behind him with no expression in his voice whatsoever.

Mike sputters out a laugh, instantly not caring that he's dis-covered.

"Beer's bad enough," Joseph adds, still motionless. "That other shit makes you wish you died in your blackout."

"I don't care," Mike feels at his defiant best, and takes two more slugs to demonstrate exactly his not caring.

"Good!" Joseph condones spiritedly, and tips back his flask for a sip, himself. "So, Mike..." he pauses...and there is only the subtle sensations of the night, and moonglow... "How does this sound: 'RED'S CONVENIENT DRUGS AND MILK: HEADQUARTERS FOR WORLD COMMUNIST DOMINANCE'?"

"Red sells bubblegum," Mike turns half around toward the infield, again. "He's no Communist!"

"Doesn't matter. I've got a deadline. Gotta get some sorta topical crap down on paper – "

"Thought you hadda tell the truth," Mike challenges, leaning back with elbows up on the next level, as before.

"Oh. You mean he's *really* not a red Commie? Oh, my."

"You knew that."

"He was, you know, Mike. At my age, Red was a hippie-Commie, insufferable anti-establishment dildo. Now he's a fifty-year-old hard-drivin' capitalist-realist prick."

"So why don't you write that?"

"I am. But I gotta start with that pinko thing, or the new Red doesn't sound as good," Joseph explains.

"Why you tellin' me this – hey, Joseph! Don't even think 'bout tellin' my story, eh?"

"No, I know your story, and it's just started."

"Jus' ended," Mike immediately disputes. "Far as this town's any part of it."

"Hey, I'm surprised you're still here. I told my friends you were long gone."

"You're not gonna tell everyone you saw me..?!" Mike interrupts drinking to finally voice his now recurring unrestrainable alarming thought.

"No do," Joseph swears, his hunched, black form still not budging up there. "I'm with you, Mike. It's your life. And you've had too much to deal with. My theory is: time to do what *you* need to do."

"Maybe I deserve tuh go tuh jail," Mike now poses with unconvincing self-pity, trolling for Joseph's opinion on that.

"If Ray seizes up dead, maybe you should. But if he makes it, your parents will likely have it all erased."

"Good. Then I'll be free when I'm out there runnin' 'round free," Mike waves one of his bottles toward out there. Then he twists to face Joseph squarely again (almost falling off the bench) and begins forcefully, "One thing, though..."

Joseph waits, but nothing comes. "Mike! Fuckin' what one thing?"

So Mike tipsily mounts the bench to face up to Joseph. He states his one thing: "I don't want Ray tuh make it."

The four-year-older young man and generally insightful writer reacts – after a troubled moment: "Whuh."

"Wait a minute!" Mike suddenly thinks of something. "What're you doin' here? Are you fuckin' off, too?"

"Ho!" Joseph hoots. "No, not yet, Mike. Tell you the truth, I think it's okay, here – but then, my family supports me...incessantly. Still, I'd like to make it in the big world, someday, though."

"But I meant whattayuh doin' sittin' here?"

"Same as you: can't stand reality, that much. Not without hiding inside this hard liquor and thinking about it a lot."

"Know what that means," Mike grumbles.

"So you're not alone. In the world."

"No, you're right," Mike nods one big nod then sips again. "I knew that, anyway. There's kids like me livin' on streets all over the fuckin' place."

Joseph thinks that one over, briefly. "You shouldn't have to live that kind of life, if you don't want to – what did you ever do to deserve having to live like that?"

"Nothin' – 'til recently. But y'know, Joe, the way I figure it..." he puts it on hold to gulp another big shot...

"Yes Mike, I'm here..."

"Where else do I start – to learn how tuh live a real life..?"

...

Mike soon wanders off, sleepy but anxious not to lie down somewhere and wake up in open daylight. He somewhat recklessly retraces his route right through the downtown, stopping often to observe familiar old things...in his current more profound and saturated state. Back at the hideout, he perches awhile on the garage peak, witnessing the first light of dawn push away the night sky...and recalls that Joseph asked nothing about where he's staying, what he's eating, or where he got the beer. Good guy, Joseph, he registers. Moments later, having inched along then down into the loft and onto the cushions, he begins to stare, in that softest of light – with all types of feelings jolting his determination back and forth – at the knife still stuck upright in the board... then conks right out.

...

Joseph, meanwhile, has left the bleachers, having finished pondering the Firmament, the Great Undertow, his next article, his article coming out in print this morning, and the Hilarity and Outrage of some lives.

"He's not a threat to anyone else," Chuck responds to the Watsons' repeated concern about Mike having a knife.

Mister Watson is standing in the bright fluorescence squarely in front of the police chief at his desk. His wife is waiting timidly just inside the open door. Behind her, a warm morning rain tries to soothe with its patting of countless splatters.

"Then you tell me why he took it," the dad asks as though an official should officially know.

"Impulse," Chuck doesn't have to think about it. "He left in a moment of defiance, and the knife went with the feeling."

"*Moment* of defiance?" Mister Watson scoffs. "He's been gone..."

"Four days," his wife has to remind him from behind.

"Seventy-two hours," Chuck makes it accurate, implying that he is paying full attention to the problem.

"And Ray was getting better...but now..." Mom stirs her own anguish, her reddened brown eyes wet with tears.

"He's stable!" Dad quickly affirms to her without turning, as though if everyone went along with his positive attitude, their son would soon be well.

"It's fifty-fifty, the doctors..." his wife trails another thought.

"Well, let's just hope and pray," is about all Chuck can suggest. "Sure wish I could tell you something – anything at all – about

Mike," he switches crises, leaning back, firmly lacing his fingers together on his stomach. "We haven't found one single thread, yet. No sightings – ten counties wide."

Mister Watson reacts, "But you said before, the longer he goes unseen all around, the more chance he's still right here in town! – so then where's he staying? What's he eating?!"

"We've been checking," Chuck responds evenly, holding back all tone of temper (well aware that this caring father has not searched one square inch for his missing son). "We've checked every house and garage and building, and we're doing it all again starting this afternoon. And we'll keep making the rounds indefinitely. If Mike's around, we *will* find a clue." (And he adds to himself: If he's not staying with some friend, Mike sure is good at self-disciplined survival.)

"My wife here thinks he probably killed himself!"

Chuck can't help grimacing at Mister Watson's insensitive choice of words. "You want me to answer that? As though I'm supposed to know?"

"He's right!" Mrs. Watson stops her husband cold. "Now, you leave him to his work," she orders, glaring at him. "Chief Cintz isn't to blame here. He didn't cause this and he's no magician to fix it. I want to go now. I want to see Ray!" And she twists through the doorway out into the rain.

"If Ray dies," Dad now feels he can ask with his wife gone, "do we charge Mike?"

"Have to."

"And if not?"

"That can be up to Ray and you two," Chuck puts it to him.

Mister Watson hesitates, then turns and strides out, too.

And though the mother's point of view is clear, and he can see she is acting entirely from the heart, Chuck is again left with no conclusive idea of what the father really wants to happen in the end.

"W hat *is* this shit?"

"Ah, com'on, Norm! It's good!" Ba-dee in his apron aims his big smile of challenge down at Norm on the opposite side of Nick's luncheonette counter.

Norm raises the newspaper again, and with a doubting scowl up at Ba-Dee, then at Howard three stools away, and at Joseph, the object of his query three stools the other way, he reads the column heading once more:

INFINITE GRAINS

"Hey, we talked about that one night!" Howard now recalls that particular back-road philosophical conversation sometime last year (merely one of their many potentially endless verbal searches).

"Oh, yahh?" Joseph reacts mockingly. "Somebody copyright it?"

"Listen!" Norm silences them, then preambles, "It didn't sound like drivel out loud a year ago, but..."

Joseph, calmly, believes in his work: "Just read it, Norm-nuts."

So Norm quotes:

> We're little specks, all of us here, in our little town, in our little county of this big country on a wide world amidst an overpoweringly vast universe. Little ambulatory mushy blobs of awareness.

Minds of consciousness that, for all the experts know about the nature of consciousness, could be the size of tiny grains within our brains. Or, could be the size of our whole living bodies, you could imagine. Either way, still mighty small, in Creation.

But think of what you think: We can comprehend any possible thing within the infinite. We know, or could choose to know, any possible thing about our world – our neighbors, our governments. What we don't know, we could soon find out, or eventually find out. What they won't tell us, we could still comprehend if they did. The only thing we can't seem to find out is anything beyond 'is' – as in: the future. Plus death. But that's all. Nothing much.

Of course, though, the way personality (character, disposition) works, some things sink in with some people, but seem to flush right out of others. Still, that's fine – otherwise, we would all be closer to identical, I suppose.

But (my point), what about some of the basic, commonsense things like:

WE ARE ALL BORN EQUAL

Why do some people ignore or forget or feel they are above that obvious characteristic of humanity? (Don't tell me it isn't so.

I have yet to see real blue blood.) Or over-
look that the true reward in life is:

HELPING OTHERS

– with food or shelter or, most profoundly,
friendship. (Com'on, everyone out there,
we all believe in these things, down at our
true self! Why does it so often get buried?)

Last year, our friend Wilf Granger said
something I thought is a good starting
point in our need for trying to understand
ourselves:

"What a delicate web of human interaction a small town is."

So true, Wilf.

We can comprehend that – it can get-
complex. And takes some work, sometimes.

But again, individualism (what you
would likely argue here, Ed Donald) dic-
tates we take in what we see and hear...to
then see what we feel and think, and let it
change our views, or we ditch it – *solely* to
fit our desires.

Well, what happens?

What happens, sometimes, is cruelty,
indifference, greed, rage...

Rage. There's one (we've seen recently)
that can maybe – often be entirely someone else's fault: someone snaps, wholly under another's cruelty, indifference.

THE THING IS: to look for that kind of reason, before judging. And, as was true in my sermonizing last week, judge your own shortcomings and weaknesses – and outside pressures, too – alongside your usual daily acts of jurisprudence against humanity.

Remember, little grains, you can grasp it! Both sides!

"Whuh," Howard reacts Norm-like.

"Preachy!" Norm is now more specific than "shit". "Joseph Welt's How-To-Do-A-Perfect-World column!"

"That John Sing guy lets you print this in his paper?!" Howard is actually incredulous.

"No, I snuck it in there," Joseph counters, blankly amused.

"It's the same stick-poking as last week!" Norm won't let up.

"It's as good as last week's," Ba-Dee stands by Joseph.

"Well," Joseph concludes, watching his supporter remove his apron, ending his Monday afternoon shift, "last week's earned me three hundred and forty dollars."

"You got thirty-four positive calls about it?!" Norm can't believe the number.

"Mostly positive, some more neutral – John Sing talked to them all."

"Whuh," Norm reacts characteristically.

"Is he sorry he made that deal with you?" Ba-Dee thinks money.

Joseph believes, "No, don't think so. He said he sold quite a few more papers last week. Enough to justify hiring me on mere possibilities."

"So...good article!" Norm now thinks money, too.

"Then maybe the big bucks are proof that Joseph really is saying something powerful," Howard relents.

"Something worthwhile," Ba-dee has another word for it.

And Joseph just smiles a little, thinking about Mike Watson, Nelson Nelson, Sid the cop, ex-mayor Jimmy Jimms, baseball Jackie, Gene their murdering ex-friend, Mayor Susan Granger, her husband Wilf, Chief Chuck Cintz, Lucy of Lucy's, each of the ol' boys, and three thousand other worthwhile life lessons to go.

Mike's eyes open focused right on the carving knife. Outside, it's still bright – he guesses four o'clock. So he stays motionless, the ad for his hunting knife coming to mind: "THE LEATHER HANDLE WILL NOT SLIP. THE BLADE IS SHARP AND SLIM." ...The extra pillow there is a help – didn't even think about him screaming out – just squish it down on his sleep-ugly face... The knife slides in pretty easy. He violently tenses – his whole body. Wonder what his face looks like now... Holding him down is easy, too...maybe he passed out from the pillow. The blood came gushing out around the knife... gushing out...

Mike wonders how he actually stabbed someone – his own brother! He feels that grip of shock, again – that he really did it! He also still feels pissed that Ray made him end up doing it...

But there must be lots like me on the streets like this, running away from some sort of impossible shit...

Gotta live – couldn't go on living like that, forever. In fact, I'd do it all again, if it meant my life against some *fucker*...

Curious if he has a hangover, Mike slowly sits up. His unsynchronized head thumps a bit, but it's nothing much. He rummages through his grocery bags for a juice box. He finds the magazine article he was into (rating the safest cities to live) and half reads it as he thinks about what to do tonight. Then, an hour and two more articles later, he hears voices...

It's somewhere near the front of the garage – a man and woman abruptly started talking. The woman's voice is plainly a greeting. Mike strains to make out what they're saying, but can't quite catch it.

I'd better slide open the window to hear this, he thinks. He works it up carefully. He pushes himself partway out, bracing on a tree limb. Stretching up to near roof level, he aims an ear at the voices out front... It's Chief Cintz! Talking weather with...gotta be the lady next door...

Mike has to believe the police are searching around here again. He squirms back inside and pulls his stuff together – being extra cautious to not clunk the empty beer bottles together (he was conscious enough last night to not carelessly toss them on someone's lawn) or, when he wiggles it free from the wood plank, to not clink the knife against them, either.

Four plastic bags soon hooked on a thumb, Mike stands hunched at the window, checking around for signs of his presence. With his foot, he slides the cushions over to cover the little cut in the gray wood where the knife was. He's sweating, now. His head suddenly hurts. Did he put the key back? – yes, I did. I always do. First thing.

Slowly slithering out, Mike strains an arm to embrace the tree trunk, switching the bags to that hand so he can turn and close the window. The Chief is still talking.

There's only one direction to go, and Mike looks up. He sees a way to climb higher.

The bags rustle. There is no wind. Drops from the morning rain still fall from the leaves. He knows he has to go high, in case the police chief does the loft this time and looks out that window. He hoists himself another limb higher, then rests and listens.

When he's only ten feet up he hears the conversation stop, then each voice says, "Seeya". Seconds later, Mike recognizes the Bennetts' back door closing. That's good, he breathes easier: Chuck's searching the house first, again.

Mike scrambles higher – he wishes this tree was *way* bigger. Reaching as far as he can go, he squints down at the garage window...now he's about twenty feet up from it. And the skinny trunk top he's clinging to is swaying a foot.

Peering out around, he's startled to see the back door of the house – patches of it through the leaves... Oh, well, if Chuck looks up, he looks up, Mike sighs – he still might not see me in this dark jacket and jeans...and he tries to tuck the white bags more behind him. Then beyond: the whole town! Or a good part of it, anyway. Wow, he thinks, great view! So he wonders if he should come up here again, when he can relax about it.

Chuck soon steps back out and strides right to the garage. A minute later the little window opens! Gaping straight down, Mike can see the top of the Chief's gray head...it twists back and forth as he scans the ground around all the sheds and garages along the fences below...then disappears back inside.

Whoa!, Mike exclaims to himself. Now if he just doesn't examine anything too closely – like under those cushions or the window for fingerprints...

Only a few seconds later, Chuck pulls the garage side door shut and hooks the key back on the nail under the house steps. Next, he stands in the middle of the driveway and gazes across the yards both ways...but doesn't look up...then plods down the driveway and disappears along the street.

"Close one!" Mike whispers as he breathes normal again. And he holds up where he is, trying to figure out how to avoid having this happen again.

He doesn't budge for an hour, and leaves all his bags ready by the window when he does wriggle back inside. Once it's dark, he slips into the house and strips. With his clothes soaking in the basement laundry tub, he streaks upstairs (feeling really stupid walking naked through this old couple's home) and cautiously runs a bath. Like his clothes, he soaks in the dark for two hours. Taking a big chance, he then tosses his clothes and the towel in the dryer (though pulling the vent pipe apart to keep the outside noise down). It's one in the morning before he's dressed to go out...

But he has no place to go. And he suddenly feels lonely.

Sitting on the sofa again, staring through the streetlight into the emptiness, thin lips tensed together and brown eyes wet, he wishes he had someone to talk to – even for a few minutes, like Joseph last night. But he can't chance anything...and so decides that tomorrow night he is leaving town, starting by walking the ten miles to Elston City. And that plan makes him feel better.

Soon, Mike leaves the house, simply to walk around outside, to see how things feel now.

...

About four blocks away, Looker is silently descending his stairway for a late-night (early-morning) walk. The air is invitingly sweet, and he is restless from struggling with poem words. And he is also very curious about what he observed a few hours earlier, before sunset (and plans to pass by that way) when he glanced out his kitchen window as he stood at his sink cutting up vegetables: not far in the distance, right above the slopes of the rooflines, someone was teetering at the top of a tree! Retrieving his birdwatcher's binoculars from the balcony, he lifted them to his eyes there at the window and knew instantly who it was.

On Lucy's side of the dividing highway, one block behind the restaurant, the street quietly rests in the warm midnight air. In jeans and no shirt, Wilf has just flopped on a porch chair in front of the darkened living room window. Sue eases out a minute later, her long, honey hair a jumble of curls on the shoulders of her robe.

"It's my dumb brain," she grins at her husband as she sits beside him in the enclosing deep shadows.

"I know," Wilf chuckles a little.

"You're okay?" she questions for the fourth time since waking and following him from the bedroom to the kitchen and then out here, sensing that his dreamy cuddling was intended to lead somewhere – subconsciously, at least. "Did I push you away?" she adds a more direct try before he can respond.

"Not really."

She catches him winking, sleepily. "Well, sorry to confess I was dreaming something about men, about men being rough – not your type..." she pauses to lean close to see if he's dozing off. "Must have been from talking with Beth tonight about that Town Talk column – it sure churned up her feelings." ("Tonight" having been another evening gathered with Beth Cintz and other good friends at Lucy's.)

"That abuse from her father?" Wilf is actually alert and concerned, eyes wandering the contrasts of their streetlight-accented neighborhood.

"Chuck never told you the worst of it," she reminds him. "All the physical things we knew – the rape, then him hitting her until finally she would – *God..!*" Sue stops a second to hold firm against tears. "When she starts on about those details, though, it's not so much the physical stuff she ends up crying over, it's mostly kind of a mental thing – that he even thought he had any right to use her, or believed he was supposed to force her – like that's why he was a stronger human, or something. Then so much of what she feels comes out in that newspaper today, and exactly like the article says, it's the basic human nature of it that she can't understand – why people turn out that way."

"Turn out like her father? No one knows what causes the human mind to go that far off, do they?" Wilf doubts. Then he assumes, "So you woke up tossing and turning about that?"

"Probably," she frowns. "Beth sure was upset."

"All from the column?"

"Well, actually, no. She's also been talking so much with Chuck about Mike Watson...so everything surfaces again, because she thinks Mike's feeling what she felt."

"But Chuck doesn't believe there's anything sexual with Mike."

"No – well, nothing visible. But how abuse manifests seems kind of secondary to the emotional damage that's done. It's that 'one human demeaning another human' thing in Joseph Welt's article."

"I can see that... But you wonder why some handle it better – like Sid," Wilf notes.

"He had help from his mother. But Beth had no family help. And we can imagine Mike now believes he hardly has anyone in the world."

"We could help him!" Wilf is (as always) quick to try to do his part. "And isn't there something the town can do, Your Honorette?" he lightly jests, though most serious with his question. In the faint light, their eyes meet.

"Lots. We could find a room for him, if he wants. Help support him, see him through school."

"Long as he doesn't have to go back and live with Ray."

"Or in that house with Ray gone, by his hand," she notes.

"But he'd be a murderer..."

"Oh, he's still a minor. And when you talk to people like Beth who have solid justification – "

"You mean you would let him off?" Wilf asks gravely (and at that moment sees someone walking along the few visible feet of Main Street a block away – must be Looker, he's sure – he keeps those writer's hours).

"From what I know right now, I might. But it depends on Mike's attitude – all he intends."

"Well, it's a tough one. And I guess like Beth, it never completely goes away – especially for Mike if Ray dies," Wilf supposes.

"When Chuck called the hospital tonight he said it seemed to the nurses that Ray was close to consciousness. I think he'll live."

"Hope so. Time will tell. Anyway, better get some sleep. Gotta be rested to think up another witty line for my buddy Joseph's next column." And Wilf stands and shuffles back inside, to the sound of Sue's scoffing giggles.

By Tuesday noon, Wilf is up to one hundred percent full of doubt about who it was he witnessed through last night's wee-morning-hours veil of darkness – from his porch, through the gap between houses – walking along Main Street. What's bothering him are the short (it seemed) haircut and the jacket – the guy appeared to have on a dark gray jacket. And he can't recall ever seeing Looker wearing something like that.

So, heading home for lunch from his schedule of telephone tests, Wilf stops in at the police office.

"Something's bothering me, too," Chuck reacts to his friend's report of his odd sighting. (At the bright window, pale blue eyes straining to follow the movements of the street, and with arms crossed and blue shirt with dark pants plus severely brushed-back hair...he sure looks official. Only his old white sneakers allow him comfort, today.) "In fact, I was about to call you."

"Here I be," Wilf stands firm right beside him, his serene eyes also drawn to the motions of the street. "What's buggin' you?"

"Two things, actually – oh!, how could I forget: Ray's conscious this morning. Looks good, now."

"Great! That's a relief... All we need now is Mike."

"True. Anyway, this morning I'm searching around again, so I decide to double-check the dance hall. And what I notice is this ladder in the storage area back of the stage there, up against the wall under that small window..?" He eyes his taller friend to see if he recalls the window. (Wilf nods.) "So I climb up and look, and was more than a little surprised when the thing just slides right up – and then one pane falls out..."

"That window hasn't been opened in nine hundred years!"

"Exactly. And if it was a break-in sometime lately, we sure weren't called in on it – we would've been, obviously. And no one would sneak in there without stealing stuff or vandalizing the place, right?"

Now Wilf is steadily nodding agreement. "Got it. What's the other thing?"

"Well – oh!, and they're going over to the hall this afternoon to see if any bottles are missing from their list... Then the other thing is, Nick was just here telling me about his buns – "

"Ho!" Wilf bursts with delight. "Did you tell him about yours?"

"Hee hee." "You know how stingy he can be – maybe he could make a real living there if he quit feeding his bowling-ball kids – "

"Now, now."

"Anyway, he tells me how his buns don't add up to his patties. He says he always matches up his hamburgers with his bun orders. So I walk up there and check – there's no money missing from the cash register, at least. But the only clue I can find is a sunk-in bucket under the back washroom window, as though maybe someone stood on it to squeeze through."

"So the theory here is that Mike broke into Nick's for a bite and into the hall for a beer?"

"Yeah. Added to that phone call the other night to the hospital plus what you maybe saw last night, I'm sure now he stayed in town."

"So you were going to call me to..?" "We're doing a full search – where's that mayor you're married to, anyway?"

"Matter-of-fact, she went to visit Ray Watson this morning."

"Well, I'm getting every volunteer I can find – we start right now with anyone who can come. We'll do one-half the town, then the other half, comb it close – nothing overlooked, nobody's word taken at the door. If someone doesn't want their house searched, they get put on a list."

Wilf squints at the street. "It's getting serious..."

"This is for Mike's sake – if we don't find him and help him out, who knows what he'll do next..."

And thinking of the knife Mike took with him (and imagining it smuggled into the hospital to open another life-draining hole in Ray Watson's guts) plus his talk with Sue last night, Wilf again feels a deep compassion for the confused sixteen-year-old fugitive kid. "I'm with you!" he declares. "My work can wait – my lunch is in the fridge at home, I'll be right back."

...

An hour later, Lucy's bench is filled to overflowing with helpers. Bert and the ol' boys are all there, along with Lucy, Reverend Fisk, Jimmy Jimms, Sue (back from Elston), plus Beth, Norm and Howard and two dozen others – including Frank Watson who rode home with Sue.

Chuck soon quiets them down (people driving by are stopping, and have to be shouted the details of what's going on) and explains his plan while Sid and Wilf hand out notepads and pencils. Everyone will start in one corner of town – behind the Varmint Hall – working their way along that side of Main, writing down the house numbers of those they can get into and search, and those they can't. Newcomers, Chuck adds, will start at the other end. He even stations frail old Mel on Lucy's bench in case – it pains him to make the analogy – "Mike scurries like a rabbit across the highway".

As a mob, everyone except Mel turns and starts toward the curve (still causing most passing cars to stop – several of the occupants wanting to sign right up are told to wait at Lucy's for the Chief). Who, meanwhile, drives to the ball diamond and has Jackie supervise a search of the weed field past the outfield fence then the small forest beyond, plus the two other little woodlots along that edge of town. He tells them, "If you spot him, or any signs of him, do nothing. Go over to Lucy's and wait for me."

Next, Chief Cintz phones the hospital and talks to Mister Watson. Dad is glad to hear about this intense new search, but declines to drive home and help. (Just as well, Chuck thinks. If he should be the one to find his youngest son, he'd likely overdo the thing and get himself stabbed, too.)

Though slow to start, the sweep is soon advancing well. With two or three people combing each property, it appears efficient. (Chuck estimates well under a thousand homes, altogether – mostly houses, maybe a hundred apartments. He really doesn't care exactly how many.) And volunteers number eighty after only one hour.

By three o'clock, searchers start emerging on Sideroad 93, the county road that quarters the town as it crosses Main Street, Highway 3. Sid directs them back to Lucy's.

By five, that whole side of town is finished (with Chuck and Sid, between supervising rounds, probing business buildings and Reverend Fisk's church).

"Nothing!" a few voices respond to Chuck's "Nothing?" in front of Lucy's. Splitting them up (there are now over a hundred volunteers) he reemphasizes his feeling that signs of Mike's presence are all they'll likely see. The two throngs fan out both directions across Main Street, notepads in hand.

The Chief starts Sid on the remaining stores, while he sorts the slips for the inaccessible houses (ninety-two – he'll send people back to look when the owners are likely home from work). And here, again, he can't help think about his own list of seven places he had originally considered as best possible hideouts: the dance hall is one, the other six are vacant or temporarily vacant houses.

Chuck now decides to give in and trust his insistent intuition, and aims for the Varmint Hall first, feeling the need to examine the roof. (The workers who set up for the dance did report "no noticeable" missing liquor or beer.)

Up on top of the rear extension, Chuck can see from the outside that the window putty looks as though it was recently pulled off from around that one loose pane. Back down inside, he scours every corner and cupboard. He even checks the empty beer bottles in their cases...one brand has seven in a row in the top box with their caps set back on. He tries to imagine some habitual recapper at last Saturday's dance turning in his empties all at once. (To balance the books, they ask for an empty before selling anyone another – though they're often missing one or two.) Nah, he thinks, who around here is capable of doing that? Along with the window, that oddity has to be because someone broke in. With nothing questionable at all like that – for years – reported from the staff here, the one and only suspect, he flatly feels, is Mike.

Chuck then revisits the two houses he listed on that side of Main. At one, the volunteers couldn't get in because the real estate agent had the keys. Chuck soon locates him, but discovers nothing inside.

It's now after six. The Chief feels confident they will finish before sunset. He's less sure they will actually find anything.

A half hour later, on the other side, with his teams again flanking in toward Road 93, Chuck reaches Fuller Street and the first of the final four houses on his own list. That one is clean and bare (a hesitant neighbor watching over it has a key). His next one, across the street – a squad of three has minutes ago inched across its yard – belongs to the vacationing Bennetts.

For the third time, Chuck takes the key from its hiding place under the Bennetts' back step. Starting to feel worn out, he trudges through the house again, examining everything he examined before, trying to summon even keener eyesight this time. From the attic down to the basement, he registers nothing significant – except maybe it means something that there is no soap in the bathtub soap dish... Maybe (he stretches conjecture) if someone were to use it, he would not put it back because it would take so long to dry hard...maybe.

He is soon standing on the outside back steps, again. In front of him, between the trees, the sun is blazing lower in the haze of the warm evening. The air is still; the leaves of even the topmost branches aren't quivering, whatsoever. For a moment, he watches the strange sight of a dozen people meandering yards both ways.

Crossing the yard to the left side of the garage, Chuck thinks about the last time he searched here: the dirt floor and junk, the small loft...and it suddenly strikes him that – exactly like the window of the dance hall – the little window up there actually opened right up! Shouldn't it be seized shut, too? This garage is ancient – why would the Bennetts ever open it..?

He quickly unlocks the door.

It's dim and hot inside. The tree-shaded glow from the window up there barely lights the clutter on the rough floor. Chuck heads straight for the loft steps. The wood creaks with his weight...

Only two steps up, his eyes poke above the loft's floor level...

Not a sound, not a motion. The few dusty boxes tucked under each roofline seem like forlorn props for an uneventful era. The faded yard furniture cushions on the floor between them look undisturbed from the last time – and for years. Chuck turns and tries the window...it slides as easy – or maybe easier than before. He sticks his head out...and looks up...and sees one broken twig ten feet above him... Nothing else. Next, back inside, he pulls away the cushions one by one...and there, under the bottom one, is a half-inch scar in the gray surface showing the tan wood inside – from a knifepoint!

Now Chuck is positive. He figures that, living only a block away, Mike must have cut the grass and taken care of this place sometime over the years. So, he knows where the key is. And the key fits the house, too, and Mike took the soap – shoot! The boy is clever – and he's diligent!

But... (Chuck now stands there, pushing his fingers through his hair over and over, wondering) where did he go? Did he somehow know we were searching around today? No, only if someone somehow quickly told him... Then where could he run in the daylight? So, he must've left during the night last night... Then he could be anywhere, by now... Chuck finally realizes he should go check Mike's home.

Up on the next block, he finds Frank at home, alone. The Chief tells him about what he's seen at the Bennetts', hoping that, if Mike's closest brother secretly knows anything, with this hiding place discovered he'll give it up.

Frank appears tense (from too much seriousness for a seventeen-year-old, Chuck believes). His pure brown, intelligent eyes and coal-black, combed-back hair accent a handsome face that is so different from his younger brother's, the Chief notes. (He takes after his mother, it's plain.) Frank reveals only one new but significant detail:

"Mike had some money stashed," he tells the Chief when they're back on the porch (after the obligatory house search). "Mom and Dad didn't know – Mike bugged me not to tell, for some reason. All I knew was where he always kept it."

"It's gone?" Chuck doesn't really have to ask.

"Now. But it was there the first morning he was gone – I looked. And..." Frank hesitates, as though guilty.

"Go ahead – we're trying to help him, Frank, not track him down to shoot him, or anything."

"It was there yesterday morning. I've been watching it all the time..."

Chuck's eyes widen at the sight of fitting pieces. "And because all of you go in to see Ray..."

"No, well, we've been there every night. But he hid it in the basement, so he could've just snuck in after dark anytime, I guess, last night."

Chuck pictures Mike creeping around like a burglar in his own house (and again is impressed by the young man's intuitive timing: clearing out right before the big search). He asks, "How much did he have, do you know?"

"Hundreds. He saved like a packrat."

"Right... Did you search..?"

"Can't see anything else gone. Dad would've got unreal if he found his own money missing...he took some more for lunch again, today."

"You mean..?"

It takes a second for it to register with Frank that it's okay to tell the police: "Well, yeah, Dad keeps his big cash wad in a shoe in his closet. He only carries some with him everyday – including today, so it must have been all there. Ray said he would bust our nuts if we ever touched it –" Now he turns self-consciously red for repeating the exact words.

"I get it... Ray's not too compassionate, I hear."

Frank lets slip one tight little laugh at Chuck's choice of words.

"So what do you think, Frank? Is Mike gone?"

"Definitely was around town until yesterday – last night."

"Any ideas – like relatives or friends anywhere?"

"I wondered that, too. Nothing, really," Frank concludes, eyes now appearing restless, having said everything he knows.

"Well, how about staying here, in case..?"

"He shows up? That's why I came back home, with everyone tracking him down."

(Oh my, don't say it like that, Chuck feels it full-force. Here is the closest person on Earth to poor Mike and he sees him as a hunted animal.) "We'll help him Frank. It's not like that. And anyway, Ray..." He's not sure if he should say it...but it's Frank, after all: "Ray deserved it, I think. Didn't he?"

And in a wordless reply, seeping tears suddenly fill Frank's eyes.

...

It's two hours later and the search is over. Some folks have gone home, but twenty or so are still hanging around outside Lucy's. Sixty more are hanging around inside Lucy's.

On a chair by the curb, in the peaceful dusk, a welcomed hot coffee embraced by both hands, Chuck tells everyone out there everything. They are owed it, now.

And with enough clues to know pretty much where Mike has been all along, the one and only problem the chief of police now has is where to look next.

entle starlight glimmers through the true-color endless black sky while below, the warm, thick, early-summer air is empty of daytime bugs and birds and wind. On the sandy gravel of the dark lonesome road, the car hunches, without a twitch. Along both sides, the young cornstalks, in the stillness, the serenity, are silent.

"Dork," Howard continues.

"Wraith weasel," Joseph instantly counters, fitting it in between beer slurps there in the sightless pitch of the back corner seat.

Howard hesitates again, slouched in the front passenger side, still straining to think of a crushing slur. His last one was of desperation, after their unbroken ten-minute volley of debasement drifting out the open car windows profaning the sacred land.

"Time's up," Joseph declares.

"Time's never fucking *up* calling you shit!" Howard manages.

The car goes quiet.

They started this at midnight, with Howard objecting to Joseph's loud "FREE THE PRICK ERADICATOR!" chant. Howard now believes Mike Watson should be charged and put away – even assuming Ray stays on this side. Norm in the other back corner and Ba-Dee driving (his own car – "Me again?!") have stayed relatively neutral.

"Proprietary," Joseph now utters without the slightest relevance. "Ichneumon."

Again, calm country-night air dominates –

"There!" Howard breaks the silence, spinning almost unseen to face the pain-in-the-ass journalist. *"That's* what I mean!"

"What?" Ba-Dee speaks for all three who don't get it.

"Joseph's always doing that!" Howard whines. "That uppity, thinks-he-has-the-answers-to-all-human-nature shit! Then he says something lofty!"

"You're vilifying my human nature...Howie Hamster," Joseph responds with a tone of indifferent superiority.

"See?!"

"He's supposed to be like that, Howard," Norm imagines creative character.

"I've got a right to be and do me," Joseph makes a stand, sounding like he's grinning wide.

"Actually, Joseph," Ba-Dee does have one objective point about this, "you've been a little snooty since your first column came out."

"Snooty?" the writer reacts, tasting the word.

Norm joins in, "Yeah, Sir Snooty. And where were you today for the big search?"

"Looker's."

The other three are caught off guard.

"He's a writer, you know," Joseph notes, then adds: "He knows things."

"What the fuck does that mean?!" know-nothing Howard is now livid.

"Mike things," Joseph immediately seizes all three into silence again.

When Joseph doesn't automatically elaborate like a normal person, Norm prompts, "Well?!"

"I think there's a question here of...ethics, if I say – "

"Then why did you even say *anything* – ?!" Howard interrupts.

And Ba-Dee interrupts Howard to claim: "Mike's hiding at Looker's!"

"Nohhhh!" Joseph tries to stop the madness.

Ba-Dee tries again: "Looker saw Mike crawlin' around town – "

"With that big kitchen knife clamped in his teeth!" Howard sounds as if he's beginning to like this picture a lot.

Joseph this time stays mute, as though he dissolved into the night.

"So Looker *did* see Mike!" Howard reads Joseph's lack of reaction.

Now Joseph follows through (he mentioned it in the first place because he truly respects his friends, and wants all trust to include openness): "Fuckin' awright!" he moans, yanking another beer can off the last of their two six-pack clusters. "What he saw...Looker saw Mike up a tree..."

"Right!"

"Sure!"

"Wait, listen!" Norm insists, the only one willing to give it a try.

"Really!" Joseph uses the all-time all-powerful it's-the-truth word. "Looker was looking out his kitchen window yesterday, and off in the distance he looks and sees Mike up a tree – he looked at him through binoculars and got a real good – "

"Which tree?" Howard asks as though he thinks Mike is still there.

"Couldn't find it," Joseph relates. "In the direction of Mike's house, maybe a block away from it."

"No shit..." Norm tries to fathom why Mike was up a tree.

"He was scrambling to avoid being seen – "

"From Chuck snooping around?" Norm won't let Joseph miss a detail.

"Guess so – what else? He stayed up there for a while, Looker says. And he had some plastic grocery bags with him – "

"Ohhh!" Howard takes a turn. "He was camped out – in someone's garage, or something!"

"Anything else, Joseph?" Ba-Dee pushes onward.

Again the informant hesitates, deathly speechless. "Okay," he soon caves in. "Looker went strolling around when he saw Mike up the tree, but he couldn't see him once he got over there, or even figure out which tree it was. So then later, about one or two in the morning, he says, he was restless and went walking again. He was coming up to Lucy's – alongside it – when he reaches the corner of the building and Mike's right there! Mike's just marching past Lucy's in the middle of the night like nothing ever happened and he just owns the street...

"So now they're both stopped frozen face-to-face, five feet apart. Looker says Mike seemed a bit spooked, so he gives him a little wave. Mike gives him an automatic 'Hi' then starts out down the street again. But Looker stops him...somehow, and gestures at Mike to follow him – which he does."

Norm can see, "Looker's not about to write out notes standing in the street in the dark."

"Right," Joseph says, pausing to glug beer. "So over at his place, Looker types out something about understanding how Mike feels – Looker saved it and filled in roughly what Mike answered and showed it to me. Then Looker pounds out a brief version of his life story, and Mike gets it: they both come from the same place, in a way. Looker was treated with painful indifference as a kid, with his father getting tough, sometimes, and he thinks Mike's problem is not so much Ray but how his parents didn't...parent him – intervene and give Mike some self-worth, and all that shit. So Mike doesn't react, until Looker starts up about his brother Bill and how great it must have been to have an understanding and loving older brother – though Looker knows

Frank and Mike couldn't be closer, but Frank isn't the type of adult-aged influence – "

"We get it," Ba-Dee assures Joseph.

Joseph sighs, as though it's the toughest story he has ever told. "That's when Mike gradually starts spilling. He begins crying – from Looker's compassion about Bill, probably. And he says that's really how it was, and it's true about his parents and Ray. And then – because Looker doesn't talk – can't interrupt or lecture or condemn Mike, is what Looker told me allowed Mike to open up – even if he typed something, the kid wouldn't have to look at the screen – and then Mike spits it out, talking non-stop for two hours."

"So they're soul mates..?" Howard can barely imagine the two of them being in any way the same.

"You could say," Joseph accepts the concept.

"So what's Mike's plan?" Norm jumps from pasts to futures.

"Well, Mike told him where he's been hiding out, and that when they met up he'd just ditched his groceries and was about to walk to Elston. Leaving town for good was his only plan, he said."

Ba-Dee asks, "Did he say where he's aiming?"

"Only Elston – as a start, I guess."

Norm thinks to question, "So what's Looker going to do? Tell Chuckie Chief?"

"No. Not now, anyway."

"What's that mean: 'not now'?" Howard catches.

"Yeah!" Ba-Dee adds. "And where exactly right now is Mur-der-Mike Watson?"

"Gone..." Joseph answers vaguely.

Norm puts something together, here: "Wait a second! Mike was there at Looker's all night. You were there today – !"

"Mike was sleeping!" Joseph finally confesses the last of it, irritably. "I didn't talk to him. I didn't even see him – well, I saw him through the bedroom door cracked open – "

"Oh, shit! You and Looker are accomplices!" Howard sits up and groans. "And now so are we!"

Joseph scoffs, "Don't get your pecker pretzeled all up, Howie. I think Chuck is entirely on Mike's side – especially now that Ray looks like a live one."

"How do you know *that?!*" Norm fields this revelation.

"John Sing was talking to Lucy who was talking to Reverend Fisk who was talking to your brother Jeff who was talking to Frank Watson."

"Oh," Norm now knows... "We really don't need telephones, do we?" he repeats an observation.

"So!" Howard refuses to forget. "When and where exactly is 'gone'?"

Joseph figures, "Gone for a walk, tonight. Right now. To Elston."

"He'll get caught," Ba-Dee thinks. "They're watching for him there, too."

"Well – hey, wait a second, here! Keep in mind Looker and I didn't know about the big search – his place faces farmland, re-member? So we didn't see anything all afternoon. And my guess is that when they got around to his place this evening, because it's Looker's they didn't even go up his sidewalk. So anyway, Looker told me he would give Mike some money, and tonight was going to tell him what he knew about life on the run – as in: hobo...ing... or something. And he'd give him some of his clothes, and a hat, and then tell him how he could change his looks..." Joseph trails.

"Disguises?" Norm is intrigued.

"Sorta. Whatever little changes he can do. Said maybe Mike can't grow a beard yet, so he gave him fake glasses and an eyebrow pencil – "

"Whoa! What's Looker doing with that stuff?" Howard sounds shaken.

"I told you," Joseph tells them again, "how he was tracked down by his parents. Looker was desperate. No way he'd ever go back home – to 'that house', he called it. Which he pointed out was what Mike called his home, too: 'the house'... Oh, also, Mike said he would leave that kitchen knife with Looker, too."

And so, into the deeper night, out there under the stars, heartfelt thoughts about those two town lives keep the four friends talking it over. Also, from their distance, it's repeated more than once before the dawn, in similar words to Norm's first asking the answerless: Wonder if Looker did the right thing...

The entire time the four hometown young men were talking about him, Mike had no trouble ducking the rare late-night car streaking by him as he marched down the highway to Elston City.

Now at the edge of the grid of lights and streets, he feels excited – and not lonely or desperate or homesick whatsoever. From out there, he again has no problem at all slipping out of sight of the three patrol cars he encounters as he strides all the way downtown.

The sidewalks are mostly deserted. He passes two all-night coffee shops with no one in them (except workers behind counters who have seen almost every human thing and no longer care to notice much of anything). Further into the city he meets some stragglers, plus a couple of drunken types (homeless, with the bars closed). And he is cruised by two separate carloads of young guys. (In Looker's black T-shirt and ball cap, Mike feels he projects a street-normal cast. And don't do the challenge thing and eyeball them, he also knows.)

In the heart of the city, after wandering for an hour, he comes across a small building, an aging two-story factory or warehouse on a side street near a popular main business section. On its concrete steps are ten or so people. They're just talking.

A thin, short girl calls "Hi" to Mike as he's about to veer toward the curb and cross the street to avoid them. He almost stops walking, but then coasts a little closer instead.

They're all mostly young, he sees in the streetlight. The girl who noticed him is about his age. Two or three are maybe twenty; some have long hair and ragged jeans. It seems half of them are smoking cigarettes. Without thinking, he moves a few steps nearer.

"Hi, I'm Lucretia," the girl now opens right up, as though she has a trained eye for her kind. "You can come sit down here. I've never seen you around, right?" (None of the others are paying much attention – or at least they're not staring, Mike observes.) "If you're looking for a place to flop, there's lots of room inside – everybody just curls up on the floor, though..." Gazing at him, she waits to see if Mike talks.

"Oh...who owns it?" He eases toward the bottom step where she's folded up against her knees. He glances repeatedly at the others sitting around and above her.

"The father of one of us, the rumor is. But nobody ever bugs us... Well, the posse comes 'round once in a while to look for milkers..."

"Milkers?" Mike asks with a start of a grin.

Lucretia smiles easily now, too, her pretty eyes brightening an otherwise plain face. "Yeah, you know: missing kids with their pictures on milk cartons, and things. But we've got hiding places in the buildings out behind – you hafta jump the roof, though. Anyway, you can stay, it won't cost you anything – not even your name, if you don't want." (By his manner, she's now fully aware he's new at this.)

Mike nods with understanding, but not commitment. (In his heart, though, he feels overwhelmed with a potential: a sense of life that is unimaginably fuller than the exhilarating freedom he felt in the Bennetts' garage loft!)

"Sit down," she says so unaffectedly, he does. "Most here work some, and they help out others who don't, or they're new here. But just food, right? Everybody moves on, eventually, but lots come back, someday. There's some real fucked-up life stories here!" she adds with the delight allowed by self-made security.

"Guess I'll fit in, there," Mike now fully smiles at her for the first time.

"Hey, group!" she calls, turning her head to the group. "This is..."

"Mike," he softly blurts, eager to be at least that much an insider (rather than a nameless outsider).

A couple of them say, "Hey, Mike." Most everyone offers a quick smile, and some add a sincere little wave.

...

Several hours later, Mike is tranquilly asleep on a rug against a wall of the warehouse's nearly empty second floor.

Outside all around him, the song of the traffic plus the blazing, cheery sunshine perpetuate the dynamics of a center of hopeful and immersing life.

Ray Watson, this time, must not get emotional: doctor's orders. Around his bed are Mom, Dad, Frank, and one mean and scrutinizing young female nurse. Plus Officer Sid and Chief Chuck Cintz.

"Then I being the victim have my inhabitant (inherent) right to press charges, irregardless?!" Ray wants Chuck to answer this exact same question a third time. His hard, dark eyes, up at the end of the scant bumps of his small frame under the blankets, are fixed coldly on him.

(Standing aside, with lips sealed tight, Mom and Dad promised the nurse they would not argue with their oldest and now evidently recovering son.)

"Yep. It's your right." Chuck can't, by local law, argue either.

"So *do* it!" Ray seems to believe that here as the center of things, he has power.

But with that raising of her patient's voice, the nurse abruptly herds everyone out, barking "No no no no!" while wagging her forefinger at equally angry looking Ray.

...

All the way back home, Chuck repeatedly restates to Sid at the wheel how his arresting and charging Mike Watson would be the low point of his career, and maybe would prove to be the low point of compassion and understanding for anyone ever in their town.

The next day, Thursday, Chief Cintz is busy with bulletin acknowledgements and reports from every police station in a hundred mile radius.

No sign of Mike Watson. The official criminal search, however, has just begun.

Then, late in the morning, Joseph Welt materializes in the police office asking for the Chief, elusively claiming it's important. Sid is on duty, but Chuck is across at Lucy's picking up lunch. Sid hustles over and gets him – and is equally startled going in as Chuck is coming out to see Looker openly, though expressionlessly, sitting right there, alone, on Lucy's bench. (Looker was never ever even that much a part of things here, before – though it's known he is 'talking' now with Joseph and his friends.) So, logically, it's him behind any reason Joseph could have for seeing the police chief.

As soon as Chuck steps back inside his office, Joseph – standing stern at the window – hands him a big knife.

Puzzled for an instant, Chuck starts putting it together: "Looker's with you?"

"Yep."

"Looker got this from Mike – was Mike over at Looker's?"

Joseph is all cooperation: "Yep." And he pokes back his thick specs.

"Then he was there Tuesday when we were searching – after clearing out of Bennetts' garage – shoot, he's got intuition! So how did he get together with Looker?"

"Met up with him on the street," Joseph explains simply.

"Like old buddies – oh wait!" Chuck now suddenly sees it, grimacing across the fluorescence-bathed office at Sid, arms spread wide. "They come from the same place, the same kind of troubled home – Mike and Looker – !"

"Nelson," Joseph clarifies. "Nelson Nelson."

"Yeah, I heard," Chuck shifts his gaze back to Joseph in front of him, then adds as though trying it out: "Nelson..."

Joseph proceeds to give him every detail, including Looker's feeling of conscience (regarding the Watsons as well as the law) that made him decide to turn in the knife and tell what he knows. He then ends it by declaring that neither he nor Looker has any idea where Mike is now. Presumably, it's somewhere out of town.

Chuck thanks Joseph and asks him to please thank Looker and tell him he might have to talk to him soon, then insists they both say nothing about the knife until he informs the Watsons about Mike.

An hour later, Chuck is outside Ray's hospital room reporting to the Watsons the recent whereabouts of their youngest family member and, subsequently, the recovered knife. Mrs. Watson collapses in her chair with relief and has to be readmitted to the hospital.

...

By Thursday evening, almost everyone in town has heard all the details concerning Mike, and in every neighborhood conversations about him are either full of rage or full of reflection. (Chuck believes, because it's their town, they have the right to know anything he does, if it's safe to say.) Chuck is then pleased to hear, when he calls the Bennetts up north, that they are not concerned at all about their property, that they feel for young Mike Watson, and (sounding somewhat apologetic) that there was "nothing of value in their house worth taking that he could use".

...

By Friday afternoon, with some people settled firmly into feeling nothing but sympathy for Mike, and others having decided he needs to bear the consequences of his act (charged and given a record) – but with everyone very concerned about his welfare and well-being – the subject of their compassion – Mike Watson himself – has been discovered and is now sitting in Chief Cintz's police office spare chair.

"They just saw me on the street," Mike strokes his buzz-cut hair once, staring absently at the floor as he, that briefly, explains how the Elston police picked him up. Though he would rather be back there at the warehouse, he was not so disappointed to hear Chuck say Ray is recovering nicely – because now he sees that if he's not charged here, he has a hopeful life to go to there.

(Sid, across the office at his desk, is all smiles. He is so happy this is working out without more tragedy.)

Chuck starts, "Your mother is a wreck – "

"Yeah, so was I," Mike is quick to counter, without raising his eyes.

"No, I didn't mean to rub guilt in your face, Mike. I should've said that she's resting okay in the hospital and she'll feel better when she sees you..." (Mike doesn't react.) "She cares for you, above everything – it's not a contest, you know, when you're a parent. Parents care so much for each kid, each one differently."

Mike squints his pale eyes up at him, his expression saying he has never thought of it that way. He merely nods.

Chuck now has to tell him the bad part: "Ray wants charges pressed."

"Don't blame 'im," Mike mutters, somewhat surprising the other two with his acceptance.

"Most of us – Sid and I, plus your mother and Frank...well, most of the town, actually, would like to see Ray give it up – "

"What about Dad?" Mike catches the omission.

"I think he's with Ray, but your mother has a choke hold on him."

"Figures – about him being against me, I mean," Mike is back to focusing on the floor.

Chuck next explains, "They agreed to a kind of house arrest again, Mike. You stay confined to home, until things get resolved. Sid and I phone you regularly there. The alternative is the Youth Offenders' Detention Center in Elston – "

"When's Ray getting out?" is all Mike wants to hear now.

"At least one more week. Let's try the home thing until – "

"Let's try this," Mike sternly interrupts, abruptly staring straight into the police chief's patient eyes. "I want to charge fucker Ray with abuse."

Chuck...is overwhelmed. In the swell of emotions that rise in him, he feels mostly added respect for this young man – a new pride in Mike as he takes this stand for his rights!

"We can get out the lawyer list!" Chuck can't hold in his unexpected enthusiasm (though now he starts studying Mike to see if he genuinely means to follow through).

"Good," Mike is clearly very serious about it. "Right now."

And as Chuck rummages through his jammed desk drawer for the list, Sid eases to his feet and crosses to stand beside the teenager. "Mike," he starts gently, patting him on the shoulder. "Just a thought, okay? But when I was sixteen, too, I started seeing how all what my parents couldn't do for me and all they did wrong didn't have to rule my life..."

Mike blinks his eyes up at friendly Sid beside him, then with a hint of a smile, nods his head. "Sure..."

"And," Sid finishes, noticing Chuck's pleased look, "I realized I'm always perfectly free – to go or stay. And most of all, I guess I had enough of a brain to see that I could always keep choosing, you know? To do the right thing for me...and then everyone..."

...

Mike is soon home – at the "house". Sid will stay with him until his parents return. (Everyone now seems willing to let Mike stay entirely on his own, when his parents visit Ray again. But they won't tell Ray that.)

As Mike wanders the house again, one moment nostalgic, the next, anxious to leave...then feeling sad for his mom – and even for his father, somewhat – he eventually feels...prevailing, about himself: he can and wants to go on and find his life, away from this little world of others' making. And freed from all doubt that he did the right thing for himself – that he acted with righteous outrage against oppression that for years kept him smaller than human – Mike is now not one drop sorry for Ray.

Looking for changes around the place, he finds none. But some things sure appear a little strange to him – especially the wicker chest he hid in that night, plus the tidy-made bed where Ray, only nine days ago, lay spurting to death...

From those days trapped in turmoil here, to the exhilarating independence of the Bennetts' garage loft, to the compelling future of Elston, Mike feels, in nine days, he's changed worlds.

This time, instead of closing himself up in his room, Mike heads back downstairs and talks, at length, with Sid.

MARY DUPLEIX WATSON

It was a difficult beginning. Mary Dupleix and Clayton Watson were young and unemployed, and chose a new life together risking all they had ever known. Against the wishes of every member of both of their families, Mary (hers, affluent, Catholic) and Clayton (his Protestant, honest yet poor) had found, dated, and wholly embraced each other, and of course, married. So, based on firm family standards, on religious principles, each was ostracized.

But now they had each other and their lives of promise ahead of them. They did not sense very clearly how they had no support.

Moving far away from their childhood homes, Mary and Clayton soon found jobs – low paying, but a start. And before long, they welcomed their first baby.

Raymond was born healthy and strong, and they adored him. He was theirs alone. (And Mary was never more radiant: intelligent and warmest brown eyes showed her whole being now sweetened with her joy, and her smiles were wide with contentment.)

Then, a year later, came William – little Bill. He was delightful, too, and Mary loved him and Ray so deeply.

But life became even more difficult, with Clayton the only one working now and two babies to raise (a time when most young couples get so much help from the proud new grandpas and grandmas). So Clayton simply worked harder (too hard). It was all he could do.

At two years old, Bill got sick and almost died. In the hospital for months, he was alone half the time, with no help at home for Mary to be with him. (And with no insurance, doctor bills started coming in, adding to Clayton's stress.)

Mary, understandably, was frantic. She cherished her boys beyond words, and to see her little one so weak and suffering... She cried constantly. She began to doubt God and any purpose to life and Creation – why give a mother such joy and love, only to overshadow it with torturous anguish? Why was humanity blessed with the fulfilling exhilarations of love, only to be emptied by the hollowing apprehension of loss..?

But little believer Bill gradually recovered, and became...an angel. Spirited, open, loveable and likeable, he grew older as everybody's buddy and (automatically – no consciousness involved) everyone's favorite.

When Ray was five and Bill four, Frank was born. A year later, the fourth and last: Michael – baby Mike. The family on Fuller Street was complete: four boys – Mom had her challenge. And noble Dad could only keep on working hard.

Through the years, with the two little guys, Mary had her best help around the house from Bill. He kept an eye on them, guided and taught them, and, most satisfying of all to see, regularly enjoyed playing with them. Ray, it was evident from an early age, had his own life. And Dad was home less and less.

But as time passed, Mary began to feel confusion. With the boys no longer demanding all her attention she could take time to think, to feel her life. And her uncertainty grew. She began to suspect she was two people at once: one loved her family (though she missed her exciting young groom) and felt content enough with what she had. (She had no close friends – with four boys, after all.) The other Mary caught up with her as she sat blankly watching television in the evening, or found her in bed unable to fall asleep: it was her childhood deeper self, her young girl's dreams.

Not that she could do anything about it, she believed. So many years had gone by, and her parents were gone, brothers and sister so...distant. Maybe, she lamented, if she had started a career...

But the boys never stopped growing and eating and demanding at least a good part of her time and energy; then Clayton would come home needing supper, most nights, and a clean shirt pressed before he had to go out again. So life was full of responsibility for her – thank heaven we always have our health, now, she kept reminding herself to be grateful for all the good things.

More years sped by, and Ray finished school. He tried various jobs, but always ended up back home. They don't listen out there, he would complain. They can't even understand common sense.

Bill then graduated from high school, too. He took a basic store clerk job and rented a small apartment downtown. And when he wasn't hanging around his "real home", as he liked to call where he grew up, he seemed to be always driving off, in his tiny first car, to Elston City with his friends, to see all their many new friends.

Though Mary believed strongly in independence, that her sons should have self-reliance and try to be dignified men, she was quietly pleased that Bill stayed so close and that Ray knew he was always welcome back home. And Frank, she felt confident, would succeed – he had a clear sense of future and had already chosen a profession. Mike, though, was opposite: he seemed to have no heartfelt direction (but had capability enough, once he got into something, she was sure). She often wondered, having Dad and three older brothers over him, how Mike would sort out which role model to follow. (Thankfully, she also reasoned, though Ray was tough on Mike, at least he bullied him down from straying into trouble.)

In no time, her two young ones were teenagers, and then Frank was driving and was almost finished high school. Soon he would be off to college, she sighed. Where were the years going so fast?

But then...but then...

It was ten at night. Mike and Frank were up in their room studying. It was late spring, and exams were near. Mary was in bed, reading. She was tired, tonight. Clayton had just got home.

The doorbell rang. Mike went down...it was a policeman, from Elston. Mike didn't recognize him. The officer inquired if he had the right house: the Watsons. Mike answered yes, and was asked to get his father.

Mike found Dad in the kitchen, then went back upstairs. The officer and Dad talked for a minute or two, then Dad came up to talk with Mom...

Suddenly, Mom weakly screamed, then wailed loudly, repeatedly, uncontrollably, and began hysterically weeping –

Bill was killed.

Dad came in to tell Frank and Mike – they were already numbed by Mom's strange voice of shock: "A car crash, the highway," Dad clumsily explained. And he left to try to comfort Mom.

Ray was phoned at different friends – they said they would go find him. Frank had to drive Dad in to identify...Bill.

While waiting, Mike felt nothing. He couldn't feel it, or even imagine it. He tried to talk with Mom, to help her stay calm. She did, for him.

Frank and Dad were back in an hour, with Ray – who first thing took his two brothers aside and gave them instructions on how to behave now. He said be strong, above all, for Mom's sake. Stay out of her hair. Help her around the house, he told them. Nothing much more.

The hours inched by. Everything was changed. All routines stopped: no school, no work for Dad or Ray. People – strangers, some of them – came into the house to help, though none of Mary's or Clayton's family ever appeared.

Mary, more than anyone, felt it and could not bear it. She could not understand it: Why, so close to death as a toddler, was Bill allowed to live, only to have it come to this end – at just age twenty? All his young life, racing headlong only to this tragic end – at this glorious stage of his fresh life! Why didn't He take him back then? -- before the times of cherishing and laughing and feeling so good (that this fine boy is her son!) could build all through those eighteen years in between to such a level of mother's true contentment?!

Still, more than not understanding her loss, she could in no way feel anything outside the overwhelming pain of it. Life, so sacred, so inherently hopeful...so cruelly, so suddenly, ended. All those years, and days, and minutes, caring for, watching over, being with...lovable Bill. How can you go on living and have those feelings die away, instantly cut off from continuing? – but all the love is still in you...yet the one it's for is no longer there to give it to...

Mary's life, solid and stable enough before, came undone. She couldn't eat or sleep. She couldn't talk without unraveling. At times, she couldn't face her three remaining sons. When she could, their loss was not discussed. She spent most of her time in her bedroom, sleeping, reading. Alone.

Weeks later, she was unchanged. But then abruptly she did start going out daily – only to visit Bill's grave, where she would cry with unabated torment and say aloud, "Little one, where are you now...where, in Creation, should I believe you've gone? Sweet eager son...everything is so changed, without you... I'm so sad all the time, so lost what to do... If you could only be right here, now...for my emptiness..."

Days later, her routines came back a bit, but she was still mostly frozen – at the moment of Bill's death.

Months later, Mary was sometimes a little cheerful (but she would never again be fully what she was). Clayton was kind to her, attentive, but still was away from home so much. And his heavy drinking turned chronic. (But how else, she sympathized, can a man bear loss? And remember, too, years left to go: the old hospital payments for Bill's infant illness – how a man's strength is tested!)

Then tragically, again, it happened...

Ray lay dying.

And a third son was as close as the thickness of a killing blade to being a murderer!

Mary's life felt even more desperately futile to her, now.

Though, still, she visited Ray all possible hours, praying for his life and dreading another loss. And she anguished over Mike – poor Mike, baby of the family, confused, unsupported. Is he even still alive? – oh *no, no*, Michael, don't take your life from us! You're forgiven – *I* forgive you, Mary beckoned to him over and over in her heart...

Yet unforeseen and incomprehensible to her, when Ray began recovering and Mike was found alive in Elston, Mary could not rise out of her depression. Some part of her knew she was supposed to be overjoyed that Ray would live...but she could not manage to feel it. She just acted it. And Mike...well, he wouldn't really hurt himself, would he? Most of the time she knew he was only running. So now, it's almost as though she understands Mike, and actually hopes he can find his happiness away from the past year's tensions of their home.

Still, she's lost Mike forever, intuition tells her. He's so bitter. He may come back around home, at times, or live nearby, is all she can reasonably expect. (Mostly, now, she prays for and needs Ray to give up his mindless determination to have Mike "put away in infinternal lock-up!")

And Frank – sensible, likeable, and wisely caring Frank – will soon be away at school, and then will probably head off somewhere to a proud profession...perhaps on the other side of the world.

But it's Mike leaving home that makes her feel so alone. Plus his hatred for his oldest brother – to the brink of murder – makes her family seem so...forlorn, and fatally weakened.

Mary can see little hope.

...

But all along, and forever to come, what Mary doesn't see is that every human thing that she was, is, and expects to be is visible to and worshipped by Ray, is sensed and loved so much deeper by Frank, and is felt most profoundly – through empathy – by her youngest son Mike.

D arkness has filled all the volume of clear air, replacing the daylight. The street is quiet.

The bench outside the restaurant window is empty, and Lucy leans on his long oak bar pensively watching nothing, out there. The police office across the way is bright, its door wide-open, with no one inside. Both Sid and Chuck are right here, across the counter.

Lucy straightens, stretching away the stiffness from another long day of standing. He returns to where he was leaning before, right in front of his good bud Chuck. With his warming wide grin, with friendly blue eyes above a short frame – eyes almost level with Chuck's where he sits – he rejoins the conversation in his gentle, raspy voice:

"It ain't right."

Chuck slumps himself against the stool backrest, his stare narrowing into the eyes of a man who has seen it all. (Bartenders and restaurant front-liners should be made special advisors to judges, he once honored Lucy out loud, to his eventual regret. Not that his ego took over. It just labeled his mystique.) Around him swell and ebb a soft roar of voices – including his wife Beth's from the same side booth where Mike Watson sat steaming and muttering sixteen days ago. (If there's forty people here tonight, he poses to himself, forty are talking about the Watsons.)

"Course it ain't right," Chuck finally agrees. "There's gotta be some balance. We know Mike didn't stab Ray for absolutely no reason. But then Ray sure has a right to have his assailant charged."

Wilf, on the next stool past Sid to Chuck's right, has a question: "Won't Mike charging Ray for abuse cause Ray to drop his assault charge?"

"It's Ray Watson," Ed on Wilf's right reminds the other four who's involved.

Lucy reiterates, "Well, it ain't right. It'll tear poor Mary apart."

"How else does it get settled?" Chuck asks.

"I don't know – privately, somehow," Lucy still readily concedes he's not the best judge.

Chuck huffs, "Well, sure! That's the sensible way. Question is, which person in all this is sensible?"

"Mary and Clayton are sensible as can be," Ed leans forward on the counter to enforce his claim with a glare at the others (saying the core thing that's been or is being said many times over today and tonight in this restaurant and town).

"Well..." Sid rattles them here with this, "some families are sensible only from the outside lookin' in."

With the debate still simmering, and most people in there working on more coffee or beer or drinks (this being Friday night), Chuck is too worn out to go on. So he says goodnight to his friends and wife and starts for home. Before aiming up the side street beside Lucy's, though, he crosses to his office and phones to check on Mike. Mary answers, plainly sad and weak. Chuck asks how she's doing, how Ray is, and how Mike seems. "Fine," she replies listlessly to all three. Then she strains her voice a little to say, "Did you want to talk to Clayton? – I'm afraid he's out..." Chuck answers no, then hears that Mike went to sleep a while ago in his room. He thanks her and says good night.

Walking home in the cool and fresh late-evening air, alone on the unusually quiet weekend streets, Chuck rolls it over again in his mind: the question – his and Sid's question – of which member of that Watson family, with the possible exception of seemingly quite realistic Frank, needs more help.

"**N**eurasthenia. Repression: reprobatory; expiable," Joseph tosses out apparent possibilities as he reaches down beside him for a fresh full beer. In the distance, there is only the starlight-punctured canopy of night above the blacked-out sleeping corn. Barnyard lights glimmer here and there, away across the unseeable rolls of farmland. To the right, a glow of civilization – the energy of the hive: Elston City, ten miles off.

To Joseph's right, Howard requests (rather sedate and compendiously for Howard), "Speak fuckin' English."

Norm and Ba-Dee are there in front of them, half-sitting on the balcony railing, attentive.

They're at Looker's.

Looker is in his favorite chair on Joseph's left, keyboard in hand, the monitor screen between them positioned so Joseph can read the words aloud to the three others.

"Why," Norm now suddenly breaks in Norm-like, "is there so much space in space?"

"Why not?" Ba-Dee leans out over the balcony rail a bit and looks straight up, as though to see for himself.

"The stars would bump together – " Howard starts.

"What about my good words?!" Joseph reinterjects, plainly offended that he was denied a response.

They had been talking about Mike Watson and his family (of course) and were digging deep for meaning (Looker all the while offering no script, only appropriate facial expressions).

"There's no figuring it out, Joseph," Ba-Dee gazes down at him through the soft spill of light from the living room window. "It just has to work itself out."

"Or *in* – like a knife!" Joseph can't pass it up.

"Mike made his point," Norm notes, prepared for the back-wash of pun-groans that comes. "He won't wanna do any more physical damage."

Now Looker speaks: "He's damaged his well-being much more than it already was," he types as Joseph reads.

"Yeah," Howard returns to his justice frame of mind. "He could have charged Ray with abuse anyway – without gutting him."

"That's it," Looker responds. "Getting physical justice cuts himself down a notch, too."

"What is this, cheap pun night?" Ba-Dee grins.

Here, Joseph turns to Looker and bores in rudely, "What about you, Nelson? Was there someone you wanted to stab?"

Looker smiles understandingly, while the others watch only half-ashamed of Joseph (their unashamed halves, by their usual standard, feel anything is fair in words). He keys, "Not even myself. Thanks to my uncle, Admiral Nelson..." (Joseph guffaws again, like he did when he first heard the uncle's name. The other three chuckle too, hearing it direct from Looker, now.) "Who gave me perspective – that my life is principally my own and to see everyone as rocks – "

"Rocks...*rocks?!*" Joseph reacts with over-dramatized disbelief to what he's reading aloud.

Looker sips some beer, then explains: "Rocks: distinct weights and 'influences', my uncle calls it. People who can either anchor you or weigh you down, and even crush you, but cannot or should not ever be you – enter your individuality."

"Good one!" Norm says. "Rocks – you don't have to be a big one to have identity!"

"Or be a big one to bruise others up!" observes Joseph.

While all of them try to picture more homo-geologics in their minds, Norm can't help drawing the lame connection: "So, if all stars have planets which are basically rocks, why are they so far apart?"

"To give unlimited exploration challenges for all to try for," Howard has one.

"Keeps us little grains humble," Ba-Dee recalls Joseph's column.

"To leave enough room for the True Engine of the Universe," Joseph attests: "Chaos!"

To all of which Nelson bangs out the obvious real reason: "So no other beings can see what we're doing."

1 t's Saturday evening and Ray Watson is standing right there in front of Lucy's Large Lunch spilling his guts:

"I din deserve this! F'he had bugs up his ass, why din he jus' say so?! Jesus Haych Christ! He's the one who's downright abusive – the way he walks around with that goddamn attitude pissin' off our mom and everyone! Moody li'l no-good punk! Who's he think he – ?"

'Shouldn't you still be in the hospital?" Sid, standing at the other end of the bench, doesn't really sound as concerned as the words to his question would normally imply.

Bert, Mel and Shooter (waiting for their wives and their traditional Saturday night Lucy's supper) plus bachelor Chase, all cranked their heads synchronously from wobbly Ray to the officiating police officer. Norm, Ba-Dee, Joseph and Howard are clumped near the door, having held off going inside when they saw Ray hobble across the street. Chuck is sitting tilted back at the curb, observing. Wilf is right beside him. (Their wives are inside with their usual group, filling up on pre-dance coffee and conversation.) Reverend Fisk and Jimmy Jimms now walk up. And inside, Lucy has his nose pressed against his screen door, listening.

"I jus' signed myself out!" Ray exalts, smiling gamely back at Sid. "*They* don't know when a man's ready to go – yuh gotta know

I know how good I feel more'an they do!" He then grins ingratiatingly at each and every one of them. (Chuck doesn't smile back, with his unplanned trip to Elston Youth Offenders' Detention Center today still fresh in his mind, with its feeling of having to drag poor Mike there – only because Ray came home so abruptly – still churning his own insides.)

"You gonna be okay?" Chase pushes his red ball cap up above the lowering sun line so he can see Ray basking.

"I'll feel lots better when I get my way," Ray seems a bit hesitant to say it more specifically.

"How's your mom?" Reverend Fisk asks from Sid's end of the bench.

"She'll be better now!" Ray smirks wider (some in the group probably adding in their heads the implication "now that I'm home" and others "now that Mike's gone").

"Good," is all the Reverend comments.

"Well, better sid'own before I fall down!" Ray chuckles forcefully and continues his awkward walking. "Hope this place's coffee doesn't kill me, now! Ha!" And he disappears inside, Lucy holding the door open for him.

...

Mike Watson is let in, and he sits on one of two mid-floor sofas in the Youth Detention Center common room. At a small corner table, three teenagers are playing cards. On easy chairs at the end of tall bookracks set right-angled to the walls, a few more are sprawled or curled up, reading. (Only this room is open to both sexes, with everyone allowed in various hours of the day.) There are no windows; the two steel doors are locked. Five security cameras monitor the bright room; somewhere outside it, two supervisors do little else but watch.

On the beat-up sofa opposite the old one Mike is on, a tall skinny guy, maybe fifteen, is stretched out watching the TV mounted high on a side wall. He is ragged, with a torn-up white T-shirt (its emblazed-in-hellfire-red "YUH FUCKED WITTA FUCKUH-MAN..?" query still intact across its front) complementing shredded blue jeans and the last scraps of black sneakers. His dirty-brown hair would likely reach his shoulders, if it wasn't all over the armrest, yet his face looks clean and actually quite ruggedly handsome. Overtop the fixed TV natter, without a glance, he flatly asks:

"What'id *you* do?" His deep voice doesn't fit his apparent age, and his opening line is well practiced, as though it's automatically and always the greeting, here. "First time ever, huh?" he adds before Mike can even decide to answer. "C'n always tell."

"How?" Mike sincerely wonders.

"Yer lookin' at us all. Insteada starin' at the fuckin' walls, or somethin'."

Mike glances around at everyone again, and realizes he's right: absolutely no one was or is watching him. "Oh yeah."

"So what'id yuh do?"

"What did *you* do?" Mike answers with a good question, without emotion.

"Fuckin' pounded my no-good fuckin' dad to an inch of utter death," he bluntly explains it all in one line, his apparently newly acquired size alone fleshing out the part about having to first save it up enough through all his small and defenseless years.

"No shit?" Mike accents that heavily with respect.

"Yeah. So what'id *you* do?" the other one patiently tries again, this time angling just his eyes across the space between the sofas.

"Stabbed someone – "

"Cool," the guy reacts, already positive Mike did it for good reason.

"Ending up in here ain't so cool," Mike finally slumps down a little on the sofa.

"This ain't nothin'. This place's jus' daycare. Everybody comes 'n' goes here – like, nobody's really that pissed at us."

Mike stares at him, eight feet away...

"Erskine Fontaine Schuppe."

"Huh?" (Mike believes it's an introduction, but he can't be sure.)

"My fuckin' name! Great, huh? No fuckin' wonder I almos' kilt the prick, huh?" Erskine now grins with great inner amusement.

"Mike Watson."

"Hey, Mike. So tell me 'bout it. Who'd yuh do? – call me Bean – bee, ee, ay, enn – f'yuh want."

In his head, Mike guesses beanpole or string bean. Or even human bean.

"As in Coulda," Bean obliges. "Coulda *be*-ing, yuh know? Like I coulda *being* so fuckin' *giant* at this or fuckin' *gigantic* at that – I was enrolled in first-year university, " he adds in normal English.

"You were? – how old – ?"

"Fifteen. But bright doan make yuh so smart."

"So they nicknamed you Coulda Bean here?" Mike smiles a little, feeling suddenly a bit at home.

"'Bean' was easier – someone downtown – yuh know the warehouse?"

"Oh yeah! I stayed there," Mike now feels he's talking to a long-lost buddy.

"Great, huh? No one fucks with yuh there – yuh got yer own life, there."

Now Bean sits up, facing Mike squarely. Hunched forward, elbows braced on knees, his intelligent amber eyes lock sincerely onto Mike's. "Yuh know, my so-fuckin'-called father would push me down, then he'd start hittin' me – real hard. Then when he was drinkin' he'd..." he hesitates for Mike's sake, mindful of this new kid's own possibly painful experiences, "...and, you know..."

Mike knows. "If he'da ever tried to do me I'da knifed him *full* of fuckin' holes!" he angrily gauges his rights.

"Yeah, good one," Bean grins wide, showing his perfect teeth. "Yeah but, I'm glad I dint knife 'im or anything, now. He's still tryna put me away, though...the fucker... Hey, so yuh dint say who yuh did – father, right?"

"Oldest brother – "

"Thinks he's yer father, right?"

"Yeah – my dad's way better than him. Dad just mostly does nothing," Mike says it aloud for the first time in his life.

"Yeah, well, none of my biz'ness, but maybe that's yer real problem," Bean leans back and gazes around the room. "Well, at least from what I see 'round these here fucked-up lives, anyways... Think yuh knifed the right guy?"

Though Mike has thought a lot about his parents' role in making or not making his attitude, so far he never really faced what Bean now said. Tears of self-pity wet his eyes, but he tries hard not to cry.

"Hey!" Bean focuses back on Mike and smiles the most understanding smile. "Don't worry 'bout lettin' it out here, Mike buddy! Everyone does alla time, yuh'll see – best thing yuh can do. Hey, d'yuh wanna break outa here and go kill 'im for good – what's-his-name?"

"Ray," Mike chuckles once as he wipes away a tear.

"Yeah, *fucker Ray!* Fuckin' ugly human fuckin' bein'! One less ugly human on this good Earth!"

That remark grabs Mike – the "good Earth" part. "You sound like everyone at the warehouse...about that."

"Good Earth? Sure! Hey, fucker Ray ain't the whole world – ain't even part of yer life or mine, f'we don't want. Jus' get 'im completely outa yer head, is all, and then the world's jus' a big-ol' good time!"

That's what Mike found so compelling about the warehouse: everyone has a sense of future – everyone talks with a personal feel of hope that belongs solely to them. But then he thinks to ask:

"Do you still want your father dead?"

"Only when 'is time comes – he'll get 'is retribution."

"Retribution?"

"Yeah – punishment. Over there, yuh know?"

"I don't know about all that religious stuff – "

"Yuh will. Yuh doan mess with them kinda thoughts now 'cause they seem like yer parents' ideas. When yuh first re'lize y'aren't smart 'nough tuh even begin tuh know any of the big reasons *why* in this whole universe, then yuh begin tuh feel somethin' real – jus' keep an open mind. Yuh doan hafta do no fuckin' organized cult thing tuh believe in creation – it's all jus' right in front of us! Believe what yuh feel, and stick to it. Then it'll happen..."

Mike waits for Bean to say it... (Or maybe he's supposed to fill in the rest himself. Regardless, he sure likes what he's hearing.)

"What'll happen, my good buddy Mike, is fucker Ray won't fit inside yer life no more."

...

Ray has chosen the exact center stool to sit on, down along Lucy's long counter. No one is to his left...until Joseph, Norm, Howard and Ba-Dee enter a minute later and perch on the four stools at the far end; Lucy now leans on the front end, to watch. Ol' Jerry soon begins placing white 'Lucy's' mugs, steaming with coffee, in front of each of all five new counter customers. Behind them at the mostly-filled tables and booths – except for little Rebecca zippin' around serving and cleaning up – a stillness has settled...

Chuck Cintz now comes in, carrying his empty paper cup, and wordlessly parks on the stool closest to Lucy by the register.

"So how yuh doin', Ray?!" It's Joseph who's the one who asks it enthusiastically with a thick-glasses stare from nine stools away, finally deflating the awkward-silence pressure that was filling the big room.

Ray flicks a look at him while raising his mug. "Okay," he smirks (as if indulging in any and all concern, even from townspeople who never said anything except maybe hi to him ever before).

Joseph's fuzzy eyes continue to bear down on him. "So, Ray..! You're not dead!" Instantly, Norm beside him pokes him hard in the ribs.

"Heh-heh! No, guess I'm the sa'vivor kind, lad," Ray responds, gazing straight ahead at the wall of shelves and Looker's MY TOWN book of poems...which happens to be right there.

"I see..." Joseph is still perfectly motionless (though Howard is now reaching across Norm and pinching Joseph's arm with all his might to get him to shut up). "That's good, Ray. So...how's everyone? – your mom and dad and Frank and young...thingamabob..."

Ray, with sideways glance and cordial kind of smile, thinks to ask, "Who're you, anyways?"

"Joseph! Joseph Welt! Ray, your neighbor down the street four houses!" he guffaws theatrically.

"Oh, a'course," Ray frowns. "Well, Mom's still kinda rough, some. Dad's okay. And...hey, you the one that writes in the paper?"

Everyone in the restaurant heard that question, and though Ray seems oblivious, their recurring murmur of voices has now dissipated to nothing. And Chuck adjusts his plumpness nervously on his big, brass stool.

"The paper! – yes, that's me!" Joseph now searches Ray's face for indicators of suspicion or inclinations towards capitalizing on print-exposure martyrdom. Behind Joseph, the three pairs of eyes sticking out around him are examining, too... There is definitely no suspicion.

Ray grins again, slurps some coffee, then cautiously rubs his side (as though, Joseph thinks, a phantom knife is being twisted in there). "Well, that's it. Jus' Mom, I guess. But the...problem's mostly solved."

"Oh," Joseph contemplates. "I see. But you still are in the process of charging and imprisoning...the 'problem'..."

Chuck tenses to his feet. Lucy and every single one else freeze a little straighter. Even Jerry slows his wiping dishes.

"Listen, you gotta beef with what goes on in our family?" Ray now points his head down in Joseph's direction, but still doesn't talk eye-to-eye.

"Ray!" Joseph hints at a scoff. "It's a free country! – but then, it is your business. I'm simply sort of wondering, you know...wondering if maybe your little brother is also on this status list you just started giving me – is he okay? Do you have any idea?"

"Mike needs'ta be straightun'd out!" Ray simmers, not noticing Chuck edging slowly in behind him toward no-man's-land (though the Chief does not appear necessarily intent on stopping this).

"'Straightened out'... is he bent, Ray? Is he twisted?" Joseph knows his use of double-entendre words is lost on single-minded Ray Watson.

Ray spins on his stool a quarter turn, grimacing with the pull on his wound. Now he sees Chuck standing in between, and finally realizes what he's been drawn into.

"Jus' le'me take care of it," Ray scowls at Joseph, though he reestablishes his fixed-smirk expression. "It's *my* family. I'm the only one ever knows what it needs an' what's ever wrong..." And he picks up his mug as he stands, heading for the one empty back booth.

As Ray passes within four feet of him (with three friends' hands now openly gripping different parts of his clothing), Joseph observes, "But Ray! Maybe what's wrong is one and the same with why he knifed you!"

Though Ray hesitates as he strains by, he decides against confronting. Also, Chuck is positioned exactly between them.

Ray Watson soon settles into his booth, and two women wisely cross over and start nicely asking about his health, and then about his folks. Chuck, meanwhile, nicely proposes to Joseph that he and his buds best leave for a little while – for Mary Watson's sake, he reasons.

As Joseph stands, a foot overtop Chief Cintz, he gulps his entire coffee and whispers with a smile, "Don't feel bad, Chuck. We weren't planning on staying, anyway...though maybe if that fucker had died... *Hey!*" he then decides to very loudly suggest, "If that booth over there empties out," Chuck turns his head to look where he's pointing, "ask Ray Watson to try the view from there. It's where Mike sat just before he stabbed him..."

Sunday afternoon, Mary Watson is followed by her son Frank, and by Joseph, Norm, Ba-Dee, Howard, Sid, Wilf, Mayor Sue and Looker into the well-guarded visiting-hours lobby of the Elston Youth Offenders' Center. Mike is sitting there waiting.

After Mary visits with her son a half hour, she and Sid leave (doctor's orders: avoid too much mom-stress). Now the others huddle around Mike, telling him about the tense moments last night at Lucy's. (Though appreciating their support, Mike here silently worries that Ray would be even more overbearing with Mom.)

They then tell Mike about later on at the Varmint Hall, how Ray was out on the floor trying to dance, ill-advisedly drinking shots and stumbling, and had to be helped back to his table three or four times.

Mike merely nods, with a serious and knowing expression, nothing more. He then tells them how he's doing, mentions his peculiar new friend Bean, and adds that he would really rather be locked up here than at "the house". They all understand.

After an hour of visiting, the support group rises as one to leave, offering Mike cheerful encouragement and promises to do whatever they can to convince his brother Ray to put and end to his heartlessly off-balance obsession to have him imprisoned.

Mike, in turn, smiles with appreciation, but surprises them by saying he isn't worried, that talking with his own lawyer last night, he is assured that his abuse charge against Ray is "guaranteed solid".

...

Mary Watson sits drooped in one of the wooden rocking chairs on their broad front porch. Her husband half-sits on the window ledge in front of her. And on the old pullout sofa bed near the other end, Ray is laid out, eyeing them as they talk. It's late Sunday afternoon.

"Why can't we drop the whole thing?" Mary frets, asking the same question she's asked for the last several days in exactly the same way (using "we" as though not to focus pressure on her oldest, and as though she and her husband are required by blood to be part of Ray's civic duty to prosecute Mike).

"It has to stand, Darling," Clayton starts his positioning with the usual touch of impatience in his voice. An emptied shot glass rests beside him on the ledge. "Because of the assault counter-charge," he sidesteps using Mike's name, "we need Ray's charge to at least balance it out."

"You mean one could cancel out the other?" Mary asks with a heaving breath of weariness, willing to agree if it could neutralize legal conflict between her oldest and youngest sons.

Ray stays rigid on the sofa, but his voice is full of rage: "I got my needs here, Ma! I don't wanna live the rest of my life thinking no justice was ever mine to have – don't matter whatever he says, anyway, 'cause there's no two ways about him criminal attacking me!"

"Ray, we understand that," Dad now tries to calm this, some. "And we understand there's the issue of having Mike pay for his actions. But Mother's question is about ending this quietly, rather than having things...broaden..."

Right then Frank walks out onto the porch, sipping a can of soda.

And the other three fall silent.

...

Bean beams, eyes sparkling with the thought: "Yuh really got-ta case?!" he asks as though wanting Mike to just simply repeat all what he just said. (It's Sunday night at the Detention Center, minutes before the common room lock-up and lock-up-in-their-tiny-rooms time for all the evil youth offenders.)

"Yup," Mike assures him from the other sofa – the same positions they were in when they met. "The lawyer said sure thing. Last night."

"Fuckin' fair! Hey, I should do that!" it occurs again to Bean. (Erskine has pursued precisely that counter-tactic right to the limit, then stopped himself and his lawyer short, for his mom's sake.)

"You should," Mike supposes, smiling with brave self-righteousness and that much more confidence.

"Well, yah, I did. But it didn't – I didn't..."

"You didn't go through with it?" Mike can't imagine Bean letting his hated father get away with it.

"Still should, yuh know... Maybe I will – see how you do, first," Bean gives him all his happy white teeth as encouragement.

"Okay, we'll take 'em all on – "

"Whoa a sec!" Bean now gets snagged on why he didn't do it. "What about yer mom an' things? Yuh could do serious mood-squooshin' there!"

Mike doesn't need to think it over. "So? – I mean, I don't want to hurt her – or Dad, I guess. But I've got a whole life to live, don't I?"

And Bean can't help recognize: "Yep, gotta stand up for yerself now, Mike, 'cause it sure sounds like Mom and Dad created that monster Ray by not doin' right-much for yuh all along!"

...

521

"He's in on it," Ray concludes to his dad as he slowly rises from the sofa bed, heading into the house for the night.

"Frank? On what?" Clayton Watson asks, still quite coherent even after his many drinks, staying out there on the porch after Mom went to bed early.

"What Mike's doin'," Ray tries to sound nonchalant, saying it as he puts on a show of steadying himself standing.

"You mean both your brothers cooked this thing up about you – your so-called abusing Mike – together?"

"Yes. A'course," Ray acts indignant. "G'nite."

"I see...good night," Dad allows thoughtfully, though he's too tanked to summon the obvious question: If there was no abuse from Ray, what possible reason in the world would have compelled Mike to do what he so desperately did and to furthermore now grind through the whole ordeal of charging him?

...

Monday morning, Mike is informed by his lawyer that a hearing is scheduled to review his charges that Ray abused him: it's in four days. All his family must be present before the judge.

Mike is also told that his family was given a date for the hearing regarding his alleged attempted murder of Ray: it's in three days. He is required to be present, too, amid his family.

CLAYTON HERMAN WATSON

The proper thing (cautiously poor or not) was to somehow keep young Clayton in school. With his older brothers working and sisters always helping Mother plus babysitting and such, ten-year-old Clayton was the first – and as the youngest, the last – with a chance to finish a post-high-school course. There should be enough money coming in to see him through.

And Clayton did eventually graduate, but in the dying small city where he was born and raised (where, he assumed, he would follow family tradition and live his entire life) there was no work for him whatsoever – all the year he tried.

So Clayton Herman Watson left the only few square miles of geography he had ever known and seen, and ventured to the big city. He didn't stop to feel if he was full of hope.

He found no work there, either, suitable to his education. But his family borrowed a little money and (on their confidence he would someday do well) sent him allowances monthly.

Then, amid all the gray and stagnant hours and days, Clayton met pretty Mary Dupleix. He fell wholeheartedly for her dark, fine face, her questioning intellect, the charm of her smile, and her compelling honesty. So he wanted a life with her, instead of what he believed he was missing back home.

But there was a serious cost: both their families were outraged – culture, religion, status – more opposite partners could not be imagined!

Young Mary and Clayton had to commit or separate. Yet above all, he reminded her how no one should be in charge of their lives but them. And they turned their backs on home, on Clayton's allowance, on Mary's family security.

And fortunately, very soon, Clayton did find work: a low paying job at a large investment firm. Three years later, with Mary pregnant, he was transferred to Elston City, and they found a very reasonably priced house to rent in a town only ten miles away. (Though Clayton would have likely found better positions at other companies had he tried, he felt loyalty to Head Office for giving him employment when he was desperate.)

But then it surfaced: with the birth of his first son Raymond, Clayton felt trapped. He should have recognized it was in part because his past family could not be part of his own future family. And (had he talked with her about it) it was what Mary began feeling, too.

Now, work was that much more an effort – with added expenses at the same meager income. Yet how could he chance leaving for a new job, with no savings and a baby to keep healthy? So, fighting the gloom, he did what seemed right: he dug in harder – tried not to think about it or let it affect him – and worked longer hours, wooing clients and bosses and inspectors at restaurants and bars to all hours of the night...for the sake (he rationalized) of business.

Mary, apparently, understood.

Soon, baby Bill was born. Another hungry mouth – but he and Mary loved him dearly, too, and they would manage...though Clayton couldn't help calculate to himself how this would set things back that much more from the possibility of Mary ever working again.

Then, disaster: At two, Bill fell deathly sick. It was a night-mare of worry and turmoil, of hospital vigils and monstrous doc-tor charges. Yet months later, Bill pulled through, with no fore-seeable reason why he should not live a long, healthy life.

Although Clayton did gain some salary increases, the hospi-tal debt canceled them out. And as more time passed, Frank was born, then Michael. And Clayton buried in his heart his regret over having two more children – unplanned (though accepted as deserving life). All he could do was distance himself from such a sobering mental torment. (Certainly, however, there would be no more babies!)

The years rolled by; he and Mary became more and more set in their ways – Clayton content with all his cronies (with usually enough money to keep himself well-enough oiled against any grating frustrations that might surface). And the boys matured fine.

But then, a parent's worst reality: suddenly, unwarned, un-imaginable – in the midst of perfect health and young-adult ad-ventures – Bill was killed. Twenty-one years old, Clayton kept thinking. He outlived his own son, the one he thought would outfight them all, after what he went through as a toddler... And Mary, poor Mary...it was plain, her special feeling for Bill. She could not bear it.

Clayton, naturally, blamed himself. He should have been a better provider – Bill might have lived if he hadn't been driving that horrifying little car..! It felt like punishment. In his mind, he looked for answers everywhere, but could find none. He could barely talk with Mary; she was always at the edge. And, with no consciousness to it at all, he pulled back from his other three boys: they terrified him – they had the potential to overwhelm him... with feelings. He could lose another son, and then Mary with him. They could drag him down with anguish – how could he work and provide for them, then? And he just bottled all this up inside... Oh, he could talk with Ray, some, but nothing at all deep. Ray was always practical, and strong. He was an ally. An ally the way his own brothers and sisters could have been – or even his much more steadfast parents, if they were still living.

Clayton tried to find solace in the Bible, but usually found it more tangibly in his liquor. He had to have something, he justified, to carry him over the strain of emotions at home and the pressures at work. At least he didn't rampage or womanize or fall down drunk. He drank (in his words) to stay within himself. That's what he needed to keep functioning. Otherwise, he would weaken...

Along with all of it, Clayton was feeling his age – middle age, his pale brown hair graying and thinning to nothing, his body turned to mush from desk work and indulgence, and all the romance of his youth – his boyhood, all the brothers and sisters, his home town, the exciting big city and his young bride – was all irretrievably behind him. He felt like running away...but that wouldn't be right.

And now this...this Mike thing.

In the same way the glorious hopes of his own past are beyond reach, Clayton now feels no accessibility to his sons. Mike stabbing Ray seemed to seal it. But who could have stopped it? Who could have repaired the anguish that Bill's loss caused and who could have dissolved the bitterness between two so-different sons? Maybe Mary (his most private objectivity had to question) was simply not the complete mother they could have had – oh, she was always caring and kind and worked hard to maintain their home...but what was missing? He knows he was the father figure: stable, providing, stern when necessary; he tried to be a man, for them. But still, the boys seemed so...but only visibly since this Mike thing...

Independence, Clayton always believed, is the uppermost quality to give a son, and Mike is old enough to realize his actions and face the consequences. And Ray is adult and must follow through with his convictions – he was the one who was stabbed, after all, and has every right to have the proper action taken... though it would break Mary's heart to see her youngest actually sent to prison...

Well, all I can do, Clayton keeps arriving at, is try to keep things calm, sensible, to salvage the better parts of my own, my wife's, Ray's and the other two boys' lives – he will not force anyone into doing anything against their will. When the hearings come, he will try to stay neutral – he will stand clear. As long as Ray recovers his health fully, he decides, everyone in time can merely put this all behind them, and each of us can go on...living.

"Yeah, your fam'ly's shits don't stink! – worm-lips!" Heap Henry stands slumped in a lump at his fixed position in shallow center field. Though his thirteen-year-old thought processes aren't entirely sure exactly what his observation to Rick there in the dugout means, he believes it has proper weight. (All Rick yelled out at him was "Lowlife!" ... though he neglected to temper it with an appropriate "bug-eyes" or "puke-breath".)

Now stepping out of his dugout onto the sun-hot dust, tall fourteen-year-old Rick stiffens his arms at his sides and responds, "You scum-eatin' tub-a-lub turd-tongued fart-sucker!" (though from last year, Henry has stretched almost completely out of his plump era).

Keenly observing this outburst from the mound, Jackie stands firm, arms braced on hips, long, black hair flailing wildly around his head in the gusty wind. All six of his other players have withered to the ground (here, five hours into this Monday's session of their summer-long game). (So far this year, it's sixty-eight to fifty-seven for Rick's boys.)

All of Rick's seven teammates on the bench now step up onto the infield dirt, too.

Chomping his usual big wad of gum – dirty, baggy clothes flapping in the breeze, sweaty-wet hair stringing down to his shoulders – Heap starts laboring across the grass in toward them.

"You think you're so much better, don't you? Just 'cause you got a bigger house!" Heap now shows his seriousness by omitting a slur, too.

"Sure ain't no prizes in that bunch of animals at your house!" Rick stares Henry down, coldly referring to the drunks and social-assistance clan he's a member of.

"So fuckin' what?! That don't make *you* no proper fuckin' sophisticate!" Henry uses his dictionary word for the day with timely precision.

Now the two belligerents are nearly face-to-face. Jack is accelerating toward them from the mound.

"You some sorta Mike Watson wish-I-was, or somethin'?" Rick aims dagger-like. "Think you're better than where you come from?"

"Yeah, peckerless..!" Heap thrusts out and arm and shoves Rick's shoulder, both of them now realizing for the first time this season that Heap has sprouted as tall as Rick.

Right here, Jack steps between them. "What's you guys' families got to do with how you end up? Haven't you got a brain and a life of your own?" he rotates his head back and forth at them along his own restraining outstretched arms.

Neither Henry nor Rick, eyeballs still in a death lock, have a quick answer for that.

"Shit!" Jack flings his arms in the air and trods back toward the forlorn battered baseball he left resting on the pitching rubber, confident this confrontation is irrelevant (which it obviously is, since the combatants have also just turned wordlessly back toward their proper places). "Shit!" he yelps again out at the wind. "Howcome everything that happens in this loopy town ends up on this ball field!"

"So you finally got off your high-and-mighty pulpit," Howard says to Joseph as they walk down the street to Lucy's. Norm is astride just-ended-his-shift Ba-Dee right behind them. The late-afternoon sun is still fusing hard, and a fantastic fleet of white clouds builds across the sky, utterly silent...above.

"Yeah!" Norm concurs, watching the four feet in front of him pound the sidewalk. "Finally a column that doesn't try to *pound* something serious into you!"

"Hey, Lonely Len *is* serious!" Joseph reacts, defending his latest subject (the derelict who mysteriously appears once in a while on his customary stool at the hotel bar to patiently wait for liquid charity). "His life is as important as – "

"Who?!" Howard instantly contests, so wary of Joseph's disloyal observations.

Joseph stops in his tracks, causing Norm and Ba-Dee to collide with him in a confusion of bodies in a clump on the open sidewalk. "My life," he puts it to little Howie. "And Norm's here and Looker's and Chief Chucky Cintz's and Mike's and Ray's and Bungy Alwot's – "

"*Fine!*" Howard snaps, turning back toward their destination and stomping off, sorry for even asking.

"Howie!" Joseph grins. "Don't you wanna know who the fuck Bungy Alwot is..?"

As they approach Lucy's, the four ol' boys there on the bench plus Sid, Wilf, Ed, Chuck, Editor John Sing and two local farmers who sometimes hang around there stop their rumors and exaggerations and wait for: The Celebrated Journalist.

"Great story!" Ed says it first to Joseph as he and his buds coast to a stop.

"Yeah, how'd you find out all that about old Len?" Sid questions the inquirer, still openly heartwarmed from reading it.

"Bought him multi-bottles of booze," Joseph simpers as though guilty (at an equally grinning John Sing). "The tough part was getting his whole life story out before he became upright-incoherent." (Len never mumbles, or even slouches. He just keeps on drinking, sitting up straight indefinitely, as if only his vocal cords lose all control...in that, he also tends to start softly grunting, as though at some unknowable minor demon.)

"What a life," Wilf now smiles a sad smile and shakes his head. "No one had any idea where he came from, did they?"

"No," Chuck sighs, "only theories."

"So Joseph, what was it, him finally opening up?" Bert asks, from years of observing others trying.

"Oh, oiling him up, like I said, then just happened to hit the right note," Joseph relaxes some, pushing his hands into his jeans pockets. "What I told him was the Watson family story, and he started weeping – *weeping!* So I tried to draw it out some, asked him about growing up and his parents. Once he got going about how great his childhood was, with all the wealth and caring parents, he was feeling so good he kept on talking. But..." Joseph takes a deep breath, "when he started in on those early years with his wife and new baby...it was smiles to tears. And then it was how both died, and how he walked away from his business – and his fortune – hoping to find some meaning..."

"Instead he found despair," Ed interjects in a moan, as though feeling that potential in everyone.

"That's true," Joseph agrees patiently. "He could never push himself up off the bottom. He had no one to do it for... But one curious thing I left out had to do with what I named him – he didn't seem to mind me calling him Lonely Len...as long as I kept up the flow into his glass, I guess. Anyway, what he told me was this little story about a guy he knew he called Desolate Don...who hung around the bar near Len's business – a real loser, he called him, but he usually felt sorry for him and bought him drinks – until he sat down one night with him and listened to his story. Len didn't give me details, but he said he swore to himself back then that he would never end up – well, give up on life, that way... that nothing could ever be that bad – "

"Until you're there yourself," Wilf observes with understanding.

"Nah, ya gotta keep your head straight," one of the farmers scoffs. "Don't matter what hits ya, it's your responsibility ta keep on livin' – "

"To who?" Ed challenges.

"Ta God!" the man shoots back. "Livin' is the purpose of life!"

"Then you don't know how some things can affect you," Ed has a broader view. "The loss of some things."

"It's the strongest, most driving force in the world," Sid now states his position on the worst thing to lose.

"What is?" Chuck prompts him from across the sidewalk.

"Love!" Sid attests plainly and unembarrassed.

"Caring!" John Sing supports him wholly with his favorite word for it.

"Compassion," ol' Chase adds another from the bench.

And Joseph concludes for all of them, amid his three buddies nodding and all the murmurs of agreement and positive feeling – amid the surfacing of remembered moments and images of poor young Janet murdered last year, of her wounded family, of Looker's desperate life choices, of Mike Watson's struggle to be whole, and of Lonely Len and everyone everywhere who inevitably knows precisely the same sorrow:

"All true. And the way I see it, everything we are and do is human feeling. Most of us just live it, but a few people are hard as stone...and then, some others suffer terribly."

oble Earth,
      Wherein all were born...

Reared by winds,
Rains,
The fantastic dynamo Sun,
We are part
Of the ages of the whole...

"Nelson Nelson". That's me, he stops and thinks....

Aloft in breezes,
Rushing nowhere
Past horizons...

The envelope on the table beside him says it's him; the phone caller asked his landlady for two thirds of the currently locally-known him by name; and he does have papers to put him as close as any one of you can be to proving...it's really you.

    But inside, Nelson feels emptied of himself; he feels hollowed, of so much of what made him...him.

Fleeting life, the secret span

Of so few years,
Against only perceivable eternity,
Still all outside experience...

Fears, in the night, of life.
The grace, of faith.
How to soar again
Above the pulling world

Of despair, loss,
On all the currents
Of Time?
– the Creator's trick
Of distance!

Beside the envelope with his name, with his place in life print-ed on it, are two pages. Though meagerly typed and all spread out, it still could have been said in a mere four words.

But it's from an army of lawyers. Collectively, they regret to inform him, in so many words:

Uncle Admiral is dead.

"Admiral died bravely, at home, among his beloved friends, succumbing unexpectedly quick to his closely guarded secret cancer."

On page two (Looker has yet to get to it) is a statement in-forming "NELSON NELSON: Nephew" that he is now – so con-voluted as it is in wordage and so inappropriately insensitive after the stab of page one – a solidly wealthy man.

t's late Wednesday night (almost Thursday morning) and Lucy's Large Lunch is closed and locked for the day. Gathered inside, at four square tables pushed together to make one big square table, are Lucy, Chuck, Wilf, Mayor Sue, Reverend Fisk, Norm, Howard, Ba-Dee, Joseph and Looker. This is Looker's idea.

Having taken a quick flight Tuesday morning to attend his Uncle Admiral's funeral (his parents were not there), Looker came back today with a concept – something he believes his much-loved uncle would have liked. What inspired his concept was: himself. And Mike Watson. And young people like those in the downtown "warehouse" in Elston. (Looker was actually there once, eleven years ago, but didn't stay overnight.)

Unlike the warehouse, which is basically a simple shelter, he wants to fund a "school of reality" – a residence/drop-in center/ hideout for young adults. Once approved by referendum from the whole town, Nelson will buy a house and renovate it to accommodate perhaps a dozen young folks. (He has these points printed out, and this select group is reading through them one by one. He furiously scribbles explanations to their questions, which Joseph has volunteered to voice.) Adults would require permission from an overseeing committee – town leaders balanced by some youth home residents – to visit beyond an entrance common room. One professional social councilor would be hired, and the loosely structured courses would be strictly "life" courses: the psychology of families, and comprehensive looks at where and how parents are inadequate; plus: baby studies – not how to have or what to feed them, but how to behave around them, how to block all your own damaging influences on them. (Looker notes, "It's the most important impact you'll have in your life: on your own children. They, in turn, impact society entirely. But no one teaches young people how to parent them right.") Also, he sees this as a place for troubled teenagers to gain perspective, away from the power of their parents – not unlike the Elston warehouse – where they can begin to figure out their own life's worth.

Everyone likes his concept. Looker cautions that he is no expert, except by experience, and that his sketched-out structure might be counterproductive, as is. In response, Mayor Sue commits to consulting the experts. And all the men sign up for the renovations. The referendum, they believe, is the only true hurdle.

It's agreed that John Sing will publish the proposal in next week's paper (with Joseph adding that he is more than willing to pontificate about it in a column).

"We hope," Chuck then ends the meeting, "that Mike Watson is our first guest in our..." he hesitates over what they should call it.

Joseph, the worker of words suggests, "Home Near Home."

Enthusiastically optimistic – with the added impetus of a dignified name – they all leave cheerfully, with the warm hope that they might soon do a few young people out there some good.

"It'll never fuckin' work," Howard exhales wearily into the thick blackness around him in the back seat. In the distance, lightning flickers against the dark silhouette of a tree line, and the broad ember of town lights behind them barely tints the brooding cloud cover overhead. Out the rolled-down windows, crickets suspend their chorus, waiting for the coming storm.

"Lowlifes," Ba-dee postulates. "A pit of degenerates."

It's right after Looker's meeting, and Norm is driving, Ba-Dee sits beside him, and Joseph has melted, strangely silent, into the same abyss of lightlessness that Howard has embraced in back.

Norm disagrees: "Don't you two have any trust that humans inherently want to do right? That it's outside influences and pressures that can turn young adults to or away from doing the wrong things?" he observes as though he's not a young adult himself.

"Right. So give 'em free room and board," Howard groans, "and let 'em stew in their community-provided pot of revolution!"

"There was never a time you could have used a place like that?" Joseph now talks, his calm rumble stopping Howard cold with that picture-it-for-your-own-self counterpoint.

"Yeah, imagine those times your mom or dad or someone really pissed you off," Norm rallies. "Wouldn't it have been good to have somewhere to go – to get it out of your head?"

"That's why we come out here," Ba-Dee notes, implying that all young people will find their own ways.

"Sure. Beer-guzzling, inane-questioning sheep, hiding in the dark," Joseph tries brutal objectivity.

"That's if you're heartlessly objective," Howard sees. "But you don't actually believe that, Joseph."

"No," the journalist is honest, "but the real problem is that there's no place for most of them to go..." Then thinking about that makes him angry: "Take Mike – cowering in a garage, for fuck sake!"

"He wouldn't have been arrested hanging out at the Home At Home?" Ba-Dee questions rhetorically.

"Home *Near* Home," Joseph corrects. "And the idea is, he would have found answers there before it came down to the pillow-on-the-face, skewer-with-a-harpoon solution."

"Does this mean we won't have to come out here anymore to drink beer and talk drivel?" Ba-Dee pictures, selfishly thinking about saving wear and tear on his car.

"The four of us are past any home-beside-home salvation," Norm answers at the wheel. "Anyway, we'll soon all be able to go legally sit right beside Lonely Len and drink beer and talk drivel there all night."

"I'm lookin' forward to it..." Howard enlists, gazing forlornly out his window at Creation, as though all is pointless.

"See? There! That's where we're at!" Joseph catches Howard's acquired frustration "If we would've had some stabilizing place to turn to in our lives, we wouldn't see things as bleak, half the time."

"You mean we'd have optimism and purpose?" Ba-Dee asks with a big grin in his words.

"Pointless..." Howard mumbles.

"Well, tomorrow's Mike's hearing," Norm says leaning against his door, as though settling in for the wait. "Hope dipshit Ray backs down."

"I'll say it again," Joseph says it again: "Without some other place to go to here, this town has lost Mike Watson, either way."

And with that, they decide to leave, having already agreed to accept Looker's invitation for a get-together – to talk over Mike's hearing results – at his place tomorrow evening.

"There was no denting him – I went at him for an hour this morning," Chief Cintz apologizes to Mike Watson as he officially drives him (blue uniform shirt and tie, even) from the Detention Center to the Elston courts building. Around them, traffic is heavy, and some people scowl at the passing police car's sixteen-year-old degenerate convict. "Ray is just stubbornly determined to drag you through this..." (And Chuck is still stuck between telling and not telling Mike about Looker's proposal – bad timing, plus it's still only a concept.)

"Whatever," Mike reacts, full of certainty, staring back at the strangers out his closed side window.

"But he might give it up right here – I mean with the whole actual legal system in front of him now."

"Doesn't matter. Tomorrow matters," Mike reminds Chuck about the hearing for his charges against Ray, his eyes strikingly calm. He strokes his buzzed hair once, and adjusts his posture to sit straight again. (He's wearing his newest favorite black-abyss T-shirt.) "If it has to go to a trial or something, I got more shit to say than him."

They're soon there, and Chief Cintz escorts Mike from the parking lot through to the courtroom. The first thing Mike sees inside – from ten feet outside the open doorway – is Ray's hard brown eyes right on him...

Mike could not feel more at ease. He keeps in mind all what his new buddy Bean said about owning your own place in creation, plus all his clearly surfaced truths he felt while hiding out in Bennetts' garage and more still while locked up. This despicably bleak human, he assures himself with knowing eyes fixed on his ex-brother's, is no longer an influence in my head.

Mike has to sit at a side table, alone with a totally unknown new Youth Center legal counselor. Settling back in his chair, he shifts his focus from his case worker's explanations to see, fifteen feet and ninety degrees away, the straight row of all his family's eight eyes fixed right on him: Dad, Mom, Frank, and two seats further down their long table, beside his lawyer, is Ray – still glaring at Mike. (Even Mom, he notices, is dressed business-like the same as Dad and has assumed an environmentally appropriate expressionless air.)

Chief Cintz took a seat in the first row of the empty little visitors' gallery. A uniformed guard stands at ease near a side door. Everything except the ceiling, Mike notes, is solid, polished wood. And a court reporter sits waiting, front-and-center... Then suddenly, grabbing everyone's attention, a great-big husky large-mustached robed judge enters swiftly and immediately barks:

"Awright, record this: I just found out about this other thing tomorrow with you people – nobody ever tells me anything! Well then, I'm not about to go an inch into this one with that one pending tomorrow. It's all one problem, ain't it?" He then raises his gavel as though this is a trial to end, but stops it mid-air to add, "And if you – hey, cut that out, now, Irene..." he leans forward and instructs the reporter to stop recording, "...if you, Mister Ray Watson," (he now frowns judgmentally straight at him) "intend to drag your little brother through all the inevitable court sessions that are coming – because just like me, the guy tomorrow I swear won't touch that one without this one, you see? – well, let me advise you here that the scales of our justice has two sides, and though it's true there's something perfectly real backing your side, you should be prepared for the unimaginable weight of social conscience – that's already piled up! – on young Michael's side, from what I hear. And though I know your pain is physical and valid, Mister Ray Watson," he now stands and finishes with the same flourish as when he entered, "you're the only one who could right here call this game even and by doing so save everyone along that line of folks beside you a whole brand-new mountain of pain! That's it!" And he's gone.

Everyone is stunned, except Mike. Since his very first thoughts of righteousness in this, he feels no surprise that things are going his way. All he's thinking now is how his lawyer can use this in their case tomorrow. Then, looking away from the door where the judge evaporated, his gaze meets his mother's, and she's crying. Clearly, she was tormented that things came this far, and is for the moment relieved that this part didn't happen. But plainly, too, it's still up to Ray – to prevent the most anguishing stage...and it's there in her eyes: the apprehension over two of her three remaining sons each being tried and sentenced out of her life.

Next, Mike shifts his attention to Ray...who is searching down through the wood table in front of him. He looks shocked. No way he believed his case – his victimizationing – was any way unsolid. Ray thought he was pure right, and Mike – the stabber – was hundred percent wrong.

Mike, however, now feels whole.

After a quick visit with just his mom and Frank in the emptied courtroom, Mike is driven back to the Center by Chuck – who confesses his full support for him and then eagerly tells him about Looker's youth home idea.

Mike now feels better than he ever has.

...

With the next day's hearing canceled too, a court date will be set once all lawyers for both sides reconfirm the charges.

...

"Suck-ay-truck!" Bean grins with his great teeth amid his wrecked hair, Thursday night in the Center common room. "Now what?"

Mike is flat-out on the opposite sofa. "I guess the big one: judge 'n' jury."

"Woo! Think it'll get tuh that?"

Mike smiles wide at the thought and answers, "Hope so!"

"I git it!" Bean chortles and stretches out on his sofa, too, sharing Mike's confidence. "Glad yuh sliced 'im now, right?"

"Right..." Mike spontaneously responds, yet trails off as though never forgetting his guilt.

"Glad he lived, too, right?"

"Yeah, true," Mike feels both sides of that – the other side being: Otherwise he wouldn't be around to officially admit what a low human being he is.

...

"I know, Ma! I know, I know!" Ray sits tensely on the porch rocker, one hand over his wounded side as though holding in his innards. "It could drag on months – I know – Dad said!"

"So think of all the embarrassment alone to us, Ray," Mary pleads. "Hasn't our family been through enough..?" And she starts softly weeping, again. (Clayton is out at some meeting, somewhere, and Frank just left for a long-postponed date with a girlfriend, so Mary saw her chance here to pressure Ray, mother to son.)

"I comprehen' all that stuff, Ma!" Ray stiffens, as if with the physical strain his emotional tension is causing. "But what about me? I want some..." he stops short.

"You want some what?" she presses. "Do you only want vengeance? Or are you afraid now that if you drop it, his attack will look justified – is that it?!"

Ray doesn't answer. He squints out through the screened porch end beside him. (Only Mom can occasionally challenge him effectively enough that he submits.)

"So you think if you at least go to court, you appear to believe you're right and he's wrong!"

Ray shakes his head – with frustration.

"Ray, don't do this!" Mary now begs. "Maybe Mike – "

"Maybe he's right?! Is that it?" He now pushes painfully to his feet against the armrests, but still doesn't meet her eyes. "You haven't seen every goddamned thing going on in this house all up 'til now like I've done! Does the whole thing add up here like he's right about this to you?!"

She's suddenly enraged. "Don't you *dare* try to deny that you're sometimes hard on Mike – Frank too!"

Now he turns and makes eye contact. "You'd testify that?! You'd take his side against me?!"

"Oh, Ray, this isn't about sides!" she wails. "Don't you understand we're supposed to be a family? And that families work things out – to support each other!" she cries in her hands cupped at her face.

"And then I'm s'posed to call him brother – after he tried to cold-bloodily kill me!"

"Ray, Ray!" Mary shouts. "He didn't do it for no reason at all!" And then she screeches at the top of her voice, *Why can't you see he hates you for real reasons?!*"

...

As Mike settles down on his hard bunk, up against the concrete wall of his locked and dim little room, he tries to picture several things in succession: He imagines what his mom is doing right now – if she's hurting real bad or if *Dickhead* is pissing her off, more. He then visualizes the warehouse...and Lucretia – wow, how I miss that place, he feels, can't wait to go live there, if... And next he wanders his home town in his mind, much like he actually did those few nights...and sees Chuck trying to help him, and then Frank being a real brother and friend to him, plus his regular friends laughing and hanging around the bowling alley, and Lucy's, too, and then the Bennetts' garage...and Looker – with his idea – his great idea! It's such a good concept, Mike dreams, and he feels a heartfelt pull to be part of it.

riday rolls over into Saturday, uneventful. Saturday evening, the ol' boys are patriarching as usual on Lucy's bench, with most of the young and older young men around them just loitering, putting in time (as are the women inside) while waiting, as usual, for dance hour – except this evening there is considerable energetic talk, both under the lowering sun as well as inside coffee-and-conversation haven, about Looker's proposal. (Actually, Nelson is in there, too, in a booth with Norm and his buds, blending with the citizenry most easily.)

Chuck and Wilf have been detailing the discussion out on the street, telling the others all about Sue's quick progress getting professional advice plus her plans for the referendum (next Friday looks good). The only hints of objections, both inside and out, are from those who have sense enough not to openly condemn the concept too heavily anyway, because if they did they would appear to be perfect parents who see no need.

When eight o'clock comes, everyone senses the Varmint Hall doors opening. Most start wandering down the sidewalk toward there right away, Wilf and Chuck with Sue and Beth, Joseph with Howard, Norm, Ba-Dee and Looker, Ed and his wife...and many more.

...

The dance hall is quickly crowded. (As always when something new is going on, or during some crisis, people come meet here, to be part of their town.) The usual attendance of one hundred and ten or so Saturday-nighters is averaged upward by tonight's gathering of one hundred and fifty already, so far.

At their familiar front table, Chuck and Beth are circled with generally the same ten or twelve friends and regulars as usual, while deep in the shadowy back corner beside the doors, the journalist and his college buds scan the dim hall with their honed nocturnal eyeballs and particular observational slant – with Looker amongst them adding perceptual clarity, tonight.

Everything's normal; everyone is just having fun. Until ten twenty-five:

When Ray Watson squirms in.

He limps his scrawny self straight to the ticket table up at the right, tosses down some cash, then orders a beer at the kitchen bar in behind. (From anywhere around the hall, his smile looks attached, and clearly contains an extra twist of the lips intended to ingratiate.) He turns and sips beer, surveying faces for friends... sees some midway along the opposite wall. So (in a "pathetic display of victimization," Joseph points out to his friends) he labors diagonally across the dance floor, expecting all the winged-feet persons in his way to clear a path... They do.

Though everyone in the hall sees Ray...no one is really watching him for anything he might do. Chuck does his professional best to welcome him...in his thoughts. Norm, Howard, Ba-Dee and particularly Joseph do rudely stare, full of theory, right at him, but they are too buried in darkness to be seen by him.

The general noise level, however, has noticeably hushed – as though enthusiasm for the proposed youth home for all their kids, in Ray's ironic presence, has to be checked.

But then, as the minutes pass, everything seems fine, and the weekly let-loose joviality and community party regains steam.

And Ray Watson merely sits quietly with two school-days friends, nursing his bottle.

An hour later, Frank Watson strolls in.

Frank is with three others (a bud and girlfriends) and as a group they head straight to a table where other friends wait, along that same wall between the denizens of the corner and the Dark Presence. Subsequently, they sit, they rise to dance, they sit and drink sodas, and they talk. Everything's still fine...

Until Frank is dancing with his sweetie, snugglin' and shufflin' – and Ray strains by, in a heroic excursion to the bar... Something is said. To those pirouetting around them, it sounds like Frank teases with "gimpy" – a greeting, a salutation, it seems, a light brotherly joke...maybe.

Ray seizes to a stop. *"What?!"* he chooses to challenge rather loudly.

Frank doesn't respond. His face tenses seriously, and he leads his dance partner quickly away.

Ray scurries along with them. "If you got somethin'ta say..!" he barks, elevating his empty beer bottle level with his younger brother's face.

Frank stays silent.

"Spit it out!" Ray now reaches to clutch Frank's shirt.

Frank looks hurt, intimidated. His eyes strain, as though full of tearful emotion. But he abruptly flings out a defensive hand and brushes Ray's arms away.

In reaction, Ray tosses his beer bottle in a little loop through the air at Frank. It bumps him on the chest, then clatters to the floor. Everyone nearby seems to think it just slipped.

"Fuck off," Frank now surprises himself saying it, amazing himself even more by the cool calm way he said it.

Ray grabs him two-handed, the pain of his wound immediately showing in his eyes. *"What's your goddamn problem?!"* he shouts the few inches up to his younger brother's face.

Now people stop dancing.

And from the mysterious back corner where all were observing this keenly, Joseph rises and strides briskly out across the floor.

At the stage end of the hall, Chuck stands, too.

Frank's date has backed away, bright eyes wide on him – he couldn't look more tense...or handsome... (Though he's unraveling inside, he is at least as brave as Mike:)

"I said go fuck yourself," Frank again makes his frame of mind clear.

"So you too, ayh?" Ray glares.

Chuck's now right there. Joseph halts opposite him, within reach of the poised brothers. The music has stopped. And dozens of others are hovering closer.

"Me too *what?!*" Frank leans forward.

"You an' Mike!"

"What – against you?"

"You're tryin' to decredit me!"

"You can't *discredit* an asshole – an asshole is just a shit-spittin' asshole!" Frank pops some folks' eyes saying it (still looking coolly self-contained). "What makes you think anyone's trying to make something out of nothing?"

Ray doesn't get it. "Jus' because I'm you two's older brother, you think everything I did was too hard on you!"

Chuck, fearing the worst, steps in. "Ray, why don't you save this for court – "

"*No!*" Ray spins a quarter turn shouting. "This is not Mike! This is *him!* – I jus' wanna know *his* problem!" he demands, stabbing a finger at Frank.

"Maybe it's your cumulonimbus charm he can't handle," Joseph cannot resist, tantalized – grinning, beneath mirth-filled goggled eyes.

"Joseph!" Chuck snaps at him, and several hands reflex out to hold the wordy one in place.

"Mind your own goddamn bis'ness!" Ray twists partway, but doesn't look at Joseph. He is too intent on proving himself above Frank, as he stares daggers at him: *"Well?* What's your problem, li'l Francis *asshole?"*

Instantly, right here, Frank – out of nowhere – with a big roundhouse left, thumps Ray full in the face. Ray flies sideways through the air and lands elbows-first on the floor. "Nothing, now," Frank quietly answers.

Ray climbs to his feet, plainly trying to act untouched (and noticeably no longer favoring his stab wound). "Yeah, sure!" he seethes. "Spit it out! Say it'n words!"

Chuck can't help feel sympathy, so he braces Ray where he wobbles – but sees Ray grabbed his beer bottle on the way up...

Frank stands firm, controlled. Punching his brother was obviously the emotional part, and now he wants to say something correct – that fits:

"You've been inhuman all along, how could you suddenly understand any real truth now?"

The entire dance-hall crowd moans with that last blow.

Ray strikes back: "You two've been nothin' but a pain in the ass t'me an' Mom an' Dad – nobody wanted both you two! *You're goddamn mistakes!"* he roars as though triumphant.

Tears well in Frank's eyes, not from any truth in the words but because he sees his brother's real nature suddenly surfacing more and more.

Joseph has to say it: "The real Ray Watson breaks through his shedding skin – "

"Back off!" Ray snaps, eyes darting at Joseph.

"Not while you're damaging humans," Joseph leans his big frame over him, and sneers.

Tightened fists at his sides, Ray demands, "This is no way your fam'ly business – "

"You don't own them either, Ray," Joseph notes, focused.

Ray gives up on Joseph and angles back to Frank (everyone's synchronized eyes following him). "Nobody wanted you! You were no use to our fam'ly!"

To which Frank has the right response: "But we sure ended up with more worth than you, *loser!*"

That did it. Ray leaps at Frank, clamping his neck. The whole pack of onlookers sways in their same direction, some arms raising futilely to hold them back.

Like in a spasmodic waltz, the brotherly couple grapple and lurch and throttle their fists at each other across the dance floor. And (as though at a routine primal ritual of supremacy) the observers simply stand back and wait for an outcome. But it doesn't come:

Because, so soon into the tussle, Clayton Watson storms through the doorway and across the hardwood then pushes through the throng to wedge his hands between his two sons, bellowing, *"Enough! Enough!"*

(At ringside, between the enoughs, could be heard Joseph's softly spoken but distinct, "It's about time." And seen by some is Chuck's quick nod of agreement.)

The round wall of people now tightens closer.

"What does this solve?" Clayton takes charge, his boys now separated.

"He started it!" Ray points at Frank as he straightens his clothes.

"*He* started it seventeen years ago!" Frank zings back, pointing in retaliation through his father's restraining arms. (An "Ooo!" swells through the crowd: another direct hit for young Frank.)

But then – like the parting of the seas – the multitude now slowly opens wide, cleaved by the very presence – alone and tiny at the double doors – of Mary Watson. It takes an awkward moment, but every single body settles silently still.

From forty feet away, Mary proclaims, "Ray, I've decided you mistreated my boys – yes, that's right: they're *mine*, not yours!" And her voice quakes, a hundred and sixty-some pairs of antici- pating eyes above lips gasping or squeezed shut holding breaths for her next words... She takes one little step forward. "And Frank, I also think we need to learn to understand Ray's shortcomings. Maybe we have to teach him, now, and not condemn."

Clayton's arms droop to his sides. (He would love to have said exactly those words.) And Frank and Ray are both staring, en- tranced. (Among the horde of marveled onlookers, only Joseph, and Looker beside him, are smiling.)

"Since we lost Bill," Mary really wants to say it all, regard- less of impending sobs, "we've been such an incomplete family, haven't we? We should have pulled together, but instead each of us has closed up..." Then, her face quickly draped with tears, she adds, "And I think that idea – for that place for young people – is very good. I wish it could have been there for my Bill...and for you, Ray..."

"And for Mike, now," Clayton adds, "we hope – "

"Oh, there's more than hope," Mary stops him, "if we all help create it." And wiping away her tears, she states with a little smile, "And exactly because we weren't very...skilled parents, I would like to help with that idea – in honor of my four boys."

The place erupts. From the moody low of Ray's treatment of Frank, Mary's words dramatically raise everyone's optimism for the future of their kids and their town...perhaps because it was her boys who needed help most.

"That was great!" Norm repeats through his early-morning bleariness as they wait to assure another dawn out there on their starlit, country-road watch (repeats what all four keep restating and the fifth one keeps nodding to over and over since they cracked their first beers coming out here from the dance).

"Yeah," Howard agrees again. "And it was great that they all stayed awhile – I thought ol' Clayt was gonna drag 'em all home." (It soon turned back into a dance, Ray returning wordlessly to his table, Frank to his, and Mom and Dad sitting a few minutes at Chuck's before leaving together.)

"Yup, that was great," Norm again reasserts what he's resaid repeatedly.

But from the middle of the back seat, Joseph questions, "So that was a better outcome than me pummeling Ray Watson down to a shapeless gob of jelly on the dance hall floor?"

"That would've been *great – !*"

"Nohhh!" Ba-Dee cuts Norm off. "It couldn't have worked out better than it did."

Looker in a back corner taps Joseph's arm and hands him a note he's written in the dark against his beer bottle. Joseph flicks on Looker's little flashlight and reads, "A lot to fix."

Howard can sure picture that. "Maybe it'll never really be fixed completely – especially between Mike and Ray."

"But they got past the worst part: the big hump of exposing all of it out in public," Ba-Dee still is most positive.

"Plus the first words about fixing things," Norm adds.

After a brief and lightless silence (of contemplative acceptance), Joseph makes it personal: "So then it now begs the question: What fuckin' use are us beer-slurpin' infidels going to be to our good bud Looker here's new monumental spendthrift project?" He then slurps many ounces of beer, characteristically, as though a reward for saying something critically pertinent.

"I'm in!" Norm rustles again in the front passenger seat. "Whatever I can help do – painting, whatever. It'll be – "

"Great!" Howard cuts him off, huffing. "Here's us shining examples of youthful males volunteering to be brotherly help to lost-soul kids. Hee-hee," he scorns with his standard little sardonic laugh.

"Nohhh!" Ba-Dee groans again. "We don't do any of that. We just do menial stuff."

"Just us volunteering will be doing that something-pivotal thing of just supporting it," Joseph points out.

Now Howard comes around: "Hey, that's right! If everyone like us cool guys are part of it, it'll be the cool place to be and they'll all come around!"

Looker scribbles/Joseph reads, "Exactly!"

Norm now brightens even more: "And we could have a discussion group – us five – and pose to all the little youths the true profound universal mysteries – !"

"Great!" Joseph runs with it. "And if there's a garage there, we could park an old car in it and keep it all dark – with a box of beer always on the back seat! – and we'd sit there waiting for kids to come 'round to listen to all this wisdomly shit we do!"

Howard gets enthusiasm, too: "Yeah! We'd be like the five new wise old men on the mountaintop –"

"The five swilling blots in the darkened car!" Ba-Dee sees the picture, too.

"We'll be loved and respected by everyone!" Norm now sums up. "The back-road, beer-breath-belching...big brains of brotherhood!"

...

"Big bulbous beautiful bare breasts," Norm utters pleasurably as he softly strokes Suzanne's naked nipples on her utterly nude body, the blazing summer sun an hour up into the lush cover of trees surrounding the peaceful pond. (Norm didn't feel like sleeping, so from the back road with his friends he went stealthily to Suzanne's bedroom window, compelling her out to the swimming hole, to the glorious sunrise, and to stripping every last stitch of clothing.)

"Wish I would've had something like that..." she dreams.

"You do. You have two of them."

"Nnnoo!" she giggles softly, curling his hair with a finger as he lays his head on her silken tummy. "I mean Lookerhaven."

"Ohhh," Norm purrs sleepily in the warm morning breeze. "Yeah, me too."

"There's this assumption our society has that trusts all parents to know all there is about raising well-balanced and well-rounded offspring."

"That's it, you know," Norm uses her "you know" adder. "It's as though as long as they're physically healthy, you're a good parent."

"Right! But who has the psychological wherewithal? Who has any idea about all the emotional and social problems a child will go through – changing problems that come up faster as the years go by!" (Suzanne is getting worked up.) "I wish I'd had a place to go to for answers..." she laments again.

"Looker foresees a center for lost parents, too," Norm relates.

"Good! That gives me hope that I might not be a fucked-up parent myself!" she sighs deeply, as Norm raises his eyebrows and tilts his head back to meet her eyes...'tween her gracefully arching flesh.

"Right, good thought!" he firmly agrees.

"So then, be with me here," she now pulls away smiling and stands, indicating with one hand the calm pool of cool water and with the other her physical center of female gravity,"deep in the pure waters of Eden..."

And as one, they slip through the unrippling liquid, beneath the dark glass, into the volume of primal fluid...

ike feels like a child, maybe for the first time ever. The news from last night's dance – an evening centered, evidently, around his family – causes pangs of longing, of need, for the moments that were good. It's as if he'll be missing his rightful share when there's more of them.

But at the same time, he believes he will never go home again, as though now, vindicated by everyone's recognition of the need for help for families (ignited by him – thrust in motion by him), he thinks at least one part of all of it is resolved. So, now I can go on to live exactly the life that feels right, free to be positive... Unless I'm in jail.

As he sits on the cot in his closed-up room, long after Mom and Dad then Frank and the others left him in the visiting room, he tries to picture Frank punching Ray – tries to experience it how Frank did... It's just the same as his own rage, he knows... though Frank is such a different person. But then, that's what makes it feel good: that we're alike and understand so much together, from experience, but we're so individual in direction and wants. And, huh, what did Bean say, when I told him about the dance and my valiant brother Frank? "Hey, yuh know it's one of those caring-runs-so-deep things – that yuh don't tune to it 'til somethin' megaton happens."

...

In his weekly stampede of written words, Joseph's column the next day is full of imperative for Lookerhaven (Suzanne's compact name for it was passed along by Norm.) He implores, for the sake of their all-inspiriting sense of future, that everyone vote yes in the now scheduled Friday referendum.

John Sing, not so surprisingly, this week sells a record number of papers, countywide.

...

On Wednesday (four weeks to the day since the stabbing) Mike's court date is set: eight days away. (They want to rush it up, to get Mike out of the Detention Center – one way or the other.) Ray, through his veneer of righteousness – despite some better talks about it with Mom (Dad still can't face issues directly with his sons, very well, and maybe never will) – leaks no drops of blood-tie, charge-dropping compassion.

...

Friday's referendum turnout at Reverend Fisk's church is satisfyingly full. (The question is only about the concept; no financing or legalities are stated.) Out of an estimated fifteen hundred eligible adults (twenty and older), thirteen hundred and ten vote. Out of an estimated six or seven hundred "youths" (ages twelve to nineteen), four hundred and ninety-one respond to their separate poll.

Predictably, every single youth casts a "yes".

And surprisingly, only twenty-eight adults say "no".

Mayor Sue Granger immediately sets the physical project in motion.

It's a hot July Thursday morning. As the broad floor of the Elston courthouse lobby fills with the inevitable morning swarm, Chief Chuck Cintz sits with Mike Watson on a designated bench outside a courtroom. (They're an hour and a half early.) He's telling Mike about Lookerhaven's progress: A house has already been chosen, appropriately right on Main Street four doors up from Nick's Bowl, and Looker's fund has been put in place. Its bedrooms can be used as is, but some renovations are planned for the rest. The legalities seem clear, and applications are already arriving for a resident staff counselor.

Mike is pleased, but hearing all about it gives him little distraction from the imminent possibility of prison. (He's decided this week that the issue of his freedom is as big as any principle.) Though his lawyer –wherever he is – has been solidly confident, Mike has that feeling that anything can happen.

Across the lobby, Mayor Sue, Beth, Lucy, Norm, Joseph, Looker and twelve other hometowners are now gathering and talking, each occasionally facing Mike's way and smiling, winking, or thumbs-upping.

And then Mike's family arrives...

Filing through the doorway, Ray is in front, with Mom and Dad arm-in-arm behind, and Frank a few steps back.

Suddenly, Ray's lawyer appears out of nowhere and pulls him aside. Talking for only a minute, they return to the three Watsons left standing in a knot ten feet inside the doors. (Mike and Chuck are watching this closely from their bench, as are Joseph and the others from their side of the lobby.)

The lawyer seems to extract some kind of agreement from Mary and Clayton, then leads all four down a side corridor and in through a doorway. He soon reappears and crosses the marble floor to Chuck and Mike.

"Hi, Chuck, Mike," he reaches to shake both their hands. (Alan Friar: tall and thin, black suit, prematurely gray hair and quick eye and hand motions give the impression of someone obsessive about work.) "You know I'm representing Ray, right?" Chuck smiles and nods at his old acquaintance. "Tim" (Mike's lawyer) "is in there with your family, Mike. What we're doing here is one last try at resolution – you can turn it down right now..."

Mike doesn't respond at all, so Alan continues. "Tim and I have talked about your family situation a lot, Mike. You know there's only one guaranteed way of no one getting hurt – hurt some more, that is – and that's if we can settle this thing some-how without taking it inside there," he points dramatically at the courtroom door. "We'll have to go in anyway, but only to have it dismissed. Your folks and Frank and even Ray, and everyone else over there, want to at least indulge us lawyers and talk about it. We've got one hour."

Mike eyes Chuck, then peers over there at the others – more specifically, Looker...

"Okay," Mike forces out the word, with clear reluctance.

In less than a minute, Mary, Clayton, Ray, Frank and Mike Watson are settling down together at a table for the first time since the stabbing. Mike and Ray sit diagonally opposite. They each pretend the other isn't there. (Frank is across from Mom, beside Mike, and as he sat he patted him once on the back. Mike smiled.) Lawyers Alan and Tim anchor the ends of the ten-chaired table, each of them closest to their respective client. And Chuck takes the stool beside the door. A court clerk is summoned then dispatched to inform the judge what they're doing.

"No question," Alan begins, "there's wrong done on both sides – right, Tim?"

Short, fair-faced Tim answers with a firm "Right."

"And Ray," Alan now stares him down, "as your legal counsel, let me officially inform you that the case against you is no less real than yours is against him." He points forcefully again, without looking, this time at Mike.

Ray swallows, perhaps with uncertainty.

Tim takes over, in his oddly soft voice, gesturing to them all, saying, "People in your situation are always here for past stuff. They don't concern themselves enough about the future stuff..."

Mary's brown eyes are shifting back and forth. Her lips are tight together, and her expression is stone. Clayton focuses on his hands overlapped on the table, as though experience with meetings gives him presence. Mike, Frank and Ray each stare straight ahead at the blank walls.

"So that's what this is really about, right here: the future," Alan gives them his experience. "Now somebody tell Tim and I where this part of the fight will get each one of you in the long run."

That request unnerves all five Watsons. None of them replies.

"Despite all the serious reasons that brought you here," Tim joins back in, "this right now is by far the most serious under-taking and life-determining decision of your lives. Mike, give us something," he orders his client.

Mike freezes for a second, then remembers his rage. "I just want to show everyone I did it for good reasons." (Ray doesn't even blink at that.)

"You did. No question. Everyone knows that now," Tim responds, eyes glancing at Ray. "So Ray gets convicted. Then what?"

"It's over," Mike thinks.

"But he's imprisoned?" Alan asks.

Mike doesn't answer. The plain room seems emptier.

Alan obliges, with his experience: "So then Ray has a record, forever. Mom suffers all through it. Then years from now she has to watch Ray try to start a new life. Dad's in the same boat, plus his name in business in his mind is forever tarnished. Frank has to bear it, too, all his life. And then Ray gets out angrier than ever."

Mike nods an inch with understanding.

"Well, then it's the same if Mike is...imprisoned," Mary tensely sees, watching Ray.

"Yes," Alan and Tim both flatly and simultaneously acknowledge.

"*Wait!*" Ray sharply reacts. "How'um I'ta get *justice* here?!" he loudly states his whole position (still stiffly staring at the wall).

"Ray," Dad now seems to finally face a consequence, "it's a trade – forgetting past wrongs for a better future!"

Tim brightens a little. (Chuck by the door is the only one who notices.)

"So now I'm jus' suppose'ta forget about this having been stabbed!" Ray whines, hotly.

"*No!*" Dad flares. "We use our past problems to – "

"To show us how to do better!" Mary finishes for him.

"Right," Alan agrees. "You don't wipe the slate clean. You leave it on there as something to start working with."

Here, Frank surprises even himself by speaking. "I don't want to live in a house that's all full of anger for years..."

Mom's eyes wet with tears. "Oh, Frank, none of us really do..."

"So we can choose some cooperation," Dad encourages. "We can choose to try and get along... And be happier."

"Takes strength. Honesty, humility," Tim warns.

And Alan adds bluntly, "But less effort and pain than fighting your never-ending war."

"Well, we could get help...dealing with it, couldn't we?" Mom can see.

"It would be mandatory," Tim notes.

Mike is now slowly nodding. It appears he has firmly won his case, already.

But Ray is still scowling.

"Ray," Dad sees the look, "they're right. Don't tell me you want more years of anger – of having your mother live through more grief... Can't you imagine some harmony..?"

"Some love?" Mom pleads.

Ray sits unmoved.

Now Alan commands his client: "Ray, tell us that's the price you'll make all of your family pay to get what *only you* want in that courtroom!"

"No, tell *you* what!" Ray erupts. "I only want *him* ta pay!" he half stands and thrusts an arm and finger diagonally across the table at Mike. "So maybe all the rest of you jus' have'ta put up with it like *I* did! – for my avengence here!"

Mom and Dad both sigh. Mike, the lawyers notice, is glaring back at Ray with a look that could kill.

"For you, this isn't about being stabbed, is it Ray?" Tim tries to suggest.

Ray misses the whole point. *"You wanna see here?"* He yanks out his shirttail, exposing his raw scar. "If it isn't 'bout this, what in the goddamn Jesus Christ hell is it about?!"

"Man, he's ignorant!" Frank mutters.

Ray hears that and flings himself down the table at him. Several hands, including Chief Cintz's, react to stop him.

"Shut your little mouth!" Ray threatens, now physically restrained.

"Sit down!" two lawyers and Clayton all shout almost in unison. Alan leaps and circles behind his client to push him back down onto his chair. He then leans on the table straight in front of him and confronts:

"It's real plain now who the only obstacle is here, Ray. So I'm telling you outright – look at me!" he insists as Ray keeps firing vengeful stares across at Frank and Mike. "You, Ray, *cannot win!* If your assault charge against Mike has weight, it is at least equaled by all the nasty, hard-ass things you did to him over the years! The way the courts look at it today, Mike was justified – *justified!* Do you understand that word, Ray?" (Ray, startled, blinks with acknowledgement.) "And I said *at least* equaled! If not equaled, it is weighted *against* you – you win your point but lose your war! And you take any and all hope and promise and sense of future for every member of your family down with you! *Get it?!*"

Ray looks shaken. His own lawyer is slashing holes in him.

For the next few minutes, both attorneys hit Ray – and Mike – hard with more assurances, from their experiences, of what exactly to expect.

Then Mike – thinking mostly about freedom...independence, *really living*, a future thoroughly past this, of the Elston warehouse and Lucretia and Bean and others he met who are exactly like him and so positive to be with...plus some freedom for Mom and Dad and Frank from all *this* – relents:

"I'll give it up if he does."

It's all he has to say.

Mary immediately exhorts Ray to do the same – that if Mike is willing to put bitterness behind him, Ray, the oldest and "more mature" she poses, "should be at least as willing."

"No," Ray decides.

(Right here, the court clerk returns, indicating in a whisper that they have ten minutes.)

Mom turns bright red. Clayton reaches over and squeezes her hands. Tears of anger stream out as she reacts in a controlled, firm voice:

"Well, so, Frank is right. Who would want to live in our home if it's always full of anger..? I don't want that, either. But *I* am *not* about to leave..!" She hesitates, weighing her whole maternal life. "The memory of my Bill is in my home. And unlike you, Ray, he was so full of love, and need and caring..." Weeping, she stops, but raises a hand so no one interrupts. "I want to still live there, for Bill...and for you, Clayton, my love..." she embraces him with caring eyes, smiling with belief – a way she stopped smiling some time ago. "And for you, Frank, my angel," she leans across the table to caress his hand. "And for my brave and noble Mike..." her eyes close tight, then open to warmly gaze at him. "And if everyone else is willing to live with me – to just be there and try to live with caring – everyone except *you,* Ray – well, then I guess you can't be part of that..." she now stares fiercely at him. "I know, in your mind, Ray, you try to do what's best for me, and us. But what you've all too often done, and what you're doing right now, is so wrong. It's the opposite of what's needed... So, Ray, if you insist on going through with this, then *I* insist, right now...that you *never* come home again!" And she ends with a gasp of absolute resignation to more loss in her life.

All of a sudden Ray appears pathetically wounded. It's as though he's finally heard and comprehends the truth of their lives: that he is directly responsible for unhappiness, not harmony. At last he sees the possibility that the consequences of his actions alone – not as any part of what he's so often taken action against – are real and damaging.

The room is anxiously quiet. A minute passes, and nothing is said. More seconds go by, wordlessly...

The clerk opens the door, and signals it's time.

Tim stands, and moves with Alan to the door. Chuck is on his feet, holding it open.

At the doorway, the two lawyers stop and turn. Four Watson's are poised in their chairs watching the fifth...

So Ray speaks:

"Alright!" he caves in.

Alan beams. "Good! Let's go – we don't keep this Your Honor waiting!"

And the family rises and files out behind him.

...

Charges in both directions are summarily dropped – with all kinds of conditions. Mike is granted probation, and is released to the custody of his parents – with Ray's oath of good behavior, same as Mike. And Frank.

It's all over...

It's all over except for the work of forgiving, forgetting, and remembering to care.

L ooker walks by the youth home. Beneath the last defiant blaze of autumn maple color, he stops and thinks, "Wow, this house is attractive." Fresh paint, tidy yard – thanks to dozens of volunteers working through late summer and early fall. There are two young men and one young woman staying here at the moment, and an average of thirty others drop in daily. Mike Watson is not one of them.

As he passes his project, then Nick's Bowl (his buds Ba-Dee, Howard and Norm gone back to college, now) he wishes only that it could have been here for the one teenager who inspired him to do something in the first place...

In front of the police office, he nods at Sid through the window. At the corner, he waits for the walk signal, zipping up his jacket against the cool wind. The stoplight changes, and he is soon stepping inside Lucy's.

It's Monday, and Joseph is waiting for him at the mid-point of the long counter with a copy of The Town Talk opened at his column. Lucy says hi to Looker and reaches under the cash counter for the poet's new laptop computer. (Being wealthy, Nelson now owns two, keeping one here for conversations.) He sits beside the journalist.

"Nelson! Winter tweaks the turncoat wind!" Joseph does his over-dramatized imagery thing.

Nodding and grinning, Nelson flicks on his voice and types up, "What's your weekly spew about this time?"

"'Spew'?! Nelson – 'spew'? Not so, you literary-elitist snot! This biting brain-muncher is, as ever, the heartbeat of our commonality!"

"I read it," Nelson clicks.

"Oh. What'dya think?"

"How is Mike really doing and remind me who Bean is?" Nelson asks in one line about Joseph's Friday night stay at the Elston warehouse. The quiet gray eyes of his strong-featured face then rise to meet his squarely.

Joseph thinks a second, recalling the depths of what he did not put in his column. Meanwhile, Lucy wanders by with Nelson's coffee. He is still concerned about Mike, too. (As well, he is a new sponsor of Lookerhaven and, like Nelson now, a financial contributor to the warehouse.)

"Mike's mostly okay," Joseph begins. "Like I wrote, he's feeling good about life there on his own – he sure has the wherewithal to be that independent. But he misses his home here, more than he imagined he would, he says. And it pisses him off that Ray won't shut up – all the bullshit Ray's saying that he only gave in for their parents' sake and he'd still press charges if it wasn't for them."

"Mike doesn't come back here often," Lucy has heard.

Joseph takes a thoughtful deep breath. "No, especially when there's a chance Ray might be home, too – it's a good thing Elston is big enough that they don't bang into each other there... But Ray hangs around with those lowlifes he works with in that industrial new-concept-ghetto suburb, anyway." He stops for a gulp of coffee, and to get back on track. "So Mike still feels that hollow youth feeling, I think, so much so that he has to stay away... it overwhelms him by contrast, now, whenever he comes home. But the three normal Watsons go see him regularly and are happy for him, with all his weird friends and his working in that thrift store. And they're getting along better – closer, was the word he used... Oh!, he does have a weekend booked at Lookerhaven, though, in a month."

"Good!" Nelson types, pleased enough. Then he suggests, "It could have ended much worse."

As Joseph nods to the appearing words, Lucy reads them too, then notices above: "Bean". "Who's Bean?"

"That strange one in the Detention Center, remember? The Brain that Bounced?" Now both Lucy and Nelson remember, bobbing their heads. "Well, he just got out and went straight for the warehouse. Mike was thrilled. I think he sees Bean as some sort of role model on how to be your own self. They're inseparable, now... Actually, it appears they're the current darlings of radical individualism amongst all fifty or sixty frighteningly different individuals I saw there."

As Joseph started saying all that, Chuck Cintz came in and sat beside Nelson, with Lucy quietly serving him a coffee while they listened.

"Mike couldn't be better," Chuck adds his professional perspective. "For Mike – from that family mess – he's doing okay."

"Agreed, Chief Cintz," Joseph concludes as well. "And he'll get and stay better, too." Then he thinks to add, "And Clayton and Mary, by all appearances, are happy as larks – I see them walking around our block holding hands, all the time...mushy old fools!" he jokes, knowing Chuck and Beth also walk around all over holding hands. (Chuck just winks at him.)

"Happy enough ending, minus one," Nelson observes.

"Maybe Ray will never understand completely," Lucy poses, his raspy voice toned with disappointment.

Nelson replies, "He may understand, in his own way. But his character will have to unwind completely before he is capable of change."

"Don't see that happening," Joseph believes. And he then leads them on to concerns about the teenagers currently staying at Lookerhaven, plus the few others in town they're working with who are struggling to be part of their families and community.

"You goin' over?" Rick asks against the cold November wind.

"Yep," Jackie replies. "Right now."

It's the official (barring one or two more warm-enough Saturdays) bottom half of the final inning of their fall post-summer-season baseball game (Rick, with his remaining out, is hopelessly behind 81 to 57, though he and his team squeaked out a win in the summer-long classic, 556 to 547 – avenging last year's loss to Jack) and Rick is asking from his dugout as Jack answers from the mound. They're talking about Lookerhaven.

"Eddie, you goin'?" Jack finds him in the late-afternoon, autumn shadows of the dugout. (Eddie Ogden, with his long history – all through his young life – of family problems, was the first youth to wander into Looker's youth center unscheduled. Now he goes regularly, to share his thoughts and to just be with the normal other everyday "fuckups", as they like to refer to themselves – in order to try and stay "unfuckedup", of course.)

"Yeah," Eddie affirms, too. "My mom's bringing over food," he announces, which, because of her good cooking, perks the others' interest.

"Hey, dipshit," Jack next turns toward Heap Henry in center. "You?"

"Ineluctably... Throw the ball, bug-nuts," Henry suggests.

And Jack does, resulting in a ground-ball out and a diamond-wide ambivalent end to this year's baseball.

Leaving the field as one big pack, all sixteen boys head for downtown, having agreed to jam into Nick's Bowl for a season's-end soft-drink celebration. Jack, Rick and Eddie walk shoulder-to-shoulder.

"What's a haven?" Rick, with zero senior-kid ego, openly asks younger Eddie, the reading fanatic.

"Just a safe place," Eddie answers simply, without attitude.

"I don't need no safety," Jack declares, brushing back his ever-longer black hair.

"That's not the whole point, I guess," little Eddie glances up at him, adjusting his thick glasses (as though tidying up, same as Jack). "I mean, maybe someday one of us will really need it, like Mike Watson did before he stabbed the wart-head." (Everyone in town has some degree of criticism, or feelings of total condemnation, for Ray Watson.) "For us, it's supposed to be someplace we can go to get different ideas."

"You mean to prove our parents are wrong?" Rick asks, flipping the old baseball up and snagging it. (He and Jack have been to Lookerhaven only two or three times each, briefly.)

"No, scum-skin!" Jack knows better. (His mom volunteers her computer plus keyboard skills to help the youths churn out their little internal newsletter.) "Parents help it out – it wouldn't even exist if parents were locked out and bad-mouthed by the kids in there all the time."

Eddie adds, "Yeah, and like all the books they have there, the idea is to just work on problems you have with your emotions, and things. And the psychologist is there to answer things your parents probably don't know."

"Oh," Rick now understands better. "Good idea."

"It's not for everyone," Jack thinks.

"Well, no..." Eddie wonders. "You don't even have to have problems. It's like, you can hang out there and learn what the fuckups are going through, so you'll know."

"Yeah, I see," Jack says. "Or just be around other guys – more ordinary kinda guys like us...to feel real."

And as they walk out of sight of the ball field, Eddie Ogden laughs a bit at that, from knowing exactly what it means.

EPILOGUE

"Nascency," Joseph notes. "Remedial. Collocate." (He is spurting out words as though squeezed from him, as he sits squashed between Norm and Ba-Dee – with Howard wedged in at Ba-Dee's end – on one of the three-seater sofas of the Lookerhaven living room. He is apparently groping for applicable words.) "Sympatrically."

"The Christmas decorations look nice," Ba-Dee observes through the thicket of milling bodies attending this first open house for Nelson Nelson's project.

"Cool," Howard agrees.

All four have paper coffee cups (cups and contents courtesy of Lucy) balanced on a knee...

"Wish it was dark in here," Norm utters.

"What? Like the back road?!" Joseph reacts incredulously, twisting his frown at him. "Norm! Get a hold of yourself! We're in the realm of the living – "

"Wish it was dark and I had a beer," Howard sides with Norm.

"Beer isn't ethical here!" Joseph yanks his head one hundred and eighty degrees toward Howard.

"*You're* the big glug-a-lug!" Howard snipes back.

"If we would've had a nice place like this, we wouldn't be here right now," Norm says Norm-like, changing depths.

"What the fuck does that mean..?" Joseph asks with a caught-in-the-middle blank stare and intentionally meek overtone.

"He means we would have always had some place respectable to go loiter," Ba-Dee answers for Norm.

"But *why* wouldn't we be *here* now?" Joseph hates it when he doesn't grasp something.

"We wouldn't be here on this sofa," Norm means. "We'd be milling around too, in demand, popular, like productive contributors to society – "

"Instead of huddling like antisocial rabbits wishing we had beers to catalyze our courage," Ba-Dee finishes nicely for him.

"Antisocial rabbits?" Joseph ponders, now. "Beer-drinking antisocial – "

"Mike Watson's here, you know!" Suzanne slips out of the mob right in front of them to report...looking alluring in a low-cut, simple black dress. She winks at Norm.

"Mike's here!" Chuck breaks through from the side to inform the four of them, too.

From the other sofa, Lucy stands and repeats in a question, "Mike's here?"

In thirty seconds (the way it happens in gatherings of people) twenty others have circled around Joseph and his buds, picking up on the good news there that Mike came. The four young men wide-open to it are now fully in the thick of things. Beerless.

Mike wanders into the room – dark T-shirt, hair outgrowing his buzz-cut, he is accompanied by Erskine Fontaine Schuppe – the Bean. They approach the tightening cluster of folks. Somewhere in the crowd, ol' Bert – gathered with his cronies Mel, Shooter and Chase – officially announces loud enough for everyone in the whole house to hear: "Hey! It's Mike!"

Sid, Wilf and Sue, Beth, Ed and his wife and John Sing now close in, too. Margaret and Carl – parents of slain Janet (it's been a year and a half, already) – have stopped in, as well. Their daughter Jennifer is standing over there close beside a friend: Norm's younger brother Jeff. Several of the baseball kids, fronted by Jackie and Rick, bunch near the sofa, gawking. Then Reverend Fisk appears with Jimmy Jimms, and beside them: Frank Watson, here to show his younger brother the work he helped do here, too. (Mom and Dad Watson are right now volunteering in the kitchen, again.)

Looker is let through and he crosses the open floor in front of the sofa, indicating to Mike to follow. He hands a big note to Joseph.

"Ohph! – Looker's babbling on again!" Joseph rumbles ominously to the crowd as he unfolds it, causing a wave of laughter (as much for openly calling him "Looker" – now that everyone knows to call him "Nelson" – as for his tasteless joke about his voicelessness.) "Here it is, everyone!" he bellows.

A current of silence rushes through the whole downstairs, as people from every part of it, including the kitchen, press toward the front room to hear Nelson's dedication. Joseph waits for complete quiet – brandishing a wide grin of potential spoken-word power.

Joseph repeats, "So here it is!" He glances, eyes twinkling up at his good friend Looker, then reads:

"Having merely looked around for ten years here," (tension-breaking enthusiastic giggles erupt) "it finally sank in that I have a home here, with all of you. But, like everyone on Earth, I carried the confusion of imperfect childhood around in my head, and couldn't clearly see today, or tomorrow. Well, this house is intended for both today and tomorrow – the realities of right now and its problems, and how to deal with them..."

Spontaneous applause spreads.

Joseph smiles...waits...

And reads on: "Still, it took something outside of me to make this reality clear. And it's here now, in front of us. It made me feel like I was that child again, secretly enraged and helpless. It's something that should never happen to us, or our children – to sacred new life, the little ones we bring into the world and raise and bequeath our communities to..."

Joseph beams broadly now, and reaches up to pat Nelson's arm, as though to say no one on Earth could have worded this better.

"The starting point for this, for me, was Mike Watson, running from his own confusion and lack of our understanding. So, though in memory too of someone I loved and who I knew all along always unconditionally loved me and affirmed it in the end, I want to dedicate my little project for our future here, to Mike..."

(Mike is unashamedly wet-eyed. And so is Bean, right behind him.)

Joseph finishes, "Well, here's to Mike! And putting aside Suzanne's practical but unsolicited good name 'Lookerhaven'," (Suzanne laughs through her tears, too) "let's now officially call this home-near-home..."

Joseph makes them wait for it:

"Mike's Hideout."

The big gathering again bursts with laughter and cheers, and soon they start chanting for Mike to speak. Self-consciously, he does:

"I think I know...well, some kids are, anyway," he begins awkwardly, eyes searching the floor, "their family isn't always enough – I mean, I know parents can't see everything... We need friends – friends like all you guys!" Now he gazes at faces all around, and with everyone smiling and thumbs-upping encouragement, he adds, "I know too what I ended up having to do wasn't smart...but maybe there's gotta be someone around to tell you different – tell you a way out..." (Though blushing red, he is determined to say it right...and finds his parents' pleased faces to help him.) "With so many of us messed-up kids around – ay, Bean?" he smirks at his outrageous, fantastic-smile dear friend. "And Looker, too, right?" (Nelson nods emphatically.) "Well, an idea like this can't go wrong, so thanks!"

And as everyone loudly claps, he holds up his arms to stop them, saying, "I almost forgot. Bean and me made this in the shop, locked up there in Elston – maybe we can stick it on the wall here, somewhere..? Jus' something Joseph here said to me a while ago – I kept thinking about it...like it's a good thing for everyone to think about doing more of – show 'em, Bean!"

Bean opens a plain plastic bag and pulls out a wooden plaque, raises it high and rotates it around to reveal to everyone its two carved profoundly simple and appropriate, resolving and conclusive tear-wrenching words:

HUMAN KINDNESS

www.ingramcontent.com/pod-product-compliance
Lightning Source LLC
Chambersburg PA
CBHW051928020726
47501CB00001B/25